THRONE OF SCARS

(Lost Kings MC #20)

AUTUMN JONES LAKE

COPYRIGHT

ALSO BY AUTUMN JONES LAKE

THE LOST KINGS MC™ SERIES

Slow Burn (Lost Kings MC #1)
Corrupting Cinderella (Lost Kings MC #2)
Three Kings, One Night (Lost Kings MC #2.5)
Strength From Loyalty (Lost Kings MC #3)
Tattered on My Sleeve (Lost Kings MC #4)
White Heat (Lost Kings MC #5)
Between Embers (Lost Kings MC #5.5)
More Than Miles (Lost Kings MC #6)
White Knuckles (Lost Kings MC #7)
Beyond Reckless (Lost Kings MC #8)
Beyond Reason (Lost Kings MC #9)
One Empire Night (Lost Kings MC #9.5)
After Burn (Lost Kings MC #10)
After Glow (Lost Kings MC #11)
Zero Hour (Lost Kings MC #11.5)
Zero Tolerance (Lost Kings MC #12)
Zero Regret (Lost Kings MC #13)
Zero Apologies (Lost Kings MC #14)
White Lies (Lost Kings MC #15)
Swagger and Sass (A Lost Kings MC Novella)
Rhythm of the Road (Lost Kings MC #16)
Lyrics on the Wind (Lost Kings MC #17)
Diamond in the Dust (Lost Kings MC #18)
Crown of Ghosts (Lost Kings MC #19)
Throne of Scars (Lost Kings MC #20)
Reckless Truths (Lost Kings MC #21)
Rust or Ride (Lost Kings MC #22)
...and many more to come!

Nothing stops a Lost King from claiming his woman in the latest installment of the Lost Kings MC series by USA Today bestselling author Autumn Jones Lake.

The strongest souls carry the deepest scars.
I thought I was beyond redemption. Too far gone to fall in love again.
Somehow, Serena soothed my soul and slipped into my heart.
Every day I spend with her chases the ghosts that still haunt me away.
With her, the future I never thought I'd have seemed to be within reach.
But the pain of her past threatens to rip our present to shreds.
Time might heal all wounds, but some scars never fade.

This is part two of Grinder's story and should be read after Crown of Ghosts.

GLOSSARY OF CHARACTERS AND TERMINOLOGY

The Lost Kings MC™ World © Autumn Jones Lake

Grinder's (*Crown of Ghosts* and *Throne of Scars*) can be read as a standalone duet. He's never had a book or short story written about him before. We've seen and heard about him through other people's eyes throughout the series (see what I did there, *people* not characters!) But *Crown of Ghosts* is the first book where we are in his head.

The series has had some shakeups in the last few books. I've updated the glossary to reflect certain events. Obviously, I can't cover every detail here or we'd be reading a million word glossary instead of a few pages!

The following may contain spoilers if you are not caught up on the series or have skipped books.

Please note, this glossary only pertains to *my* romantic fictionalized motorcycle club world. It should not be construed as applicable to any other fictional club or a real-life motorcycle club.

THE LOST KINGS MC: UPSTATE, NY ("Empire," NY)

President: Rochlan "Rock" North. Leader of the Upstate NY charter of the Lost Kings MC.

Sergeant-at-Arms: Wyatt "Wrath" Ramsey. Protector or enforcer for the club.

Vice President: Blake "Murphy" O'Callaghan. Murphy was the road captain up until *White Lies* (*Lost Kings MC #15*)

Treasurer: Marcel "Teller" Whelan. Handles the money and investments for the club.

Road Captain: Dixon "Dex" Watts (newly appointed to the position in *White Lies*)

Grayson "Grinder" Lock: The former sergeant-at-arms of the New York charter. We saw a little about his relationship as Rock's mentor in *Wheels of Fire* (*Hollywood Demons #3*). We first "met" him in *Corrupting Cinderella* (*Lost Kings MC #2*) and have seen him a few other times throughout the series, most recently in *Zero Regret* (*Lost Kings MC #11.*) He has been mentioned throughout the series by the brothers as they looked forward to his release from prison.

THE LOST KINGS MC: DOWNSTATE, NY ("UNION" NY)

- **President:** Angus "Zero" or "Z" Frazier. As of *Zero Apologies* (*Lost Kings MC #14*), Z is the president of the Downstate, NY charter of the Lost Kings MC.
- **Vice President:** Logan "Rooster" Randall
- **Sergeant-at-Arms:** Steer
- **Treasurer:** Hustler
- **Road Captain:** Jensen "Jigsaw" Kilgore

THE LOST KINGS MC: PORT EVERHART, VA

- President: Cypress "Ice" Caldwell
- Vice President: Farmer
- Sergeant-at-Arms: Pants
- Treasurer: T-Bone
- Road Captain: Wings

THE LOST KINGS MC: DEADBRANCH, TN

- President: Digger
- SAA: Squiggy

We haven't met anyone else from Deadbranch...yet!

OTHER LOST KINGS MC MEMBERS

Cronin "Sparky" Petek: Sparky is the mad genius/hippie stoner behind the Lost Kings MC's pot-growing business. He is rarely seen outside of the basement, as he prefers the company of his plants.

Elias "Bricks" Serrano: We have seen Bricks and his girlfriend Winter throughout the series. He's one of the few members who does not live at the clubhouse.

Sam "Stash" Black: Lives in the basement with Sparky and helps with the plants.

Thomas "Ravage" Kane: We've gotten to know Rav and his snarky humor a little bit better in each book. Ravage is a general member who helps out wherever he is needed.

Sway: Former president of the downstate charter of the Lost Kings MC. We've seen Sway and his wife Tawny off and on in the series since *Strength From Loyalty*, usually annoying Rock in some fashion.

Hoot: We've seen glimpses of him since *Slow Burn* when he was a lowly prospect. He finally got his full patch, but still gets a lot of the grunt work.

Birch: We also met him as a prospect. He's been voted as a full-patch member but shares in a lot of the grunt work with Hoot.

Priest: The Lost Kings MC's national president. We first met him and his wife, Valentina, in *After Burn*.

Malik: Soon-to-be prospect for the Lost Kings MC. Helps out at Crystal Ball. Owns the Lucky Duck pawnshop in Ironworks.

THE LADIES OF THE LOST KINGS MC

Hope Kendall North, Esq.: Nicknamed *First Lady* by Murphy in *Corrupting Cinderella (Lost Kings MC #2)*, Hope is the object of Rock's love and obsession. Their daughter is named Grace after Rock's mother.

Trinity Hurst Ramsey: Wrath's angel. Former caretaker of the club. She now has her own photography and graphic design business. She is married to Wrath, fiercely loyal to the club, and best friends with Hope.

Heidi "Little Hammer" O'Callaghan: Murphy's wife and Teller's little sister. Heidi just graduated from college and works at Empire Med. Murphy officially adopted her daughter, Alexa Jade.

Charlotte Clark, Esq: Teller's sunshine. Often credited with taming the brooding treasurer of the Lost Kings, Teller.

Lilly Frazier: Z's brave and devoted siren. The new queen of the Lost Kings MC's downstate charter. One of Hope's best friends. Z and Lilly's son is named Chance.

Shelby Morgan: Rooster's sassy little chickadee. Country music singer from Texas. We first met Shelby in *Swagger and Sass*.

Serena Cargill: Former downstate club girl. At one time, she was broken-hearted over Murphy. We first met her in *Strength From Loyalty*, got to know her better in *White Heat* and *More Than Miles*. She has appeared here and there in the series since then. Mistreated by Shadow, the former VP of the downstate charter, we have not "seen" her since *Zero Regret*.

Swan: Lost Kings MC club girl and dancer at Crystal Ball. Swan has found a new calling as the yoga teacher for the old ladies of the Lost Kings MC and is slowly moving away from dancing at Crystal Ball.

Willow: Bartender at Crystal Ball, but once or twice we've caught her sneaking in or out of the basement with Sparky.

Tawny: Sway's ol' lady. The former "Queen B" of the downstate charter of the Lost Kings MC.

Anya Regal: Porn princess of the Lost Kings MC, Virginia charter.

Stella: Pornographic film actress. The downstate charter is the sole investor in her production company. Ex-girlfriend of Z. Current...*something* of Sway. Her *Sex in Every City* series sometimes requires members of LOKI to work as bouncers on her film sets.

Shonda: Club girl from the Lost Kings, MC Virginia charter.

OTHER RECURRING CHARACTERS RELEVANT TO THIS STORY

Russell "Chaser" Adams: President of the Devil Demons MC in Western NY. (*The Hollywood Demons* series contains his story.)

Mallory "Little Dove" DeLova-Adams: Chaser's wife. Daughter of mafia boss Anatoly DeLova.

Angelina Adams: Mallory and Chaser's daughter

Linden "Stump" Adams: Chaser's father. Former president of the Devil Demons MC.

Sullivan Wallace: Jake's brother, and the owner of Strike Back Fitness. He's a significant character in *Bullets and Bonfires* and has his own book, *Warnings and Wildfires*.

Remington "Ruthless" Holt: Owns "The Castle" with his best friend, Griff. It's an underground fighting ring Murphy used to participate in. We've seen him most recently in *Lyrics on the Wind*. He is the caretaker of his younger sister, Molly and runs a bar that his grandparents left him, where the Lost Kings have recently had some interesting events happen.

Griffin "Stonewall" Royal: Remy's best friend and business partner.

Eraser: Owns Zips, a racetrack near the Lost Kings MC territory. Married to Ella. Most recently seen in *White Lies*.

Roman "Vapor" Hawkins: The book *Cards of Love: Knight of Swords* is his story. We first met him and his wife, Juliet, in *After Burn*.

Jake Wallace: One of Wrath's business partners in Furious Fitness. Jake has appeared off and on throughout the series since *Tattered on my Sleeve*. He sometimes holds self-defense classes for the ladies.

The mysterious "Quill" who we met in *Diamond in the Dust* and is Chaser's half-brother.

Anatoly DeLova: Mallory's father. Leader of Russian mafia. Sometime business associate of the Lost Kings MC.

Dawson Roads: Famous (fictional) country music singer in the Lost Kings MC world. He's been mentioned here and there since *One Empire Night*, but we didn't "meet" him until *Rhythm of the Road*.

Carter Clark: Charlotte's goofy, often inappropriate, younger brother.

Loco: Business associate of the Lost Kings MC. He covers the Ironworks area of the Lost Kings MC's territory. He has appeared throughout the series and become a strong LOKI ally.

OTHER MCS: FRIENDLY CLUBS:

Devil Demons MC: Based in Western NY. Long-time friend of the Lost Kings MC. Their clubs are intertwined and share a lot of history. More of this is explored in the *Hollywood Demons* series.

Wolf Knights MC: Mostly an ally of the Lost Kings. Runs Slater County but has had a number of shake-ups in the last few years. Whisper is their current president. Claimed to be dissolving their charter and turning Slater County over to the Lost Kings but we haven't seen them fully exit the area yet.

Iron Bulls MC (From the *Iron Bulls MC* series by Phoenyx Slaughter): Southwestern outlaw club. Meets up and does business with LOKI once in a while.

Savage Dragons MC (From the *Iron Bulls MC* series by Phoenyx Slaughter): Texas outlaw club.

ENEMY CLUBS:

Vipers MC: Used to run Ironworks until the Lost Kings took over that territory. Still active in other parts of the country.

South of Satan MC: Vermont MC who has stirred up trouble for LOKI in the past.

LOST KINGS MC TERMINOLOGY

LOKI: Short for LOst KIngs

War room: Where the Lost Kings hold "church."

Property patch: When a member takes a woman as his old lady (wife status), he gives her a vest with a property patch. In my series, the vest has a "Property of Lost Kings MC" patch and the member's road name on the back. The officers also place their patches on the ol' lady's vest as a sign that they always have her back. Her man's patch or club symbol is placed over the heart. Rock's patch is a crown. Wrath's is a star. Murphy's is a four-leaf clover. Teller's is a dollar sign. Z's is the letter Z. Rooster's is a rooster wearing a crown. As a joke, Wrath gave Rock and Hope a "product of" patch for baby Grace. Maybe it will catch on as more kids are born into the club? We'll see.

PLACES IN THE LOST KINGS MC WORLD

I use a mix of real and imaginary names to describe the places in my series. Again, I bend and shape geography to my needs as this is a *fictional world that I have created.*

Empire, NY: The territory run by the Lost Kings MC upstate charter. This is a fictional version of Albany, NY, the capital of New York State. Many of the Lost Kings MC's businesses are located in and around Empire.

Slater, NY: Loosely based on Schenectady County. Until recently it was the Wolf Knights MC's territory.

Ironworks, NY: Loosely based on Rensselaer County (Troy, NY).

In the beginning of the series, it was run by the Vipers MC. It is now considered territory of the Lost Kings MC.

Union, NY: A fictional area two hours south of Empire, NY, where the "downstate" charter is located.

Crystal Ball: The strip club owned by the Lost Kings MC and one of their legitimate businesses. They often refer to it simply as "CB." Located in Empire County.

Furious Fitness: The gym Wrath owns. Often just referred to as "Furious." Located not far from Crystal Ball.

Strike Back: Owned by Sullivan Wallace but members of the Lost Kings MC have worked there in the past.

Johnson County/Johnsonville: Fictional area where Heidi grew up. About an hour west of "Empire." Where Strike Back Gym, The Castle, and Zips are located. Possibly the new home of a Lost Kings MC support club? We'll see!

Zips: Racetrack owned by Eraser where all the illegal gambling/racing in the area happens.

The Castle: Formerly a juvenile detention center. The building is now used to house the underground fighting ring run by Remy and Griff. Murphy used to fight here. Other LOKI members also blow off steam in the cage here from time to time. Located in the middle of nowhere, NY, it once-upon-a-time housed Griff, Vapor, and possibly Teller during their "troubled youth" days.

Kodack, NY: Another *fictional* NY area located in Western New York. Somewhere near Buffalo, perhaps. This territory is run by the Devil Demons MC.

Empire Medical Center: Local hospital where all the Kings receive medical treatment. Heidi also works there now.

OTHER MC TERMINOLOGY

Most terminology was obtained through research. However, I have also used some artistic license in applying these terms to my romanticized, fictional version of an outlaw motorcycle club. This is not an exhaustive list.

Cage: A car, truck, van—basically anything other than a motorcycle.

Church: Club meetings all full-patch members must attend. Led by the president of the club, but officers will update the members on the areas they oversee. (Some clubs refer to the meeting room where they hold church as the "chapel." My club refers to it as their "war room."

Citizen: Anyone not a hardcore biker or belonging to an outlaw club. "Citizen wife" would refer to a spouse kept entirely separate from the club.

Cut: Leather vest worn by outlaw bikers and adorned with patches and artwork displaying the club's unique colors. The Lost Kings' colors are blue and gray. Their logo is a skull with a crown. The *Respect Few, Fear None* patch is earned by doing time for the club without snitching. *Brother's Keeper* patches are earned by killing for the club. *Loyal Brother* is for a brother who's spent more than five years with the club.

Colors: The "uniform" of an outlaw motorcycle gang. A leather vest, with the three-piece club patch on the back, and various other patches relating to their role in the club.

Fly colors: To ride on a motorcycle wearing colors.

Muffler bunny or "bunnies": A girl who hangs around to provide sexual favors to members. Old ladies in my series will sometimes refer to them as "friends of the club," depending on the girl in question. Some clubs refer to them as club whores, patch whores, or cut sluts. These terms are not regularly used in my series. Sometimes simply referred to as a "club girl."

Nomad: A club member who does not belong to any specific charter, yet has privileges in all charters.

Old lady/ol' lady: Wife or steady girlfriend of a club member.

Patched in: When a new member is approved for full membership.

Patch holder: A member who has been vetted through performing duties for the club as a prospect or probate and has earned his three-piece patch.

Road name: Nickname. Usually given by the other members.

Run: A club-sanctioned outing, sometimes with other chapters and/or clubs. Can also refer to a club business run.

I'm sure I'm forgetting something! But that should get you started!

CHAPTER ONE

Grinder

When people have taken pleasure in watching you bleed, it changes you. Turns you into the savage you swore you'd never become. After a while, you're not sure you'll make it back to who you used to be. So if you find a woman who soothes your inner beast and defrosts your frozen soul, allowing them to slip away isn't an option.

Sometimes, running away to protect what you love most can be the bravest act. I understand that. Respect it, even.

Doesn't mean I won't search every corner of this Earth until I find my woman.

"I'll drive." Z follows me down the hallway.

"You're not coming with me," I grumble over my shoulder. "My life's not a soap opera for your entertainment." But fuck if it's not starting to feel that way.

Z thunders down the stairs behind me. "Hey." He taps my shoulder when we reach the packed clubhouse living room.

I spin around to confront him in a low voice. "What?"

"I'm not looking to be entertained, brother." Z's as solemn as I've ever seen him. No dimples in sight. "I just wanna make sure you're okay. And that she's all right."

"Fine." I blow out an annoyed breath. My gaze darts around the room again, confirming no one's listening to us. "Don't say anything to anyone, though. Please. I don't need everyone knowing my business before I even know what's up."

"Promise." He holds up one hand. "Won't breathe a word to anyone until you're ready."

"Thank you."

Outside, the crisp night air slaps me in the face. Bright light spills out of the garage. The gravel crunches under our boots as we cross the lot. I catch a figure banging around inside and move faster.

"Dex," I call out.

"I thought you didn't want anyone else to know?" Z mutters.

Ignoring Z, I hurry to meet Dex outside the garage door. "You busy?"

"Always, but what's up?"

"You've been by Emily's place, right?"

"A few times. Keeping an eye on things. Haven't seen anything or anyone sneaking around."

"You mind stopping by and asking if Serena's there?"

Dex widens his eyes. "You actually want me to knock on her door and let her know the club's been watching over her?" He continues with the incredulous stare. "How do you want me to explain that?"

"Don't."

"What's going on?"

"Nothing. I can't get a hold of Serena and I'm worried about her." I try to dial down the agitation in my voice. "Z and I are gonna run by her place. Emily's is like an hour in the opposite direction, so—"

"Yeah. Sure, brother. I got you." He slaps my shoulder. "I'll head out right now."

"If she's there, just ask her to call me and send me a text to let me know."

"You got it."

I give him a description of Serena's car and the license plate. He squints but doesn't question me further.

"Let's go." Z slaps my chest.

2

"Do that again and you're going to pull back a bloody stump," I warn.

"Easy, Grinder."

I turn toward my truck but Z stops me. "I'll drive. That way, I can take off if she's there. Leave you two alone."

"Super," I grumble, sweeping my arm ahead of me in a lead-the-way gesture.

Z shakes his head, muttering under his breath about my grumpiness.

"You wanted to come with me," I remind him. "Deal with it."

There isn't much to talk about as he drives us into Empire. At least there shouldn't be. Z seems to have a different idea.

"Where's your head at, G?" he asks.

"I want to make sure she's okay." My hands curl into fists in my lap. "Don't want to get my hopes up," I admit in a lower voice.

"What are you going to do...if she's...*you know?*"

"Let her know I'm going to take care of her and our kid." I snort and close my eyes for a second. "I already used some of that cash from Quill to order a fucking engagement ring after our meeting today."

Z chuckles. "That's some irony."

"Yeah, I'm laughing my ass off over here."

His hands tighten around the steering wheel and I move my gaze to his face. Jaw clenched, eyes staring straight ahead.

"I really wish we'd killed Shadow slower," he says, voice tight with anger. "She wouldn't be so fucking scared that she felt like she had to run if—"

"Had the same thought." It stings that Serena doesn't trust me or my club. But I can't blame her, either.

A cloud of disapproval hangs in the cab as we venture farther into downtown Empire. Z steers his truck onto Serena's small street and scowls.

"How can you let her live here?" he finally asks.

"I offered to move her into a nicer place. She wasn't having it."

He lines the truck up next to a smaller car and smoothly parallel parks it against the curb. "Life's not as much fun without a good woman frustrating the fuck outta ya."

"Ain't that the truth."

His gaze scans the pavement in front of us. "Where does she usually park?"

"On the street." I examine both sides of the road. "I don't see her car."

He opens his door and steps out, while slowly studying the area.

Irritated, I slide out of the truck and slam the door. "You don't need to come up with me." The last thing I need is Serena freaking out because I showed up with a brother. Even if it's Z.

"I'm too invested in the outcome now." He flashes his dimples and runs a hand through his hair. "If she's here, I'll go sit in the truck."

Arguing with him is a waste of time. I head toward Serena's building not bothering to check if Z's following me.

"The fuck?" he grumbles as I wrench the front door open. "It's not locked?"

"No." I pull out my keys. The two of us sound like a herd of moose jogging up the stairs. If Serena's home, she'll hear us coming.

"You already have a key to her place?" Z asks.

"Yes," I growl. "Any more questions?"

"Probably. Give me a second to think on it."

"You do that, asshole." I stop in front of Serena's door and unlock the deadbolts.

"Well, at least she has good hardware."

"First thing I did when I saw this place."

"I should've guessed." He laughs.

I push the door and it swings wide. Nothing greets us but the dark stillness of her quiet apartment.

Stale stuffiness hangs in the air, as if no one's been here in a while. Makes sense. I've had Serena staying at the clubhouse since her attack. We only stopped by once briefly to pick up a few things.

I flick on the lights.

Hope bursts in my chest. Books scattered on the entertainment stand, throw pillows and blanket on the couch, even a couple pairs of her sneakers lined up by the front door. Everything appears as I remember from my last visit.

She hasn't packed up and moved. There aren't any boxes waiting to be filled. That's good. Maybe she just needs a breather. A moment to absorb this life-altering news. Some space. As much as I hate it, I can give her that.

As I'm busy cataloging familiar items, Z stomps through the living room like he owns the place.

"Take your damn shoes off," I call after him.

He returns to the front door with a raised eyebrow. "Seriously?"

One hard stare wipes the smile off his face, and he toes off his boots. "Happy now?"

My gaze drops to his feet and sticks. "Are those...*mermaids* on your socks?" I blink and stare at the colorful blue and green wool. The stress of this endless day must be making me hallucinate.

"Lilly bought them for me." He rocks back on his heels and wiggles his toes. "I wasn't exactly expecting to show them off tonight."

"You went to a meet wearing *mermaid* socks?" For fuck's sake, now I've seen everything.

"A Glock too." He pulls the pistol from the holster at his side and points it toward *my* feet. "Keep making fun of my socks, fucker."

"Where'd she even find something to fit those big-ass grizzly paws of yours?"

"I don't ask questions. She and Trinity are always shopping for stuff together." He presses his hand to his chest. "It's not easy to find clothing to accommodate men of my size."

"Jesus Christ, Wrath running around in mermaid socks too?"

"Nah." Z lowers his hands into a V, framing his crotch. "I think Trin's thing is gettin' him fancy underwear."

"I didn't need to know that."

"You asked." He re-holsters his pistol. "We looking for something here or you got more wardrobe critiques?"

"I don't know what we're gonna find. Doesn't look like she's been here."

Even so, I do a sweep of the apartment. I flick the light on in the first room.

"What's this?" Z asks.

"Where she films her stuff." I wave my hand in the air. "Those makeup videos."

"Cute." He moves closer to the long counter where Serena usually keeps her laptop and other equipment. "Something's missing."

"She brought her laptop up to the clubhouse."

"Anything else?"

I shrug. "I couldn't name half the equipment she uses if you put a gun to my head." I yank my cell phone out, checking for any messages. "I'm still trying to wrap my head around this smartphone bullshit."

His grim nod is almost worse than if he'd laughed.

I move on to her bedroom. Unfortunately, Z follows me. Can't say I'm comfortable having him in my girl's room. His gaze slides over her dresser to a small desk in the corner. He picks up a stack of envelopes and flips through them.

"Stop going through her shit," I snap.

He fans the envelopes in front of him. "Searching for a clue about where she might've gone."

"She's not close to whatever family she's got left." I snatch the envelopes out of his hand and sort through them. Bills. Lots of 'em. My gaze lands on one from Union County Hospital.

"Yeah, saw that too," Z says quietly.

I slip the piece of paper out of the envelope and unfold it. No details, just a balance that makes my eyes bug the fuck out. "How the hell does she plan to ever pay this off?"

He plucks it out of my hand but doesn't seem as shocked at the number. "If it's what I think it's for, the club should be paying it anyway." He folds the paper and tucks it into his pocket.

Since I agree the club should pay it, I don't give him shit for stealing my girl's mail.

He sifts through more papers on the desk. "Most of the important stuff she'll have on her phone these days," he mutters. His gaze lands on a corkboard over the desk with dozens of colorful squares of paper. Quotes ranging from cute to profound are scrawled in her neat handwriting over each one.

One corner of Z's mouth lifts. "'Never assume loud equals strength and quiet equals weakness.'" He nods. "I like that."

My gaze lands on another one that freezes me in place.

The strongest souls carry the deepest scars.

"Let's get going." I nudge his side with my elbow. "Obviously, she's not here."

And I won't be able to rest until I find her.

CHAPTER TWO

Serena

Free yourself from fear by forgiving your past mistakes.

THE THINGS I'M RUNNING FROM AREN'T JUST IN MY HEAD.

They're etched into my soul. Burned into my psyche. My mind is at war with my heart.

Protect my baby.

Gray is nothing like Shadow. He'd never *hurt* me, even my scarred heart knows that truth. But my brain can't stop reminding me that it doesn't mean Gray *wants* this baby.

Guilt follows me all the way to Emily's house.

Coward. Rude. An endless stream of scolding words keeps repeating in my head. How can I leave Gray without an explanation? What will he think when he returns to the clubhouse and I'm not there?

I need time to think. Steel myself for the inevitable rejection. Prepare for the worst.

I've been broken so many times in my life, I'm now unbreakable.

I tuck my car into a spot at the end of Emily's street. A large willow tree with long trailing branches shields me from view. I already called Emily and asked if I could stay with her. She didn't demand an explanation, just told me my room was ready and waiting.

The warm glow of streetlamps illuminates the way to Emily's house. Her neighborhood's safe and friendly, but I'm still anxious as I hike my backpack over my shoulder, loop my bag over my arm and sling my purse over my other shoulder. I hurry over the sidewalk that's actually been cleaned and salted. Barely any trace of the last snowstorm covers the pavement.

The bluestone path to Emily's front porch is lit up with small solar lights. Another light floods the front yard and porch, almost blinding me. Good burglar deterrent.

I hop onto the porch and jab my finger against the doorbell.

The door swings open, and Emily appears. A screen door still separates us. "Why are you ringing the bell? You know you can just come in."

"That seemed rude." I reach for the handle. The screen door lets out a low screech as I swing it open. I step inside, quickly closing and locking it behind me.

Emily's gaze roams over me from head to toe. Seeking injuries, probably.

"It's nothing bad, Em." I set my bags on the bench next to the door and kick my shoes off.

"You had me worried."

"Sorry, I didn't mean to." I glance around. "Where's Libby?"

"School. Rehearsal. She's supposed to get a ride from a friend." She glances at the clock on the wall. "If she's not back soon, I'm going to kick her butt."

For the first time in hours, I actually smile.

"Come here." Emily pulls me into a hug. "Let me make some tea and you can tell me what's going on."

As much as I love coffee, this feels like a tea kind of conversation. Wait, can I even drink coffee anymore? My hand strays to my stomach. I have a lot of things to figure out.

I follow Emily into the kitchen.

"What's going on?" She turns her back to me, standing at the sink to fill a blue enamel teakettle. "Are you okay?"

"I don't know."

"Did something happen with Gray?" she asks carefully.

"It's nothing like that, Emily," I answer quickly. Emily knows all about my history of shitty boyfriends and I don't want her thinking Gray is another in the long line.

Her shoulders drop, and she blows out a breath. "Good."

"How's work?" I ask to take the attention off me.

"Not bad." She goes into a lengthy description of her current research project. Most of it goes over my head but I nod, smile, and try to ask the appropriate questions.

"All right." She sets two mugs of hot water on the table and places a box of tea bags in the middle. I pick through her stash until I find a sachet of chamomile and pop it in my mug. "Tell me why you're so jumpy?" She perches on the chair across from me and fixes her own tea.

Somehow, it's easier to say it when she's not looking right at me. "I'm pregnant."

Damn, that feels weird rolling off my tongue.

She flicks her gaze to mine and for a brief second, pity, sorrow, or maybe disappointment flickers over her face. "Why don't we take these in the living room?" She lifts her mug and stands.

Feeling like a kitten whose mama cat is about to drag her by the scruff, I grab my mug and follow.

I sink into the corner of her couch. Turning to face her, I tuck one leg under my butt.

"How far along are you?" she asks.

"Not long. I took a test, well, three tests this morning."

"What does Gray think?"

I drop my gaze to my mug, staring into the amber liquid, searching for answers. "I haven't told him yet."

Her hand slips into my field of vision, resting on my knee. "Are you afraid he'll be mad?"

"I guess so." I lift my head but still can't meet her eyes. I stare at the curtains covering the large bay window in the dining area. Heavy, dark velvet with gold tassels. Must've been something her parents picked out. It doesn't seem like Emily's style.

"Serena?" she prods. "Are you worried he'll hurt you?"

"No. He's not like…not like that. "

She sighs. "Good. Okay."

"We just haven't been together long. I asked him once and he didn't seem receptive to the idea."

"Well, he has a lot going on, trying to put his life back together."

I finally meet her eyes. "Thanks."

"I didn't mean it that way." She brushes off my defensiveness. "I don't know him as well as you do. I only met him once. But he seemed awfully smitten with you."

I can't help smiling. "He's good to me."

"He's older, though. A baby at his age…he's probably not going to be able to help you out as much. And of course, you know, there's a good chance you—"

"Don't." I don't even want to think about Gray dying before me.

"I know you've already thought about all of this."

"Yes," I whisper.

"You should talk to him, Serena. Don't preemptively decide how he's going to feel without talking to him. Give him a chance."

"I know."

"Ultimately, it's *your* decision and I'll support you no matter what."

I clutch my stomach. "I want this baby, Emily." Tears sting my eyes. "I want it so much. That's why I'm so scared."

"Oh, honey." She scoots closer and tugs the tea out of my hand, setting it on the coffee table. "I get it. I do. You went through a lot. And this is probably bringing up that trauma."

"Obviously."

She wraps her arms around me, pulling me into an awkward hug. After a moment of hesitation, I hug her back. "Thank you for not telling me how stupid and careless I am," I whisper against her hair.

"I'd never say that, because it's not true."

Unconvinced, I shake myself out of our embrace. "I'm not scared he'll hurt me physically." Old memories threaten to burst out of the brick walls I built in my mind to contain them. I wrap my arms around my middle and rock forward. "But if I sense he's mad or doesn't want the baby or even suggests...I can't handle it."

"You can handle *anything*." She leans into my space, leveling a stern stare at me. "You're the bravest, strongest woman I know—

"I—"

"No." She slashes her hand in front of her. "You're not a good judge of yourself. I'm objective."

The corners of my lips twitch. "You're not objective."

"Well, *you're* definitely not." She pats my knee. "Seriously. You just found out a few hours ago. Take some time and let the news sink in. Steel yourself emotionally to have that talk with Grayson. You can do it over the phone if you want to keep some distance. I can go out. Give you space if you need space. Or I can stay and hold your hand. Whatever you want."

"I don't even have a job right now."

"Your channel's doing better, right?" She wrinkles her nose. "No offense, but your apartment's not really great for a baby."

"I should've taken Gray's offer to move me into a nicer place," I mutter.

"He did? Why'd you turn him down?"

"It's too soon. I didn't want to get comfortable somewhere, then we break up, and I end up homeless."

"Smart. Yeah." Her eyes light up. "Move in with us!"

"What?"

"Yes! We have more than enough room." She points at the ceiling. "That corner room is empty. It gets great sunlight in the morning, so you can film your videos." She twists toward the dining room. "Or there in the afternoons."

"I can't take over your whole house."

"We have the room. Please." She squeezes her hands together. "The little room next to yours is just storage. I'll clean it out and you can use it as a nursery. It'll be perfect."

"Emily, you don't want a baby in your home."

"Why not? I like babies." She squeezes her hip. "I don't want one shooting out of my hoo-ha, but—"

I burst into uncontrollable laughter. "Why? Why'd you have to say *that?*"

"What? It's true. Sounds like a nightmare. Oh, oops." She slaps her hand over her mouth. "Sorry."

When we finally settle down, I pin her with a serious stare. "Are you sure?"

"Honey, you have a home here with us as long as you and the baby need one." Emily rests her hand over mine. "Libby would *love* having you around more. I bet she'd help you with babysitting when you're ready, too."

"I can't ask her to do that." I consider the offer. I'd definitely be safer here. Jobs aren't as plentiful. But there is a small, local hospital. I can probably find something. "I'll pay you rent."

She wrinkles her nose. "The hell you will."

"Emily—"

She holds up one hand. "If you could help me drop Libby off at school in the mornings, I'd appreciate it."

"That's it?"

"Well…" her gaze darts around the room like she's desperately trying to think of some chores for me to earn my keep. "Help out with the groceries."

"Of course. I'll clean up around the house too. Be a good guest."

She leans in and throws her arms around me. "So, yes? You'll stay with us?"

I can't help but return the embrace. So choked up from her generous offer, I have trouble articulating the right words. "Thank you." My voice cracks.

"You don't have to *thank* me. When do you want to grab your stuff from your apartment?"

"Uh." Shoot. If I don't call Gray soon, he'll be watching my place. Or have one of his brothers sit on it. He won't accept me just disappearing—

A knock on the front door startles us apart. My head whips toward the front entrance. "Who's that?" Fear trembles through my voice.

Emily leans forward and swipes a tablet off the coffee table. She flicks the screen and taps a few times. She pauses and studies the view of the front porch that appears.

"You have a camera on the porch?" I ask.

"Damn right I do. It's just Libby and me here. I have cameras all over the place." She turns the screen my way. "You know him?"

The guy has his head tipped down and away from the camera, but I recognize him from his casual stance and posture. Broad shoulders back, one hand tucked in his pocket. He shifts and the Lost Kings MC patch on the front of his cut comes into view.

Dex. Gray's already sending people to look for me.

I can't decide if it's incredibly sweet. Or downright creepy.

"Yes, I know him," I answer quietly.

CHAPTER THREE

Serena

GRAY'S ALREADY SENDING PEOPLE TO SEARCH FOR ME.

He didn't come here himself. That means he probably went to my apartment. Guilt and anxiety go to war in my stomach.

"Is he a friend of Grayson's?" Emily asks.

"Yup."

She stares at me for a few seconds. "Do you want to talk to him?"

And say what? If I can't talk to Grayson about this yet, I'm sure as hell not going to tell Dex. "Nope."

"Okay." She lifts her chin toward the hallway and hands me the tablet. "You can turn the sound on." She taps the screen. "If you want to listen to what he has to say."

I scurry into the hallway, my socks sliding over the polished, hardwood floors. Blood thundering through my veins, I rest my back against the wall and close my eyes. My heart's torn in two. Gray's worried enough to send his brothers to look for me. I know it's a sign of how much he cares, not that he's trying to control me. But Shadow stalked, tracked, and hunted me down so many times, I can't stop the pounding of my heart.

Shadow never asked a brother to look for me. He preferred to keep his violent tendencies and stalkerish behavior hidden from the club.

The front door latch clicks, bringing my mind to the present. I shake off the fear and questions bouncing around in my head and peer at the tablet. The grainy, black and white view of the front door provides a good angle of Dex and Emily.

"Can I help you?" Emily's pleasant, don't-fuck-with-me tone calms me a notch.

"Emily?" Dex rumbles. "Serena's friend, right?"

"Who's asking?"

"I'm a friend of Grayson's." On the screen, Dex pulls his hand out of his pocket, extends it, and pauses. Emily continues staring at him, ignoring the offer to shake hands. He drops his hand to his side. "Dex."

"Is Grayson okay?" Emily asks.

"He's worried about Serena. He can't seem to get in touch with her. Have you seen her recently?"

"No," Emily lies, smooth as butter.

Dex reaches for the door. "Can I come in for a sec?"

Emily's hand tightens around the handle. "No, you can't. I don't know you."

Dex blinks and hooks his thumbs in his pockets. The corners of his mouth seem to twitch with surprise and amusement. I'm sure he's not used to women saying no to him for any reason. "Fair enough."

"I'm not sure what else I can tell you." Emily shrugs but never looks away. Libby isn't the only good actress in the family. "I haven't talked to her since yesterday."

"She was okay when you spoke?"

"She sounded good." Emily cocks her head. "Did they have a fight or something?"

Dex holds his hands up. "Don't know. I don't want to get involved in their personal stuff."

Emily slowly tilts her head the opposite way. "Showing up at Serena's friend's house seems awfully *involved* to me."

Amusement flickers over Dex's expression, but he locks it down fast. "Just doing a favor for my friend. Like I said, he's worried about her."

"Well," Emily chirps, almost a little *too* chipper. "She's not here."

"Okay." Dex hesitates, glances over his shoulder and back at Emily. "Would you mind giving me a call if you hear from her?"

Silence stretches between them. Emily stares straight ahead, like she's considering the question. Knowing her, she wants to tell him no. Or to fuck off. One or the other.

While he's waiting for an answer, Dex pulls a small white rectangle from his pocket. A business card.

My, my, isn't he prepared.

"My number's on the back." He gestures toward the black, rectangular mailbox attached to the side of the house. "I'll drop it in there."

"All right." Even though I can't get a clear shot of Emily's face, I hear the smile in her voice.

A few seconds later, the door clicks closed. I peer around the corner. Emily's leaning against the back of the wood, chin tipped up and eyes closed. A dreamy smile curves her lips.

I chuckle and step into the living room. "Everything okay?"

"Oh my word. Yes." She inhales a deep breath and opens her eyes. "Do you know that guy?"

"I know Dex." Fighting off a smile, I glance at my socks. "He's a sweetheart."

"Is he ever," she gushes. "So respectful too. I could tell he was pissed I wouldn't let him in, but he didn't push or try to convince me."

There's a reason all the club girls are eager to solve the mystery of Dex. He's always had a way of making everyone feel safe and protected, even though he keeps his distance.

"So, did you get all of that?" Emily's voice turns business-like again and she shakes off her Dex-induced fog. "It sounds like Gray's concerned about you."

"I know." I hesitate, my hands twisting together in front of me. "I'm not ready to call him yet."

"Come here." She holds her hands out, motioning for me to join her on the couch. "Let's talk about this some more."

I drop onto the bouncy couch cushion and inhale a few deep breaths. Heat burns my face. I haven't figured it out myself, yet. How can I discuss this with anyone else? Especially Emily. I'm already disappointed with myself. I don't think I can handle her disappointment too.

"I'm tired." I yawn to punctuate the statement. "Um, can we not say anything to Libby about this, for now?"

"Of course. I won't tell a soul." She shrugs. "I'll say the heat in your apartment isn't working or something."

"Thanks."

"I doubt it'll be an issue. I think she'll just be excited you're here." Her mouth turns down. "Somewhere along the way, I went from fun, big sister, to annoying parental unit."

"Aw, that's not true."

"It is," she shrugs, "but that's what I signed up for."

The reminder of all the tough decisions Emily's faced on her own tug at my heart. I shouldn't be burdening her with my mistakes. "I'm sorry—"

"You don't have anything to apologize for." She pats my leg. "You're going to stay with us. This is your home now. End of discussion."

Home has never been one particular place to me. More of a feeling. And right now, with Emily's acceptance and support, I really do feel home.

CHAPTER FOUR

Grinder

Halfway back to the clubhouse, Z and I both receive texts. Mine's from Wrath.

Church. First thing tomorrow morning.

Z's message flashes across the truck's dashboard screen.

Rock: *If you're still local, we're sitting down for church first thing in the morning.*

"At least he seems to respect your role as president," I say, nodding at the screen.

"Rock?" Z lifts an eyebrow.

"No, Godzilla. Who the fuck else would I be talking about?"

He turns his head slightly. "How'd you end up with the road name Grinder, instead of Grumpy?"

"Hilarious. You should be a comedian."

"Yeah, things are working well the way they are," he answers my initial observation.

"Good."

"I'm trying, but I still don't quite trust all of the guys downstate the same way I trust—"

After what Serena told me, I don't blame him. "Always knew Sway would cause a lot of damage if he had an ounce of power."

"True story," he agrees. "Rooster's solid. Jigsaw too. You can trust them. Butcher—he spent a lot of time up here helping out. Good brother."

"Kinda strange your SAA isn't at the top of your list," I point out.

"I trust Steer," he says slowly. "But he was an officer under Sway too."

"You didn't want to clean house when you came in?" Not that I need him to confirm or deny.

He hesitates. "Assuming Sway's role at the head of the table was a... delicate procedure."

Something Z would've been perfect for. Lotta folks underestimated him back in the day and it seems like he's used that to his advantage over the years.

"I didn't want to leave upstate," Z says. "Still burns my ass a little."

"You can't go back to VP once you've been the prez."

He shrugs. "I could give a fuck about titles." He gestures toward the screen where the text from Rock is still blinking. "I never felt stifled or anything working with Rock. And yes, I mean working *with*. He doesn't treat any of us like we're *underneath* him."

"Never was afraid to get his hands dirty."

"Right. He's always had everyone's respect." He snickers. "Well, he was rough on Teller and Murphy sometimes, but they deserved it."

"I've noticed he still is. Couldn't have been too bad. They turned into fine brothers."

"Aw, papa bear. It's so good you're home."

"Don't start with me."

The smirk slides off his face. "I mean it, G. I hate that you missed out on so much."

"No more than I do." No point in denying the obvious. Or wallowing in it.

"I know."

"If I dwell on it too long, it'll make me crazy," I warn, hoping he'll drop it.

"Sorry. I didn't mean to bring it up."

"It's always there." I tap my fingers against the back of my skull.

"That lingering feeling. I want to make up for lost time. That's why I hate this shit with Grillo holding me back."

"It won't last forever, brother. One way or another we're going to take care of him."

"He's my problem to handle."

"Problem of my brother's is a problem of mine. That hasn't changed."

Why has it always been so easy for me to *give* that advice but so hard to accept it myself?

I can't believe I'm going to say this out loud. But Z didn't have to give up his evening to drive around Empire County with me. I want him to put his guilty conscience to rest. "I feel like I have this second chance with Serena. And I really don't want to fuck it up."

"You won't." He pauses. I glance over and catch his clenched jaw.

"What?" I prompt.

"Nothing. Maybe don't pin all your hope on one girl, you know? She's...ah...at a different stage of life than you are."

"Thanks for not saying 'young enough to be my daughter' like Wrath did."

He grins. "Wrath wouldn't understand tact if a thousand pounds of it fell on his big ol' Viking skull."

"We've talked about that." I cough and shift in my seat. "Serena and I, I mean."

"You have?"

"Yes, Z." I'm not going to get into personal stuff she's shared with me. He already knows more than he should. "She's had it rough in her own way."

"Most people who end up in club life have a reason."

I growl at the mention of Serena being *involved* in the club, even though I already know all about it.

"Easy, I didn't mean anything bad by it."

"I know you didn't." I stare out the window, watching the red taillights ahead of us. "In some ways, I think she's better suited to being an ol' lady than Rosie ever was."

"Probably." He glances over. "Although, I'd keep those comparisons to a minimum, brother. Women ain't fond of that."

I snort. "Yeah. I screwed stuff up with Rosie long before I went inside. Trying hard not to do it again."

"Learning from our mistakes and trying to do better is what it's all about, right?"

"Supposedly."

"You think you're ready to be a dad?"

"Doesn't really matter if I'm ready or not."

"I guess you're right."

"But I am." I glance over. "You, Rock, and Wrath were fun and all, but—"

He bursts into laughter. "Bro, today they will throw you right back in jail if you try raising a kid the way you 'raised' us."

"Goddamn, you were such a smooth-talking little bullshitter when Rock brought you to the clubhouse."

He grins even wider. "I'm a hustler, baby."

"Were you ever." My mouth curves at the memory. Full of himself or not, Z earned my respect early with his loyalty and hard work.

Z slows the truck and makes the turn onto the narrow road leading to the clubhouse's gate.

"How'd you guys ever find this place?"

"I honestly don't remember. We needed something with the space for Sparky to grow his crops. Wanted it to be private and hard to find."

"You got that."

"I'm looking forward to you coming to see downstate."

"Same, brother."

Z slows the truck as we approach the gate. It slides open, allowing us to continue up the steep, paved driveway.

"Looks like the party must've moved down to Crystal Ball," Z says as he slides into a spot across from the clubhouse.

"Good. I wanna see what Dex found without everyone sticking their nose in my business."

The party hasn't completely died down. Rooster, Jigsaw, and Ravage are clustered in front of the war room doors when we enter.

Z claps my shoulder. "I'll see you later." He ducks inside the small office to the right and closes the door behind him.

"Grinder!" Rooster's hearty greeting erases a fraction of my irritation. I accept a quick handshake and pat on the back from him. "Life treating you good, brother?" he asks.

"Eh. As long as I'm not inside a cell, I'm good."

"Hell yes." Jiggy holds out his fist and I tap his knuckles with my own.

Finally, the brother I *need* to talk to steps inside the clubhouse. I barely restrain myself from pouncing on him. Dex takes his sweet-ass time moseying over.

"Well?" I ask as soon as Dex stops in front of me.

He flicks his gaze my way and smirks. "Emily's a beautiful woman, but she can't lie for shit."

"Aww, look at Dex noticing a woman." Jigsaw cackles and slaps Dex's back. "Good for you, buddy."

Dex slides an irritated glare at Jigsaw. "I'm runnin' Crystal Ball. *Noticing* women is literally *all* I do. All day, every day."

"I meant in the *biblical* sense," Jigsaw clarifies. "Not in a commercial way."

If I wasn't ready to come out of my skin, I might find their antics amusing.

"What do you mean, Dex?" I ask, ignoring Jigsaw. "Did you see Serena or not?"

"No, but I definitely heard two people inside the house."

"Her younger sister lives with her," I say.

"She hot?" Ravage asks.

I growl in Rav's direction and it's enough to shut him up.

"Ah, I didn't know that. Coulda been," Dex says. "Didn't see Serena's car in the driveway. Peeked in the garage and it wasn't in there either."

"Thanks for trying."

"No problem, brother."

And thanks for not asking me why.

"What's going on, Grinder?" Rooster asks. "Is Serena okay?"

"We're fine," I answer in a clipped tone that should leave no room for follow-up questions.

Thankfully, Rooster takes the hint.

"You sticking around for church tomorrow?" I ask Rooster.

"Yeah." He glances at the war room. "If Z's sticking around, I will. Shelby's over at Wrath and Trinity's house." He jerks his chin toward the stairs. "They said we could stay with them if the clubhouse is too noisy."

I huff out a sad laugh. Sleeping at Wrath's house had been the highlight of my first night of freedom. I clap Rooster's shoulder. "You should. It's quiet and peaceful there." I shake Dex's hand and tap knuckles with Jigsaw and Ravage. "I gotta head back to my place. I'll catch you in the morning."

THE NEXT MORNING, I'm torn. Stop by Emily's to ask about Serena or get my ass to the clubhouse?

Waking Emily at the ass-crack of dawn won't endear me to her. Besides, it's time I start pulling my weight with the club. Fuck knows they've been carrying me for years. I need to give back to my brothers. Especially after the way no one has hesitated to help me since I've been out. The club's handed me everything I needed on a silver platter —housing, vehicle, clothes, calling in big favors—the least I can do is show up when my president asks me to.

A pull in my chest wants me to drive to Emily's but I point the truck east and head toward the clubhouse.

Focus.

Bleary-eyed brothers are either sprawled on the couches or milling around the living room when I step into the clubhouse forty-five minutes later. The war room doors are still closed, so at least I'm not late.

Wrath's sitting at the bar sipping coffee and seems to be the most alert brother in the vicinity.

He grins as I approach. "Mornin'."

"Do I have time for coffee before church?" I barely slept last night. I'm in need of a caffeine jolt.

He jerks his head toward the closed door of the office next to the war room. "Rock and Z are having a presidential sit-down. You probably have a minute or two."

The dining room's almost empty, except for Hope and Lilly sitting at the end of one of the long tables. On closer inspection, I notice the kids playing at their feet.

"Good morning, Grinder," Hope calls out.

"Morning." I throw them a quick wave and pour my cup of coffee.

Little feet patter over the floor, stopping next to me with a squeak. "Hi!"

I glance down at Z's son. Still wearing pajamas along with an eager, chubby-cheeked smile. "Morning, Chance."

"Come see!" He holds out one of his small hands, beckoning me closer.

I follow him over to where Hope and Lilly are sitting. As we approach, I notice the kids have a blanket spread out with a racetrack for cars or something situated in the middle. Little Grace is studying a red plastic car. Chance scowls when he sees her and reaches for it.

"Ah, ah, ah," Lilly scolds gently. "Let her play with it for a minute. You have plenty of other cars."

He nods and quickly picks up a shiny, black Jeep replica, holding it out for me to inspect. I set my coffee down and accept the toy. "Damn, that's heavier than it looks."

"Open!" Chance points to the Jeep. I flick one of the doors and it opens.

"Very cool. Where'd you get that?" I lean down so I'm closer to his level. "I want one."

He snatches it out of my hands.

"Chance," Lilly warns.

"It's okay," I laugh.

"Auntie Trinity bought that for him," Lilly explains. "Because he's not spoiled enough."

"It's my duty to spoil *all* my niblets," Trinity announces as she pushes through the swinging kitchen doors and heads our way.

Hope chuckles and sips her coffee. "I like *niblets*."

"It's just easier than nieces and nephews." Trinity plunks a carton of half-and-half in the middle of the table.

While the girls are talking, Chance tiptoes toward Grace and snatches the car out of her hands.

Grace's sweet face screws into a frown and she lets loose, howling for all she's worth. It'd be funny as hell if it wasn't so heartbreaking.

"Oh no." Hope leans over and picks up her daughter, pulling her into her lap. "You're okay."

"Chance." Lilly holds out her hand for the car. Chance looks at it, then Grace, then his mom. "Chance," she prompts again.

Reluctantly, he hands it over.

"Jeep too."

He huffs but gives up the Jeep. Then turns his big, sad eyes toward Trinity.

"Easy come, easy go, little man," Trinity teases, shaking her head. "What Mom says, goes. Can't help you out."

Chance crosses his arms over his chest and scowls at Lilly for a few seconds. Grace's sniffles catch his attention, and he wanders over to her. "I sorry."

Grace buries her head against Hope's chest.

"I sorry!" Chance says louder.

Grace waves one little hand at him, in what I swear looks like the toddler equivalent of fuck off.

Hope laughs and pats her daughter's back.

Z strides into the dining room and nods at me. "We're about to go in."

"Okay."

"Daddy!" Chance shouts and runs over.

"Daddy isn't going to give you a different answer," Lilly mutters.

"Uh-oh, what'd you do now?" Z picks his son up, swinging him into his arms. "Tell me straight."

Chance lays out his argument in a rush of garbled sounds. Z seems to understand every word out of his son's mouth, though. He listens and nods along. Finally, Chance stops and stares at his dad for a verdict.

"Grace is little-er than you, buddy," Z says. "You can share with her for a few minutes. She just wants to look, right?"

Chance frowns.

"Told you." Lilly presses her hand to her mouth, trying to hide her laughter.

They're both so calm and easygoing with their son. Hell, when I was a kid, I probably would've gotten smacked *with* one of the toys to teach me a lesson. Who am I kidding, my parents didn't waste money on toys and shit.

My gaze slides to the kids again. Do *I* have the patience for parenting? Chance is cute and all, but I bet he's a stubborn little shit. Will my temper and rigid attitude end up inflicting a lifetime of damage on a kid?

Serena's sweet and calm. She'll be a good mother. I can easily picture her sitting right next to the other women, waiting for us to finish church, and playing with the kids. Is that what she wants, though? Will she be happy doing that?

Fuck, I'm too old for this.

"You all right, old man?" Z says, curling his hand around my shoulder.

God damn, why am I an open book to this fucker? I shrug off Z's question and spear him with a warning look. But his face remains impassive. He won't say anything or share my troubles before I'm ready.

"I'm fine."

While he and Lilly share a word, I say goodbye to the girls and head down to the war room. Seems like the perfect place to be considering the emotions at war inside of me.

CHAPTER FIVE

Grinder

As I enter the common area, Rock and Wrath emerge from their office with Murphy and Teller following behind.

Wrath unlocks the war room doors and opens them wide.

"All right, let's get down to business," Rock says, ushering us inside with an impatient sweep of his hand.

"Seems like everyone was waitin' on you, Prez," I point out. A good verbal spar with Rock should help me shed the complicated feelings that followed me from the dining room.

He shoots a don't-start stare my way. I respond with a smirk. Shaking his head, he slaps my back. "Thanks for coming up this early."

"You call, I answer, brother. It's time for me to step up and help my club when I'm needed."

He pauses. Around us, brothers continue chattering, taking their sweet time. Rock pulls me out of the flow of traffic.

"Your commitment to the club has never been in question," he says in a low voice. "You're contributing in the ways I need you to right now."

"I'm just sayin', I appreciate all the help the club's done to help me adjust since I got out. You've called in some serious favors on my behalf. I wanna do whatever I can to give back."

He nods once, but trouble still seems to be brewing in his hard eyes.

Brothers are still settling into their chairs when we enter the room. Rock's more patient than I am, waiting until everyone's seated before shattering the noise with a smack of his gavel against the hard wooden table.

"Simmer down." He doesn't raise his voice, but it still carries, commanding everyone's attention. The yakking stops and everyone turns toward Rock.

"Thanks for joining us a little earlier than usual," he starts.

"We love ya, Prez, otherwise I wouldn't be missing my prime beauty sleep hours." Bricks yawns and runs his hands through his thick puff of shiny black hair.

"Nah, he's missing morning snuggle time," Ravage sings, blowing a few kisses toward Bricks.

"You wish someone would snuggle with your gnarly ass."

Rock stares at the ceiling for a few seconds while the guys hurl insults at each other.

"Y'all miss your daily dose of Ritalin or something?" Rooster slaps his giant palm against the table. "Settle the fuck down."

Jigsaw snickers into his elbow. "You said *y'all*."

Rooster punches Jiggy's arm.

Rock blows out a long, slow breath. Probably counting back from ten. "We done?" he asks.

Silence.

Rock waits a beat to see if it sticks.

"All right." Rock settles his arms against the table and stares down the length of it, meeting each brother's eyes. "I got a call from Loco. He wants a meeting. Today."

"Damn, that crazy bastard's got balls." Dex whistles.

I raise my finger in the air to get Rock's attention. "I'm way overdue paying my respects to Loco." I sit forward so I can meet Rock's stare. "You mind if I tag along?"

"Loco will offer you some prime pussy on the house," Ravage announces.

I turn slowly. "What?"

"He runs a brothel over in Ironworks," Teller explains in a bored tone.

"Bro, just call it what it is, a *whorehouse*," Stash says. "No need to be fancy."

Rock snorts. "I think Loco would be offended. He's gone to a lot of trouble to turn it into a 'classy establishment.'"

"Thanks for the warning," I grumble at Ravage. "You mind if the grown-ups have a conversation? Or you gonna interrupt me again?"

Brothers cough or laugh under their breath. Ravage grins at me. "Just tryin' to help a brother out."

"Yes, Grinder," Rock says, ignoring the sideshow. "I'd appreciate it if you joined us."

Teller suddenly seems fascinated with the table as he slowly sinks into his seat.

"T and Dex." Rock's gaze runs the length of the table. "I want you with us too."

Teller groans and rolls his eyes but doesn't question Rock today.

"Why?" Ravage moans. "None of them are gonna sample the goods."

"That's the *point*." Rock's tone is full of patience born from repetition. "I don't need distractions."

Z raises his hand. "Since I'm here anyway, I'll tag along too. I owe Loco a favor, so if he's asking you for help, I should be in on that."

"Appreciate it," Rock says.

"He give any hints about what he wants?" Rooster asks.

"Nothing," Rock sighs. "He loves the cryptic spy game bullshit."

"He just needs a friend, Prez." Wrath grins. "It's nice he's bonded to you."

"Careful, wiseass," Rock growls without turning Wrath's way. "I'm not done deciding who's coming with us."

"Please?" Ravage bounces in his seat and waves his arms around.

"Pick me! Pick me!" Stash mocks in a girlish voice.

"Damn right, pick *me*," Rav answers.

"He probably wants to borrow some extra muscle for outcalls,"

Dex says. "Malik says Loco brought on new girls. They're meeting dates outside Loco's place. But he wants a driver for the girls. No one goes alone."

"While I can appreciate that he wants to keep his girls safe," Rock's jaw tightens with irritation, "we have enough things to handle without adding bodyguard chores. If it's a one-off, we'll see what we can do for him."

Jigsaw raises his hand and lifts his chin at Z. "If Loco needs help this weekend, I'm around."

Z nods.

"Thanks for stepping up, Jigsaw," Rock says.

Jigsaw's mouth curves into a sly grin. "If I'm gonna be listening to someone going at it this weekend, it'd probably be more fun if it's strangers and I'm gettin' paid for it." He jerks his thumb toward Rooster.

"You could just," Rooster strokes his hand over his beard, "oh, I don't know, *not* be a fuckin' creep."

"I don't think you understand how *loud* you two are," Jigsaw protests.

"I mean, Shelby *is* a singer." Ravage shrugs. "But I haven't heard anything—"

"Careful, Rav," Rooster growls.

"It's not her, it's *him*." Jiggy elbows Rooster.

"Shut the fuck up."

"Oh my God, *all* of you, shut the fuck up." Wrath's voice shakes the windowpanes.

"Sparky, when will you have some product for Loco?" Rock asks. "I know he'll want an update."

Sparky squirms in his seat for a second. "Well, boss. Production is a little low. I diverted some of the last harvest to our edibles division."

Rock grits his teeth. "How's that going?"

"Good, good. Willow knows a guy who distributes to a few of the college campuses in the area. We're setting something up."

"Okay," Rock says slowly. "But it's easier to wholesale our harvests to Loco, isn't it? You're getting tied up baking and making edibles and now distributing them instead of *growing*."

Sparky slumps against his chair like Rock just told him unicorns don't exist. "It's a new outlet for my creativity," he protests.

Rock, Wrath, and Z share a look, then Rock's inquisitive eyes turn Teller's way. Teller shrugs.

"All right. Is it making you happy, Sparky?" Rocks asks.

That right there is why Rock's probably managed to stay president for so long and earned the brothers' undying loyalty and respect. Not many bikers would tolerate Sparky's eccentricities.

"Yeah, boss. And I'm providing treats for the clubhouse too."

"Yes, you are, bro." Rav leans over and offers Sparky his hand for a high five.

"Is this exposing us to more risk?" Rock asks.

Sparky scratches the side of his head. "I dunno. I don't think so. It's legalish now."

Teller leans forward and scribbles something on a notepad in front of him, then turns toward Sparky. "Catch me afterward."

Rock lifts an eyebrow. "You gonna have Charlotte look into it?"

"Yeah, but I want to get a clearer picture first."

"Thanks." Rock scans the table again. "All right. Bricks, you're opening CB today, right?"

"Yup." He nods. "You'll let me have Dex later, though, right?"

"I'll be there," Dex promises.

"Anyone else have business?" Rock asks. When no one raises their hand, he nods. "All right."

Murphy clasps his hands together and turns his gaze toward the ceiling. "Thank you, Jesus."

"Don't go thanking your magical sky daddy yet, I got plenty of work for you," Wrath warns.

"When'd you find religion, brother?" Bricks asks Murphy.

"Probably when he started praying that Heidi's baking a boy in her oven," Ravage answers.

"Don't talk about my wife's oven...or anything else," Murphy snarls.

"Are we done here?" Teller asks, scowling at Ravage.

"Yeah, everyone can go." Rock nods at Teller. "Let's meet up outside."

"You got it."

The volume of chatter in the room rises as brothers shuffle out of the room. Rock stops Ravage with a quick, short whistle.

"Rav." He curls his fingers in a "come here" gesture.

Rav's eyes widen and he glances over his shoulder.

"We only got one of you, get over here," Rock says.

Rav jams his hands in his pockets but lifts his chin and squares his shoulders as he approaches Rock's end of the table.

"Prez, I was only kidding around," he says in the most serious tone I've heard the fucker use since I've been here.

"No, you've got a point, crude and annoying as it is," Rock adds.

"*That* should've been his road name," Murphy says. "Crude and Annoying."

Rav grins and flashes his middle finger Murphy's way. "Fuck off, Ginger Yeti."

"Great, glad that's sticking." Murphy shoots a glare across the table at Wrath who grins at him.

Rock pulls Ravage away from the table out of earshot. Doubt whatever they're discussing affects me one way or another.

CHAPTER SIX

Serena

A new day is your opportunity to make it better than yesterday.

IN MY FIRST ACT OF EARNING MY KEEP AT EMILY'S HOUSE, I'M UP EARLY to drop Libby off at school.

I can't tell if it's the early hour or usual teenage sullenness but she's quiet and busy checking her phone while I stick to the local thirty-mile-per-hour speed limit.

"Everything okay, Libby?"

"Yeah," she mutters, staring out the window. "Thanks for taking me. Em likes to sleep in after she works late."

"No problem."

We haven't told her *why* I moved into their house. Libby seemed excited about it. She'd given me a big hug before heading to bed last night and that was it.

Today, she seems indifferent or distracted. I always thought she liked school. Maybe she's just not a morning person.

"What's wrong?" I try again. "And don't lie. I can tell something's bothering you." I don't take my eyes off the road. Somehow, I think it'll be easier for her to spill whatever she's bottling up if I'm not looking at her.

"Nothing." She sighs. "There's this new kid at school. Kyle. I thought we…I don't know. He was supposed to call me last night and he never did. He just sent me this lame, 'oh sorry, I forgot' text. And asked if I'll meet up with him after school."

Maybe all the hard lessons I've learned over the years can finally be of some use. "Can I give you a piece of advice I wish someone had given me at your age?"

"Don't date until I'm twenty-five?" Libby scoffs. "Emily says that all the time."

"No, although, that's not bad advice either." I pause to make sure she's listening. "*If he wanted to, he would.* It's as simple as that."

"What does that mean?"

"If he *wanted* to talk to you, nothing would get in his way. If you're important to him, he'll make the effort. Don't accept the bare minimum. Anyone who 'forgets' isn't seriously interested, so don't waste your time or energy on him."

"Whoa." Out of the corner of my eye, I catch her rubbing her temples. She purses her lips and lets out a dramatic explosion noise. "Mind blown, Serena."

"Don't make fun of me. I'm serious."

"No, no, no," she insists. "I mean it. His fingers aren't broken. If he wanted to talk to me, he would've called. Why bother dissecting his motives?"

"Or wondering if something is wrong with *you*—because there isn't, by the way," I add. Boy, had I wasted a lot of energy worrying about *that* when I was younger. "The amount of effort he puts in reflects his feelings."

"Thanks, Serena."

Warmth spreads through my chest. I wish I'd been as smart and open to advice when I was her age. Or had anyone in my life who cared enough to give me *good* advice. "Spread the word to all your girlfriends."

She giggles. "I will."

I flip my blinker on and turn onto the long driveway to the high school. "Do you want to be dropped off in the front or the back?"

"Front is fine." She leans forward and squints through the windshield. "I see my squad."

"Good." I slow to a stop behind someone's station wagon.

Libby unclicks her seat belt and leans over, quickly kissing my cheek. "I don't know what happened but I'm happy you're staying with us."

My throat tightens and I can't form an answer. It doesn't matter, anyway. As quick as it came, the moment's gone. Libby flings her door open and jumps out. "Thanks, Serena!"

"Text if you need me."

"Okay!" She slams the door and skips toward her group of friends.

Guilt prods me as I drive away from the school. My phone has been off since yesterday. Grayson's probably worried about me. As soon as I can, I pull my car off to the side of the road.

Fear ruled all of my decisions yesterday. Today is my opportunity to do better. I might need some time to digest that I'm pregnant. But Grayson has no idea what's going on. He returned to the clubhouse and found me gone. Shame washes over me. How immature.

I turn on my phone and sure enough, I have several voicemails and texts. My lips curve. For a man who claims he doesn't like to text, he sure sent me enough.

My thumb hovers over the screen. I'm too chicken to listen to the voicemails. I scroll through his texts. Nothing scary or threatening. Not that I expected threats from Gray, but old habits, fears, and traumas are hard to reason with.

What do I even say? I freaked out because I'm pregnant and scared how you'll react? That seems unfair. I don't want to tell him through a text either.

Finally, I tap out a few words.

I'm okay. Sorry for making you worry. I just needed a breather.

I press the send button before I chicken out.

My message invites more questions instead of providing any

answers. *Time for what?* I don't know what else to say, though. At least, hopefully, he won't worry.

Not feeling any better about the situation, I tuck my phone into my purse and steer my car onto the road again.

Groceries. I promised Emily I'd help out and that means not leeching off her food. Maybe I'll make dinner for us tonight.

I stop at the market closest to her house and dash inside. First, I aim my cart toward the coffee aisle.

Wait. Can I even drink coffee?

I need to schedule an appointment with my doctor.

Why are all these things occurring to me so slowly?

Frozen in place, I stare at the shelves of colorful bags and cannisters of coffee, unable to make a decision. Decaf? Half-caf? What can I have?

"Serena?"

I jump at the unfamiliar male voice.

Heart hammering and legs shaking, I turn toward the intruder.

"Theo!" I blow out a relieved breath and paste a smile on my face, hoping my former classmate didn't notice my ridiculous reaction. "How are you?"

His friendly smile widens but he doesn't move in to hug me or anything. We were friendly in school but not a hugs-hello friendly. "Good. What are you doing out here? I thought you took a job in Empire?"

I swallow hard, not wanting to admit I'm now an unemployed loser—who dated one of her patients. "I did. I was. I, um, I'm living with a friend nearby. What are you doing here? I thought you were joining your family's practice near Union?"

"I did. I'm visiting my girlfriend. She's moving down there with me."

"Oh, that's great." I can't remember his girlfriend's name. Muffy? Misty? Missy? Something with an M. "How is she doing?"

"Good!" He ducks his head and runs his hand through his shaggy light brown hair. "We just got engaged, actually."

"Congratulations." I smile, genuinely happy that someone's life is going well.

"So did things not work out at Empire?"

My shoulders twitch. How am I going to answer this question? He won't be the last person to ask. *I got knocked up by one of my patients* seems like an answer that would immediately disqualify me.

"Well, if you're looking for a job, my sister needs to hire some new therapists."

I blink. "I thought it was a family practice?" Since he grew up in a family full of physical therapists, all of our coursework seemed to come so easy for Theo. While being the first person in my family to even go to college left me struggling to figure things out.

He flashes an easy smile. "Not at all. She's looking for someone with strong patient communication skills, and you excelled in that area."

"Oh." Heat bursts over my face. "Thanks."

"If you're interested, give me your number and email. I'll pass it to her with a strong recommendation."

The thought of moving back to Union—near the downstate Lost Kings MC charter—where I had so many bad experiences isn't appealing. Besides, Grayson's here and probably not able to move any time soon.

Then again, I'm going to be responsible for another life and my employment options might be limited. Turning down his offer would be stupid. "I'd love that. Thank you." I give him my info and we say goodbye.

To avoid the awkwardness of running into him again while I'm finishing my shopping, I stay in the coffee aisle for a few more minutes. Decaf. I better go with decaf for now. I toss a bag of Green Mountain in my cart, then move to the sweeteners. Can I even use my precious monkfruit now? Something else to add to the list of things I need to ask my doctor about. I pick up a bag anyway.

What else? I slowly roll my cart toward the meat section and choose a few packages of ground beef, lamb, and pork to make meatloaf. That should last us a few days. I take my time lazily zig-zagging my way through the store to pick up the rest of the items I want. I'm sort of winging it and end up backtracking a few times. But something about the mindless shopping and wandering around the store settles my anxiety.

Finally, I've had enough and head toward the checkout counter.

My nerves return as I turn onto Emily's street. All the vehicles near her house seem familiar. No motorcycles or big black trucks. I can't hide forever, and I'm not lugging the groceries all the way down the street, so I back into Emily's driveway. The whir of the garage door opener fills the air as I'm lifting bags out of my trunk. I turn and find Emily standing in the middle of the wide garage entrance with her arms crossed over her chest.

"I was getting worried about you."

"Sorry, Mom." I chuckle at the scowl flashing over her face and nod to the bags. "Help me carry these in, please?"

"Serena, you didn't have to go to this much trouble." She hefts one of the bags into her arms. "You don't have to stock the fridge in order to stay with us."

Sometimes, Emily knows my people-pleasing ways a little too well for my comfort.

"I'm not here to sponge off you." I grab two other bags. "And I'm making my famous meatloaf tonight."

Her eyes sparkle with interest. "Oh, *reallllllly*? Okay, I can get on board with that."

She helps me unpack the bags. A good thing since I'm not exactly sure where everything goes in her kitchen.

"Have you talked to Grayson, yet?" she asks over her shoulder.

I falter mid-step. "No. Why? Did he stop by here?"

"No."

"I can't talk to him yet. But I sent him a text so he wouldn't be worried. He left a bunch of voicemails and texts," I admit.

She sighs and turns to face me. "I get it, honey. I really do. But he's not Jimmy."

Just the mention of Shadow's real name sends a shiver of revulsion down my spine.

"And you're not alone this time," she continues. "I'm here for you no matter what."

Tears prick my eyes. Why couldn't Emily and I have met years ago? Her tough love could've helped me avoid a lot of bad decisions. Or would I have been too stuck in learning things the hard way and dodged her friendship?

I sniffle and nod. "Thank you."

"Just think about it."

"I am. Trust me. That's *all* I'm thinking about."

She huffs a soft laugh. "I bet."

"I ran into a guy I went to school with." I desperately want to change the subject. "He offered me a job but it's down in Union."

Her eyes widen. "Aw, crap. I know you need the work, but I'd be bummed if you moved that far away."

"It wasn't a sure thing." I shrug. "They probably won't want to hire me once I start showing."

"Well, you don't want to work for someone who discriminates against pregnant people anyway."

"True," I chuckle. Right about now I'll take anything, but I keep that to myself. "Lot of bad memories for me down there."

"Aw, honey." She reaches over and squeezes my hand. "You're so much stronger now. You can handle anything."

I return the gentle squeeze. "Thank you. The more you keep reminding me, the more I believe it myself."

"That's what I'm here for."

CHAPTER SEVEN

Grinder

IRONWORKS.

Damn. Last time I stepped foot on this side of the river, my presence could've kicked off a turf war with the Vipers MC.

The small city doesn't look that much different from what I remember. Maybe a little cleaner than it used to be. More cutesy shops and fancy-looking restaurants. Lots of parking meters. The one-way streets are still narrow and lined with crookedly parked cars.

"No Vipers left in this area," Rock says as if he'd read my mind. He points toward my window. "Lost Kings hold everything to the Vermont line now."

"How the fuck you doing that with such a small club?"

"Ruthless determination." He flashes a grim smile. "Murder. Mayhem. Intimidation. All the usual tools."

"Jesus, you're a scary bastard."

"That's a compliment from you."

I grunt, wishing I'd left a better legacy for Rock. Impending fatherhood must be making me question all my life choices even more than usual.

"Seriously, though," Rock continues. "We do it by building

alliances. Loco's a pain in my ass but—I can't believe I'm going to say this—we have a similar mindset in some ways."

"What ways are those? I don't remember us ever being okay with prostitution."

He sighs. "I'm not thrilled. But he seems to look after his girls. He's not trafficking minors—"

"Christ, that's a low bar."

His jaw twitches. "The girls seem to be working for him willingly. He offers them protection for something they'd be doing anyway."

"Yeah, I can't trust a man who makes a living off the backs of women. Literally *off* their backs."

"I hear you." He side-eyes me. "Crystal Ball isn't much different."

"Showing *off* your body is different than letting strangers *into* it."

From the back seat, Teller leans over and pats my shoulder. "Grandpa's lettin' loose with the harsh truths today."

"You *grandpa* me again, I'm gonna gut you," I warn, shrugging him off. The fucker's been so quiet this whole ride, I almost forgot he was back there. Then again, that's how Teller and Murphy learned so much in the early days, by being quiet and blending into the background. I shouldn't forget that. The mouthing off he's supposedly known for came later.

"You're all right with this?" I ask Teller.

"Like Rock said, Loco takes care of his girls. Doesn't tolerate any clients treating them bad or anything." He shrugs. "If you knew what the Vipers had been into and the shit they did, you'd be thanking God Loco moved into this space. Someone's gonna do it. Might as well be someone who isn't pure evil."

"Still never gonna have an opinion different from Rock, are ya?" I scoff. Wrath used to joke about him being Rock's mini-me for a reason.

Out of the corner of my eye, I catch his scowl, while Rock smirks.

"When I think he's wrong, I tell him," Teller says.

Rock tips his head, staring at Teller in the rear-view mirror. "But I'm rarely wrong."

"Don't get crazy, Prez."

"Knucklehead has no problem runnin' his mouth." Pride and affection are wrapped up in Rock's words.

"Your woman okay with you hanging out at a whorehouse?" I ask Teller.

"I don't exactly ask her permission." Teller leans against the back seat. "She doesn't ask about club business unless it's important." He chuckles under his breath. "Charlotte wouldn't waste time worrying if I'm sampling the goods, anyway." He raises his hand and scissors his fingers. "She'd just chop off my dick while I'm asleep one night." He laughs harder.

"The quiet redhead?" She didn't seem like the violent old lady type.

"She ain't that quiet," Teller mutters.

I turn and find him smirking to himself while tapping on his phone. Obviously, he's keeping in touch with his girl. After a few seconds, he glances up.

"You want to meet up with Carter this week?" He lifts his chin toward me. "He's got some sketches if you want to take a look."

Christ, how can I set up time to get inked when I don't know what the hell's going on with Serena? "Yeah, let's see how the day shakes out."

"All right." He returns to his phone.

"How close are we?" I ask Rock.

"Not far."

"Thanks. That's helpful," I grumble, pulling out my own phone. I doubt Serena bothered to answer one of the twenty texts I've sent her, but I check anyway.

My phone vibrates and a message pops up.

Buttercup: *I'm okay. Sorry for making you worry. I needed a breather.*

Thank fuck. I close my eyes and let out a quick sigh.

"Everything all right with you and Serena?" Rock asks. "Hope said she wasn't at the clubhouse last night or this morning."

Jesus Christ, the way everyone's up in my business isn't much different than when I was in prison. At least his question's coming from a good place.

"Yeah," I answer slowly. I'd rather not let more people in on my problems. Having Z know is bad enough. "We're working through some stuff."

Instead of asking more questions, Rock slows the truck to a stop and carefully eases it into a spot in front of an old brownstone with a purple front door.

He shuts off the truck and turns to give me his full attention. "You up to this?"

"Don't worry, Prez. My head's in the game." I jerk my thumb toward the purple door. "This the place?"

"Yeah, door was red last time we were here."

"He change with the seasons or something?"

Rock smirks. "Maybe."

Engines rumble through the narrow streets, reminding me of how much I miss riding.

"Soon, brother," Rock says as if he sensed my mood.

"Wanna get down to see Z's place." Was hoping I'd be able to ride with the club when we go.

"You'll be impressed."

"He's done a lot with it," Teller adds.

Z's bike is the first one to come into view. The narrow street is full of parked cars. Rock grabbed the last spot. That doesn't seem to concern Z or the others. At the crosswalk, he takes advantage of the dip in the curb and smoothly steers the bike onto the sidewalk, gliding to a stop a few feet from Rock's rear bumper. Dex and Ravage pull in behind him, lining their bikes in a neat row.

"Can't imagine the locals are gonna care for that." I nod to the other brownstones along the street.

Rock shrugs. "We'll be long gone before the cops stop by to do anything about it."

"You say that now," Teller warns.

Rock and Z share a few words, then Rock waves his hand at all of us to follow him. We crowd onto the stone steps. Rock tips his head back as he punches the doorbell. Obviously, Loco's got cameras set up around the place.

The heavy door swings open and a barely dressed young lady with golden skin and a dazzling smile welcomes us inside.

Either she has zero fear response or Loco warned her we were coming. Her sweet, but blank, smile remains in place as the six of us crowd into the narrow foyer.

"Good afternoon, gentlemen," she says in a practiced, husky voice. Her gaze sweeps over each one of us, then returns to Rock. "Loco's waiting for you in his office. Follow me."

The filmy see-through robe draped over her shoulders billows behind her, keeping us at a distance. Her bare feet sink into the thick carpet, barely making a sound as we follow her down the long hallway. We pass a parlor area full of ornate velvet and wood furniture. A few girls perched on a couch crane their necks to get a look at us. One with long, sleek black hair falling over her shoulders wiggles her fingers and blows me a kiss.

Great.

As we pass, giggles erupt through the room. I turn and find two of the women peeking around the corner. The black-haired one waves at me again.

"Hey, darlin'," Rav says, slowing to talk to them.

"This is quite an operation," I mutter to Rock.

"Uh-huh," he grunts. His irritation seems to rise with each step we take deeper into this house of sin.

We follow the girl to a glossy dark wooden door with elaborate brass hardware.

She knocks three times and twists the knob, swinging the door open wide.

"Prez!" Loco stands from behind a wide, ornate desk and opens his arms like he's planning to hug all of us at once. His dark red suit appears to be made of a similar material as the heavy drapes in the front of the house. A thick, heavy fabric with a subtle embroidered flower pattern. Never seen anything quite like it.

As we continue piling into his office, his loony grin falters. "Rollin' a little deep today, Rock."

Rock shrugs. "You sounded like it was important."

Loco's eyebrows crawl halfway up his forehead. "Oh."

"We can wait out there, Prez." Dex nudges Ravage toward the door.

"Thank you," Rock says over his shoulder, not taking his eyes off Loco.

"Tasha," Loco snaps his fingers, "find Clementine and entertain these gentlemen. On the house."

"Sure thing, boss." Tasha executes a seductive spin, snagging Ravage's hand in the process and dragging him out the door. Dex sighs and follows them.

"Thank you, Loco," Rav hollers at the ceiling.

Teller pushes the door closed, drawing Loco's attention.

"*Tellller.*" Loco draws out the word slowly and tugs on the lapels of his snazzy suit. "Haven't seen you in a minute." His voice loses its smooth confidence for a second or two.

Something about Teller seems to leave Loco unsettled and I find that funny as fuck.

Loco shakes it off and allows his gaze to slide over Rock, Z, and finally land on me.

"Grinder." His eyes widen and his anxious frown turns into a more welcoming smile. "Honored to finally meet you in the flesh. Congratulations on your freedom."

"Thank you." I hold out my hand and he grips it tight. He tugs and I get the feeling if the desk wasn't in our way, he'd try pulling me in for a hug. "Glad to finally put a face with a name. Wanted to come by and say thank you—"

"No, no, no." He drops my hand and shakes his head vigorously. "I need to thank *you* for looking out for my boy Ricky inside. Really appreciate what you did for him."

Damn, Ricky must've been released at least three years ago. "How's he doing now?"

"Not bad. Not bad. Got off parole. Moved down south. Stayin' out of trouble."

Surprised the kid's still alive. "Well, that's more than any of us can hope for."

"Got that right." He gestures to the chairs in front of the desk. "Have a seat, gentlemen."

There are only two chairs. A third one rests against the wall. Teller grabs it and sets it closer to the desk, gesturing for me to take it.

Rock drops into the middle chair and Z takes the one on the other end. Teller puts his back to the wall so he's facing Loco.

Loco stares at him as if Teller might flip into a rampage at any moment. Can't wait to hear *that* story.

Rock settles into the chair, adopting a casual pose that suggests the barest hint of interest. Z remains rigid, as if he's waiting and eager for whatever Loco's about to share. I'm somewhere in between the two of them. Curious but also wanting to get all the posturing and theatrics over with.

"Normally, I don't pay a lot of attention to what's going on inside," Loco says, flapping his hand in the air in a dismissive gesture. "Prison is its own jurisdiction."

I straighten my spine. My part of this meeting isn't over.

"Same here," Rock says.

Loco taps the back of his hand. "I understand things are different inside. Split along more obvious lines." He nods at me. "That's why what you did for Ricky means something to me." He slaps his hand over his heart. "And I know you worked to leave things in a fair way before you got out."

Fuck. "I have a feelin' that all went to shit," I say.

Loco dips his chin. "Big Chief be steppin' on a lotta toes in there."

I sit forward and lower my voice. "He's messin' with things out *here* too."

"That's what I heard." Loco shifts his gaze to Rock. "What are you doing about it?"

"We're still monitoring the situation," Rock answers in an even tone. "As you can probably figure out all by yourself, my *brother's* in a precarious position." Rock rests his hand on the arm of my chair, a subtle reminder that his loyalty to me will come before any business arrangements with Loco.

"We be standing alongside each other on this one, Rock." Loco raises his hands like he's waving a white flag of surrender.

"You got a shady parole officer after you, Grinder?" Loco asks.

"How'd you know?"

"I hear things." He sits back, a sly smile sliding over his face. "I can take care of that problem for you. That way you don't take the heat for it."

"That's one hell of a big favor." Rock leans forward. "What exactly do you want in return?"

"Ahhh, that's the businessman I know." Loco shakes his finger at Rock. "You never disappoint."

"Cut the shit, Loco," Z says.

"Zero, you're more and more presidential every time I see you."

"Let me get this straight." I tap my fingers on his desk to get his attention. "You're offering to take out my parole officer, in exchange for what?"

"Well, for one thing, I owe you," he says.

"You don't owe me shit."

"How you think I know about Grillo?" Loco says in a low voice. Now we're getting down to business.

"He's hassling you?"

"Not me. Ain't been on parole in over a decade."

I glare at him, fully understanding why Rock finds dealing with Loco so annoying. "Good for you."

"He was involved in the hit on your guys inside," Z says.

"See, Z gets it." Loco points at Z, his voice rising in agitation. "He gets it."

"We *all* get it," Rock says.

"Grillo went after my girl." And caused a chain reaction of events that probably led to my current predicament.

"Shit. You serious?" Loco asks.

"He sent someone after my girl," I clarify. "That guy's been dealt with."

Loco sweeps his gaze from me to Rock, then Z. "Who? How?"

"It's club-related," Rock says, cutting off Loco's questions.

"Bro, all this is club-related." Loco swings his arm in a wide circle over his desk. "All of this."

"Don't fuck with me, Loco. You think I don't know you've got more going on than your happy hooker house and drug hustle?" Rock asks.

Loco's mouth curls into a devious smirk. "You think I don't know you been selling half my shit to the Devil Demons MC?"

"You don't own our whole supply, Loco," Rock says in an even tone. "Never have."

"That hurts, Rock."

"Jesus Christ." Z rubs his fingers over his temple. "Can we stop with the petty bullshit."

"Just so you know, we're not selling 'half your supply' to anyone," Teller says. "We're off-loading the junk weed that doesn't meet Sparky's quality standards. So, chill."

Rock turns and shoots a glare at Teller.

Loco flicks his gaze to Teller, then back to Rock. "Demons know that they ain't gettin' the best?"

"They don't give a fuck," Rock snaps. "They're slinging it to college kids who don't know the difference."

"I dunno, some of these college bros seem to be majoring in weed." Loco barks out a laugh. "Don't worry, I ain't trying to jam you up with the Demons. Chaser ain't a bigoted fuck like his old man but we both know he'll side with the white boys."

Rock sighs. "I think we all side with the green." He rubs his thumb against his fingers in the universal sign for "cash."

"Eloquent sidestep," Loco points out. "That's why I've always liked doing business with you, Rock. You ain't trying to convince me it's not an issue but you don't participate. You dislike everyone equally."

"Indeed," Rock answers slowly, to drive home the immediate focus of his dislike.

"You mind if we veer back on track?" I ask. "I ain't got as much time left as you all do, and I'd like to spend some of it outside."

"Aw, come on, Grinder, you'll probably outlive us all." Loco pounds his fist against the desk. "But yeah, let's get to it. Grillo sent someone to rough up your girl. She okay?"

"Yeah," I answer. "She's fine now."

"Look at you, sly old man." Loco whistles. "You been out for a heartbeat and already got yourself settled down with a woman?"

"Like I said, making up for lost time over here." I roll my hand through the air in a hurry-the-fuck-up gesture.

"You dealt with the one who laid hands on her?" Loco asks.

"Yes," Rock answers.

"Grillo set up my cuz." He stabs his finger against the desk, then drags it in a straight line forward. "Which led to him being sent to Pine. Which led to his demise at Big Chief's hands. Blood for blood."

I get what he's saying. His loss is greater. He should be the one to take Grillo out. Since I don't give a fuck who actually pulls the trigger, I just nod along. "I hear you."

"I'm just saying. You come across him first, I need you to let me know." Loco cocks his head. "He might be privy to some other information I need."

"Don't kill him." Z says. "That's what you're asking?"

"That's all I'm asking."

"Done," I say, then hesitate, realizing I should've let Rock make that call.

He doesn't seem bothered by my gaffe. He nods slowly. "Anything else?"

Loco's gaze skims over the three of us, then briefly flicks Teller's way. He rests his elbows on the desk. "I do have a small request."

Rock nods in a way that says "no shit" without uttering a word.

Loco frowns. "I'm aware there were...issues with the Vipers when they asked you all to hire their girls at Crystal Ball."

"Understatement," Rock mutters.

"Ransom sent his girls to our club to start trouble, not to work," Z explains.

"He was turning his girls out any which way," Loco spits. The judgment rolling off him is pretty funny considering we're sitting in his whorehouse.

"Turning tricks was the least of it," Z says. "But yeah, we won't risk the exposure by having girls pull that shit in a business we own." Z's tone makes it clear, that better not be the favor Loco's seeking.

Loco touches his fingers to his chest as if he's offended by the suggestion he'd ever do such a thing. "I understand the need to be discreet."

The purple front door on this brownstone says otherwise, but whatever. I did my part. None of this other crap concerns me.

"Go on," Rock encourages.

"A few of my ladies would like to *transition* into dancing. Eventually, they want to get away from adult entertainment services altogether—"

"But you want to use Crystal Ball as part of some hooker twelve-step program?" Z asks.

Loco snorts, then chuckles to himself. "You could say that."

"Dex can probably explain better, but business has been slow," Rock says. "I trust that any girl you recommend isn't coming to stir up drama. Or troll for clients to bring back *here*." Rock levels a pointed stare at Loco and waits for him to nod. "I'm willing to give anyone you send us a chance, but I want to be honest with you right now about the state of our business."

"That's fair. And I appreciate your candor." Loco flashes an evil smile. "Maybe some brown sugar will sweeten up your joint."

Z cough-laughs. "Maybe that's what we're missing. Yeah."

"Well, y'all got lots of pale, bony blondes twirlin' on them poles," Loco points out. "Variety keeps things interesting."

"I'll let Dex know," Rock answers, barely hiding his irritation. I haven't been to Crystal Ball since I got out so I can't agree or disagree with Loco's assessment. Couldn't care less. Greased up girls humping my leg for dollar bills didn't interest me before prison and it doesn't interest me now.

"We're having success with our girls downstate who are camming," Z adds. "Our Virginia charter's got something similar going on. Startin' to make bank."

"You know how to set all that up?" Loco asks. "So it's safe for the girls?"

"Yeah. I can do it." Z grins. "Rooster's got more recent experience, though. He and I can work out something for you if your girls are ever interested in exploring that option."

"Eh." Loco waves his hand at the door. "What they do in the bedroom is one thing. Once it's online it's out there forever."

"True," Z agrees. "The girls we have doing it were going back and forth from films, so they were already comfortable with that."

"I'll drop the suggestion at our next house meetin'," Loco promises.

Rock sits forward. "I'm sorry, what?"

"House meeee-*ting*," Loco enunciates slowly. "Hoe church. Bitches bring all their complaints and suggestions to my attention, and we work shit out."

"How democratic of you," Z chuckles.

"Don't tell me you don't have a sit-down with your dancers."

"I don't." Rock touches his chest. "Dex probably does."

"You really not runnin' things there anymore, Rock?" Loco asks.

"Nope."

"Ah, right. You got that fine as hell wife." Loco closes his eyes for a second like he's savoring whatever memory he has of Hope. God help the fucker, Rock's about to snap. "You knock her up again yet?"

"No," Rock growls.

"Sorry, sorry." Loco holds up his hands but doesn't look one bit apologetic. "Forgot you're touchy about personal shit."

"I haven't knocked up my wife again yet, either," Z says. "In case you're keeping track."

Behind us, Teller choke-laughs.

I'm not finding the conversation as amusing.

"Anyway, you think you can help me out?"

"We'll do our best," Rock says.

"Good. Good. Thank you." He stands and offers his hand to Z, then Rock. "What's my man Sparky cookin' up these days?"

Rock actually chuckles. "He's dabbling in edibles."

Loco scowls. "I can't sling that on the street."

Z glances around the office. "You could offer them to your customers here."

Loco nods. "Guess you're right. Nice add on. Upcharge. Whatever the fuck."

"He's still working on his unique strains," Rock adds. "Don't worry. We'll have new product coming soon."

"That's what I like to hear." Loco claps his hands together.

After more posturing, endless chit-chat, and a long round of handshaking we're finally released from Loco's office.

Cloying perfume hangs in the hallway. A high husky voice and two lower rumbling ones come from the first room we passed on our way in.

"I suppose we should go collect Rav and Dex," Rock says.

Teller shrugs. "I don't think Rav will be upset if you leave him here."

"Nope. We be like Fletcher Park up in here. Carry out what you carry in. Ain't got time or space for clingers." Loco claps his hands behind us like he's trying to scare a hawk away from his pet rabbits.

"That a problem?" Teller asks. "Guys don't know when to leave?"

"That's why I grab their credit card up front," Loco says.

Rav grins at us from one of the couches. Two lingerie-clad ladies are occupying his lap. I recognize one as the girl who opened the door for us. Dex is talking to another young woman, with a couch cushion's worth of space between them.

"Ahh." Loco beams at Rav and Dex. "Good taste, gentlemen. While we're all assembled here, this young lady is one of the ones I mentioned." He points to the woman sitting with Dex. "Patience."

Rock nods, but I think his own patience is about to snap. I know mine is.

"I leave the hiring to Dex," Rock says.

Dex smoothly stands. "If it's all right with you, Loco, I asked Patience to come in and audition sometime this week."

"Yes, yes. Excellent." Loco shakes Dex's hand. "Thank you, Dexter."

Dex scowls then forces a smile.

One of the girls in Rav's lap raises her hand. "Me too."

"Yes, Clem." Loco arches an eyebrow at Dex who nods.

A gentle touch brushes my shoulder and I jump.

"Easy," Loco says. "The man just got out of prison. Don't be sneaking up on him like that."

Thanks for broadcasting my business, asshole.

"Sorry," the raven-haired beauty who'd waved at me earlier says in a low, husky voice.

"Ya know what? Y'all stay. Get to know each other," Loco encourages. "I got work to do."

"Thanks, Loco," Rock says. He sends a murderous glare at Rav who doesn't seem to be taking the hint.

"I'm Serenity," the girl next to me says.

The universe really enjoys fucking with me, huh?

"Did you really just get out of prison?" she asks with wide, curious eyes.

"You should be careful asking men you don't know questions like that, sweetheart," I warn.

"Oh, sorry. I'd love to show you a good time." She wraps her fingers around my bicep.

I swear to God I hear Z and Teller giggling behind me. *Fuckers.*

My skin's crawling with discomfort. Not from the girl. She's lovely. Twenty-five years ago I would've let her lead me by the dick straight to her bedroom. My body's frozen. How the fuck do I handle this? It's not like I've been around a lot of women in the last fifteen years. Sure, a muffler bunny here and there have hit on me up at the clubhouse—they're easy to blow off. But most of my time's been spent obsessing over Serena.

I don't want to *offend* this woman and risk causing a problem with a business associate of the club. But I really want her to get the fuck away and stop touching me.

"We need to go." Rock drops his gaze to where she's clinging to my arm. "Another time, sweetheart."

I shoot a glare at him. There won't *be* a next time.

Finally, I shake her loose, and pull myself free from her grasp.

"Okay." She leans up on her toes, pursing her lips like she's planning to kiss me.

I swerve away like she just threw a snake at my face.

This is ridiculous. I need to get out of here.

Without another word, I stomp out of the house and down the front steps.

"Fuck." I kick one of Rock's front tires. I'm stuck until he gets his ass out here.

"Don't take it out on my vehicle." Rock's rumbling voice is somewhere between concerned and amused. He stops and rests his hand on my shoulder. "You all right?"

"No. I'm old, awkward, and not used to hanging around forward women." I blow out a frustrated breath. "And I didn't want to be rude to one of the girls and have it fuck up your relationship with Loco."

"Don't worry about it."

Z and Teller join us. Both of 'em grinning like idiots.

"Serenity would like you to have her phone number." Z presents me with a small black business card.

"Fuck off with that." I slap the card out of his hand.

"Christ, Grinder, you could've just told her you had a girlfriend and weren't interested," Teller chimes in. "You didn't have to act like she had cooties."

"You can fuck off too."

"It's okay, G. We're not questioning your *virility*, we're questioning your manners," Z says between giggles.

"Enough," Rock groans. "Where are my other two fuckwits?"

"Present!" Rav hollers, pounding down the steps and jumping onto the sidewalk. Dex follows at a slower pace, hands stuffed in his pockets.

"I think Tasha likes me." Ravage grins and turns to wave at the girls watching us from the window. "She was extra chatty and cuddly."

Dex rolls his eyes. "She was probably hoping you'd tip her."

"Of course I tipped her." Rav's offended tone actually lightens my foul mood. "I'm not a scrub. Just 'cause Loco says it's on the house doesn't mean I'm gonna stiff the lady." He ducks his head. "Well, not monetarily anyway."

"What a gentleman," Teller grumbles.

"Nah, give him credit where it's due," Dex says. "Most guys wouldn't bother."

"Again with the low bar," I mutter.

Teller catches my eye, smirks, and nods at me. "Charlotte's friend Mercy is always saying 'the bar is in hell' and now I understand what she means."

"Damn, Mercy is *fine*," Rav says. "When you having her over to your house again? I wanna be there."

Rock smacks him in the back of the head. "Didn't your dick get enough attention today?"

"I don't understand the question, Prez."

"Let's go."

Finally.

I'm itching to get back to the clubhouse. As soon as Rock stops the truck, I open my door.

"If you don't need me, I have a few things I want to take care of." I hate runnin' out on Rock but now that business is out of the way, I can't sit still for the recap of the events I just sat through and all the other assorted bullshit that will drag on for the next two hours.

"Yeah, go ahead." Rock clasps my shoulder and stares at me for a second. "Need anything?"

I open my mouth to snap at him, then stop myself. "Nah, brother. I'm fine."

"Thanks for coming today. It helped a lot."

"Careful, Grinder, Rock will start making you go meet with Loco on the regular," Z warns.

I huff a laugh. "Whatever you need, I'm here for it."

"I know you are," Rock says in that serious tone that gets under my skin for some reason. "If you need something, call. I'll be home. Not planning to go anywhere else today."

Teller snorts. "That's code for—"

"Don't start." Rock throws a warning glare Teller's way.

"I'll catch you later." I wave and head toward my truck without waiting for an answer.

Someone's boots crunch over the gravel behind me. Bet it's Z. I don't slow my pace, though.

At the truck, he catches up to me. "You going to look for Serena?"

"Yes." I turn and pin him with a stare. "Alone."

He shoves his hands in his pockets and glances at the ground. Probably smirking. Asshole.

But when he finally lifts his head, his mouth is a firm, determined line. No dimples in sight. "If you find her, will you let me know? Send a text or whatever."

"Yeah, brother. I can do that." I hold out my hand. "Thanks, Z."

"No problem." He takes my hand but pulls me in for a hug. "Sorry for giving you shit back there."

"Eh. I deserved it. Could've handled it better."

"I get it, bro. You're still adjusting."

Yeah, and every time I think I've moved forward, I end up taking two steps back.

CHAPTER EIGHT

Serena

"The most common way people give up their power is by thinking they don't have any." -Alice Walker

After the emotional talk with Emily and the stress of waiting for a text from Grayson, I'm exhausted.

Emily curls her arm around my shoulders. "Why don't you go upstairs and take a nap? You've been through a lot of emotional stuff in the last two days. And I bet you haven't slept well."

"I haven't." I yawn and stretch.

"Go on. If you're not up by four, I'll come wake you." She flashes a wicked grin. "I'm not missing out on the meatloaf you promised."

"Deal."

Upstairs, I strip off my clothes and slip into a soft T-shirt I borrowed from Gray. His subtle scent is woven into the fabric and even though I'm the one putting the distance between us, it helps me feel close to him. I crawl under the covers, sighing as my head lands on the pillow.

A few minutes later, I'm still awake. I stare at the ceiling. A million questions and worries run through my head.

I need to make a doctor's appointment. I tug on my T-shirt that's gotten tangled around my waist. I'll need maternity clothes at some point. Baby stuff. Emily's offer is sweet, but I can't stay here forever. I might need to take that job in Union if I can't find anything else. I need health insurance for the baby. I should sign up for some sort of class or something too. Oh my God. How does any woman do this? It's so overwhelming.

Eventually, I drift into an uneasy half-asleep, half-awake state.

A vision of chasing a little blue and white bundle through a choppy slideshow of different phases of my life takes over my mind. Every time I'm about to scoop the bundle into my arms, it disappears. I'm left running through my grandmother's house searching for my baby. Then it switches to my mother's apartment. My old high school. The roof of a building that I long ago considered jumping from. Hospitals. Downstate's clubhouse. A jumble of other places I recognize but can't name. Each time, no matter how careful I am, the baby disappears. I want to cry, but my throat is too tight. My voice stolen. I can't call for help and my anguish goes unnoticed by the faceless people around me.

I startle awake, blinking at the ceiling. My heart hammers. I concentrate on what happened in the dream but the more I try to focus, the fuzzier the details get. The suffocating sense of helplessness remains, and I'm left with a hollow despair ringing in my chest.

With my hand over my heart, I sit up and drape my legs over the side of the bed. I love my baby so much already. I'm going to be a good mother. I may not have any family to help, but it's not like they helped me through any other phase of my life. My mother set a terrible example growing up. Her actions were everything I *don't* want to be as a mother. I'd never sacrifice my child's safety for a man. Never.

The doorbell echoes through the house.

Not sure where Emily is or if she's even still home, I shake off the last of my nightmare and pull on a pair of leggings. I stuff my feet into my favorite fuzzy boots and pad downstairs.

The doorbell rings again.

I bump into Emily at the foot of the stairs. My gaze drops to the gun in her hand.

"Emily, what are you doing?" Fear compresses my voice into a harsh whisper. "Who's at the door?"

"Your gangster boyfriend."

"Wait, what?"

She pins me with eyes full of annoyance. "After you went upstairs, I looked up the name of the club stitched on the guy's vest yesterday. Lost Kings MC. There isn't a ton of information out there but what I did find was terrifying."

Embarrassment and guilt settle over me like a soggy blanket. "It's not like that."

"Your boyfriend hired *bikers* to look for you at your friend's house, Serena. That's so fucked up. You should be scared."

"*He's* a biker, Emily. He didn't hire anyone. It's *his* club." Even as I try to explain, I feel her invitation for me to move in being rescinded.

"Jesus. Are you serious?" Her eyes bug as the vague pieces of my past that I've shared with her slip into place. "Oh my God. Is this the same organization your ex was part of?"

"They're not all like Jimmy. Gray's nothing like him."

Her eyes are full of pity as she shakes her head. To her, I'm another woman stuck in a pattern of bad decisions.

"Emily—"

"No. You stay here."

"What are you going to do?"

She checks the safety on her pistol and tucks it in the back of her pants. "I'm going to talk to your gangster boyfriend. And if he tries to break in, I'm going to shoot him," she whispers back.

"Emily!" I admonish in a harsh whisper. "That's not funny."

"Do I look like I'm kidding?"

"It's really not like that."

"Stay here," she orders.

CHAPTER NINE

Grinder

I TOLD YOU, YOU COULDN'T RUN FROM ME.

There it is. Serena's car. Smack in the middle of Emily's driveway.

Found you.

The urge to storm into the house and claim my woman surges through me. I stare at the sidewalk for a minute, wishing like fuck we were doing this another way.

But I can't let my girl hide from me for another second.

I park the truck and trudge up the walkway. I give the doorbell an impatient jab and wait. Wind chimes tinkle nearby, but otherwise the house is quiet. Maybe they went out together in Emily's car? I glance at the garage but can't tell if anything's in it from this angle.

A creak. Movement inside of some sort. I squint, but can't make out anything through the screen door or the pane of frosted glass in the front door.

I jab the bell again.

Finally, the interior door swings open. Emily stands on the other side of the screen door. "Grayson. What are you doing here?"

Lines of tension and apprehension tighten her face as she studies me. Serena's told her something. I'm not sure what or how much but definitely something that didn't paint me in a good light. The friendly woman I'd met before has been replaced by this fierce, protective one. Hard hazel eyes drill into me, like she's considering blowing a hole through my skull.

"Hi, Emily. I'm sorry to bother you. But I'm looking for Serena, has she been by?"

"Did you two have a fight?" she asks.

"No. I need to talk to her, though." The need to see Serena burns in my chest. She's close. I feel her presence.

"She's not here." All the acting ability in the family went to Libby. Emily's voice falters and she glances over her shoulder.

Still, something in Emily's posture puts me on alert. Every instinct I have says I need to handle her carefully. "Emily, I just need to talk to her." I turn toward the driveway. "That's her car. Where is she?"

She shifts, holding one arm at an odd angle. Concealing something behind her back.

What the fuck?

"It's okay, Emily," Serena's soft voice soothes all the tension in my body.

Serena walks up behind her friend. "Give me a second, Gray. I'll meet you outside."

Emily swivels her head from Serena to me. She sighs and reaches for the locked handle. "No, it's okay." There's a click and she swings the door open. "Come in."

She steps aside, making room for me to enter.

I catch a black shape in her hand. I slow my movements the same way I would if I'd encountered a cobra.

Did she answer the door with a gun? To protect Serena from me? Jesus Christ, this woman's brave as fuck and she just earned my admiration and protection for the rest of her life.

Emily catches my eye and carefully tucks what is indeed a pistol into the pocket of her sweatshirt. "Feel free to use the living room. But be aware, I'll be nearby if Serena needs me."

"Thank you, Emily."

She nods and turns away, stopping to say a few words to Serena before disappearing around the corner.

Then, Serena and I are left to stand there staring at each other.

"What's going on, buttercup?" I finally ask. I don't want to ask about the pregnancy. I want to wait and see if she confesses on her own. If she doesn't, we've got bigger problems. "I got back to the clubhouse and you were gone. Won't answer my calls or texts." I tilt my head. "You know how much I hate to text."

The corners of her mouth lift. Fear still lingers in her cautious eyes, though. "I don't know."

I step closer, holding out my hands to her. "You can do better than that."

Sweet relief flows through my veins as she slides her fingers against mine and tugs me toward the couch. She drops onto the corner cushion and tucks one leg under her so she's facing me. I arrange myself on the low, uncomfortable couch in a similar way, so I can see her. The back of my hand brushes her knee and she inches closer.

"So, I have to ask, why does Emily seem to hate me now?"

She rolls her eyes. "Well, after Dex's visit," she slants an incredulous look at me, "she did a little Googling and uncovered some unflattering Lost Kings MC stories."

I burst into harsh laughter. "Well, shit. Good to know our reputation still precedes us."

She nudges me with her knee. "It's not funny. She was worried you hired Dex to come find me. I had to explain that's *your* club," she whispers, as if she's worried she did something wrong.

"I'm proud to be a King, honey. You don't have to hide it. They're my brothers. Dex wasn't going to drag you up to the clubhouse or anything. I was just worried about you." In hindsight maybe sending Dex here wasn't the smartest choice.

She nervously bites her bottom lip and twists her fingers in her T-shirt, one that I recognize. The corners of my mouth lift. "Did you steal my shirt?"

Her eyes snap up to meet mine, like she's worried I'm mad. "I like it. It smells like you."

"Well, I'm sitting right next to you, now." I slide my hand over the cushion and wrap it around her leg, tugging gently. "Come closer."

She scoots a few inches.

"Closer."

Her leg bumps up against mine.

"Closer." I pull her into my lap. "That's better."

Stiff and unsure, she perches on my leg and crosses her arms over her chest.

"Did I do something wrong, Serena?"

"What? No. It's me." She touches her forehead. "I'm all messed up and needed to think."

"You had me worried."

Her body relaxes a notch, her weight sinking into me. She turns and finally looks at me. "I'm sorry."

Serena

I feel lower than low. Unable to express what's really wrong.

But oh, being in Gray's arms is a flame melting away the ice-cold fear surrounding my heart since I saw those three positive tests.

He shifts, leaning forward to kiss my cheek.

"What did I tell you?" he rasps against my ear.

He slides his hand over my hip, splaying it over my belly. My heart rate speeds up.

"What?" My quivering whisper barely breaks the silence.

"You can't run from me, Serena." He pushes my hair out of my eyes. "I'd never hurt you for any reason. And I'll always find you."

I nod but can't force any words out of my mouth. Gently, he tugs up my shirt and rests his palm against my stomach again.

Just like the day we met, I'm frozen in place when our eyes meet. "Are you really pregnant?" he asks.

There's so much hope tied up in his quiet question.

Maybe this isn't the disaster I thought it would be.

But I'm still cautious. "Why would you ask me that?"

"I found...those stick things. At the clubhouse. They were yours, right?" The spark of hope in his voice falters.

Oh. My. God. He found the tests? I can't do anything right.

"You found them?" Heat crawls over my cheeks.

He huffs out a humorless laugh. "You didn't exactly hide them, buttercup."

How could I be so careless?

"Three of them. All positive." He stares at me and the weight of the question he's asking seems etched into every line of his face.

"Yes, I took the tests. I'm pregnant." I hold my breath waiting for the inevitable "are you sure it's mine" question.

But it doesn't come. He curls his hand around mine, lifting it to brush his lips across my knuckles. "Thank you."

Thank you.

"You're not mad?"

"That we're having a baby? Hell no."

"You really...you want to do that with me?"

"Fuck, yes. I want to do everything with you." His jaw ticks and he glances at my stomach. "Are you sure? Have you seen a doctor? I'm worried about getting my hopes up here."

Getting his hopes up? "Not yet. I took several tests."

"Yes, I know," he answers dryly, "I found them, remember? Three sticks and no woman to give me the good news in person."

"You...you think it's good news?"

"The best."

"But when I asked you...about having kids. You didn't sound thrilled. At all."

"When did you...oh, right. I was distracted with all that shit going on." His voice falters. "I've always wanted a family. But I thought I missed my chance. At a certain point, I made my peace with it. Prison and all the time I lost stole the possibility of a family from me."

Tears of shame slide down my cheeks. I can't believe I handled this so badly. "So you're happy about this?"

"Yes." His jaw tightens. "Don't you know me better than that by now? I take care of my responsibilities, Serena."

"I don't want to be a responsibility."

"You're more than that to me and you know it."

Air fills my lungs as if a heavy burden's been lifted from my shoulders. "Where do we go from here?"

Grinder

Where do we go from here?

I'm still trying to transition into a semi-normal life. But it's not like we can ask the baby to wait for a more convenient time.

"First, you're going to give me all of your bills." Like fuck am I gonna have her stressing about financial stuff I can easily handle.

Serena shifts and pulls away, staring at me with shock in her eyes. "Excuse me?"

"You're carrying *my* baby. That's means huge changes for you. I don't want you under any additional stress. Besides, you're out of a job because of me."

The corners of her mouth curl up. "Not because of you."

Directly because of me. She got attacked at her job because some lowlife thought that was a way to get at me and that's how her boss found out about us.

"Yeah, buttercup. It's my fault." I stroke my knuckles over her cheek. "Besides, I take care of what's mine."

"But you're only working part-time yourself. You're still trying to get back on your feet."

Fuck, that's a painful sting to my pride. She's not exactly wrong, but she doesn't have all the facts, either. "I'm able to take care of both of you, Serena. I promise."

"I like my job." She hesitates. "*Liked* my job. I worked so hard to get there."

"And you'll find another one. No doubt in my mind, Serena. You're a healer. It's what you're meant to do." I rub my hand over her leg. "But right now the most important thing is to take care of *yourself.*"

"I don't want to learn to depend on you." She lifts her chin. "I still need to have a way to support myself and my baby. Have my own money."

"I'll never stop taking care of you." Another thought slams into me. She's trying hard not to point out one obvious issue. "If something ever happens to me, the club will take care of you, Serena."

She snorts. "I definitely don't want to depend on *that.*"

Can't blame her. It's gonna take a long time for her to fully trust my club. I get that. "Look, I appreciate you worrying about me, but I'm able to take care of you. You're not a burden or whatever else you're thinking."

She sniffles. "I'm not an incubator, either."

"Honey," I laugh. "Where'd you come up with that idea?"

"You wanting me to not work and just, what? Stay home and knit baby booties?"

I'm aware of the age gap between us but is that really what she thinks of me? "Do people still do that?"

"I don't know." She side-eyes me. "I don't know how to knit or anything else. Just so you know."

"I don't think knitting is a requirement for motherhood." I sigh and glance around Emily's house. Big home for someone her age. Old, but sturdy and well-crafted. Neighborhood seems quiet and tidy. Serena should be safe and comfortable here until I find us a more suitable place.

"You're not comfortable staying at the clubhouse, are you?" I already know the answer, but I want to be sure.

"Not if you're not with me."

"Okay." I blow out a frustrated breath. "I want to be with you, but this stuff with Grillo needs to be sorted first. And I'd like to move somewhere with more room." My gaze drops to her stomach. "One way or another, we'll need a bigger place than I've got now."

Fear slides over her face and she shifts away from me ever so slightly.

"Too much?" I ask.

"A little," she whispers.

"Nothing's changed, Serena. The way I feel about you hasn't changed."

"You mean that?"

"By now, you should know I don't talk to hear myself."

She stares at me.

"We need at least four bedrooms."

"What?" Her eyes widen. "One baby at a time, please."

I can't help laughing. I never thought I'd have *one* kid, let alone two. "I want you to be able to set up your studio to film your stuff in."

"Oh." Her lips twist in sad disappointment. "I'll probably have to give that up. It's silly anyway. I won't have time for playing with makeup."

The dismissive way she says it pisses me off. "It's *not* silly. You love doing it. You're good at it. You've got a lot of people who love your videos. Having a kid doesn't mean you have to stop doing what you love. Unless it doesn't make you happy anymore."

"I can't hold a baby in one arm and blend eyeshadow with the other," she scoffs.

I hold out my arms. "My hands ain't broken, Serena. I *do* plan to take care of my own kid. Not just chain him to you and skip away."

A slight smile curves her lips, and she ducks her head. "You said *him.*"

"I don't want to call the baby an 'it.' That feels wrong."

Sweet laughter finally flows past her stubborn lips. "Oh my God." She curls her arms around my neck and kisses my cheek. "You're really excited about this?" She rests her head on my shoulder and nuzzles against me. Damn, it feels good to finally have melted her resistance.

"Excited. Happy. All the good feelings," I assure her. She doesn't look any different. Her stomach's still flat but I can't help touching her anyway. "I can't wait until you're showing."

"Really? You won't think I'm all fat and gross?"

"What?" My face twists with confusion. "Are you out of your mind? Don't say shit like that."

Her cheeks turn red, and she glances away.

"I'm serious. I've heard some women worry about that kind of stuff. But I think you're beautiful no matter what. And I'm looking forward to seeing you fat with my baby."

Her nose wrinkles.

"I'm a crude fucker, I know. Stop acting surprised."

She leans in. "I like that side of you."

"Good."

"Do you want something to drink?"

"I don't know. Is Emily going to shoot me if I step foot in her kitchen?"

"Probably not." She grins and pops another kiss on my cheek. Can't get enough of them. "I'll be right back."

Serena

In the kitchen, I find Emily staring into the freezer.

"What are you doing?"

"I was melting from your talk and needed to cool off," Emily whispers.

I let out a soft laugh. No surprise she overheard us.

She slams the freezer door shut. "Your man is an extremely rare breed, Serena." While it sounds like a compliment, the catch in her voice makes it seem like she still has reservations.

"He is. And I feel bad that I can't seem to let go of all my past issues."

"It's going to take time, honey." She gives me a sympathetic smile. "And it sounds like he's a patient man who understands."

"Don't worry." I reach for her hand. "I plan to stay here with you guys…if that's still all right with you?" She seemed pretty bothered by the motorcycle club thing, so I won't be surprised if she's not comfortable having me here now.

"Of course it is. As long as you want." She squeezes my arm. "Hey, I mean that, okay? Don't rush into anything because you feel pressured."

"I won't," I promise.

I return to the living room and find Gray standing. "I actually need to get going, sweetheart," he says.

"Oh." I set the glasses on the coffee table. "Okay."

"You need to make a doctor's appointment tomorrow."

I bristle at his stern tone. "I know that."

His mouth pulls at one corner but otherwise doesn't respond to my sharp answer. "I want to go with you, so let me know when it is."

"What? Why?" Shadow had wanted to go to the doctor with me too. So he could badger the doctor about a paternity test. My body trembles at the reminder of that cold humiliation. The looks of pity from the doctor. I was so mortified, I couldn't go back to that office. I had to find a new doctor. And then…it didn't matter anyway.

He freezes in place. "Don't fathers go to doctor's appointments sometimes?"

"I guess." I shrug, trying to reel in my defensiveness. "I don't know."

"I don't want you to go alone."

"Why?"

Frustration twists his face. "Because I'm worried about you and want to make sure you and the baby are okay."

"I'm not lying."

"What?" He frowns. "I never said anything about lying."

"It's yours." I resist the urge to glance away. "The baby is *yours*."

He stares at me in confusion. "I never thought otherwise."

"I just…you know…in case…because…" I stammer out a bunch of sentence starters but never get out a full thought.

We're not making progress. I want to be happy that he's offering to take me to the doctor, but too many past memories make anything but fear impossible. "I'll call you when I have an appointment."

"Can we get together tomorrow?"

"Ah, sure."

"Let me take you to dinner." His tone drops to something soothing, like you'd use to capture an injured animal. I guess in some ways that's exactly what I am.

"Do you need help cleaning out your apartment?" he asks.

"Emily and Libby were going to come over and help me pack. I'm going to put some stuff in storage. And try to sell some other things online."

"Why don't you let me take care of moving stuff to storage." While he phrased it like a question, it sounds more like it's a done deal in his head. "And if you sell stuff online, don't have anyone come to the apartment unless I'm there."

It's useless to argue that Emily will be with me. "I won't."

"Do you have everything you need here?"

I point to the ceiling. "I'm in the guest room. There's another spare room, Emily said I can use it as a nursery..." Hurt flashes in his eyes and my voice falters. "When the baby comes," I finish in a whisper.

"Serena, by the time the baby comes, the three of us are going to be under the same roof."

I can't answer.

As much as I want to believe him, and as much as my heart wants to be with Gray twenty-four seven, my brain refuses to stop flashing a yellow caution light.

CHAPTER TEN

Grinder

THAT DIDN'T GO QUITE AS WELL AS I'D HOPED IT WOULD. BUT BETTER than it could have. I want Serena with *me*. Want my eyes and hands on her every second of the day.

But I also need to give her space. If I pressure her, it'll only backfire on me later. That's one lesson I've learned over the years.

"Wait, Gray," Emily calls out.

I lift my head and spot Emily hurrying around the side of her house and over the lawn.

She catches up to me at the truck and tosses a hasty glance over her shoulder toward the house.

"Is this where you put a bullet in me?" I ask with a wry twist of my mouth.

Her cheeks flame red, but she defiantly pulls her shoulders back. "Not yet."

"Good to know." I lift my chin. "What's on your mind?"

"I heard some of what you said to Serena."

I figured she was probably listening in and don't give a fuck. I don't have anything to hide.

"You said all the right things and so much more." She glances at the pavement. "Serena and I haven't been friends for long. But she was there for me and Libby during a dark time. I love her like a sister. I don't want to see her get hurt. If she wants this baby—and I know she does—I'll do everything I can to make sure they're *both* safe."

She doesn't say "including shoot you, if you hurt her" but it's definitely implied.

Anger threatens to boil through my veins, but my rational side understands she's not attacking *me* personally. She's trying to protect Serena. How could I ever argue with that?

Her expression hardens. "She's a good person with a good heart. She'll be a wonderful mother."

"I know," I say gently.

"Your words and promises were a nice start—"

"But you need more than words from me to stop answering the door with a gun?"

She snorts. "Nah, I do *that* all the time."

All this courage seems to be new to her. She's fidgety but determined. Takes a damn strong woman to confront a man like me on a shadowy, empty street all by herself.

Honesty will go a long way with Emily. Even if it's the ugly truth. "I don't know how much Serena's told you about me. But I just got out on parole. Spent the last fifteen years locked up with some of the worst men society ever produced. I understand the situations you're worried about better than you think."

Her eyes widen. "Serena mentioned parole but…"

Maybe Serena didn't say how *long* I'd been inside. Fifteen years isn't a simple stretch. Time like that changes a man and not for the better. A smart woman like Emily would realize that. "You're worried I want to use her to get readjusted to society then ditch her and let her raise our child alone, or that I'm a bum who will live off of her, draining her youth and bank account like some ex-con vampire."

A brief smile flickers over her lips at that last one. "Maybe not quite that vivid, but along those lines, yes," she admits.

"I've heard it all, Emily. The tricks and traps. The cheating, games, lying, and stealing that cons do. And I have *nothing* in common with those kinds of men." Maybe a few things in common. But deliberately hurting women isn't one of them.

"Good. I'm sorry, Gray. You seem nice and all. If you were just dating, I wouldn't…" She glances at the house again. "But the stakes are so much higher now."

"Don't apologize for being a good friend. I respect the hell out of you for having the nerve to say any of this to my face."

Her anxious frown flips to a hesitant smile. "I really do like you."

"I appreciate you letting Serena stay here. I wanted to move her into a nicer place months ago but she said no and I didn't want to push." I pull out my wallet. "If you're not charging her rent, I'd at least like to help you with expenses."

"I can't take your money." She studies me with her shrewd eyes. "Please understand, Serena and the baby have a home with me, no matter what. I don't want Serena forced into a situation where she thinks she has no options."

Neither do I. I want Serena more than anything. But I also want her to *want* to be with me. Not feel like she's obligated to move in with me because I knocked her up.

"I'm glad she has you, Emily."

She presses her hand against her chest. "Wow. Huh." She tilts her head to the side, staring at me through narrowed eyes. "I expected you to get defensive."

"Eh." I shrug. "The impulse was there for a second. But I get it. You don't know me, and you want to protect Serena. We want the same thing. There's nothing to be defensive about."

"Hmm." She nods slowly, still assessing me. But I'm winning her over.

"Let me have your number." She pulls her cell phone out of her pocket. "In case there's ever an emergency."

All the things that could possibly go wrong strike cold fear through my chest. We exchange numbers but it doesn't feel like enough.

"I'd still like to help you out, though," I say. "If you won't take money, is there something else I can do for you?"

Again, she seems taken aback. What kind of men have been in this woman's life that basic decency seems so shocking?

The kind of men who make her open the door with a pistol by her side.

She blinks for a second and glances at the yard. "How are you with a lawn mower?"

AFTER EMILY LEAVES, I sit in the truck for a second to send Z a text. He's the only one who knows the situation and he cared enough to go with me to Serena's apartment. I should at least let him know she's okay.

Found her. Everything is fine.

Fine. Not good. Not great.

I fire up the truck and head toward Strike Back Studio. Been neglecting the job Wrath called in a favor to get for me and it's time to spend some time there being useful.

At least Emily's place isn't far from work or my apartment. If Serena needs something, I can be there in fifteen minutes. Much better than her apartment in Empire.

Sure, keep telling yourself everything is fine.

As I roll to a stop at the sign at the end of Emily's street, the entire cab of the truck rings.

"What the fuck?" I stare at the screen in the dashboard. It takes me a few seconds to remember the instructions Murphy gave me. I hate this shit.

I punch the "accept call" button. "You tryin' to get me killed?"

"I thought you hated texting, Grumpy, I mean, Grinder." Z chuckles. "Figured it'd be easier to call you."

I turn right, moving slow through the quiet residential area. "I'm headed to work."

"This late? Figured you'd be celebrating with your girl."

"Sully needs me to close the place. I've been shirking my responsibilities there. He doesn't ask for much, so ..."

"Yeah, I feel you. So what happened?"

"Are you bored or something? My life ain't your personal soap opera."

"Nope. I got plenty to keep me busy. Just lookin' out for my brother."

Pile on the guilt, why don't ya. "Nothing happened. She freaked out like I thought."

"Did you explain the club will take care of her, if she ever needs it?"

"Thanks for planning my death, fucker," I growl. "Yeah, she's got a hard time believing that, though."

"Fuck," he mutters. "I don't blame her. Where'd you leave things?"

"I'm going to go with her to the doctor when she gets an appointment. And for now, she's moving in with her friend."

"That a good thing?"

"Yeah, she's got a nice place. Only ten minutes from my apartment."

"Good." He pauses. Almost sounds like someone's talking to him in the background. "G, the club has…funds. If you want to buy a place or build a house on the club's property, we can help you do that."

More charity. "Club's done more than enough for me since I got out, Z. I'm not taking any more from my brothers."

"It's not *taking* if it's freely offered, Grumpy."

"Keep it up, fucker. I said no."

"All right. All right. I'll let it go."

I doubt it'll be the last time he mentions it, though.

CHAPTER ELEVEN
Serena

"Does this look okay?" I execute a full spin. The skirt of my dress flies out in a circle around me, swishing around my knees when I stop.

Emily taps her finger against her bottom lip. "Beautiful. That melon color gives you the whole peaches and cream glowy thing." She pats her cheeks. "Love the heels too. You're lucky Gray's so tall, you can wear whatever you want and he still towers over you."

"I was thinking the same thing as I went through my shoe collection."

Libby perks up. "Can I go through your shoe collection?"

As much as I love Libby, that's not happening. "I don't think we wear the same size, kiddo."

Her mouth turns down. Emily reaches across the kitchen table and taps her sister's arm. "Cut it out. You have enough shoes."

"Yeah, but I neeeeed a pair of knee-high boots like Serena's."

Oh, boy.

The doorbell rings, saving me.

Wringing my hands, I hurry to the front door and open it. *Why am I so nervous tonight?*

Gray's on the other side and smiles as soon as he sees me. "You look beautiful."

"Thanks." I twist my fingers in the material of my dress then stop, worried I'll leave sweaty fingerprints on the light-colored fabric.

He thrusts a large bouquet of cheery, bright yellow sunflowers at me.

"Oh! Thank you. They're so pretty." Realizing he's still standing outside, I step back. "Come in. Let me put these in a vase."

"I know they don't have a lot of scent." He shrugs. "But I saw them and they looked so sunny and hopeful, they reminded me of how I feel around you, so I had to get them."

Whatever nervousness I answered the door with fades. Gray always has such a thoughtful reason behind everything he does. "I love them. They're one of my favorite flowers." I step closer and lean up to kiss his cheek. "Thank you."

I take his hand and tug him toward the kitchen. One corner of his mouth lifts. "Emily's not waiting in there for me with a shotgun, is she?"

"She and Libby are in there. But no shotgun that I know of."

I bustle into the kitchen, my heels clicking over the tile. Libby twists around in her chair and grins at us. "Hi, Mr. Lock!"

"Hey, Libby."

"Oh, how pretty!" Emily hurries to one of the cupboards. "Let me find a vase for you."

"Thanks." I set the flowers on the counter and unwrap them from the bright blue tissue paper.

"Oh, are these from the little shop next to Strike Back? The owner is so sweet," Emily gushes as she fills a cobalt blue vase with warm water. Her voice is a shade higher than usual. Is she nervous around Gray? Or is she feeling guilty for being so hostile to him yesterday?

"She always donates to the drama club," Libby adds.

"Don't know if I met the owner or not, but whoever helped me was quick and efficient," Gray says.

I chuckle. It figures those would be two qualities he'd admire.

Emily fluffs the flowers into place and sets them on the counter.

"Thanks."

"I'll bring them up to your room if you want," she offers.

"It's okay. I'll take them up with me when I go to bed later." Gray's standing so close, I feel a slight shift in his body. Was he expecting me to come home with him tonight?

After a few more seconds of small talk, I link my hand with Gray's and we head outside.

On the front porch, I check my purse to make sure I have my keys, then Gray leads me to the truck.

I stop and stare at the running boards. Doing a quick mental calculation of where to place my foot so I don't slip. Between the heels and the dress, I'm worried I'll end up flashing the neighborhood.

Gray seems to sense my dilemma immediately. He stands behind me, close enough to feel his breath on my neck and his heat against my back.

"Up you go." He grips my waist and boosts me into the truck. Problem solved.

I cross my legs, smoothing my dress over my knees while I wait for him to walk around to his side.

"Sorry, I wasn't thinking." I wave my hand toward my shoes. "It was just finally nice out and I never dress up, but I swear I'm not always so high maintenance." Why am I so nervous I can't stop babbling? It's not like we haven't gone out before. *I'm carrying his baby for fuck's sake!*

His brow wrinkles. "What are you apologizing for? You look beautiful."

"Thank you." I gesture toward the house as he starts the truck. "I really love the flowers. They're so pretty." I can't remember a man ever giving me flowers before. Or coming to the door to pick me up like a normal date. It must've happened once or twice in my life, but I can't recall.

"Oh! I have an appointment Friday. It's early—"

"I'll be there." He glances over and flashes a quick, warm smile. "Is that okay? Murphy says he goes to all of Heidi's appointments, so I don't think it will be weird. Hope said Rock went with her."

"You…you asked about that?" *I thought we said we weren't going to tell anyone yet?*

"Hell, no. I just overheard the girls talking about it, that's all." He chuckles. "It's hard not to know everyone's business."

"I bet," I mumble. How I hate the thought that I'll be the topic of conversation at the next Lost Kings gathering. *Serena finally trapped a brother. Har. Har. Har.* No thanks.

He flips on his blinker and makes a left turn into a small parking lot. "Sully says this is the best place in the immediate area. The joint they all hang at after work is a bar. Figured that'd be too noisy."

"I'm not picky."

He shuts off the truck and turns toward me. "How are you feeling? Is everything okay?"

Baby, he's asking about the baby. "No morning sickness or anything like that, yet."

"Good, good. If you ever need me to bring you something, just let me know."

I duck my head, feeling heat spread over my cheeks. "Thank you. I will."

He opens his door and steps out. "Wait for me to help you out of the truck."

My mouth curves. I grab my purse and wait patiently. A few seconds later, my door swings open. I swivel in my seat and as I'm about to place my foot on the step, he plucks me out of the truck and gently sets me down.

"Careful of your shoulder," I murmur.

He rolls it a few times. "It's actually a lot better. I've been doing the exercises you gave me, and Sully helped me add a few more."

I blink, a little shocked he's kept up with it. Then again, working out and taking care of himself obviously isn't something new.

"You seem surprised."

"A lot of my male patients can be pretty stubborn." Especially the older ones who can't believe a female has the nerve or credentials to tell them what to do. Then again, Gray has never treated me that way. Probably why it's been so easy to fall for him.

"I'm not the typical anything," he says in a low voice.

Did I offend him?

"Definitely not," I agree.

It's dark inside the restaurant. Gray steps up to the hostess and murmurs a few words to her. Apparently, he already has a reservation.

We're led to a table in a quiet corner.

"You take the sitting in the corner with your back to the wall thing to heart, huh?" I say after the hostess leaves.

"Learned the hard way," he grumbles, picking up his menu.

"I'm sorry. I didn't mean—"

"It's fine, Serena. Stop apologizing."

"I don't know why I'm so nervous tonight." I pick up my own menu and run my nail around the metal-tipped corner without opening it.

"I don't either. We've been out before, buttercup."

There it is. He hadn't called me buttercup once since picking me up. I slide my hand over the table, resting it over his. "Tonight feels like a date-date."

"We've been 'dating' all along, haven't we?"

"I know." I shrug.

We both order steaks. As soon as the waiter drops a basket of bread off, I grab a roll. It's warm and fluffy. I smother it in butter and stuff half of it in my mouth quicker than socially acceptable.

Gray watches me with an amused smile.

"I'm starving."

"I could've picked you up earlier."

"It's okay."

"What'd you do today?"

"Ran over to my place and packed my clothes, shoes, and makeup. Brought back a carload."

"I told you I wanted to do that with you."

"You said packing and moving stuff. I assumed you meant the heavy stuff. This was clothes and shoes. If anyone breaks into my apartment, they're not stealing my Doc Martens or my makeup collection."

He chuckles. "We can replace your *stuff*. Not you."

"Nuh-uh. Some of my Docs are limited editions. You can't find them anymore. Same for most of my eyeshadow pallets. Priceless."

His eyes are still crinkled at the corners with amusement. "Is there more there?"

"Yes, but the rest can wait."

"Good. We can stop there Friday, if you want. I can have a few of the guys meet us if you want to clear out the place."

"Not yet. I have until the end of the month. Maybe you could help me pack and sort what I'm putting in storage and what I'm keeping, though? That way, I'll be ready." I sense he really wants to be able to do something for me and I would like the help.

"Sure thing."

After our dinners arrive, I spend a chunk of time shoving bits of steak in my mouth. I wasn't kidding about being hungry all the time. And craving red meat. I should probably mention that to the doctor. Maybe I'm anemic or something.

When I finally finish and set down my fork, I find Gray watching me.

"Do you want me to order something else?"

Heat sears my cheeks. I probably looked like I'd never seen food before in my life. "No, I'm stuffed."

He slides his hand over the table and covers mine. "I meant to ask...how did this, uh, happen?"

My cheeks grow hotter. "Gray, I think you're old enough to know how babies are made."

His serious expression doesn't change. "I'm serious. I thought—"

"I didn't do it on purpose," I say quickly. "When that guy attacked me and I was staying at the clubhouse, I didn't have my pills with me." I lean forward and lower my voice. "I'm not sure which day or which night, but you spent a *lot* of time inside me, so I'm guessing *that's* when it happened."

The corners of his mouth curl and fire burns in his eyes at my reminder. Then the feral expression turns to something more like concern or curiosity. "I thought…even after you stop taking the pill sometimes it takes a long time…"

"Well, apparently not for me." I bristle, unsure of where he's going with these questions. "I must've been out of it because I didn't even realize I'd forgotten them until we went to my apartment. But I didn't know what to say."

"Serena," he says in a tone low enough not to be overheard but stern enough to grab my attention. "Stop thinking I'm mad at you." His mouth curves into a wry smile. "I'm relieved everything still works at my age."

"What? You're not that old," I sputter. "You've certainly never disappointed me in that area." I've been with men half his age that didn't have his stamina or had some other weird sexual dysfunction. I doubt Gray will appreciate that comparison, though. "Besides, you always hear about some celebrity fathering kids into his nineties or whatever."

He scoffs. "Please, half the time, it's probably donors. Stories made up to soothe their egos and deny their impending visit from the grim reaper."

"Ewww." My nose wrinkles but I can't help laughing.

"That's better." He pats my hand and sits back. "Do you want dessert?"

"I do, in the worst way." I turn in my seat, checking out the restaurant. "Do you think they have cake and ice cream?"

"Let's find out."

Grinder

This is so fucking weird. Conversation with Serena feels like trying to capture a feral kitten tonight. She's so suspicious and defensive. I keep trying to remind myself it has more to do with her past experiences than me, but it's hard to watch her struggling so much when all I want to do is hold her in my arms.

I want things back to the way they were. Before her attack. I still haven't processed that the guy who hurt Serena is dead. His brains blown out right in front of me. Not that it matters, I'm used to gore and death. And in my life there always seems to be another enemy waiting to be dealt with.

The waiter stops at our table and clasps his hands in front of him. "Can I interest you in dessert tonight?"

"Yes," I answer quickly, worried Serena will change her mind out of embarrassment or something silly. "Do you have any cake?"

"Oh yes." The guy's eyes light up, like maybe he baked them personally. "We have a decadent chocolate blackout cake. Moist layers of chocolate cake smothered between thick frosting and—"

"That," Serena says. "I'll have that."

"Excellent choice." He turns toward me. "We also have—"

"She wants ice cream with the cake." I nod to Serena.

"Oh, yes. I can do that. The cake is very rich, though—"

"Do you have strawberry ice cream?" she asks.

"Ah, we have a raspberry gelato."

"Oh, that sounds even better." Serena beams at him. "Can I have them separate?"

"Absolutely," he answers without skipping a beat. "Sir?"

He rattles off a list and I pick tiramisu.

"Coffee?"

"Yes, two."

"Decaf for me, please," Serena says.

I raise an eyebrow but don't ask.

After he leaves, Serena leans over the table. "I'm not sure if I can have coffee." She blinks quickly. "Shoot, maybe I'm not supposed to eat chocolate either." She reaches for her purse, hooked over the back of her chair, and pulls out her cell phone.

"What are you doing?"

"Googling it. Although, you get so many contradicting answers, I don't know what to think." She pauses, staring at her phone and flicking her thumb over the screen. "Moderation. Big help," she grumbles, tucking her phone away.

"I'm sure pregnant women eat chocolate all the time."

"I know." She glances down. "I just want to do everything right."

"I can't imagine having to worry about small things like that every day for the next nine months," I say quietly. "And I'll never be able to understand what it's like. That's what I meant about wanting to take care of the things I can. So you can concentrate on all these other things that I *can't* help with." Since she didn't seem to take me seriously yesterday, and last night I thought about how to express it better, it makes sense to bring it up again.

"Like what?"

"Like your bills." I wiggle my fingers in a *give it to me* gesture. "Put all your monthly expenses together and hand them over Friday. Unless you've got something that needs to be paid right now."

Her jaw drops. Damn, she's awfully cute when she's surprised. Although, I don't know why it's such a shock. Real men take care of their responsibilities.

"But I'm going to find another job. I already had a sort-of offer…"

My jaw works from side to side. "You were struggling to pay everything *before* you lost your job. Let me help you get caught up, then…you're going to need to take some time off."

She stares down at her hands. "I don't have a lot. Rent and car insurance. My student loans are a big one, some medical bills, oh, and I have to pay the full tab for my health insurance from the old job until I find a new one. Definitely going to need that." Her mouth turns down. See, she's already getting stressed thinking about all this shit.

"Doesn't sound like anything I can't handle, buttercup."

She tilts her head.

I'd rather not mention that I flipped through her bills when I was at her apartment the other day, but she'll find out eventually. "To be honest, I looked through some of the stuff on your desk when I went to your apartment."

There go her cheeks getting all red again. Might as well disclose everything.

"Took your hospital bill. Club should be covering that one, anyway," I growl.

She opens her mouth. Then closes it. "Fair enough," she finally mutters.

Now she's gettin' it.

"I didn't do this on purpose so you'd take care of me, you know."

Or maybe she's still not hearing me.

"No shit, buttercup. Trappin' an old man who works part-time as a janitor is a piss-poor plan. You're smarter than that."

"Gray—"

"Here we are." The waiter sets our desserts on the table and returns a few seconds later with our coffee. "Anything else?"

"Just the check."

"Sure thing."

Like before, Serena hurries to take a huge bite of the cake. "Oh my God," she moans. "It's so good."

Chuckling, I fix my coffee, stirring it slowly while I watch her alternate between forkfuls of cake and spoonfuls of the dark red gelato.

"Do they go well together?"

"Yes. Perfectly." She nudges the dishes in my direction. "Try it?"

"I'm good." I hold up my hand. "If you want some of my dessert, say so now, though." I tap my fork against my plate.

She takes a sip of water. "I have more than enough here."

I can't get my fill of watching the delight she takes in enjoying something so simple. Two things that, to me, don't seem to go together.

Kind of like us.

After paying the check, we step outside. The cool night air washes over us and I take a deep breath. Hadn't realized how stuffy it felt inside until now.

"Can we walk a little?" Serena asks. "Down Main Street."

"I don't think anything's open this late."

"I just want to look. I haven't really poked around here in a while."

Johnsonville isn't a particularly prosperous area, but downtown is a quaint collection of small businesses and offices. Reminds me of something out of a history book about the Fifties.

I glance down at her shoes. "Sure you don't mind walking in those?"

"I'm fine."

I take her hand and we stroll at a slow pace. As we approach a tea shop, she stops to stare in the window. "Emily's a tea drinker. I'll have to stop by when they're open and get her something as a thank you."

I tuck that bit of information away for the future. "She's a good friend."

"She is. I'm sorry if she—"

"Nope. No need to apologize. I'd probably feel the same way if I were in her shoes." We continue walking. "How'd Libby feel about you moving in?"

"Already trying to steal my boots." She laughs. "Thank God we're not the same size. I'm kind of stingy about sharing shoes." Her steps falter. "I never really had my own. My mom would grab hand-me-downs from random people when I was a kid. Half the time, they wouldn't fit right or would already be falling apart, so I'd get blisters and get made fun of. When I was older, we were the same size, so she'd let me borrow hers. But I always hated it." She shrugs.

"I don't think that's stingy." Even as broke and abusive as my parents could be, we always had the basics.

"Maybe not, but I love Libby. I don't want to be mean about it. Maybe I'll save up and buy her a pair of her own Doc Martens for her birthday or something."

"That's sweet." I lean in and kiss her forehead.

We cross the near-empty street to the opposite sidewalk and start walking back to the restaurant.

The wide picture window of the florist where I bought her sunflowers earlier is dark now. Strike Back is only a few doors down. Also dark.

"Oh, this is your place." Serena stops and nods toward Strike Back.

"That's it."

"How do you like it?"

"It's good. It's a small gym, so you get to know the regulars pretty well. It's just Sully, his brother, and his fiancée working there, so I'm actually helping him out. The schedule is flexible, and he lets me use whatever equipment I want when it's slow."

"Sounds like a good situation."

Nothing I did on my own, since Wrath's the one who got me the job, but I don't feel like getting into that now.

She turns to face me and brushes her fingers over my shoulder. "Do you think it would be okay if I stopped by to have lunch with you one day?"

"Yeah, I'd like that."

"Let me know your hours and when would be best."

"All right." I tug her toward the parking lot. I'm not ready to say goodnight yet. But the evening's been perfect so far. I don't want to push when she's still skittish but slowly warming up again.

The drive to Emily's seems to be over too fast. I step out of the truck and ask her to wait.

I open her door. She beams at me and turns in her seat. I can't say good night without kissing her at least once. I step into the open space and rest my hand on her leg.

Before I have a chance to do more, she slides to the edge of the seat and wraps her arms around my neck. "Thank you for such a nice night," she whispers in my ear.

"You're welcome, buttercup."

She pulls away and I brush a few strands of stray hair off her cheek. I lean in and press my lips to hers. She sighs into my mouth and melts into me, tightening her arms around my neck.

Reaching behind her, I fumble for the dome light to shut it off, but the stupid truck doesn't have them in a normal location. I grunt in frustration and pull away. "Don't want to put on a show for all the neighbors," I explain.

"I don't care." She pulls me closer for another kiss.

I slide my hand up her leg, grasping her thigh. I'm so fucking close to asking her to come home with me.

She sighs and pulls away. "Are you going to lift me out of the truck again?" She tilts her head, a soft smile playing over her lips.

"Sure thing." I grip her waist and pull her toward me. She lets out a happy shriek, followed by laughter.

"I feel like a tiny little doll when you do that."

I set her down on the sidewalk. "You are tiny compared to me."

I reach for the door and slam it shut, then take her hand.

"You're going to walk me to the door?" she asks, surprise coloring her tone.

"It's late. Of course I am."

A warm yellow glow spills over the front steps and into the yard. Brighter lights burst over the sidewalk as we approach the house.

"Careful, the lights are blinding," she warns. "I almost fell on my butt the other night."

"She's got good security."

"I knew you'd approve."

Still rather have her living with me, but this is a vast improvement over her apartment.

On the front porch, she turns and faces me. "Thank you for such a nice evening."

"Any time, buttercup." A strange awkwardness settles over us. "It's been a long time since I 'dated.' Trying to remember all the steps."

"You do fine." She presses her body against mine and tips her head back, almost like an invitation. I stroke her cheek while studying every curve and angle of her face. I skim my finger down the perfectly straight slope of her nose. "I hope our baby has your nose."

She tilts her head. "You really are excited, aren't you?"

"You have no idea." I nod to the door. "Let me watch you go inside."

"Okay." She searches through her purse and pulls out her keys, holding them in the air and jingling them in front of me.

Serena

I close the door behind me and lean against it, fighting the urge to run after Gray. It feels all kinds of wrong to say good night and go our separate ways.

After a few seconds, I peek out the window, watching his truck pull away from the curb.

I sigh. My eyelids feel heavy. It's been a long day and I'm dragging.

I kick off my shoes and bend over to pick them up, carrying them with me.

Light flickers in the living room and I spot Emily on the couch with her laptop. Only a low murmur comes from the television.

"Hey, Em."

She jumps and pulls out her earbuds.

"Oops, sorry."

"It's okay." She waves for me to come closer. "How was your date?"

"Nice." I drop onto the couch next to her. "Really nice. You weren't waiting up for me, were you?"

"No." She closes her laptop and sets it on the coffee table. "I can never sleep so I come down here and get some work done, you know?"

"Makes sense." I yawn and stretch. "I'm going to head upstairs. I can barely keep my eyes open."

"Good night."

CHAPTER TWELVE

Grinder

I'M NOT LOOKING FORWARD TO MEETING WITH GRILLO TODAY. IT'S gonna be hard to keep my mouth shut and not tip him off that I know about him working with Big Chief.

I step into the raggedy, dark office and cast a glance around the waiting area. Fellow parolees with their heads down, anxiously waiting to be called in for their piss test and game of twenty questions.

One guy looks up and nods at me. I return the gesture and keep walking to the bulletproof glass window.

"Grayson Lock, here for my ten a.m. with Grillo." Ten in the morning, during the week. The most inconvenient time for anyone trying to adhere to the conditions of parole by holding down a job. Just what employers want to hear. "Hey boss, I gotta take off in the middle of the morning to go meet my parole officer. No idea when I'll be back. That cool? Thanks." It's like the system was designed to keep criminals from ever advancing into productive members of society.

That the club found me a job where I could come and go with no questions asked is a blessing I'm grateful for every time I have to come here.

The girl behind the window nods but doesn't say anything. No indication of how long I might have to wait.

I take a seat and quietly count back from one hundred to cool the anger burning inside me. If I punch Grillo in the face, there is a one-hundred-percent certainty I'll be returned to prison. Can't have that when I need to look after Serena and our baby. I plan to be by her side holding her hand when our child's born, not rotting away in a cell because I couldn't control my temper.

In prison, I got really good at sitting still and letting my mind wander. On the outside, I try to avoid doing that as much as possible. But it comes in handy in situations where killing time can't be avoided.

"Mr. Lock?" an authoritative female voice calls.

I blink out of my trance and turn my head toward the voice. Tall black woman with a head full of bouncy, perfectly spiraled curls gleaming under the fluorescent lights and an impatient smile stretched across her red lips. She flicks her fingers, motioning for me to hurry.

Christ, what fresh hell am I in for now?

"Rena Lewis." She holds out her hand for a brisk shake, then jerks her head to the side, indicating I should follow.

A tall woman, she walks quickly and with purpose, navigating the crowded office space with ease. We pass Grillo's office. The door is closed and it's dark beyond the frosted glass window. Huh.

She stops at an open door to a corner office, turns to make sure I'm still behind her and steps inside.

"Have a seat." She sweeps her hand toward the chair in front of the desk and quietly closes the door behind me.

I'm on edge as I drop into the cheap wood and vinyl chair. Has she read my file and already assumed I'm an asshole? A black woman in a male-dominated profession, she probably has to work ten times harder than jackasses like Grillo. How's that going to impact *my* life?

Most men probably start running their mouths as soon as they see her and realize the power she's going to have over their lives. I keep mine shut and wait to see what she says.

"Mr. Lock." She drops into her chair and rolls it closer to the desk, grabs a blue folder and flips it open. "I'll be taking over your case while Mr. Grillo is…on leave."

On leave. So, he's not dead. Pity.

"Is he okay?" *I should at least pretend to give a shit, shouldn't I?*

"I don't have many details." She pins me with intense brown eyes. "And if I did, I couldn't share them."

"Okay." *I truly don't give a fuck, lady.*

She thumbs through pages of notes. From my angle, I recognize Grillo's sloppy handwriting scribbled over the forms.

"So far, it seems like you've been a model parolee." Her tone is even. Businesslike. She flips another page. "Drug tests have all been clean. You're maintaining employment." Her eyebrows rise. "Employer only has compliments for your performance."

Embarrassment slithers through my chest. I hate that Grillo's been in touch with Sully, asking him about me. I knew it was a probability, but still hate it. Hate even more that Sully's never mentioned it.

"That's good to hear," I say to fill the silence.

"Haven't missed an appointment." Her nose wrinkles. "I see Mr. Grillo has made several home visits."

My stomach knots while I wait for her to continue. What kind of bullshit did Grillo write about me? Did he mention that I was fifteen minutes late one night when I came home with Serena? Shit, did he put Serena's name in my file?

"No issues there, either," she says slowly, like she's trying to come to some sort of decision. Finally, she sets the file down and laces her fingers together on top of it. "Let me be frank with you, Mr. Lock."

I nod to let her know I'm listening and won't interrupt.

"I already have a heavy caseload." She tilts her head toward four tall filing cabinets against the wall. Each with stacks of folders precariously piled on top. "Having Hank's cases thrown on me was unexpected." She lifts her chin toward the door. "So far, it looks like you've been compliant with all the terms and conditions of your release."

Except for that associating with other felons thing, yeah.

"You seem to be making good progress since you've been out." She pauses as if she expects an answer.

"I'm trying, Ms. Lewis."

"Good. Half the offenders we supervise have already had an interaction with law enforcement by now. Probably more than half. Another large percentage are already incarcerated again. As long as you don't make my life more difficult, I think we'll get along fine. Continue what you're doing. Make your appointments on time, clean tests, stay out of trouble, and we can reduce your visits to seeing each other every two weeks."

Fuck, that'd be nice.

"Then once a month," she continues. "And if things go well, I'll see if I can get you discharged early."

"I didn't realize that was possible."

"It's up to my discretion. I'm here to supervise and guide you in your rehabilitation. But if you're making progress, it seems counterproductive to continue dragging you in here. There's no reason to keep you from moving forward with your life."

This took an unexpected turn. I swallow hard and nod. "Appreciate that."

Her jaw clenches, like she doesn't give a fuck about my appreciation. Despite her hard-ass demeanor, I like her. All business and no games or bullshit. So far. We'll see how it goes. But Grillo had been nonstop assholery from day one. Already, Ms. Lewis is an improvement.

"I don't give the most attention to the squeaky wheels, though," she adds. "You should still be prepared for me to drop by your apartment or workplace unannounced."

"Not a problem."

"Good." She stands and walks around the desk. "Is there anything you need from me? Or any issues you'd like to discuss?"

Grillo never gave a shit if I had any issues. "Not that I can think of." I jerk my thumb over my shoulder. "You need me to go take a test now?"

She cocks her head and stares at me for a second or two. She's a tall woman and wearing heels so we're almost at eye level. I maintain eye contact while waiting for her answer.

"Not today, Mr. Lock. Next visit. I'm just trying to touch base with Hank's people today."

"All right. Thank you."

Her eyebrows jerk but she doesn't say anything, just leans past me to open the door, motioning for me to exit. I feel her at my back as I navigate the office. The waiting area is considerably more crowded than it was when I arrived. No chairs left. People nervously twitching and looking around. Thank fuck I got here early.

"Next week, same time, Mr. Lock," she says. "Does that work for you?"

No one ever asks what works for me. "Yes, this is fine."

"All right." She holds out her hand again and I give it a quick shake. "Next week." She dismisses me and calls for her next appointment.

I shove the heavy glass and steel door open and step onto the sidewalk. My eyes squint at the sunlight and I slip on a pair of shades. It's the first time I've left here not feeling like a piece of shit or ready to murder someone.

Early discharge. That'd be nice if I could be a completely free man by the time my kid gets here.

I pull out my phone and send Z a text as I walk to my car.

Got a new PO today.

He answers a few seconds later.

Interesting.

Yeah, it's interesting all right. Did the club have something to do with the switch? Or did Loco make a move on Grillo? If Grillo had been murdered, Ms. Lewis would've said he was dead, right? Not just "on leave" like he might pop in at any time.

I hoist myself into the truck cab and start the engine. My hand rests on the gearshift but I don't put it in drive. Instead, I stare out the windshield, not really looking at anything in particular. Could Grillo's bosses have figured out he was dirty? If he's suspended, fuck knows what stories he might tell to save his own ass. People came after Serena once before because of Grillo's big mouth. I can't have that happen again.

Especially now.

CHAPTER THIRTEEN

Grinder

Mid-week, Rock calls me up to the clubhouse. When I arrive, the parking lot is full. I spot Z's bike, then Rooster's. Looks like downstate came to play too.

"How's it going, brother?" Wrath greets me right inside the door. I slip off my coat and hang it in the closet before answering.

"Not bad."

"Sully still treating you well?"

"Yup. Even gave my P.O. a glowing report, which was a big help. Got a new one and I think the recommendation from my employer impressed her."

His eyebrows shoot up. "That's good."

"Thanks for going out of your way to get me the job."

He cocks his head. "Don't gotta thank me, brother. Happy to help any way I can."

"What's going on today?"

He shrugs. "Rock just misses everyone."

"Bullshit," I grumble.

The door opens and Rock steps inside. He nods at me. "Thanks for coming up."

"No problem."

He stops and says a few words to Wrath.

Everyone takes their time getting to the table. But the chatter dies down quicker than usual. Rock doesn't even have to bang his gavel.

"First, the new dancers from Loco's harem start Thursday night. I'd appreciate a volunteer—"

Several hands shoot in the air before Rock finishes the request. His gaze narrows and he studies the guys, then turns to Dex. "Your choice, brother."

"I'll take all the help I can get." He pins Rav, Stash, and Hustler with a hard stare. "I need you to stay on 'em."

"Not a problem," Rav smirks.

"I'm serious. Make sure they're not pulling any tricks and watch that our regular girls don't haze them. Swan will be there to supervise in the dressing room, so if she calls for help, I expect one of you to move like lightning."

The smirk slides off Rav's face. "You got it."

Dex's gaze slides to Stash. "No flirting with Willow all night, either."

"Come on," he says in a slow, lazy drawl. "You know me better than that."

A few more guys from downstate volunteer. Dex doesn't grill them as hard, but he and Z nod at each other, so I'm guessing Z will have a chat with his members later.

"Good, glad that's settled. Thanks for stepping up." Rock nods to each brother. As if they need to be praised for volunteering to spend the night at our strip club.

"Now." Rock slides a piece of paper out of an official envelope. "I got a notice from the zoning board about the new clubhouse. Apparently, we're missing a permit or some shit." He glares at everyone down the table. "Now, those of you who asked for that new clubhouse to be built were supposed to make sure it didn't end up *my* problem."

"That's my fault, Prez." Teller lifts his hand in the air. "I was supposed to take care of it."

"Nah, I was part of the group asking for the place to be built. I was supposed to remind him," Rav says.

"Spare me the mutual stroke fest, and get it done."

"Got it." Teller reaches for the paper and Rock hands it over.

"Z," Rock nods. "All yours."

"With Grinder's permission, downstate would like to throw you a welcome home party."

I wasn't expecting to suddenly have everyone's eyes on me. I sit up and glare at Z. "Sure, brother. I want to see the place. You know the reasons I haven't been down there yet."

"I do. I do." He glances down at the table for a second. "Also, Priest is planning to attend."

"What now?" I lean forward. "Why?"

"Because you spent fifteen years inside for the club?" Z says in a slow, mocking tone.

"Watch yourself," I warn.

"He's asked about you a lot over the years," Rock says.

"Eh, he came to visit once or twice early on but not since he took over National."

Rock raises his eyebrows as if he wasn't aware Priest had paid me any visits. Been so fucking long ago, I rarely think about it anyway.

"Do we want to make more progress on our support club before Priest gets here?" Wrath asks. "That's been on his agenda for a while now."

"Is this Rooster's fault?" Steer shoves his VP. "Priest was on his dick all summer sending him to different charters to spy on 'em and shit."

Rooster slowly turns his head and glares at Steer. "I wasn't spying on anyone and I'm pretty sure your ego got plenty of strokes from National, so shut the fuck up."

Steer shakes with laughter but Rooster doesn't seem as amused.

"Fault implies there is a problem." Z leans forward and glares at Steer. "You have a problem with our national president paying us a visit?"

"No, Prez. Not me."

"Good." Z turns to me. "He understands about your parole limitations. That's why he hasn't pushed to come up earlier."

"Well, thank fuck for his understanding."

"I'll let you know when we've got it all set. You think this new parole officer is gonna be a problem?"

"Don't know yet. She seemed no-nonsense but fair."

"Wait, hold up." Rav raises his hand. "You got a female P.O. now, Grinder?"

"Oh, fuck that's hot," Stash adds.

"I assure you, there is *nothing* fun about being on parole." I wouldn't even wish it on these two clowns.

"Yeah, but does she, like, carry handcuffs and shit?" Rav persists.

"Jesus Christ." Rock rubs his hand across his temple.

"She hot?" Hustler asks.

"Don't you start with that shit now too," Z warns.

"She's attractive but authoritative," I answer.

"I love the bossy bitches." Hustler rubs his hands together like a fucking deviant.

"Does 'don't start' mean *tell us more stuff we don't need to know* where you were born?" Z asks.

"What? I'm just saying. If she's looking, hook your brother up."

"Yeaaah," I answer slow and irritated, "we're not really there to discuss her dating habits."

"What happened to Grillo?" Rock asks.

"Finally, someone asking the question that matters." I turn toward Rock's end of the table.

Wrath's eyes are shut tight and he's quietly shaking with laughter. If I were closer, I'd fucking kick him. "What's so funny, Giggles?"

He swipes under his eyes and grins. "Nothing. Just the more they obsess over every chick mentioned, the more obvious it is they've never—"

"Don't you dare say it!" Rav stands and points at Wrath.

"Never made a woman come," Teller finishes Wrath's sentence. "Yes, that's what *all* of us were thinking."

I shoot a glare at Rock. "Kinda letting this train run away from you, Prez."

He shrugs. "Go on."

"I don't know. I showed up for my weekly appointment. She said he's on leave but wouldn't elaborate. She made it clear she won't take any bullshit from me but also seemed like she'll be fair and reasonable."

"Give me her name," Z says.

"No. I don't want the club gettin' involved. She said she thinks I'm making progress and she might recommend I get released early if I stay out of trouble. You'll blow my reformed criminal image if you try to bribe her on my behalf."

"Fair enough, brother." Z holds up his hands. "I'll stay out of it for now. But if she gives you trouble…"

"I'll keep it in mind."

Rock stares at me, then Z, then Teller. "You think Loco went for Grillo already?"

"Seems awfully fast," Z says. "I barely got the dude's schedule."

"You've been tracking Grillo?" I ask Z.

"Damn right I have." He crosses his unapologetic arms over his stubborn chest.

"Who knows how many enemies he's got," Wrath said. "All his people have done hard time. Fucking around with their freedom's a good way to get killed."

I hadn't really given a lot of thought to anyone else Grillo might've screwed over. Too concerned about my own damn freedom.

"Any other business?" Rock's gaze slides down the length of the table and back.

Even though I don't want to start another round of fuckery, I raise my hand. Rock sits back and nods at me.

"We got any prospects around?" I haven't seen any yet. But Wrath said something about them not being allowed at the property until they'd been prospecting for a certain amount of time.

"Only a couple at the moment," Wrath answers.

"What do you need?" Rock asks.

"Serena's staying with a friend of hers. She needs some yard work done. I said I'd take care of it. I can do it myself, but—"

"I'll do it," Dex volunteers.

"Bro, you don't have enough to do?" Murphy says.

"Whoa, whoa, whoa." Ravage stands and waves his hands around in a slowdown gesture. "How hot is this chick if Dex is willing to give up his free time to do manual labor?"

"Jesus," Dex mutters. "It's got nothing to do with that."

Teller cough-laughs into his fist. "Okay."

"Thanks, brother." Ignoring the comments, I lean forward to look at Dex. "That would help me out a lot."

"Not a problem."

"I'll pay you for your time."

"The fuck you will," Dex snaps.

"She's got a big yard."

Rav opens his mouth.

"Don't," I warn him. I return my attention to Dex. "A lot of hedges."

Rav lifts his hand and opens his mouth again.

"Don't do it, bro," Teller warns. "Grinder came locked and loaded to kick fuckin' ass today."

"Damn right." I nod at Teller. "I also need someone to help me move stuff out of Serena's apartment."

"Why isn't she moving in with *you*?" Steer asks.

I can't tell if there's sarcasm coloring the question, or I'm just irritated that Steer opened his mouth. "Because I'm still dealing with drop-ins from parole and other shit."

Jigsaw lifts his hand. "I can help you, G."

"Thanks. I'll have more details after Friday."

"Notice Dex ain't volunteering for *that* one," Murphy mutters loud enough for everyone to hear.

"Fuck off." Dex flicks his middle finger at Murphy.

"All right. I think we're done here." Rock smacks his palm against the table to end the meeting. "My officers stick around, please." He glances at me and nods. I take it as a cue to keep my ass where it is.

Z shuts the door behind the guys and returns to the table, taking the seat next to mine.

"For real, what do you think happened to Grillo?" Rock asks.

"Got no fucking clue. She said he was on leave. I asked if he was okay, and she said she didn't know. Sounded like it was unexpected. She wasn't pleased to have his caseload thrown on her, I could tell that much."

Rock glances at Wrath, then Z.

"You think we need to pay Loco another visit?" Teller asks.

Rock groans. "Yes. But this time, let's just stop by the diner. I'm gettin' sick of going all the way into Ironworks."

"Wait, he owns a diner along with the whorehouse?" I ask.

"Legit income." Wrath rubs his fingers together. "The burgers are pretty good, too."

"Dex, can you ask Malik to set something up?" Rock asks.

"Yup. I'll do it as soon as I get to CB."

"All right." Rock stands. "Anyone need anything else?"

When none of us answer, he nods at Teller. "Get those permits done."

"I'm on it."

Z touches my arm, stopping me from getting out of my chair. "Helping her move, huh? That's a big commitment."

"Is it?"

He shrugs. "How long is she staying with her friend?"

"Until I get a bigger place. I don't know. We haven't really gotten that far."

He stares at me, then flicks his gaze across the table. No one's paying attention to our conversation, though. "You'll have to get there sooner rather than later."

"No shit."

"Still planning to propose?"

I sit back and stare at him. "Why? You planning to come watch or something?"

His shoulders lift in another casual shrug. "Just wondering where your head is at, that's all."

"Were you this involved when Rock was courting his girl?"

"Yes," Rock answers in a tired voice.

"I'm sorry, did you say *courting?*" Murphy laughs.

So much for no one paying attention to us. "Don't you all have other places to be?"

Z stands and clasps my shoulder. "I gotta be up here Friday. I can stop by and help if you need an extra set of hands."

"I'll let you know. Thank you."

I stand and also prepare to leave. Don't like that inquisitive look on Rock's face. If he probes too much, I'll break and spill all the things eating me up inside.

CHAPTER FOURTEEN

Serena

"Someone's going to think I'm *your* father." Gray casts a suspicious glance around my doctor's office. No one's paying attention to us, though.

I can't lie. I'm concerned about that myself and I don't want anyone to make him uncomfortable today. So, I squeeze his hand and tug him toward the receptionist's window.

"Serena Cargill. I have an eight-fifteen appointment."

"Sure." She barely looks at me but taps my information into her computer and loudly asks for my information. Gray hovers protectively behind me. I lean in to give her what she wants, then pass her my insurance card.

"Have a seat, someone will be with you soon."

"Serena?" someone calls.

"Guess we won't have to wait long," I say.

Gray follows me to the open door and the waiting nurse. "Hi, my partner's going to join me. Is that okay?"

She eyes Grayson up and down before nodding and waving for me to follow her. She stops at a scale, and I groan.

"Look away," I whisper to Grayson.

He rolls his eyes in an *are you kidding* expression but turns slightly.

I squeeze my eyes shut and wait for the nurse to tell me she's done.

"All right, follow me." She tucks her tablet against her chest and power-walks through the hallway.

We stop at the last door on the right and she opens it, breezing inside.

Thankfully, it's a larger room but with the three of us inside, it still feels awfully cramped.

I shift on my feet, waiting for her instructions.

Change into the gown, pee in this cup, wait for the doctor.

About what I expected.

"You can use the restroom right through there and leave your sample on the windowsill," she instructs.

The door closes behind her.

Gray and I stare at each other.

"Not as exciting as you thought, huh?"

"Do you need help?"

"No." I lift the gown, clutch my cup in my other hand and duck into the bathroom.

Why am I so nervous? I'm a medical professional myself. This isn't anything unusual.

I leave my sample where the nurse told me to and change into the gown.

Is it anxiety I'm feeling or fear? Maybe if I can correctly identify my emotions, it'll help.

Fear. If I'm wrong and not pregnant, Gray will be pissed at me for putting him through all of this and I'll lose him.

You don't need a man to survive, Serena.

I step out of the bathroom and lean against the door for a second, taking a long, deep breath. *No matter what happens, I'll be okay.*

"How'd it go?" Gray asks from the chair across from me.

I slowly open my eyes. "Nothing exciting happened yet."

Anxiety. Gray seems unsure himself. His gaze darts from the door to the window. Every noise from the hallway has him sitting straighter. Maybe his unease is putting me on edge. At least I sort of know what to expect from this visit. He has no idea.

I hop onto the exam table and face him.

"Did you ever...go to the doctor with Rose?" I ask to smooth over the awkwardness. Although, once I hear myself say the words, the situation feels even more uncomfortable.

"Once," he answers in a distant tone. His gaze shifts to the window, then back to me. "She had a miscarriage. We never had a chance to try again." He shrugs. "Now, I'm glad we didn't."

Considering everything he's been through, that somehow seems tragic. "I'm sorry."

"Don't be." His gaze lands on my feet, as I swing my legs back and forth. The corners of his mouth lift. "Every part of you is cute, you know that?"

"What?" I glance down and wiggle my toes.

"Your little sparkling gold toenails are cute."

"Oh!" I stare at my feet and grin. "Libby, Emily, and I had a facials and pedicures night."

"Sounds fun."

"It was."

Silence descends on us again.

But at least the quiet feels less awkward.

Someone knocks and a few seconds later, the door pushes open. "Hi, Serena. I'm Dr. West. How are you today?"

"Good. Dr. West, this is my...partner, Grayson Lock." I sweep my hand in Gray's direction, wanting to establish from the beginning he's the baby's father. Not mine.

She turns and offers her hand. "Nice to meet you. Thank you for joining Serena today."

"Thank you."

Once that's out of the way, Dr. West focuses her full attention on me. "So, your urine test was positive. I see you're not that far past when your last period was due..." she hums as she scans the information in my chart.

"I...um...had a miscarriage last year, so I, um, was worried and wanted to come in as soon as possible," I stammer.

"I'm so sorry to hear that," she murmurs, still studying her tablet. "Oh. Oh my. Yes. Okay." She casts a glance at Gray.

"Gray wasn't the father of that baby," I whisper, absolutely mortified. I'm sure the details are colorful and unflattering.

"Well, okay then." She sets her tablet on the counter and unwraps the stethoscope from around her neck and listens to my heart. "Sounds good." Next, she wraps a cuff around my arm and checks my blood pressure. "Are you nervous?" she asks me.

"A little," I admit.

A warmer smile tugs at the corners of her mouth. "Try to relax. We won't be doing a lot today."

She unwraps the cuff and sets it aside.

I take a deep breath and blow it out slowly.

"I'm going to do a blood draw to double-check, and we'll call you in a couple days with the results. Otherwise, I want you to manage your stress. We'll get you on some pre-natal vitamins as well. Your blood pressure is a little high, so I'll want to monitor that. How do you feel otherwise?"

"Tired."

"Morning sickness?"

"Not really."

Gray sits forward. "Are we going to see the baby today?"

Dr. West shakes her head. "Not today. We'll confirm the pregnancy with the blood test and in a few weeks, I'll have her come back for a scan. We should be able to see something then."

"Oh."

Gray looks so disappointed, I feel bad for dragging him here. Why couldn't I have just handled all of this like a damn adult?

The doctor talks to me for a few more minutes. Going over diet and expectations.

"Let me take your blood pressure again." She reaches for the cuff, and I stick out my arm.

"Better," she says when she's done. "But still a little high. I want to keep an eye on that."

"I've never had high blood pressure before that I know of."

"Are you under a lot of stress?"

I shrug. "I wasn't expecting this, so it's been a bit of an adjustment."

"How's work? Physical therapy can be a high-stress environment."

"Ah, I'm between jobs at the moment."

"That in itself can be stressful," she says sympathetically. "Do you think you'd benefit from talking to someone?"

My cheeks heat up again. "I have a therapist I can call."

"Good." She turns toward Gray. "Do you mind stepping into the hallway for a moment?" While she says it as if it's a pleasant request, she opens the door, indicating 'no' isn't an answer she'll accept.

Gray's eyes meet mine. "Is that okay?"

I nod quickly.

He nods and steps out of the room. Dr. West closes the door behind him.

My stomach knots.

"How are things at home, Serena?"

"Ah, well, I just moved into my friend's house. I'm living with her and her sister."

"So you don't live with your partner?"

"No, not yet."

"Okay." Her shoulders relax.

"My apartment was in downtown Empire and not really safe or baby-appropriate, so my friend invited me to live with her," I explain.

"That was nice."

"Yeah, she's a good friend." I lift my chin toward the door. "It's closer to Gray's apartment too."

"How is your relationship?" she asks carefully.

"Good." I blow out a breath. "We haven't been together that long, but he treats me very well."

"I'm glad to hear that." She pauses, studying my face. "Were there any problems when you told him you were pregnant?"

Her questions are slightly vague. Designed, I think, so that I won't feel defensive. I'd be offended if I didn't understand why she was asking. "Not from him." My lips tremble into a sad smile. "I can guess what information is in my file." I nod to her tablet. "So this brought up some feelings connected to that for me."

"I understand." She raises an eyebrow as if she wants me to continue.

"Gray was…excited. Happier than I expected him to be." I curl my hand over my stomach. "He's been trying to do whatever he can to make things easier for me."

"Such as?" she prompts.

Wow, she's not screwing around. "Uh, my bills. He wanted to take over some payments while I'm between jobs. Clearing out my apartment. He hired people to do that for me." *Hired* is a white lie. But I don't think "asked his biker brothers to help out" will ease her mind. "Found and paid for a storage unit."

"So, he supports you living with your friend?"

"Yes." I pick at little white balls on my cotton gown. "He never thought my apartment was safe enough."

"Good." Finally, she seems satisfied. "I'd like to have you return in a couple of weeks and we'll call you if there are any issues with the blood test."

"Okay."

She opens the door and pokes her head into the hallway. "Hmm. I think he might have returned to the waiting room. Do you want me to send him back?" she asks.

"Would you, please?" I gather my pile of clothes. A few seconds later, the door opens and Gray gives me a warm smile.

"Everything all right, buttercup?"

"Yes. Sorry about that."

"No problem." He shrugs and closes the door. "I felt like a bear blocking the hallway, so I just went back to the waiting room."

I hurry into my jeans and yank my sweatshirt over my head. "Sorry this wasn't more exciting."

"Please stop apologizing." His face is full of nothing but concern when I emerge from the dark confines of my sweatshirt.

"Sorry."

His lips twist and he steps close, wrapping an arm around my waist and dragging me closer. "What am I going to do with you, hmm?" He presses a quick kiss to my forehead. "Come on. The doctor said you need to go next door for the blood draw."

"I hate needles," I grumble as I slip the strap of my purse over my shoulder.

"No one likes 'em. Let's get it over with, then I'll take you anywhere you want to go."

"Anywhere, huh?" I follow him into the hallway and to the reception desk where they hand me a slip to have my blood drawn.

The clinic is empty and they take me in right away. Gray waits in the doorway, watching from a distance.

"This will be quick, I promise," the tech assures me.

I stick my arm out and focus my gaze on Gray. Before I know it, I'm done.

"You're good to go." The tech slaps a cotton ball and piece of surgical tape over the small puncture. "Someone will call you in a couple of days."

"Great. Thank you." I jump out of the chair and hurry outside.

"Slow down," Gray calls after me, catching my hand in his. "You all right?"

"I just want to get out of here."

He opens the truck door and helps me into the cab.

"Where do you want to go?" he asks after settling behind on the wheel.

"You said you'd help me pack some things at my apartment." I shrug.

"I was thinking more like going somewhere to celebrate. Or buying you something to celebrate."

"Celebrate?"

"The doc confirmed you're pregnant. We should celebrate." He starts the truck and smoothly backs out of our parking spot. "Besides, I want you to relax. We can pack tomorrow."

"I'm too anxious to relax."

"Another reason you need to. You heard what the doctor said."

"I'm going to have a lot of doctor's appointments. Are you planning to buy me something to celebrate after each one?"

"Yes," he answers in his firmest, no-bullshit tone.

"That's ridiculous. I'm pregnant, not curing cancer."

His jaw tightens but he keeps staring straight ahead. "You're growing a whole human being inside you. Creating life, Serena. I can't do that." His voice picks up in speed and intensity. "I'm not the one who has to make all the extra doctor appointments. Or get poked, prodded, and invaded every couple weeks. So can you please let me do the one thing I *can* do, which is take care of you?"

I sniffle and dab my finger under my eyes. "That's what I told the doctor when you stepped out. That you were trying to make things easier on me."

"That's all I want to do, honey." He tilts his head, side-eying me. "What else did you talk about?"

"Nothing bad. I think a lot of doctors like to probe a little to make sure domestic violence isn't an issue." I swipe my tongue over my bottom lip. "With my history...and having you there, she was probably concerned."

"Good."

"You're not mad?"

"Mad? No. I don't have anything to hide." He glances over. "I spent time locked up with men who murdered their wives, girlfriends, and children. Some of the absolute scum of the Earth. So, if someone out here is trying to stop *that* in whatever way, I'm all for it."

"That's...a lot of men would be mad and get defensive."

He shrugs. "Like I said. Got nothing to hide." He slows to a stop at a red light. "Now, where would you like to go?"

The anxiety from the appointment is wearing off, leaving me fatigued. But there is something I've been meaning to get. "It's silly. There's something I wanted to grab but I can do it another time." Now that I think about it, I have more than one thing on my list.

"Why are you so difficult?"

"I'm not trying to be. But it's a beauty store. I can go there with Emily or on my own this weekend. No biggie."

He slides another impatient side-eye my way.

"Okay, okay. I want to go to Ulta. I think there's a store in Johnson City. Otherwise we have to go to Slater County." I peer at the road signs and mentally get my bearings. "You know what, we're closer to the one in Slater. It's right off Central Ave."

"Good. Finally." He flicks his blinker on and shifts into the right lane. "I don't remember how to get there, so help me out."

It takes me a second to look up the quickest way, but I finally figure it out and talk him through it.

"See, this is beneficial for me too." His lips quirk. "You're helping me get reacquainted with the area. Everything has changed so damn much, I feel like I've returned to an alien planet some days."

I haven't lived in the Capital Region long enough to consider how things might have changed over the years, but I understand why it might be frustrating for him. I reach over and rest my hand on his leg. "Happy to help. Although, I don't know if finding your way to the best makeup stores is how you want to reacquaint yourself with the area."

"Sure, it is." He slows to a stop at another red light and points to the left. "Look at that. Now I know where the closest Harley dealer is."

I burst into giggles.

Grinder

It might've felt like pulling teeth to get Serena to admit where she wanted to go, but once she gets inside the store, she's a focused hunter, stalking her prey. And here I am lumbering behind her like a polar bear who accidentally ended up at a tea party. Who knew there were entire stores dedicated to…pretty packages of beauty stuff? No wonder Serena's makeup channel is so popular.

At least I can act as her human shopping cart and hold all the items for her—a plain-looking glass jar with a pristine white and black label full of what looks like rainbow ice cream swirled inside, a bottle of nail polish remover with flowers floating in it, rounds of cotton, a bright blue tube of eyeliner, bottles of purple hair stuff, a tub of hair "pudding," red glow serum, and beauty sheet masks.

"I thought companies send you stuff too?" I ask.

"They do. But I'm sort of picky with my regular-use products." She bites her lip. "And sometimes, I'd just rather buy my own stuff, so I don't feel obligated to give glowing reviews, you know?"

"Sure. That makes sense."

"Ooo. I almost forgot the big thing I came for." She hurries to a row of appliances. Hair appliances. Good Lord, there are enough to fill a tool chest.

Serena whips a long, wide, shiny blue hair straightener off the shelf. "My last one died on me," she says in an apologetic tone. "You really don't have to—"

"Whatever you need." This wasn't quite what I had in mind when I said I wanted to buy her something to celebrate. I envisioned a trip to the jewelry store where she could pick out a pair of earrings or something more enduring than...*sulfide-free shampoo*. But she seems happy and that's all I care about.

As the salesgirl rings up everything, Serena pulls out her wallet.

"Don't you dare," I warn her in a low voice.

She slides a store rewards card out and taps it in front of me, her mouth slightly curling at the corners. "Unless you want my bonus points?"

I rumble with laughter. "No, that's okay."

"Oh my God! *Tranquil Sparkle!*" The salesgirl flaps her hands in the air. "You're Serena Sparkle! Oh my God. I can't believe this. I love your channel so much!"

Serena blinks for a moment before slipping into the relatable, friendly persona she uses in front of the camera. "Aw, that's so sweet. Thank you."

"I follow you under *GoldenGills420* but my name is Alice." She fluffs her short, blond curls. "This color will look so *ahh-may-zing* on you." She wiggles the bright blue eyeliner pen Serena bought between her fingers. "Are you going to use it in one of your videos?"

"I was planning to, yes."

"Oh!" Alice clasps her hands under her chin and rolls her eyes to the ceiling. "We just unpacked this gold glitter liquid eye paint that looks soooo gorgeous with the teal. Do you want me to find one for you?"

"Ah," Serena's nervous gaze darts my way. "No, that's okay—"

I nudge her with my elbow. "I like you in gold."

She lets out a thin laugh and nods to the salesgirl. "Sure. Let me see it."

"Be right back!" Alice scurries around the counter and runs down one of the aisles.

"You're a celebrity," I say to Serena.

Her cheeks turn a shade pinker and she glances over her shoulder. The woman behind us has her face pinched in annoyance, huffs, and glances at the clock over the register.

"Got it!" Alice shouts, holding a small gold tube in the air like she's carrying an Olympic torch as she runs behind the counter again. "Phew. Sorry about that." She hands the tube to Serena. "It's got this subtle gold to bronze patina-like shift in different lights. So pretty."

"Sure. I'll try it. Thank you for the rec, Alice."

"That's what I'm here for. If you ever need anything, call me." She flicks her hand in the air dismissively. "Although, you must already have a hookup with corporate."

"Not yet." Serena winks at her.

"Well, I send all my customers to check out your tutorials. They're the best."

"Thank you."

"Oh my God, and you're just as pretty in person." She leans over the counter toward Serena and whispers, "A lot of people aren't, you know."

Serena shifts uncomfortably and sends me another anxious glance. This one seems to be less about my comfort and more about her unease at being recognized by such an enthusiastic fan.

"Oh!" Alice shouts, picking up the jar of ice cream-looking stuff. "The *Unicorn Magic for Pregnant Bellies Butter Whip* is great for shaving too!" Her smile falters and her eyes ping-pong between Serena and me. "Uh…ah…you know, and stretch marks." She shoves the jar in a bag and rings up the next item.

"Here I thought it was a dessert or something," I say to Serena.

Serena shakes her head. "No."

"You're uh…not going to shift the focus of your channel, are you?" Alice asks. "A lot of my favorites started doing baby stuff when they had kids, you know? Ugh. So boring."

Serena's pink cheeks darken to red. "No, I, uh, I'm committed to the makeup stuff."

"Good, good!"

Finally, Alice recites a total. A trip to the jewelry story would've been cheaper. I hand over my card without comment.

"That was so weird," Serena whispers once we're outside. As if Alice might have supersonic hearing and Serena doesn't want to hurt her feelings.

"Rooster said you had something like half a million followers?" I remind her. "You're bound to run into one sometime, right?"

"I guess."

I stop at the truck and open her door. "I feel like I should be driving you around in something much fancier now, Ms. Sparkles."

"Stop." She playfully swats my chest. "I'm so embarrassed I ran into someone when I'm not wearing *any* makeup."

"Why? She didn't seem to notice. I think you made her day." A sign in the store next to the one we just left catches my eye. *Maternity clothes*. "Do you need any clothes?"

"See, if you'd helped me pack today, you'd know how silly that question is," she teases.

"I'm serious."

She follows my gaze. "Ohh, you mean *maternity* clothes." She pats her stomach. "As much as you're dying to see me fatten up, I don't think I'll need to worry about that for a little while."

I roll my eyes skyward. "You say *fatten up*. I say, provide a nice cushion-y home for our baby."

"Cushion-y." She shudders but can't hide her laughter.

"Get in the truck, smart-ass."

"Hey." She loops her arms around my neck and stares up at me.

"Thank you for being so patient. I know that must have bored you silly."

Damn, I could stare at her beautiful face all day long. "I'm never bored when I'm with you."

She kisses my cheek, then darts away, hopping into the truck.

"Seat belt," I remind her.

She shoots an exasperated glare my way. "Have you ever seen me *not* wear a seat belt?"

"Can't help it." I shut the door and jog around to the other side.

The parking lot is a pain in the ass to navigate through. "What happened to shopping malls? You could park in one place and not have traffic coming at you from every direction," I grumble.

"They're dying a long, slow death." Serena points to the left. "Turn here, it'll be easier to get onto the highway."

"Thanks," I mutter, flipping on the blinker.

Once I'm on the highway headed toward my apartment, Serena lets out a long yawn.

"You all right?" I ask.

"Just sleepy."

"Go ahead and close your eyes. I know where to go from here."

She reaches over and rests her hand on my leg. "I'd like to go back to your place."

My heart stutters. That's exactly what I wanted to hear. "Sure. You can take a nap there."

"I'd like that." She yawns again. "So, are you planning to be overbearing and overprotective until I give birth?"

I snort with laughter. "We've met, right? Buttercup, I plan to protect you until they put me in a box six feet under."

CHAPTER FIFTEEN

Serena

SLIGHTLY DISORIENTED, I WAKE FROM MY NAP IN GRAY'S BEDROOM. IT'S shadowy but some daylight still peeks around the edges of the blinds. At least I wasn't out for too long.

Low murmurs from the living room draw my attention. I toss the covers away, stand and stretch. The T-shirt I borrowed from Gray brushes against my thighs. I search the bedroom for my clothes, then decide I don't feel like putting my jeans on. Maybe I should've taken Gray up on his offer and bought a few stretchy pants or something.

The TV is on in the living room. Gray's on the couch reading and glances up. "Hey, how was your nap, buttercup?"

"Good. Give me a second." I hurry to the bathroom.

A few minutes later, I emerge and find him waiting outside the door.

"Were you afraid I fell in?" I ask.

"Yes." He rumbles with laughter. "Come here."

I yawn and slide my arms around his waist.

"Still tired?" he asks, running his hands up and down my back.

"A little. But I want to snuggle with you."

He lets out a happy sigh and lifts me in his arms.

"Gray!" I hurry to wrap my arms around his neck and hang on tight.

"Shh, I got you." He settles into the couch with my body draped over his lap. "Better?"

"Yes." I reach for the blanket folded over the back of the couch and pull it around us. "I'm chilly though."

He tucks the blanket around me until I'm wrapped like a burrito while holding me close. I rest my head on his shoulder.

"Thank you for everything today."

"You don't have to thank me. I had a nice day with you." He brushes hair off my cheek, tucking it behind my ear.

"You were so...patient."

Everything Gray's done since I told him I was pregnant lands on me like blocks of guilt. Shame for running away and making him worry still claws into me every time I think about it. How could I leave with no note, no nothing? He's been kind and generous toward me from the beginning. Still, I let fear dictate my actions.

"I'm so sorry," I whisper.

His hand squeezes my thigh. Firm but comforting. "What are you sorry for?"

"Running. Instead of talking it out with you. I—"

"Serena, be honest with me." His stern tone snaps my head up. "What *exactly* were you thinking? The first thought that popped into your head?"

I wrinkle my nose. "Why am I so damn fertile?"

One corner of his mouth quirks but he doesn't laugh. "When you decided to leave, what was the one thought driving you to run?"

My hands automatically cover my stomach. "To protect my baby," I whisper. Tears sting my eyes. "But not *from* you...I don't know. I just couldn't let anything—"

"I thought so." His knuckles graze my chin and he tips my head to the side, for me to look at him. "Listen to me and let what I'm saying sink into your scarred soul."

Fear flutters through my chest. "Okay."

"Your first instinct was to protect my...protect *our* child. That's the *only* kind of woman I want having my baby. One who will do anything to protect him from every threat, no matter what."

"Him?"

A brief smile flickers over his face. "Or her." He turns serious again. "Your first impulse was to *protect*. That's what a good mother does. I'll never be angry at you for wanting to protect our child."

His words and characterization of my actions give me strength. "I couldn't help it. It's instinct. Whenever I've been scared, I ran. When I was little, I'd hide under my mom's bed. No one ever thought to look for me there. When I got older and things were bad, the bed wasn't big enough to hide under anymore, so I ran away. I hid in the locker room at school for weeks until one of the coaches caught me…" My voice trails off as I fight to keep those memories locked away.

"You're brave. And smart." Gray's raspy voice anchors me in the present. "A survivor, Serena."

No man has ever seen me as any of those things. *Hot, pretty, fuckable, good girl, sweet ass, nice tits.* Those are the compliments I'm used to receiving, the only things I ever thought made me worth caring about.

"Thank you," I whisper.

"I'm not mad at you for running," he continues. "We haven't been together that long. And I think I understand some of what you've lived through."

"Thank you for not using it against me."

He frowns. "Why would I…never mind. Run when you need to run, Serena. That same urge to get away runs deep in my soul. I understand the need to be free and unchained. Just know that I'll always come find you."

"You're really not mad?"

"No. At the core, I'm a simple man. When I say I want to take care of you, it's because I care about you. Not because I want you dependent on me. If you ever want to leave, leave. But I'm still going to take care of my kid."

"I don't want to leave," I whisper.

"Good." His voice lowers. "Because I don't know what I'd do without you."

Love for him explodes in my chest, but I'm too scared to open my mouth.

He slips his hand under the blanket and runs it over my calf. His rough fingers dip into the ticklish spot behind my knee and finally grip my thigh. "I should've said this sooner, buttercup." He squeezes my leg gently. "Look at me."

My heart beats faster as I lift my gaze to his.

"I love you. I've never felt like this before and never expected to feel this way."

"Grayson," I sigh and cup his cheek. "I love you too. I've been too scared to say it. In case this didn't last."

He touches his forehead to mine. "Ah, Serena. How could you not see my love for you? Feel it?"

It's too sad to say out loud. But I know the answer.

Because I've never been loved before.

CHAPTER SIXTEEN

Grinder

It feels good to finally man the fuck up and tell Serena exactly what I feel. Even if I don't want to admit it, part of me held the same fear. That she didn't feel the same way I feel about her.

I keep stroking my hand over her thigh up to her hip. "I wish I could give you more, Serena. You deserve more than a man who can't even spend a night away from home without getting in trouble."

"Shh." She presses her finger against my lips. "No one can choose a convenient time to fall in love. We'll get through it."

"I don't want to make all the mistakes of my past *your* problem. You shouldn't have to deal with any of it."

"Our pasts shape us into who we are. Mine's screwed me up in ways I'm still trying to unravel every day."

"Don't say that." The things that have her messed up were done *to* her, not choices she made. I chose all of my bad decisions with open eyes.

"Gray, why'd you tell me you love me, if now you're going to tell me all the reasons you shouldn't?"

"I don't think I deserve you."

"You've been punished long enough." She runs her fingers over my chest. "It's time to start living again."

Under the blanket, I slide my hand from her hip to her belly. She shifts her body to make room. "I want to create a life together."

"Well, we did that." She laughs softly and rests her hand over mine.

"You know what I mean. I want to buy you a nice house. Come home to you every night. Give our kids the things I never had."

"I'd like that," she whispers.

"Good. I was worried you were going to argue with me for a second."

She presses her palm more firmly against my cheek. "Kiss me."

But she's already closing the distance between us, her lips crashing against mine. Like she's taking a sledgehammer to whatever walls she was trying to put between us.

She shifts her body, tossing the blanket aside.

"I thought you were chilly?"

"Not anymore." She lifts herself, planting her knees on either side of me and slowly lowering herself until she's straddling my lap.

"Mmm, I like this view." My hands slide from her hips to her rib cage, slowly pulling her shirt up.

Must be too slow. She grabs the hem and whips it over her head, tossing it aside.

"Aw, fuck," I groan. "Even better view." I cup her breasts, lazily flicking my thumbs against her nipples.

"No fair." She pouts and drags my shirt up to my neck, exposing my chest and abdomen.

"You want this off?" I grip the back of my shirt, teasing her.

"Yes." She rolls her hips, pressing herself against the fly of my jeans.

I flick the shirt off and rest my arms at my sides, letting her take a long look. Been a while since I enjoyed a woman's appreciation, and I can't get enough of Serena's hungry eyes roaming over my skin.

She trails her fingers over the ink on my chest, then dives for my fly, tugging at my belt.

"Easy, buttercup. Slow down."

"I want you inside me," she says in a breathless rush. "Then we can go as slow as you want."

I let out a deep groan of defeat. Who can say no to a demand like that? "Sounds like you have it all planned out."

Her lips curl into that sweet little pout again. There isn't a damn thing in this world I'd deny this woman when she looks at me like that. I lift up, freeing myself and she helps push my jeans over my hips.

"You takin' those panties off or do I need to rip 'em?" I nod to the skintight purple fabric blocking my path.

Bracing one hand on my shoulder and holding my gaze, she lifts herself and works her underwear over her hip. Impatient as fuck, I yank them lower and help her free one leg. The other will have to wait.

I slide my hand between her legs, finding her slick with desire. "Fuck, you're drenched."

"I…I know." She bites her lip and I work my fingers back and forth. "I've been hot for you all day."

"Why didn't you say so earlier?" I twist my hand, slowly slipping a finger inside her. "I would've happily taken care of you."

She inhales a long, shaky breath and watches me with dazed eyes. "I wanted to gather my strength."

I'd laugh, but since I'm ready to pound her into the floor, it was a solid plan. "Good thinking."

"Make me come."

"Fuck, I love when you say that."

She tilts her head. "Do I say it often?"

"Not often enough. I dream about you begging for it, every night." I tug her hip closer. "Come closer if you wanna get on this ride."

One corner of her mouth slides up. "I do."

She rises on her knees and leans forward, trapping my cock. I let out a groan when she slowly sinks down on me. "That's fucking good, buttercup."

I'm trying to stay calm but am so close to unraveling. She's tight, hot, and wet. Pure heaven and absolute hell as she takes her sweet time. She rests her hands on my shoulders and rises up again, slowly sinking down, taking more of me each time. I focus on her serious, determined expression.

"Easy, buttercup. Nice and slow."

She whimpers as she rolls her hips. "Feels so good."

Thank fuck I've spent time mastering the art of restraint. I need every bit of it not to hold her down and jack my hips up off the couch.

"Gray?" She moans and bites my earlobe. Her hips work faster. I'm drowning in her hair softly sliding against my face and chest.

"Mmm?"

"I love the way your key fits my lock." Her voice quivers. She shifts her body every which way, seeking her pleasure. "Your cock was made for me. You hit all my happy zones."

I twist her head to the side and catch her lip for a kiss that silences her. If she keeps singing the praises of my cock, I'm gonna blow right now.

She clenches around me, throbbing and fluttering.

The familiar warning tingle begins. I hold off until she finishes. Then that sweet, familiar blend of agony and pleasure lashes down my spine. My release is brutal and intense. Serena's wild, bucking and moaning. Her teeth scrape my neck and shoulder, her nails dig into my arms.

Breathing hard, she collapses on top of me.

"Fucking hell, you trying to kill me, buttercup?" I smooth sweaty strands of hair off her forehead and cheek.

Her lips curl into a deliciously devilish smile. She slides her fingers over my heart. "You sound alive to me." Her nails graze my nipple and I jump.

"Easy." I capture her roaming hand and bring it to my mouth, kissing her fingertips. "Come shower with me."

"Okay." She slides out of my lap and strips off what's left of her underwear.

"Don't bother," I demand as she bends over to pick up our scattered clothes.

On our way to the bathroom, she stops. "I want to grab something."

"Go on, I'll start the shower."

I have the water beating against the tile when she enters and sets her bag from the beauty store on the counter. "I want to try this." She holds up the purple bottles of shampoo and conditioner.

"Bring it." I wave her closer, then stick my hand under the spray to check the temperature.

I step in first and offer her my hand, turning her toward the cascading water to wet her hair. "You feel all right?" I ask.

"I'm still tingling all over."

I huff a soft laugh and pour some body wash into my hands, working it over her shoulders and down her back and sides. "Same, buttercup. You know how to work your man up. Especially with all that lock and key talk."

She bursts out laughing and covers her face with her hands. "Oh my God. I don't know where that came from. I'm sorry."

I grab her elbow and gently turn her around to face me. "Why?" Red splotches dot her neck and chest. I pry her hands away from her cheeks. "Compliments to my cock are always welcome, darlin'," I tease. "You had me ready to blow with those sweet words."

"You always make me feel *so* good," she says with this amazed lilt in her voice.

"Mmm, same, buttercup." I pull her toward me and kiss her forehead. "Come on, let's finish up."

She yawns and I slide my hand to her stomach. "Do you feel okay? I didn't hurt you, did I?"

"No, never." Her lips slide into a half-smile. "I'm just tired again."

"What else do you need to do?"

"Condition my hair."

"All right. Turn around."

"You don't have—"

"Turn. Around."

"Okay, okay." She holds her hands in the air and spins in a small circle.

"I want to find a place with a bigger shower," I grumble.

"Ooo, we could have fun with that."

"Yes, we could." I tap her ass. And now I can't stop thinking about bending her over. Her hands against the wall...

"Gray?"

"All done."

She ducks her head under the spray, rinsing her hair one last time.

"Go ahead, I'll be right out."

I step aside to give her room, but she slides her slick, wet body against mine. "Don't be long."

"I won't." Damn right I won't take long. Can't stand being away from her for more than a few seconds.

I finish and slap the shower off.

She's standing in front of the mirror with a short blue towel wrapped around her middle, working a comb through her long, wet hair.

Keeping my eyes on her, I rough a towel over my head and wrap another one around my hips.

"This will only take a minute," she says over her shoulder.

Stepping behind her, I curl my arm around her waist and kiss her damp shoulder. "A lot of work taking care of all that pretty hair."

In the mirror, she blinks and stares at me as if I'd threatened to shear her head bald.

"I like watching you." I tease my fingers through the wet ends, already drying into gentle waves. "And I love your hair. It's beautiful." I kiss her shoulder again. "Really like how the ends tickle my legs when you're riding my dick."

"Oh my God." Surprised laughter bubbles past her lips.

My gaze lands on a colorful jar on the counter. The stuff we'd bought earlier with the ridiculous name. "What is that?" I tap the top.

Her cheeks flush. "It's probably silly but I read it's supposed to be really good to protect my belly from getting stretch marks." She flips her towel open and rubs her hand over her stomach.

"You're not even showing yet."

"So? I thought I'd start early."

Love how much thought she's putting into this. It was unexpected and maybe not the best time but she's taking it so well. I curl my arms around her middle and squeeze. "Thank you."

"For having you buy me belly butter?"

I'm too choked up to laugh, so I hold her tighter instead. "No."

When I'm sure I won't blubber like a baby, I unhook her towel the rest of the way and dab it over her back and legs.

"Come on."

She wraps another towel around her and follows me to the bedroom. I slide open a drawer and pull out a T-shirt.

"Don't steal this one," I tease.

"I'm sorry. I'll give you the other one back."

"I'm kidding, buttercup. Take everything of mine you want." I hold up the shirt. "Arms up."

She lifts her arms and lets me drape the shirt over her, then fluffs her wet hair and yawns.

"You want to give Emily a call and let her know you're staying over?"

Serena blinks up at me. "Am I staying?"

"I'd like you to."

"All right."

"I'd like you to come up to the clubhouse with me tomorrow, too."

Her gaze slips to the side. "Are you sure?"

I hate the note of fear returning to her voice. "Yes, I'm sure."

While today might have fixed some issues between *us*, how she feels about my club is a different story. That trust was broken long before we even met.

Am I a greedy fucker for wanting all the facets of my life to coexist peacefully? A family of my own *and* my MC family?

What's broken can be fixed. I just have to figure out how.

CHAPTER SEVENTEEN

Grinder

Asking anyone for permission to do anything always irritated the piss out of me. Bikers are known for not giving a fuck. They do what they want, when they want, and fuck the consequences. After spending time in prison, I was convinced that the bikers who advocate that "fuck the law" lifestyle had never seen the inside of a cell. All that blustering big talk means shit once your freedom's taken away.

So, as much as it stings my pride, the next time I visit my new parole officer, I have a question for her.

I don't have to wait long this time. She greets me and takes me into her office quickly. After the same general questions she asks if I need anything, and I seize the opportunity like a panther pouncing on a rabbit.

"Somewhere in my paperwork, I saw something about permission for family trips. How's that work?"

She raises her eyebrows. "You have somewhere you need to go?"

Yes. Anywhere.

"Not *need*." I shrug but I've never been good at the bumbling *aw, shucks* method of getting my way. "I want to take my girlfriend away for a three-day weekend or something. Not out of state. Just a short getaway."

She drums her nails over her desk, the sound like irritating nails being pounded into my fuck-off coffin. "You're dating?"

"Uh, yeah." Surprised Grillo hadn't stuck *that* in my file since he'd been so obsessed with Serena.

"How is that going?"

Peachy, we're having a baby we didn't expect or plan for.

"Good." No reason to give her details she doesn't need.

Her serious expression remains. "I ask because dating and all that comes with it can be a difficult adjustment after such a long sentence."

Her tone is casual, not cruel or condescending. Unusual from what I've encountered in the system. "You're right. I still feel a little feral at times. But she's patient with me. My biggest challenge has been how much technology and stuff has changed, though." Although, figuring Serena out hasn't been easy either, but at least she's a pleasant challenge.

"A lot of my clients struggle with technology." She gives me what almost looks like a sympathetic smile. "I struggle with it myself some days. I need my teenager to program my phone for me."

"The receptionist at my job is good with all that stuff. She's helped me out a few times." Aubrey seems like a safer person to mention than any of my club brothers—since technically I'm still not supposed to be associating with any of them.

She glances at her desk and then the calendar hanging on the wall. "Do you have a date and place in mind for your trip?"

We're back to that. Good sign, I hope. "I was thinking next weekend. Maybe the Catskills. To do some hiking. I just want to be outside as much as possible these days."

"I can understand that. The Catskills. That's close." She nods. "Call me with the dates and an address for where you'll be staying. I'll leave an approval letter with the receptionist. You can pick it up before you go. Just keep it with you in case you get pulled over or something."

I open my mouth but I'm not sure what to say. I hadn't expected this to be so easy. Thankfully, no guilt from lying plagues me. "Thank you."

"Believe it or not, I *want* you to get back to normal. And not go back inside."

"Well, we want the same things, then."

AFTER MY APPOINTMENT, I return to Strike Back ready to work.

"Everything go okay?" Sully's brother, Jake, asks.

"Yeah." I shrug, uncomfortable talking about it, even though Jake always acts like taking off to visit with my parole officer is no big deal. As if he hangs around tons of felons and it's totally normal.

I get to work, cleaning what needs to be cleaned, and helping Jake with the few things on his list. Sully and Aubrey won't be in until later in the afternoon, so I keep an eye on the front door and help clients who need instruction on different equipment.

Around one, the bell over the back door goes off. The hair on the back of my neck prickles. The slow, tentative steps over the hardwood floor send my pulse racing.

"Grayson?" Serena peers around the corner.

"Thought that was you." I can't hide my grin. God damn she's a sight for my jaded eyes.

I close the distance between us fast, sweeping her into my arms and slamming my lips against hers.

"Oh!" she shrieks and laughs against my mouth, pulling away. "I'm happy to see you too."

I set her down. Keeping my hands around her waist, I draw back to look her over. Hair pulled into a high ponytail swinging down her back. Tight black leggings that end above her ankles, a thin purple hooded shirt, and black sneakers with purple stripes. "Did you come to work out or drive me nuts?"

She glances down. "What do you mean? I'm running errands. It's comfy."

"You look beautiful."

She tilts her head in that adorable way she does when she's uncomfortable with a compliment. "Thank you." She runs her hand over her stomach. "Figured I should wear all my body-con stuff now before I start showing," she whispers.

"You should wear whatever you want, whenever you want."

She opens her mouth—probably to argue with me—but Jake's voice interrupts us.

"Everything okay, Grinder?" He turns the corner and stops dead. "Well, damn. I didn't realize..." He stops and stares.

In the short time I've worked here, Jake's made it obvious he enjoys the ladies a little too much. I couldn't care less when it's women who don't belong to me. Serena's a different story.

"Eyes to yourself," I growl.

But he continues eying Serena in a way I don't care for. Her nervous eyes dart from Jake to me.

Blowing out an irritated breath, I take her hand. "Jake, this is *my* girlfriend, Serena."

"Serena," he says slowly. "We've met before, right?"

She blushes and drops her gaze to her sneakers, then slides it my way. The way I've heard about Jake plowing through women, I'm almost dreading her answer.

"Uh, I think we met at one of Murphy's fights once," she says quietly.

Murphy. Fine. I already knew about that and set it aside.

"Right." Jake snaps his fingers, then taps the side of his head. "I never forget a pretty face."

"Useful skill," I grumble.

"One of my many talents," Jake agrees with an impish smile. Christ, he's almost as much of a dick as Wrath. No wonder they're such good buddies.

"Murphy is missed at the Castle," Jake says.

"I'm sure he is," Serena murmurs as if she's done talking about this. I know *I'm* done with it.

"We're going to be out back, if that's all right." I curl my arm around Serena's shoulders.

"Yeah, go on. We won't get busy for a little while," Jake says, waving us away.

I turn, steering us toward the door.

Serena holds up a blue plaid, soft-sided cooler. "I brought lunch."

"I was so distracted by your gorgeous face, I didn't even notice."

She laughs softly, as if I'm feeding her a line, and pushes through the door. The parking lot behind the buildings is mostly empty this time of day. So are the picnic benches scattered behind each of the Main Street businesses.

Serena squints at the sky.

"Would you rather eat in the truck?" I ask her.

"No, it's nice out. I'm just going to grab my sunglasses from my car." She hands me the cooler and jogs across the lot. My lips curve when she stops at her car, parked right next to my truck. Like the pervy man she's brought out of me, I admire her while she dips inside, stretching her long, lean body over the front seat. She emerges a few seconds later, slides her shades on, and slams the door shut. As she returns, I study her figure for any signs of change.

"You didn't open it?" she asks, stepping over the bench on the other side and sitting across from me.

"I was too busy watching you."

Her cheeks flush. "Worried someone would run me over?"

"No. I enjoy looking at you."

Her face brightens into a smile. "How's your day so far?"

"Much better now."

She slides the cooler to her side and unzips it, quickly pulling out foil-wrapped items and two Tupperware containers. "I hope you like chicken."

"I like anything. Especially if you made it." I unwrap one of the long foil packages and find a sub sandwich. "Looks great." I bite into the toasty bread, getting a mouthful of flavorful chicken breast and crunchy veggies.

She watches me so intently, I grab one of the napkins and wipe my chin.

"Is it okay?" she asks.

"It's fantastic. You made it?"

She nods and unwraps a smaller version of what I'm eating, taking a dainty bite. While she's chewing, she taps one of the containers and hands me a set of metal utensils from the cooler.

I pry the lid off the container. Bow-tie pasta covered in dressing and veggies. "Did you make this?"

"I hope you like pasta salad."

"I do. But you didn't have to go to so much trouble."

"I wanted to." Her pink lips push into a pout, and she drops her gaze to her sandwich, flicking crumbs to the side.

I reach across the table and cover her hand with mine. "Hey, I appreciate it. I really do. And I'm so happy to see you."

"Sorry, I don't mean to be so needy."

"As long as it's *me* you need, I don't mind."

We're interrupted by Sully and Aubrey walking past our picnic table.

"Afternoon, Gray." Sully stops and throws a questioning look at Serena.

"Hey, Sully. Serena, this is the owner of Strike Back, Sully." I nod to his tiny brunette fiancée standing by his side. "And Aubrey. This is my girlfriend, Serena. She brought me lunch."

"Oh, that was sweet." Aubrey beams at Serena. "So happy to meet you."

"I just moved out here, so I was nearby." Serena gestures with her hands as if she's flustered by the attention.

"Oh! You're Emily's Serena, aren't you?" Aubrey opens her arms wide and skirts around the corner of the table to embrace Serena.

Serena returns the hug, and it seems to make her less nervous. The tension eases from her expression and her shoulders relax. "I think so."

Aubrey's bright eyes dance between Serena and me. "I had no idea. This is so great." She tips her head and looks at Sully. "Isn't this great?"

Sully's mouth quirks. "Sure."

"You have to come to self-defense class one Sunday with Emily.

You can meet Bree and my sister Celia." Aubrey rubs her hands together. "Sometimes we get to beat up on Jake. It's a blast."

"I don't know if he feels the same way," Sully says.

"Of course he does." Aubrey waves his concern away.

"I'd like that," Serena says. "Thank you."

"We'll let you get back to lunch," Sully says, taking Aubrey's hand again.

"I'll be done in a few—"

"Take your time," he cuts me off. "Nice to meet you, Serena."

By the time they leave, Serena's smiling again. Aubrey seems to have that effect on everyone. Part of what makes her so good at the front desk.

"They're really nice." Serena takes a sip of water.

"Why'd you seem so nervous at first?"

She lifts her shoulders and glances away. "I don't know. I didn't want you to get in trouble for having visitors at work, I guess."

"Nah, he's easygoing. Think you're interested in taking that class one weekend? I didn't realize Emily knew Aubrey."

"I would like to. If you don't mind."

"Why would I mind?"

"I don't want to...I don't know, invade your job."

I almost point out that I'm the reason *she* got fired from *her* job but don't think that helps. "Serena, I want to soak up every moment I can with you. Besides, I don't usually work Sundays."

"Oh, that's true."

"You should go." I wink at her. "I'll switch my days, so I can watch."

"I'll talk to Emily." Her lips curve again. "How did things go this morning?"

"Better than I expected." I lean forward and lower my voice. "She said she'd give me permission for a weekend away with my girlfriend."

She raises an eyebrow. "Really? Where?"

The excitement in her voice makes me wish I had better news. "Well, I told her the Catskills, but I want to be able to go visit downstate. I need to see Z's place."

"Oh, right." Her voice quivers with a lack of enthusiasm.

"You'll go with me, right?"

"To be your cover?"

"No. I want my woman by my side."

She stabs her fork into a piece of pasta over and over. "Are you sure about that?"

"Serena, look at me."

After a few beats of hesitation, she lifts her gaze.

"We already talked about this. Yes, I want you with me."

"Okay. Then I'll go."

Now I feel like an asshole. I'd only been thinking about making sure no one disrespects her at the club. I hadn't really thought about how uncomfortable it might make her to visit downstate. "Everyone will know you're with me."

"Do you think your parole officer will check up on where you're staying?"

I'd been contemplating the same thing. "She might."

"How about this, you tell me what weekend we're going," she suggests, "and I'll find a place and make a reservation. We can stop there on the way down and check in. Make sure people see us. Then stop on the way back and check out." Her eyes sparkle with excitement. "We can allude to staying in bed all weekend and that's why no one saw us."

"*That* sounds like a better trip."

Her gaze skips away as if she agrees but doesn't want me to know it. "Maybe next time."

"No maybe about it. We'll go somewhere just the two of us. Soon, I promise." It's a promise I intend to keep.

"I, uh, still want to keep this quiet, though," she says, rubbing her stomach. "For now."

Why the fuck does that bug me so damn much? It's news I'd like to celebrate. But since I'm dragging her someplace I know damn well she doesn't want to go, I won't do anything to make her more uncomfortable. "Sure, we can do that. Whenever you think the time is right," I agree, even though it feels wrong.

CHAPTER EIGHTEEN

Serena

Bliss is found in unexpected moments.

THE BUZZ OF A LAWN MOWER PRODS MY SLEEPY BRAIN AWAKE SUNDAY morning. I stretch and roll over to grab my phone. Nothing from Gray. He's always worried he'll wake me up.

Me: *Good morning!*

I wait a few seconds. No reply.

Stop being so needy, Serena. I throw the covers back and shuffle across the hallway to the bathroom. After that, I toss on an old sweatshirt, a thick pair of fluffy socks, twist all my hair into a knot on top of my head and pad downstairs.

On my way into the kitchen, I spot Emily at one of the front windows. She has one finger hooked in the drape, slyly pulling it aside to create enough space to peek through.

"What are you doing, Em?" I yawn as I change course and head toward her.

"Huh? What?" She jumps away from the window. "Nothing. Why? What's up?"

Okay, that's a weird morning greeting from Emily. "Why are you being weird?"

The lawn mower buzz increases in volume, then fades.

"*Ohhh!*" I draw out the sound to a naughty pitch. "Did you hire a hunky gardener to drool over?"

"What? No!" She takes a sip of her tea, trying to act casual, but her gaze wanders toward the window again.

Forget water and food, I have to find out what has her so frazzled. "No? Then why are you blushing and all worked up?"

She pats her cheeks. "I'm not worked up. Stop it."

"You are." I dash for the front door and yank it open.

At first, I don't see anything or anyone. Only the drone of a small engine. But as the volume increases, a wide, yellow machine comes into view, followed by the shirtless man pushing it. Dex.

"He has quite a bit of ink hiding under his shirt," Emily says, stepping up behind me. She taps my shoulder and cranes her neck to gain a better view.

"I'm not surprised." Pleased I solved the mystery, I close the door and attempt to unravel my next morning mystery. "*Why* is Dex mowing your lawn?"

"Gray wanted to give me money." She shrugs. "To cover rent for you, I guess."

"Aw, really?"

"Yeah, made me feel sort of shitty for being mean to him."

"Pulling a gun on him," I correct.

"Po-tay-toes, po-tah-toes." She flicks her fingers to the side. "I can't take money from your boyfriend. That's weird. But he insisted he wanted to do something and asked what I needed."

Warm fuzzies stir over my skin. That sounds like my Grayson.

"I asked him if he knew someone who could do the lawn because Libby and I hate doing it. I thought he'd *recommend* someone, not come over with his friends and do it personally."

"Wait, he's here too?" My heart rate speeds up.

She tilts her head. "He's out back working on the hedges."

"Oh, dammit." I hurry toward the kitchen. "He can't be doing that. I don't want him to re-injure his shoulder."

I burst through the back door where the fast whine of a small engine greets me.

To my relief, Gray isn't the one trimming the hedges. He's supervising two younger guys—one I recognize as Remy. Gray's wearing earmuffs, so I wave to get his attention.

The harsh lines of his face immediately soften when he spots me. Dear God, I'm knocked breathless every time this stone-hard man's face softens into a smile. Is the fluttering in my stomach from the baby or the usual butterflies from being around Gray? I can't tell anymore.

I press my hand to my stomach. "Yes, baby, Daddy's here," I whisper.

Gray finishes a complicated series of hand gestures to Remy, then crosses the backyard. I step onto the concrete patio to meet him.

He slips off the ear protection and flashes another quick, warm smile. "Morning, buttercup. We didn't wake you, I hope."

"What are you doing?"

He grips his shoulder. "*I'm* not doing anything. I asked if one of the brothers could help with Emily's lawn. Dex volunteered." Gray smirks and glances over his shoulder. "Then, *he* volunteered Remy and Griff to help *him*."

"Thank you. Or thank *them*."

"How are you feeling?" He runs his gaze over my body. Now I wish I was wearing something nicer than faded flannel shorts and an over-sized sweatshirt that keeps slipping off my shoulder.

"I feel fine."

"Yeah?" He steps closer, rests his hand on my hip, and dips his head to brush his lips over my bared shoulder.

"That tickles," I laugh.

"Does it?" He kisses my neck. "How about here? Does that tickle too?"

"Yes," I whisper. "But do it again, anyway." I rub my thighs together. "Now I'm thinking of certain, *other* places that tickles."

He growls, a low happy sound that warms me to my toes.

"Are you warm enough out here like this?" he asks.

"I am now."

"Yeah? Why's that?" His hand slides lower, to cup and squeeze my butt.

I lean up and kiss his cheek, inhaling the grass and sunshine scent clinging to his skin. "Because of you."

The hearty buzz of another piece of lawn equipment slices through the air. I pull away. "I'm going to go get dressed. Should I come out and help you guys?"

He rears back like I asked if I should strip naked and run through the yard. "No. We have it handled. It's just some winter clean-up. It shouldn't always take this long."

"Okay."

"I was going to take the guys out for lunch when we're done. Would you, Emily, and Libby like to join us? Nowhere fancy. Just the diner."

"Sure, I'll ask Emily." I glance over my shoulder. "Libby was planning to help me test this new violet shimmer eye gloss that was sent to me." I stop and strike a pose by framing my face with my hands. "So, we'll be all made up."

He chuckles softly. "You're beautiful no matter what, but I look forward to seeing you in purple."

"Gray, can I tell you a secret?"

"Anything, buttercup."

I lean up and whisper in his ear, "I love you. And you're a very sexy landscaper."

The growly sounds I love so much erupt from him again. He gives me another quick squeeze, then slips on the ear protection and returns to work.

The door squeaks open behind me. "What's going on?" Libby croaks. "Why are people being noisy this early? It's Sunday."

Laughing, I turn and find her squinting at the sun. She thrusts a bottle of water at me. "Em says to drink this."

I can't tell if it's Em's way to razz me for being hot for my boyfriend or she's really concerned about my hydration, but I accept it gratefully. "Thanks." I take a sip and run my gaze over her fuzzy red fleece pants and red T-shirt. "You ready for violet shimmer day?"

Her eyes widen. "Are we still doing it?"

"Yeah, why not?"

"Since your boyfriend's here...I didn't know if you..." she shrugs.

"Promise is a promise."

"Hey, Serena." Remy approaches us. "Is your friend inside? I need to ask her what she wants to do with those thorny hedges."

Libby thrusts her chin. "I can help."

"Who are you?"

"Libby. I live here and I hate those hedges." She moves into the sunlight, closer to Remy, and rolls up her pant leg, showing off a set of long, thin white scars below her knee. "They've bitten me a few times."

"They definitely need to go, then." Remy's ice blue eyes travel over Libby from head-to-toe as she covers her leg and straightens. "Libby, huh? What's that short for?"

She shrugs. "Who says it's short for anything?"

He pulls off his gloves and steps closer. "Hmm, Elizabeth?"

"No."

"Isabel?"

"No."

"Olivia?"

Libby squints up at him. "You sure know a lot of girl names."

That's my girl. I cover my mouth, trying not to laugh.

"What in the sexual harassment hell did I walk in on?" Emily groans next to me.

"Nah, Remy's a good guy," I whisper. "Besides, Gray will kill him if he's rude to her."

"Great. Just what I want her to learn—wait for men to protect you from other men." She rolls her eyes at me.

"It's harmless."

She gives me another side-eye, then marches off the porch and blasts her stern-mom voice. "Liberty Belle!"

"Oh shit." I hurry to follow her.

"Unless you're planning to help weed the garden, go inside and get dressed," Emily scolds her sister.

Libby's eyes widen and her cheeks turn scarlet. She sputters for a second, then runs.

"Was that necessary?" I mutter to Emily.

But she ignores me and focuses her big-sister-dragon-flame eyes on Remy who dials his charming smile up to ten.

"My sister is *sixteen*."

That information wipes the smile clean off Remy's face. "Just trying to be friendly."

"Yeah, I'm sure."

He frowns. "She go to Johnsonville High?"

"Don't tell me," Emily says, placing her hands on her hips as she goes into full mom-mode. "That's your favorite place to pick up girls."

He snorts and shakes his head. "No. My sister's a senior there."

"Oh."

"Molly Holt."

Emily shrugs. "Is she a theater nerd? Libby's world revolves around the theater."

"Uh, no. She's a reality TV junkie who likes to sing into her hairbrush sometimes."

Emily chuckles softly. "Yeah, Libby's one of those too."

"So, Emily—"

"Stop right there." She holds up her hand like a traffic cop. "I'm too old for you."

"You seem to be making a lot of assumptions about me."

"She does that," I say, butting in. "Can't help it."

Dex stalks over, glaring at Remy. "The fuck you doing?"

"Taking a break. Settle down."

"Break's over." Dex jerks his head toward the uneven row of hedges. "Fix that."

Emily actually picks up a lock of her hair and twirls it around her finger. "It's okay. I wouldn't notice if you yanked the hedges clean out."

"Don't tempt me. They're a pain." Dex glances at the yard. "But at least they give you some privacy."

"Mmm, yes, we need that," Emily mutters.

"Oh, Lord." I stare at the sky. "I'm going in, Em. Libby's going to help me film a tutorial."

"What? Okay." She waves me off and I leave the two of them outside staring at each other.

CHAPTER NINETEEN

Serena

I can't stop my leg from bouncing around in the truck. Gray reaches over, resting his big warm hand on my thigh.

"What are you so nervous about?"

"I don't know."

"It's the upstate clubhouse." He hesitates. "No one knows, Serena. Well, Z knows. He was there when I found the tests. Went to your apartment with me."

Shame heats my skin. "You let Z see my apartment?"

"The fucker gave me hell for not finding you a nicer place sooner."

"Sorry."

"I'm teasing, buttercup." He pauses again. "I think…and don't repeat this because I'm not sure…but I think he and Lilly are having issues getting…you know…"

"Pregnant?" From what I remember Z and Lilly can't keep their hands off each other.

"Yeah," he answers in an uncomfortable tone, like this conversation is giving him the heebie-jeebies. "Just from things he's said. And after what you told him about Shadow, he was worried about you. So, yeah, he wanted to make sure you were okay and came with me."

I'm not sure how to swallow that information.

169

"But he promised he wouldn't say anything to anyone else and I trust him."

"I trust Z too."

"Good." He glances over. "That's good. I'm not in the habit of broadcasting my business. Even though it's nearly impossible to keep anything a secret in this club. Hope noticed your absence and Rock asked me about you."

"She did? Really?"

He shrugs.

And he must be telling the truth. As soon as we arrive at the clubhouse, Hope welcomes me with a hug.

"How have you been, Serena?"

"Not bad."

Rock steps out of his office. "Gray, you're here. Good. Come join us at the table."

Gray squeezes my hand. "You all right?"

I blink at the question. Brothers don't usually check with ol' ladies. They're told to get to church, and they *go*.

"I'll be fine."

He drops a quick kiss on my forehead before leaving.

"Aw." If Hope were a cartoon character, she'd have hearts for eyes right now. "I'm so happy things are working out for you two."

My cheeks warm. No matter how nice she is, I still always have a twinge of embarrassment around Hope. "I love him very much." My voice is barely above a whisper but she smiles wider.

"I can tell it's mutual."

Grinder

Church is thankfully short. I'm not even sure why Rock bothered. But, after he dismisses the general members, he asks the upstate officers to stay put.

"Stick around for a minute too, Grinder," Z says.

Steer, Rooster, and Jigsaw look at each other, then Z, but he's busy searching through the closet in the corner for something. Rock stands and focuses on me.

"We took it upon ourselves to have a little something made up for you."

Curiosity tickles through my chest. Rock would never do something to embarrass me. Not on purpose, anyway.

I throw a hasty glance at Murphy, then Rooster. "I hope it's not one of those black kitty cat patches, because I'm still having trouble figuring out *why* the fuck you got those on your cuts."

Murphy squeezes his lips together so hard, his cheeks bulge from holding in his laughter. Teller closes his eyes and inhales a long, slow breath, like he's fighting the urge to punch someone.

Rooster just laughs and holds the patch up closer, so I can take a better look.

"It's this dumb challenge the Virginia charter came up with when we were visiting," Jigsaw explains.

"It's only dumb because you lost," Murphy says.

"I got *half* my card punched." Steer laughs. "I'm going for it again next year."

"You remember the different color wing patches some clubs used to hand out to their brothers back in the day?" Wrath asks me.

"Yeah. Different colors for different sex acts." I turn my head toward Rooster. "Don't tell me you fucked a cat in the ass to get that patch, brother."

Everyone at the table busts up laughing.

"No. What the fuck is wrong with you, old man?" Rooster laughs.

"It's an excellent question," Jigsaw says, saluting me with two fingers.

"Still looking a lil' green with envy over there, Jiggy," Wrath says.

"Envy, my ass. I'm not so homely I have to prove I can shove my tongue up my woman's snatch for thirty days in a row by wearing some dumb pussycat patch."

Everyone except Rock and Teller hoots and laughs it up. Rock just stares at the ceiling like he's begging God for lightning to strike the table.

"You don't *have* a woman," Rooster reminds his buddy. "So your gripe makes no sense."

"There *was* a patch available for single brothers too," Steer reminds them. "But you had to work harder to get it."

"It's disrespectful to your girl," Jigsaw argues.

Rooster chuckles. "Shelby thought it was hysterical. Disgusting but funny."

"Trinity said it was about time I was awarded for my outstanding contributions in this area." Wrath grins and crosses his arms over his chest. "That's why they gave *me* a lion instead of a house cat."

"Good Christ," Rock mutters.

"Heidi's take on the whole thing was that no one would have the balls to ask me what the patch was for, so she didn't care," Murphy says.

"Please stop," Teller grumbles.

"And if someone asked," Murphy continues, "she's more than happy to tell them her man—"

"Don't." Teller holds his hand up over Murphy's mouth. "We get it."

"I guess Heidi has a point," I concede. "Thank fuck it's not obvious unless someone's spending a lot of time staring at your patches in the first place." I glance at Rock. "Things must be golden in Virginia if that's the kind of shit Ice wastes his time with."

"They didn't give him much choice," Wrath laughs. "He was probably the only one who would've voted against it."

"Sounds like it ended up being a fun bonding activity for the Virginia and New York charters," Z says, standing at the head of the table next to Rock and dismissing the conversation by plunking a heavy paper bag in front of them. "Let's get to the important stuff."

"This is for you, Grinder." Rock slides the package my way.

"What's this?"

"Open it."

I untie the string and peel the wrapper aside. The scent of new leather hits my nose. I unfold the black leather carefully.

Property of Grinder.

Emotions tighten my chest. I wasn't even going to ask for a vote until I got off parole. For some reason, I keep punishing myself and denying what I want because of some arbitrary deadline set by people whose opinions don't even matter.

My brothers trust me and that's what's important.

I turn the vest over. *Grinder's Buttercup* is stitched on the front left side. My padlock symbol with a key and some added yellow flowers embroidered around it. "Embroidery has come a long way since I went inside," I say absently, touching the fine threads. "Nice detail."

"Yeah," Z says slowly.

I tip my head and find him and Rock watching me carefully. "Thank you for this."

"You got it, brother," Rock says.

I drape the vest over the table, spreading it out to see the patches stitched on the side. Rock's, Z's, Wrath's, Teller's, Murphy's, and Dex's are all there. Jesus, they got together and took a vote on this already? Did Z tell them we're having a baby? Rock knew I was planning to propose. Is that why they did this now?

"You don't have to give it to her today," Z says, recapturing my attention. "But I have a *feeling* you two are headed in that direction, so I wanted to be proactive."

"Just in case you want to have her wear it when you guys visit downstate," Wrath adds.

Steer barks out a laugh. I glance his way and he bites on his fist, still shaking with laughter.

I nail him with a hard stare. "What's so funny?"

"Nothing." Steer swipes a finger under his eyes. "Can't wait to see the look on Tawny's face when Serena shows up wearing *that*."

"Fuck Tawny," Jigsaw seethes. "She better not say a fuckin' word about it."

"Easy, Puzzles." Steer snickers at his little joke. "She's still a brother's old lady."

"An ol' lady who causes a fuckton of problems every time she opens her big mouth," Rooster answers.

Jigsaw throws Steer a middle finger.

Steer lifts his chin at Z. "You all take a vote without me?"

"As far as I know, Grinder's a brother of *this* charter," Rock answers. "So, yes, we did. That okay with you?"

Steer frowns and holds his hand in the air. "I saw Z's patch on there too, that's all."

Z meets my eyes. "Grinder and I go way back. He sponsored me. I'm honored to have his ol' lady wear my patch. Serena's loyal. We know she'll protect the club like a good ol' lady should."

That's a lot of words out of Z's mouth. More choked up than I want to admit, I nod at him until I can finally force out a response. "Thanks, brother."

"You know it."

"She's got mine too, brother," Jigsaw says.

"Same," Rooster adds. "Got no doubts about *her* loyalty to the club."

Steer eyes Rooster and Jigsaw carefully, then shrugs. Since I never expected this today, I'm not annoyed with Steer's questions. I'm surprised Z didn't mention it to *his* SAA but it sounds like he didn't say anything to his VP either. Rooster just has more respect for his elder brothers than Steer does. Doesn't matter what Steer says at the table. As long as he's respectful to Serena out there, I don't give a fuck about his opinion.

"Congrats, brother." Steer stands and leans over the table, offering his hand for a quick shake.

"Thanks."

Rooster and Jigsaw each pat my shoulder on the way out.

Teller turns my way. "Carter will be up here later if you still want to talk to him about that owl throat piece." He runs his hand over his neck. "He sketched something that's really cool I want him to show you."

Damn, I like this more mature, thoughtful version of Teller. "Yeah, I'd like that."

He stands and pushes his chair in halfway, then nods to the vest still clutched in my hands. "Congrats, brother. I'm happy for you."

"Thanks."

"So, did we surprise you?" Z walks around to my side of the table, taking Teller's now-empty seat.

"Sure did. Wasn't expecting this today." I grip the leather tighter. "Thank you."

He leans in closer to me. "I didn't say anything to anyone about… you know. That's not why we took the vote now."

Knowing how tight Z, Rock, and Wrath are, it must be killing Z not to say anything. "Thanks for letting me get adjusted to things myself."

"Yeah, of course."

We both stand but before I can make it out of the room, Rock stops me. "Z was adamant about this happening now," he says, almost as if he's looking for assurance that he didn't piss me off. "I went with you to order the ring. Figured you might want to do this first."

I glance down at my hands. Since I'm not ready to be honest about us having a baby yet, I decide to share something else with Rock instead. "I wanted to…I would've asked but I got this idea in my head that I can't be a full-patch who asks the club for things until I'm off parole and able to wear my cut loud and proud in public, you know?"

"Yeah," he answers slowly. "I get that. But it's not true." He thumps his fist over his heart. "In here, you never lost full-patch status or anything like that, brother."

"Do you need more hugs, G? Have we been neglecting you?" Wrath lumbers over to me with his arms spread wide. "Come here, old man."

"Get out of here with that shit."

Too late, the motherfucker wraps his arms around me, squeezing like a fucking python.

"I'm gonna kill you," I wheeze.

He lifts, bouncing me in the air.

"Now I'm really going to kill you. Put me down."

He finally releases me, grinning like an idiot.

"I hope you hurt your back doing that."

"Please, I could bench two of you without breaking a sweat."

"Don't ever do it again."

He grins even wider.

"Careful," Rock warns. "He'll take it as an invitation to do it every single fucking time he sees you."

"What the fuck happened in the last fifteen years that Teller is more mature than you, huh?" I slap Wrath's chest.

"Ooof." Wrath clutches his chest. "That's low, G."

"All right." Rock claps his hands together. "Let's stop it with cuddles for the deranged. I want to go find Hope."

"Find? We all know she's waiting right outside that door for you, Prez," Wrath says. They keep bickering back and forth on their way out of the war room.

Z watches them with an amused smile. "I'm concerned now that I'm not here on a regular basis to mediate, they might accidentally kill each other one day."

"Won't be no accident." I straighten my shirt and tuck Serena's vest back into the brown wrapper.

"Are you going to give it to her now?" Z asks.

"Yeah, I am."

"Good."

Serena

My heart patters faster as Gray approaches me after church.

"You doing all right?" he asks in a low voice.

"Better now that you're back. How'd it go in there?"

"Good." Something crinkles and I drop my gaze to a brown paper-wrapped package in his hands. "Feel like taking a trip upstairs with me?"

"Of course." I stand and follow him to the stairs.

"Actually, I want to take the trip we talked about soon," he says.

"You're sure it will be okay, right?" The last thing he needs is trouble with his parole officer.

"She said it would be and I feel guilty I haven't been downstate, yet."

"Oh." *Downstate.* My stomach clenches. Am I really ready to see that place again? Maybe Gray should go by himself for the first visit.

His jaw tightens. Maybe it's finally sinking in for him what having an ex-club girl for a girlfriend really means. Upstate is an anomaly. As much as Z's done to change things downstate, brothers like Sway, Hustler, and Tiny won't be able to keep their mouths shut about me. They'll make snide comments that border on disrespect whenever they think they can get away with it. They'll say it's a "joke" but everyone will know the truth.

We reach Gray's room and he opens the door, motioning for me to go in ahead of him.

Now, ol' Queen Bitch Tawny is a different matter. She'll talk trash as soon as Grayson's out of earshot. Picturing her shellacked beehive and overly made-up face makes my stomach flip. I promised myself I'd never let anyone belittle me again. But those cute affirmations and promises mean nothing in the MC world.

"Serena?" Gray sits on the bed and pats the space next to him. "What's wrong?"

"Nothing." I force an awkward smile and clutch my stomach. "Um, I guess I'll see how I feel?"

"Serena," he says in a sterner tone. "Let's not do this dance. I already know you used to spend time at the downstate charter."

Spend time. That's one way to phrase it.

I lift my chin.

"Are you embarrassed to be my ol' lady?"

"What?" Shock stabs the hesitation out of me. I slide closer to him. "Never, no."

He curls his free arm around me. "No? You sure you're not embarrassed to have the grandpa ex-con's baby?"

Tears sting my eyes. "Please don't say things like that. It's not true. I've never felt that way. Not once." I bury my face against his shoulder and hug him tighter.

He lets out a rough chuckle and pats my back. "Good to know."

"Grayson." I readjust myself, swinging my leg over him so I'm straddling his lap. He leans back, bracing himself against the mattress. "I can't wait for our baby to get here. I love you so much." I burrow against him even harder. "I don't want you to be embarrassed to be with *me*," I whisper.

"Serena." He gently places his hands on my shoulders and pushes me upright. Our eyes meet and he brushes his knuckles over my cheek. "As a general rule, I hate people in my business. But that's got nothing to do with *you*. I feel like the luckiest bastard on the planet that you're by my side. Don't ever, ever doubt that."

"Okay," I whisper, touching my forehead to his and closing my eyes.

He shifts and I almost fall out of his lap. Laughing, I roll to the side and sit next to him.

"I wanted to plan this better." He squeezes his eyes shut for a second. "Fuck it." He curls his fingers around the bundle he'd carried into the room. "I want you to have this now."

"What is it?"

"This." He unwraps the bundle and I realize it's not a random lump of satin. It's a black leather vest folded inside-out to protect the patches sewn into the leather.

My breath catches and I scoot away.

That's not what I think it is. It can't be. Not this soon.

"Serena." He smooths the vest over his lap so the back patch faces me.

Property of Grinder.

My nose stings. Tears prickle my eyes and my vision blurs. Complicated and contradictory emotions whirl through my stomach. Once, I thought I'd do anything to wear a brother's property patch. To have a place in someone's life. To belong and be respected by the club as someone precious to a brother.

After cleansing club life from my system, the notion of being someone's *property* bothered me. I swore I'd never have anything to do with a motorcycle club and their strange rituals again.

Now, I don't care about the club aspect at all. I just want to be branded by Grayson and connected to him in every way possible. *Forever.*

I'm too scared to say any of that, though. So, I sit there staring at the patch, waiting for him to explain. I don't want to assume anything.

"Will you wear my patch?" he asks in a low voice. "Wear it so every biker we meet on the road knows you're mine and I'll kill to protect you."

I blink rapidly, trying to force my tears away. "Yes. Yes, of course."

He blows out a quick breath. "Good. You had me worried for a second."

I swipe the tears from under my eyes.

"Why are you crying, buttercup?"

I rest my hand on my stomach. "Hormones. I'm so emotional about everything lately." *Forgive me, Baby Lock, but you've given me the best excuse.*

My gaze lands on the vest again. I'm afraid to stare at it for too long. Like it might disappear if I get too attached. Bright colors on the sides snag my attention. "Did the brothers...I'm sorry, I don't know what the actual process is. I've heard they vote on an ol' lady and that's how they get the patches on the sides?"

"Usually, a brother asks for votes from the officers when he wants to patch an ol' lady." He coughs and glances toward the dresser. "Z knew I had...plans and went ahead and had it made for me. Guys must've voted on their own."

"Really?" I rasp. "They did that for *me?*"

The corner of his mouth lifts in an apologetic way. "I think as a sign of respect for *me*, buttercup. Everything revolves around the brotherhood."

I laugh softly. "Right."

His expression turns more serious. "But it's a sign they trust you. A lot. Rock and Wrath wouldn't give their patches to a woman they didn't trust. Not even for me." He turns the vest to the side and runs his finger over each brother's patch. "Neither would Z."

I study each embroidered symbol—crown, star, the letter Z, four-leaf clover, dollar sign, and compass. "Dex gave me his too?" I ask.

"Yup. Rooster and Jiggy said they'd add theirs as well. Guess the two clubs do that?"

His question sounds more like pondering than directed at me, but I answer anyway. "I don't think they used to." I certainly never saw Rock's crown on Tawny's cut. Or any of the other upstate officers' patches. Then again, it's not like anyone discussed the inner workings of the club's patch system with me, either. The Lost Kings hold many, many secrets.

"I'm proud of you." He squeezes the leather. "This means a lot to me. I know it might seem like an outdated tradition but—"

"No. I'm honored to wear it." Oh my God, I'm going to cry again. What's wrong with me?

"Stand up," he says, voice rough but still gentle.

I slide off the bed and stand in front of him. My fingers nervously twist into the hem of my shirt while I wait for his next instruction.

He runs his gaze over me for a few seconds, then stands. So close, his body heat radiates over me. My heart flutters.

"Will you be my ol' lady, Serena?"

"Yes," I whisper.

He holds out the vest. "This means everyone will know you're mine. That I'll kill to protect you—and those aren't just words, Serena. If you're with me, you need to understand that's who I am. You're that precious to me. I'd sacrifice my freedom for your safety. That also means I trust you to behave around our club and other clubs."

My skin prickles at *behave* and it must show in the slight turn down of my mouth.

He sighs. "I understand how that sounds. But you must've seen girls misbehave before, thinking because they're with a biker, they can mouth off and start trouble."

One or two scenes like that come to mind. "I've always been the one being picked on, not the one starting the fights," I admit with a pitiful note tainting my voice that I hate.

His jaw tightens. "Well, that's never happening again. If anyone ever disrespects you in any way, you tell me. Immediately."

I can't picture myself tattling to my boyfriend every time someone hurts my feelings, and if I do that, *none* of the other old ladies will ever respect me, but that's not the answer he wants. So, I nod instead.

"The need to protect each other goes both ways," he says. "Maybe you won't use your fists or a weapon but there are other ways to protect your man and the club."

"I'd never talk about club business with outsiders," I whisper. "Never have. Never will."

"I know that." He touches the other brothers' patches on the side. "These mean that they trust you too. And they'll always have your back." He hesitates. "The club will take care of you if I'm not around for some reason."

Cold fear stabs through my chest. "Please don't say that."

"Not just death, Serena. Prison's always a possibility too."

"You're full of cheer, aren't you?"

He chuckles. "I really love you."

"I love you too. That's why I don't want to talk about death or prison."

"That's reality, though, sweetheart. We're both adults." He drops his gaze to my stomach. "Soon, parents."

"That's why you need to take care of yourself."

"I will. I promise." He holds the vest up. "Now, turn around for me. I'm dying to see this on you."

He's almost giddy, well, giddy for Grayson, as he urges me to turn faster. I slip my arms into it. He turns me to the side and fiddles with the laces. "I can adjust these if you want to wear something heavier when we're riding." He flicks his smoldering gaze to my face. "For now, I want it nice and tight."

Whoa. A zip of electricity shoots to my center.

I pat my belly and try to act calm. "You'll need to loosen it soon."

He palms my hips and turns me so he can adjust the other side. "My pleasure."

My heart bursts with happiness and dreams of our future together.

But the scars etched into my soul itch to life, reminding me that my dreams, like my heart, are fragile.

Both have been broken many times before.

CHAPTER TWENTY

Serena

SOME OF THE PATCHED OL' LADIES ARE WAITING FOR ME IN THE LIVING room when we return downstairs.

"Congratulations!" Hope jumps up to hug me first. Lilly joins her a second later.

"Z told us right after church." She touches my shoulder. "If you weren't wearing it yet we were just going to say we were hanging out. But since you are—congratulations!"

Laughing, I let her pull me into an exuberant hug. She hugs Gray next. "I'm so happy for you," she murmurs. The two of them step aside to talk.

Trinity approaches with a smile. "Buttercup, I like that." She nods to the "Grinder's Buttercup" patch on my chest. "Welcome."

Charlotte squeezes my arm. "Congratulations, Serena."

"Thanks." My cheeks are so hot from all the attention, they might catch fire soon.

Hope hugs me again. "I hope this means you'll be around more often?" She phrases it as a question but it almost sounds more like a gentle scolding.

"I...I've had a lot going on lately...and Gray, with parole...we don't usually go far."

"I understand. You're always welcomed, though. You know that, right?"

"Sure."

"Good." She glances at Rock. "We still need to have you guys over to our place for dinner. It'll be quieter than here."

"Not by much," Rock says. "Since everyone drops by whenever they feel like it." He shoots a dirty look Z's way and Z grins at him.

"I'd like that," I answer Hope, not wanting to get anywhere near Z and Rock's conversation.

She squeezes my hand quickly, then Rock pulls her away. The rest of the guys gravitate toward each other, then out to the garages.

Gray takes my hand. "Are you all right if I join them?"

"Yes, of course. Go ahead."

The chatter over my patch settles and the attention shifts to tonight's party.

Downstate, I would volunteer to help out. Now, I'm not sure what I'm supposed to do. Trinity used to be the one to handle household things at this clubhouse. But tonight, she seems laid back, casually joking around with Charlotte and Lilly.

Anxious and uncomfortable, I perch on the edge of the couch and fight the urge to yank out my phone to scroll through it.

"Uh…" Someone taps my shoulder.

I glance up. Heidi's inquisitive brown eyes meet mine. She flashes a quick smile and nods to the seat next to me.

"Sure, go ahead."

Anxiety burns through my stomach. Is this where Heidi warns me that no matter whose patch I'm wearing, I'll never be part of the sisterhood?

"Congratulations." She nods to my patch.

"Thanks." I press my hand against the lock and key patch over my heart. "It kind of took me by surprise." Nervous laughter follows my words and I clamp my lips together.

"I don't have a ton of memories of Grinder from before he went inside, but he's not as grumpy as the ones I *do* have." She chuckles but her smile wobbles. Is she nervous too? "Um, anyway, I wanted you to have this." She thrusts a small patch at me and the pink creeping over her cheeks deepens. "It sort of started out as a joke." She taps the crown, clover, and hammer patch on her own vest. "But Murphy made these up for me, and I gave them to our ol' ladies." She rolls her eyes and her tense smile softens. "I know it's not the same as having the patches of the brothers, but—"

"No, it's…wow." I blink away the tears threatening to form. I had noticed extra patches on the other girls' vests and wondered about the story behind them but didn't have the nerve to ask. "Thank you, Heidi." I accept the patch that I now realize is a tiny silver and green hammer from her outstretched fingers.

She blows out a breath and her shoulders relax. "So far, I'm the only one with a 'sisterhood' patch but we've been talking about getting different ones for each of us. A peacock feather for Trinity, this cool skull with flowers for Hope, a mermaid for Lilly, a sun for Charlotte and a flamingo or a musical note for Shelby. I haven't found a buttercup yet, just a sunflower or a yellow rose—"

She's already been looking for patches for *me*? As if I'm already a member of their close-knit little group? I'm close to drowning in the tears I'm holding back. "I like sunflowers and yellow roses." My voice is raw and scratchy. "Thank you, Heidi."

"I know the hammer isn't very girly." She laughs. "Charlotte keeps saying it should be a *unicorn* with a hammer."

The tension breaks and I burst into giggles. "Now *that* would be something."

"Right?" She shrugs again. "Anyway, I wanted you to have it before our trip downstate."

And I'm right back to wanting to cry again. Is that her subtle way of trying to protect me from Tawny? A bold advertisement that I've been accepted by at least *one* of the old ladies? Is Heidi that complicated? As Teller's little sister, she's always had the acceptance of Tawny and the rest of the club. Sure, behind Heidi's back and when Teller wasn't around, Tawny always referred to Heidi as a "bratty little princess" but to her face, the Queen Bee was always sweet as honey, almost motherly even, toward Heidi. So she might not realize how nasty Tawny can be when she unfurls her claws.

"Thank you." I stare at the patch and fiddle with it for a few seconds. My gaze lifts and scans the room. I lean closer to Heidi. "So, am I allowed to put this on my vest or does Gray have to do it?" I ask.

She bursts into giggles and bumps me with her shoulder. "Have him do it. *You* may be property of Grinder, but the cut is property of *the club*, so a brother should be the one to alter it."

Wow, if that sentence was uttered outside of this clubhouse, it sure would raise some eyebrows. "That makes sense."

The front door opens and brothers stomp into the clubhouse. I scan each one to see if Gray returned with them. The volume of chatter in the room increases.

Heidi pats my leg. "I'll catch you at the party."

"Okay." I hold up the patch. "Thank you."

I stay on the couch, watching everyone hug hello or tap fists. Gray finally parts the crowd like a mythical hero coming to my rescue. I sit straighter, happiness tugging at the corners of my mouth.

As he gets closer, I jump off the couch and meet him. Cool spring air clings to his shirt and I inhale as I wrap my arms around him.

"I wasn't gone that long, buttercup."

"I know. I still missed you."

He kisses the top of my head. "It's nice to be missed."

I pull away and lift the patch. "Think you can put this on my cut before we leave tomorrow?"

"Whatcha got there?" he asks, plucking the patch from my fingertips.

"Um, it's Heidi's patch."

His lips quirk. "I always thought that would've been nice for the ol' ladies to give each other patches too."

"I guess Heidi's the only one who has one right now but they're working on getting them for the other girls too."

He studies it with a smile. "A hammer, huh? Bet that's quite a story."

"Oh, I should've asked." I'd been too overwhelmed to question why

Murphy chose a hammer to represent Heidi. Every symbol or nickname in the Lost Kings' universe seems to have a funny story behind it, but you have be careful how you ask for details.

"Yes, I'll do it tonight." He pulls at the left side of my vest, slipping his hand between the leather and my body. He laced it up tight, so there isn't much room. The back of his hand grazes my breast as he tucks the little patch into my inner pocket. "Safe keeping." The intensity of his stare burns me from the inside out.

He shifts his hand, rubbing his thumb over my nipple.

"Gray," I whisper.

"Couldn't help myself." He slips his hand out and pats my vest into place. He leans in closer. "I want your nipples in my mouth, now."

"Here?"

"Fuck no."

Rav jumps onto the bar and curls his hands around his mouth to form a megaphone. "Move it along to the dining room, people!"

"Let's go!" Jigsaw shouts.

Brothers mouth off in response but the crowd seems to be shifting toward the hallway.

"Hurry up!" Steer bellows from behind us.

"Uh, I guess there's no escaping now," I whisper to Gray.

"Hmm," he growls in that sexy-annoyed way that he has.

"Come on." I tug him into the flow of traffic. As uncomfortable as I am tonight, I don't want Gray holding back from club activities because of me.

The whole left side of the dining room is set up as a long buffet. I recognize Swan and a few other girls hustling back and forth between the kitchen and table. Trinity ducks away from Wrath and heads toward the kitchen as well.

I lean up on tiptoes and whisper in Gray's ear, "I should probably go help the girls too."

He curls his arm around my waist. "Not tonight."

His tone leaves no room for argument.

Birch and Hoot are also on kitchen duty. I recognize Stitch and another prospect whose name I never learned carrying heavier trays to the table.

Z stands in front of the buffet.

"Blocking a pack of hungry bikers from food is an interesting tactic," I mutter.

Gray rumbles with laughter and kisses the top of my head. "He's got the brawn to go with his big mouth."

"All right." Z's deep voice carries through the dining room, quieting everyone. "Tonight, we're celebrating one of our brothers patching his old lady. Everyone make sure you congratulate Grinder and Serena tonight." He points in our direction. Everyone claps, hoots, or whistles at us.

Heat floods my cheeks as the cheering goes on and on. Feeling overwhelmed and strangely shy, I duck my face against Gray's chest. He curls a protective arm around me. "Thank you." His voice rumbles against my cheek. "All right, that's enough. Knock it off."

"*Knock it off* has always been code for *do more of it* around here," Charlotte says, patting me on the back.

I pull away from Gray and smile at her. "That's true."

"They'll get bored eventually and hassle someone else." She glances up at Teller. "Right?"

"Eh." He shrugs. "Eventually."

Gray kisses my forehead. "You feel all right?" he asks in a low voice.

"My stomach's a little jumpy," I admit.

"Let's find a seat. I'll get you some ginger ale."

"Thank you." My nervous stomach doesn't have as much to do with being pregnant as it does with having so much attention focused on me. It feels like having an anvil hanging over my head, waiting to fall when the first brother questions why Gray would ever want me for his ol' lady. I cling to his hand, not wanting him to leave my side. But Teller and Charlotte follow us to one of the long, wide tables. Rock and Hope are already situated at the head of the table, with little Grace sitting in her daddy's lap like it's her personal throne.

"Oh," I breathe out. "She's so cute."

"Here, Serena." Hope pats the table in front of the chair closest to her.

"Uh…" I hesitate, staring from Hope to Gray. Isn't that where Lilly should be sitting? Or Trinity? My gaze scans the length of the table. Lilly's seated in the middle, deep in conversation with Shelby. And I don't see Trinity anywhere. Or Wrath for that matter. "Okay."

Gray squeezes my shoulder briefly once I'm seated and leaves in search of my ginger ale.

"She's getting so big," I say to Hope, nodding at Grace.

"I know." She turns and scoops her daughter out of Rock's lap. He kisses Grace's cheek as Hope lifts her in the air.

"Wow, that's quite a party outfit." I reach over and run my fingers over the soft blue velvet sleeve of Grace's little bodysuit. Dainty ruffles puff over the shoulders. Layers of silver tulle trimmed in velvet fan out around her bottom.

Hope runs her hand over her daughter's head. "It came with a big silver bow, but that got lost somewhere between our house and here."

"Lost, my ass," Teller says, squatting next to Hope's chair to look Grace in the eye. "You tossed that thing like a football, didn't you?"

Grace *squees* and reaches for him.

Hope chuckles. "Probably."

"Come here, little bandit." Teller lifts Grace from Hope's lap like she weighs nothing, whispering words that make her giggle.

I blink, watching him handle Rock's daughter so easily. "She's lucky to have so many uncles looking out for her," I say to Hope.

She reaches for Teller and squeezes his forearm, drawing his attention. "Uncles, yes. She is."

Okay, weird.

"Teeee!" Alexa slams into Teller's legs. "Come play wiff meeeee!"

"I've been summoned." He hands Grace back to Hope. Alexa jumps up to give her friend a smooch, then runs away, yelling for Teller to follow.

Grace frowns as she watches them leave.

"Aw, what happened?" I coo at her.

She whips her head around and beams at me.

"Can I…can I hold her, Hope?" I ask.

"Sure."

I move my chair closer. Grace studies me before deciding my lap's a safe landing spot. Her gaze focuses on the patch over my heart and her tiny fingers touch the yellow threads. "Pee-tee."

"Thank you." Gray keeps calling our baby a "he" but *oh my God,* the longer I hold Grace, the more I hope we're having a girl.

"I try not to foist her on my baby-free friends," Hope says, almost apologetically. "Don't be afraid to hand her to me if she's too much."

"No, no, I'm fine."

As if she's agreeing with me, Grace flashes a big, dimpled smile.

"You are so cute," I whisper.

"What do you have here?" Gray's voice rumbles behind me.

He sets a cup of bubbling tan liquid in front of me. Grace reaches for it, but I pick it up and take a quick sip before setting it farther away.

"Nice reflexes," Hope says. "She's quick with her little grabby hands."

"I bet."

Gray pulls up the chair next to us and leans in to talk to Grace. She runs her little palms over his beard and tugs.

"No, no, Grace." Hope jumps up.

"I'm fine," Gray says. He holds out his hands and takes her into his arms.

Phew, he's a thousand times hotter holding a baby. The urge to fan myself strikes me. If I wasn't already pregnant, I'd jump on him in front of everyone.

"Look at you gettin' passed around like hot Sunday service gossip," a soft southern voice says behind us. Shelby leans down and wiggles her fingers at Grace. "Hey, cutie."

"She's making the rounds, for sure," Hope says.

"Hi, again, Serena." She leans over and hugs me. "I like the new threads." Her eyes sparkle with humor as she pulls away and runs her fingers over my shoulder.

I tug on my vest. "It was a bit of a surprise."

"Yeah, they're fond of springing it on us," she teases.

Curious, or nosy maybe, my gaze drops to the patches at her side. She has more than just the officers of downstate and at least two I don't recognize at all. She even has Steer's bull horns patch. Based on the amount of bitching I'd heard downstate from some of the ol' ladies, he doesn't give out his patch often.

She twists her body to follow my gaze and touches the heart with a dagger patch and another patch of a smiley face with a bullet hole in the forehead. "Oh! We spent time at the Virginia charter over the summer. And some of the guys traveled with me on tour as security, so they added their patches."

"That's sweet."

"They're good guys." She taps the smiley face. "Hoping we can talk Pants into coming out on the road again this summer."

"Doubt you'll have to do a lot of convincing," Rooster says, slinging his arm around her shoulders. "He's looking forward to it."

"You may end up having the whole club following you around, Shelby," Hope says.

"Lordy, that'd be fine with me. The guys are excellent creep repellent." She ducks her head. "It was nice having the girls along too. I liked the company."

They continue to the buffet.

"Everyone's lining up for food," Hope says. "I'll take her, Grinder."

"Nah, I got her." He jerks his chin toward the buffet. "Why don't you two go on up and take care of yourselves, first."

Hope seems torn, but finally nods. "Thank you."

I'm not even sure what's in the dishes on the buffet. I scoop some of everything onto my plate, grab a few rolls, butter, and utensils, then follow Hope back to the table.

Grinder's switched sides, sitting next to Rock with Grace in his arms.

He nods at me but continues talking to Rock. I return to my seat next to Hope and watch Grinder across the table.

"He's awfully good with babies," Hope whispers to me.

My cheeks burn. "I see that."

She doesn't follow it up with "when are you two going to have babies" which I appreciate. But part of me wants to confide in her. Pregnancy has been strange enough. The longer I think about it, being pregnant will probably be the easiest part. What the heck do I do with a baby when I bring her home? Did Hope worry about that too when she was pregnant? Probably not. She was older, married, and already had an established career. I can't think of a non-intrusive way to ask, so I stab my fork into my salad and stuff a wad of crunchy green leaves in my mouth instead.

CHAPTER TWENTY-ONE

Grinder

THE BIKE BETWEEN MY LEGS FEELS LIKE HOME.

Sure it's a lot newer than the one I had before I went inside. More refined in many ways. But with Rock and Murphy's help, I have it tuned where I want it.

Having my woman on the back, holding on tight, is an extra bonus.

She's not wearing my property patch. And I'm not wearing my colors. But I'm trying to be thankful for the things I'm finally able to enjoy instead of focusing on the things still out of my reach.

Wind in my face.

Pavement a blur beneath my feet.

Riding at the back of the pack with Remy, Griff, and their friend Vapor doesn't bother me. We're far enough away from the rest of the brothers that no one should be able to claim I'm "associating with known criminals" or anything else that might be considered a violation of parole. We'd passed plenty of State Troopers, so hanging back was a wise choice.

Flashing red, blue and white lights swirl ahead of us.

"Fuck," I groan.

The four of us slow our speed and move to the left.

Sure enough, Troopers have Steer and Z pulled off to the side of the road. In the quick glance I get it looks like they're hassling Steer. Maybe Z just pulled over to offer support.

A few hundred feet ahead, the rest of the pack has pulled off the road.

Never leave a brother behind.

The instinct to stop with them is there, but Z and Rock had been clear when we met up earlier at the gas station outside of Catskill. If anything like this happened, we were to keep riding ahead.

So, that's what we do.

Ahead of me, Remy slows and flips on his blinker. He and Vapor seamlessly move into the right lane. Griff and I follow.

After the tolls, Remy turns right and pulls off the road into a circle of gravel on the side.

"This was our exit anyway," he shouts over the combined rumble of our engines.

Maybe fifteen minutes later, the rolling thunder of the rest of the club reaches us.

"They're coming," Serena says.

"Hope it's all of them," I mutter, firing up my engine again.

The four of us wait until everyone goes by, then wait another few minutes to make sure cops aren't right behind them.

Remy pulls out first, Vapor second, then Griff and I. We ride along a country road deep in Union County. Can't remember if I'd ever been this way before I went to prison. No old memories attached to the area. Somewhere new to discover.

Remy's turn signal blinks and he slows his bike. There's a small dirt turnoff in front of a high chain link fence to our left. The gate's open so we ride through. Dust clouds around us. The rest of the two clubs are waiting in the parking lot. Most of the bikes already backed into spaces.

Behind us, two younger brothers rush to close and lock the gates. The metal clinks and screeches shut.

Z's standing in front of a spot near the front door and he waves for me to take it. I shut the bike down and curl my hands a few times. Fifteen years of not riding really adds up after two hours.

"Ooo, my butt is numb." Serena braces her hands on my shoulders and gets off the bike.

As I take my helmet off, she squeezes my bicep and leans in, kissing my cheek. "How'd that feel?"

"Good." I turn and catch her lips for a more thorough kiss. "Best part was having you on the back."

"I liked being there," she whispers.

"Good."

"Don't know how much longer I'll be able to." She passes her hand over her stomach and peeks at me from under her lashes.

Shit, maybe it wasn't a good idea to have her ride today. "Are you okay?" I curl my arm around her waist, dragging her closer. She stumbles, her arms flailing for a second. "Easy. I got you."

"Sorry, my legs are still wobbly." Thin nervous laughter follows her words.

"Are you worried?" I ask in a low voice.

"Maybe a little." An apologetic expression lifts her eyebrows.

"I'll be with you as much as possible. But if I'm not, stick with Lilly and Hope." Anyone at a Lost Kings MC party would be nuts to disrespect a president's ol' lady. Serena should be safe with one of them.

Z's boots crunch over the pavement. "You coming or not, G?"

"Yeah. Gimmie a second." I release Serena and get off my bike.

"Woo! That was a good one!" Sparky races over the pavement with his fist in the air and jumps on Stash's back.

Shaking my head, I take Serena's hand and walk over to Z, Teller, and Charlotte. "Everything go all right with the cops?"

"Yeah, they wanted to bust Steer's balls," Z answers. "Wrote him a few tickets."

Steer walks up with the tickets clutched in his hands. "Fucking ridiculous."

"I'll handle them," Charlotte offers, holding out her hand.

"She'll give you the friends and family rate," Teller adds.

Z moves in closer to me, while Steer joins the others. "How'd they do?"

"Remy? Fine. They ride well." I cock my head. "You realize I'm a little rusty myself, so not exactly the best one to evaluate other riders."

"Rusty, my ass." Z slaps my shoulder. "Riding's in your blood, Grumpy."

Serena snort-laughs, then covers it with a cough.

I peer down at her. "Think that's funny, huh?"

"Only because you're so sweet to me."

"Thank fuck he's sweet to someone," Z grumbles.

I glance at the building we're standing in front of. "Add some glass front doors and little orange towers on the roof and it would look like one of those old chain hotels." I can't think of the name right now, it's been so long.

"That's what it used to be," Z says. "Good eye."

I grunt in response and follow him to the heavy wooden front doors. One of the prospects, Stitch, hurries to open it and Z nods at him as we pass.

Serena's hand tightens around mine and her pace slows. I can only guess at the bad memories that might be coming back to her visiting this place again. I tug her closer and lean down, kissing her cheek. "Happy you're with me, buttercup."

"I'm happy I'm with you too," she answers in the most serious tone.

Anyone who fucks with her this weekend will be leaving with a cracked skull or in a body bag.

Serena

Smile so no one sees how broken you are inside.

After my ordeal with Shadow, I swore I'd never set foot in this clubhouse again.

Once Gray and I got together, though, I knew visiting here would be inevitable. It's different now. Z's the president. Shadow's...gone. But damn if there won't be reminders of that bastard everywhere.

Sway may not be president, but he's still a member, which means Tawny and her forked tongue of evil are sure to be lurking somewhere.

I didn't miss the disappointment in Gray's eyes when I reminded him to keep our baby a secret. He's been away from the club for too long. Our news will be celebrated at first. Then it will become ugly gossip. Tawny will imply I trapped Gray on purpose. She'll probably say something gross about him being desperate after being in prison for so long. Nope. I'm not subjecting Gray to that. He's been through enough.

Eventually, it'll be impossible to hide. Hopefully, I'll be prepared to handle it by then.

I'm a jumble of emotions as I cling to Gray's hand. Fear, shame, anxiety. I don't know why but I can't stop any of them. It's a miracle I held on for the ride down here.

As we step inside the familiar wide front doors, my entire body tenses. I angle myself, almost resting my forehead against Gray's arm to shield me from the memories.

Z stops in the center of the main room and opens his arms wide. "Welcome to downstate, Grinder."

I tip my head up, keeping my gaze locked on Gray's face. His wide eyes slowly take in every detail and he nods with approval.

Shock sets in as I follow his gaze.

So many things have been upgraded and replaced, it doesn't even look like the same clubhouse I remember.

I blow out a long, slow breath. Maybe this won't be so bad. The ghosts of my past can't chase me down hallways that look completely different from the ones in my nightmares. I feared reminders of Shadow would stain every part of this place. The cracked tiles where I'd once caught the heel of my shoe and twisted my ankle as Shadow dragged me to his room have been replaced with gray laminate floors that resemble wide wooden planks. The ratty, stained couches have been replaced with comfortable looking black leather pieces. The bar I used to hide behind to make myself useful to the club has colorful lighting installed above and around it now, giving it a cheerful glow.

More shelves have been added. The barstools have been upgraded to tall chairs with plushy black leather spinning seats. The wooden bar itself is the same, but it glistens and sparkles under the brighter lights.

"Wow," I breathe out.

Jigsaw brushes up against my other side and I peer up at him.

"We fixed a lot of things since the last time you were here," he says quietly.

I could take his words several ways but I choose the most obvious. "I see that. It looks great."

I risk peeking down the hallway leading to most of the members' bedrooms and the VIP guest rooms. No more thin, scratchy carpet that had rubbed my knees raw more than once. The dirty, beat-up walls have been patched and painted a soothing, soft gray.

The others take off to the kitchen or their rooms, but Z asks us to follow him.

"You can give me a grand tour later," Gray says.

"Yeah, sure." Z slips his arm around his wife's shoulders. "Lilly will find you guys a room."

"Everything all right, Gray?" Rock asks.

Gray's jaw tightens. "Yeah, I'm fine." He doesn't bother hiding his irritation.

Rock raises his hands and backs away.

Anxiety prickles over my scalp but Gray's eyes hold nothing but affection when he turns them on me.

"Let's see what we've got." Lilly captures my hand and drags me into the small room Z claimed as his office when he arrived. She grabs a binder from the top of a filing cabinet and flips it open, turning it so I can see the map of the clubhouse.

"Oh, that's neat." The officers' rooms are marked off. Even the upstate officers seem to have permanent rooms here now. "How about this one, near Wrath. He likes his privacy, so I doubt he'll bother you guys. Rooster's nearby, too."

"That's fine." As if it matters what I think.

Lilly's big, concerned eyes study me for a few unnerving seconds. "Are you all right?" she asks softly. "Being back here, I mean."

Shame heats my cheeks and steals my words, but I nod quickly. "The place looks so different."

Her expression brightens. "Z and I went to California for a quick trip. When we came back, the guys had most of the front room redone. The whole first floor, including all the bedrooms, has been remodeled. The pool area's fixed. The second floor's in various stages of upgrades. Well, you'll see. Z was touched they worked so quickly to get it done."

It meant the brothers accepted and welcomed him as their president. At least, that's how I interpret the gesture. That should be a good sign that things *have* changed down here.

"Here." Lilly hands me two stretchy bracelets with a small fob dangling from each one. "You have to put it next to the door and it will unlock. If not, let me know."

I slip one of the bracelets over my wrist. "Thank you."

As I turn to leave, Lilly grips my arm. "I'm glad you're here, Serena."

"I'll come help out after—"

"No, no." She shakes her head so vigorously, her long, glossy black hair swishes around her shoulders. "This weekend is supposed to be a welcome home party for Grinder and to celebrate him patching you. Spend time with your man. There will always be plenty of stuff to do another time."

Adjust your mindset from club girl to ol' lady, she seems to be saying. Or maybe that's in my head. "Thanks."

Gathering my confidence, I return to the main room. Grayson's dark expression lightens as our eyes meet.

"There you are." He curls his hand around mine.

"I wasn't gone that long."

"Still too long," he murmurs against my ear.

My heart flutters. I hold up the room key. "All set. Lilly says we're somewhere near Wrath and Rooster."

Jigsaw jerks his thumb over his shoulder. "That way. Past the presidential suite and before the stairwell."

We have to pass Shadow's old room but I keep my eyes straight ahead. Everything has changed so much, it's easy to pretend I'm somewhere new.

"Are you okay?" Gray's low voice is full of concern.

"Yes. It's wild how different a place can look after a little remodeling." My way of telling him I'm not reliving my club girl days without saying the actual words.

"Which way?" He nods to the fork in the hallway.

"Uh, left, I think." When they remodeled, the guys took down whatever old signs were left from the clubhouse's hotel days and didn't replace them. Makes it easier to get lost, which was probably their intention.

A distinctive rattling-thump fills the hallway. I shake my head, not wanting to guess which couple the sounds belong to. Gray side-eyes me.

"Lilly said it should be quiet down here."

"Uh-huh."

"This is it." I hold up my bracelet-key-fob gizmo, then press it to the pad on the door. A green light flickers and the lock clicks. "That's a nice improvement."

Gray pushes the door open and flicks the overhead light on. "Well, damn."

"Oh, wow."

The king-sized bed is neatly made up with crisp gray and blue bedding. The few pieces of modern furniture appear unused. A huge flat-screen television is mounted to the wall. I set my bag on the long dresser taking up the space under the television and wander toward the bathroom.

"It has a whirlpool tub!"

"Nicer than any hotel I ever stayed at." Gray rests his hands on my shoulder and I tip my head back so I can see his face.

"Are you okay?" I ask.

"Yeah." He rolls his shoulder. The slight tightening of his jaw tells me he's in more pain than he wants to tell me. "Been a long time since I've ridden. Probably shouldn't have started with such a long ride first go-around."

"Well, I was worried that might happen. I brought stuff to take care of you. Take your shirt off for me."

I push past him and head for my bag.

"You did what?" he asks, following me across the room.

"I was worried about your shoulder acting up." I paw through all my tightly packed items, unrolling the dress I want to wear later and dropping a pair of shoes on the floor.

"Why didn't you say something?"

"Because I knew you'd ride anyway." I find my property patch and unroll that, spreading it out on the dresser.

"Sorry you couldn't wear it on the way down," he says, staring at the leather.

"Not your fault. As long as I don't get in trouble for packing it away."

He chuckles, low and rough. "No, buttercup. You mind if I shower before you start working your magic on me?"

"Nope. The hot water will do you good. Loosen you up a little."

"Will you join me?"

"Of course."

The warm spray rinses off the long, dusty ride. After our quick shower, I find two robes on the back of the door. They appear brand new. I snap off one of the tags and slip it on.

"They do this for us or is it standard practice in all the rooms?" Gray asks, staring at the dark blue terry cloth.

"I'm not sure." I turn toward the sink and grab the small packets of cream I brought. "You won't need it. I want you naked anyway."

He chuckles and follows, hooking his finger in the belt of my robe and yanking me backward. "Same, buttercup," he whispers against my ear.

"No, no, no," I scold. "This is a professional matter."

He stretches out on the bed, resting his head on his folded arms.

"Very nice, Mr. Lock," I murmur, ripping into one of the packets and squirting cream in my cupped palm.

"Drop the robe." He stretches one arm and tugs on the edge, pulling me forward.

Letting out a fake huff, I slowly let the robe fall from my shoulders.

"More," he encourages.

I let it drop to the floor.

"Much better." His eyes study every bare inch of me.

I press my knee to the mattress and straddle his thighs. "Such a difficult patient," I mutter. I slide my hands together, warming the cream, then slick my palms over his shoulders.

The second my fingers touch his skin, he groans. "That feels so good, buttercup. Sorry for giving you a hard time."

I slowly dig my thumbs into his tight muscles. His whole body tenses. "Breathe," I remind him.

When the tension fades, I continue. "It's okay. I know you don't want to show what you consider weakness in front of your brothers. And you especially don't want *me* to think you're weak. But pain isn't weakness. It's your body's way of asking you to slow down and let your woman take care of you," I whisper.

He groans. "Wise words."

I work my way down each side of his spine. He freezes again when I reach his lower back. "Yup, I thought this might be tight. Deep breath, in and out."

"Jesus Christ," he sputters. "for such a delicate woman, you have iron fingers."

I resist the urge to laugh and keep working until I feel his muscles give. "There you go. Keep breathing."

"That stuff tingles." He sniffs. "Is it menthol?"

"It's a couple of different things. Just concentrate on breathing." I work my way back to his shoulders, and lean over him. "You can't resist me."

"True, you little witch." He plants his hands on the mattress and lifts himself, tipping me sideways.

With a yelp, I wrap my arms around his neck and hang on tight. "I'm not done!"

"Your magic fingers caused another problem I need you to take care of." He settles on his back and clamps his hands over my hips, guiding me over him.

"What's that?"

He glances down his body and I turn.

"Oh my. That's quite an erection," I tease.

"It hurts, buttercup."

I settle my knees on either side of his ribs and flash my fingers at him. "You don't want me rubbing this stuff on your sensitive areas."

He frowns for a second. Then, a wicked smile curves his mouth and he grabs my hips again, yanking me forward. "I have a solution. Sit on my face and keep your hands in the air."

"What?" Thrown off-balance, I brace my hands against the wall and stare down at him.

"You heard me." He slaps my outer thigh. "Spread 'em."

I inch my legs farther apart, careful not to dig my knees into his shoulders. "I'm going to smother you."

"I'll die a happy man." His eyes burn hot as I open for him. "That's it. Good girl," he praises.

The first sweep of his tongue sends a violent shiver of bliss through my body. My hips roll, pressing my center against his mouth.

"Mmm-hmm," he encourages, gripping my ass and pulling me closer.

"Oh God." I arch into the pleasure, leaning back and resting my hands on his shins.

"Perfect," he mumbles between kissing and licking. He slides one of his hands over my belly, settling it between my breasts.

"Gray," I whisper desperately. "I'm already...I think..."

He hums urgent, encouraging noises and pulls his hand away from my chest. I squeeze my eyes shut, concentrating on the fiery waves crashing against my center. He slides a finger inside me, twisting and curling to the exact spot that makes my toes curl.

"Right there!" I gasp and shackle my hand around his wrist.

Sparks of heat pulse through me and explode. I ride out the orgasm until I'm limp and trembling.

"Give me your hands." Gray's gruff command can't be denied. My arms are rubbery and weak, but I reach for him.

Gathering my wrists in one of his big hands, he rises and flips me to my back, pinning my arms over my head. His heavy body covers mine. A hot, blissful weight that makes me feel safe, cherished, and eager for more. He buries his face against my neck, kissing and licking. "You taste so fucking good."

A zip of electricity zings through my post-orgasm haze.

"Now, spread your legs."

I can't help but follow Gray's primal command.

"Wider." He settles himself between my thighs, slowly slipping inside me. "That's it. Fuck." He squeezes his eyes shut.

He keeps pushing, burying himself deep inside me with a long, satisfied groan.

"That's it," he praises in a deep raspy voice. "Take it." He thrusts again and again. "You're so fucking wet for me."

Each satisfied sound and compliment sinks in, filling me with a need to be closer in every way. "Only you," I whisper.

"That's right."

He doesn't get what I'm trying to say. I'm torn with the desire for him to understand my body has never responded like this to anyone else and the common sense to keep my mouth shut and enjoy the moment.

He grinds his pelvis into mine and molten heat rushes through my veins. Moans tear out of my throat and I bite my lip to keep quiet.

"Be as loud as you want, buttercup." He cradles my head with his hand and rubs his thumb over my bottom lip.

"Kiss me," I whisper.

He crashes his lips against mine, stroking my tongue and sucking on my bottom lip. Our hearts slam against each other while he relentlessly drives into me. Pressed so tight together, I can hardly draw a breath. But I relish the feeling of drowning in him. Warm skin sliding against mine. Crisp hair tickling me in various places. I arch my back and lift my legs, wrapping them around his waist.

"That's it," he says against my mouth.

I gulp in a deep breath.

He changes the angle, hitting a spot so deep and intense, my vision fuzzes at the edges. "Gray," I whisper, tumbling toward the edge of release. "Come with me."

"Not yet."

White streaks of heat blast through me, fuzzing my vision and blunting all sound except our breathing. The pleasure ripples from my center, so intense, tears leak from the corners of my eyes.

The sensation goes on and on. Gray presses his face against my neck, growling with satisfaction as his movements slow. We lay there sweating and panting in a heap of satisfied limbs.

"Jesus, I must be crushing you." He groans and rolls to the side, but pulls me close, kissing the top of my head. "You okay?"

I tilt my head and squint at him. "I'm floating."

"I hope that's a good thing."

"It is." I roll to my side, facing him. "Can we stay here all night?"

As if the universe heard my request and wants to deny it, Gray's phone rings.

He closes his eyes and blows out an annoyed breath. "I'm not a fan of being accessible by phone twenty-four seven," he grumbles. "I miss the days where people had to track you down on a landline."

As the last word leaves his mouth, his cell phone stops ringing and the black corded phone by the bed beeps.

"What the fuck?" he growls and sits up, snatching the phone off its cradle. "What?"

I can't tell who is on the other end but happy-sounding shouting comes through. I cock my head, listening for any telltale party noises from the hallway. Nothing.

There's no way the guys will let him hide in here with me all night.

"Yeah, we'll be there. Give me a minute. For fuck's sake."

I roll out of bed, wincing at the stickiness between my thighs and hurry into the bathroom.

I'm about to finish my shower, when Gray pulls the door open and steps inside.

"Everything all right?" I ask.

"Yeah, just Z wondering where we are." He rests his hands on my hips. "Do you know what you want to wear tonight?"

"Oh, yes." I grin, eager to model my dress for Gray.

"Good." He pats my butt. "You'll take longer than me to get ready."

"Are you kicking me out of the shower?"

He flashes a quick, unapologetic smile. "*Kicking out* is such a strong way to put it."

I lean up and kiss his cheek.

While he finishes in the shower, I unpack my makeup bag. I didn't bring my full arsenal but there is no way I'm running around this place bare-faced. I need as much armor as possible to boost my confidence.

The hair on the back of my neck prickles. I shift my gaze and find Gray watching me as he towels off.

"You know you don't need all of that, right?"

I glare at him in the mirror.

He holds up one hand. "Just want you to know I think you're beautiful no matter what."

"I didn't ask."

His eyes widen and he nods once. "Noted."

A few minutes later he returns, fully dressed. "Z asked me to meet him out back for a minute. You okay?"

"Sure." Then I won't feel anxious about taking so long to get ready.

He leans in and kisses my temple. "Take your time."

The door clicks closed a few seconds later and I blow out a breath. Why am I so freaked out tonight? I've always known if Gray and I were together, I'd eventually have to visit down here. *Freakin' Tawny.* I shouldn't give a shit what that bitter old bag of bones thinks of me. But I just *know* she'll try to humiliate me the first chance she gets.

I don't want Gray to be sorry he patched me.

Or second-guess our relationship.

Tawny isn't the queen bee around here anymore. Lilly is. And Lilly seems to like me. Still, I need to be prepared.

I steal a quick glance at the clock. How long will Gray be gone? Probably not that long. I skip my false lashes and layer on my waterproof mascara.

I will *not* let that woman make me cry.

Face done, I check all my angles, snap a few selfies, then start on my hair. I didn't have room for my curling iron, so I do what I can with my round brush and the blow dryer I found under the bathroom sink.

There's a soft knock from the hallway. I cock my head. Is it our door? I slip into the bathrobe and hurry to answer it.

Lilly's on the other side, absolutely stunning in a deep blue sapphire velvet dress that clings to all of her generous curves. *Jesus, I'd kill for her cleavage.*

"Hey, Grinder and Z are out back, so I just wanted to check on you." She holds up a bunch of shiny objects. "See if you needed to borrow anything since the rooms aren't really stocked with lots of girly items."

I focus on the hair straightener and curling wand she's holding out to me.

"Oh my God. Thank you. Yes, I was just lamenting that I didn't bring my curling iron." I open the door wider. "Come in."

"No, no. I have a few other stops to make."

I reach for the hair tools. "Do you mind if I borrow both?"

"Not at all. Leave them in the drawer in the bathroom when you're done, if you want. I'll probably try to keep this room blocked off for just you guys." Her nose wrinkles. "So you don't have to worry about God knows what happening in your bed when you're not here."

"I hadn't thought about that." I tap my lip. "But now I won't be able to *stop* thinking about it."

She laughs softly. "See you in a bit."

Feeling slightly better about the evening ahead, I return to the bathroom and plug in the curling wand.

While it's heating up, I section off my hair. I work quickly, only wanting to add a few loose waves. The dress I'm planning to wear is dramatic enough. I pull a few sections away from my face, pinning them at the back of my head with a black and gold bow. Finally, I run the flat iron over a few wispy, wayward strands of hair framing my face.

"Dress time," I mutter to myself. I slip into the slick black boy shorts I plan to wear under the dress, then tape my boobs into a special bra, so they'll stay put. There's nothing simple about the little black dress I chose. It's a thick, shiny wet-look material. Almost like leather with a sheen of golden sparkle woven into the stretchy fabric. A classy-ish sort of slutty dress. Or what might be considered classy at a motorcycle clubhouse. A large ruffle frames the dramatic V of the dress and wraps around my shoulders. The skintight material hugs my hips and ends mid-thigh. It's no more revealing than what Lilly was wearing, so it shouldn't be too much. I step into a pair of black heels and stand in front of the mirror.

"Not bad," I whisper, turning to the side. No baby bump yet. "What'cha doin' in there, lil' peanut?" I rub my hand over my stomach. "Hmm?"

I grab my phone, toss up a peace sign and snap a few selfies, making sure nothing too revealing is in the background. I add it to my Instagram with a "date night" caption.

The door beeps and pushes open.

Gray steps inside. His gaze lands on me and he stops.

Like a deer caught in the headlights, I stand there watching him take me in.

"Is this dress okay?" I glance down at the low V, noticing how much of my sternum is exposed. "It shows more than I thought."

Gray's still busy staring at my legs but his gaze slowly travels to my chest. One corner of his mouth slides up. "You are absolutely stunning." He closes the door behind him.

I back away a few steps. "I don't want to embarrass you."

He frowns. "You could never embarrass me. I'm standing here thinking Karma got confused because there is *no way* I've done anything good enough in this life to deserve having you on my arm."

The sweet affection tied up in his words slides over me like warm honey. "That's not true." I step closer and loop my arms around his neck. "You're good to *me*."

"You make it easy." He kisses the tip of my nose. "Thank you for coming with me. I know it wasn't your first choice of weekend getaway."

I won't bother denying it, so I nod. "I'm just…anxious about who might be here or whatever," I mumble the last part, losing my nerve.

"Hey." He tightens his arm around my waist, jerking me closer to grab my attention. "If anyone—I don't care who—says anything disrespectful to you, tell me right away."

"Gray—"

"I'm serious. Tonight, I want to set the stage for how I expect you to be treated, so there's no confusion. You're my ol' lady. Period. I won't tolerate bullshit from anyone—male or female. So tell me."

My nose tingles and my eyes threaten to water but I take a few breaths to compose myself before speaking. "I will."

"I don't want you leaving my side anyway." He drops his gaze and trails his finger from my collarbone to between my breasts. I tip my head, watching his thumb slide under my dress. "Hmm, what's under here?"

"A complicated combination of bra and boob tape."

He removes his hand and lifts an eyebrow. "Something to unwrap later."

CHAPTER TWENTY-TWO

Grinder

WHAT THE FUCK AM I DOING? SERENA'S DRESSED TO THE NINES, LIKE she should be stepping out of a limo and waving to a line of photographers eager to shoot her picture. I try not to dwell on our age difference too often, but god damn, she has no business with someone as worn down by life as me. And I'm a fucking bastard for making her come here when she's clearly uncomfortable. I promised to take care of her and ease the stress in her life. Not make it worse.

I'm on edge myself. Not looking forward to having attention on me. Not interested in talking about prison life or waxing poetic about the old days. Don't feel like dealing with brothers and their misplaced guilt that they've been out here living their lives while I was rotting in prison. None of it appeals to me. I just want to move the fuck on.

"Where's your patch?" I ask Serena.

Her big blue eyes—made impossibly bigger by all the black stuff expertly smudged around them—widen. "Here." She shifts to the side, but I don't release her. "Gray." A note of exasperation follows.

"Nah, don't wanna let go of you." To prove it, I follow her to the dresser with my hands around her waist, making laughter bubble past her lips.

Her fingers grasp the vest, carefully laid out. I watch her reflection in the mirror. "Put your hands on the dresser."

In the mirror, our eyes meet. "What?"

"Do it."

She huffs but there's a hint of a smile playing at the corners of her mouth. Leaning over and bracing herself against the wood, she raises her eyebrows. "Like this?"

"Yup. Just like that." The mirror gives a nice view down the front of her dress. And from back here I can slide the material up... "Damn, this is tight." The dress doesn't budge as easily as I thought it would.

She leans over farther, resting her elbows on the dresser. "I wanted to wear it before I start showing."

"Don't get me any harder than I already am." I run my hands over her ass and down her smooth legs.

She dances on her toes, the sharp, heavy points of her heels clicking against the floor. "That tickles!"

I tease my fingers behind her knees and she laughs harder. I lean closer and trail my tongue over the back of her thigh and she gasps, inching her feet apart.

A lick of guilt sweeps over me. I'd told Z we'd be out in a few minutes. Fuck it. He'll understand.

I stand straight and grab Serena's hips, yanking her against my groin. "A man my age shouldn't want to fuck this much."

"Do it," she whispers, staring at me in the mirror. She lifts herself long enough to carefully wiggle her dress up around her waist, then leans over the dresser again.

The building would have to be on fire for me to say no. I run my hand over shiny black material that looks more like shorts than underwear. Not something I can just slide to the side easily. I hook my fingers in the waistband and drag them down to her knees. In the mirror, I watch her eyes close and her lips part.

"You like that?"

"Yes."

"Open your eyes and watch me."

I wait until she does what I ask, then undo my belt. She wiggles her ass while I free myself. "Cut that out," I growl.

Instead of answering, she shuffles her feet as far apart as the material around her knees will allow and arches her back. With my big frame looming behind her, she looks exposed and vulnerable.

"Are you ready?" I ask.

She nods and curls her fingers around the edge of the dresser.

"That's right, you better hold on." I shove my cock inside her without any other warning. She gasps and rises on her toes, nails scratching against the dresser.

"Fuck," I groan. We did this not two hours ago and being inside her still feels like coming home.

I lean over her, inhaling the scent of her skin and hair. My hand slides between her legs. She jumps when my middle finger snuggles up to her clit. "That's it," I breathe against her ear. "Open for me."

"I can't," she gasps.

"Poor Serena," I tease, fucking her with long, slow strokes. "Are you trapped?"

"Y-yes." She squeezes her eyes shut. "Oh my God. Right there. Please." She continues begging and pleading but I take my time. My hips snap against her ass, my fingers stroke between her legs. A violent shudder works through her body. She tenses and twists her hips, her face contorting.

I back off. "Am I hurting you?"

"No," she pants in little quick breaths. "I want to come."

I let out a dark laugh. "We want the same thing."

She drills me with a hard, desperate stare. "I *was* close until you slowed down."

Now I can't help laughing even harder. "Fuck, woman." I rest one hand at the small of her back. "Give me a second."

In answer, she tightens and squeezes her muscles around my cock so fucking hard, stars dot my vision. I thrust into her again and again. Harder each time until her body tightens. This time, I don't stop. I curl my hand over her shoulder, keeping her in place while pounding into her harder.

"Yes!" she shrieks and shudders, breathing heavy like she just ran a quarter mile.

No better sound in the world than satisfying your woman, and it triggers my own release.

After a few seconds, I stagger backward. Serena still hasn't moved. "You all right?"

"Aftershocks," she whispers over her shoulder.

Fuck, if that doesn't stroke my ego. Smirking, I pull her underwear into place and slap her ass. "There. Now, whenever you get nervous tonight, just think about your man's cum leaking out of you."

She straightens and turns, resting her butt on the dresser and staring at me. I slide my hand between her thighs, and she inhales sharply. Running my fingers against her damp slit, I rasp against her ear, "I told you I was a filthy fuck. You think I was joking?"

"No," she whispers.

With my other hand, I grip her chin and tip her head back. "I love you." I press my forehead to hers. "And I like being myself with you."

She blinks several times. "I like that too."

It's a vague answer but I'll take it for now. I let my gaze roam over her. Didn't mess up her makeup or hair too much. At least, I don't think so. I hope she won't need another hour to fix herself up again. "Go, get ready. We need to leave."

Her lips twist into a smirk. "I *was* ready. You're the one who made us late."

"Worth it." I pop a quick kiss on her lips. She kicks off her heels and hurries into the bathroom, shutting the door behind her. I grab her vest and tap on the door.

"Just a sec."

She sounds close to the door. And it's not like we haven't been as intimate as two people can get, so I turn the knob and push the door open. She's standing in front of the sink, wrapping her hair around a long silver stick and carefully tilts her head my way.

"Boundaries, Gray," she scolds.

Chuckling, I lean against the doorframe. "Not familiar with the concept."

"I've noticed." She unwraps one loose curl, gently cupping it in her hand before dropping it and winding another section of hair around the stick.

"I like watching you."

"Curl my hair?"

I shrug. "Doing anything, really."

She finishes her hair and unplugs the stick. Then, she leans close to the bathroom mirror, studying her already perfect face. She reaches for a cotton swap and swipes it under her eyes, then dusts a cloud of powder over her face.

"Okay." She turns away from the mirror and holds out her arms.

"Perfect, just like before I got my dirty paws all over you." I hold out my arm to her. "Still feel like I got no business being with you."

"Don't say that. I love you, Gray." She ducks her head, her loose curls falling forward to hide her face. "I've never felt this way about anyone before."

"Same." I cup her cheek and tip her head back. Her eyelids twinkle gold with a thin line of bright blue liner above the heavy black liner. "You're wearing the gold stuff we bought?"

"Yes." Her face brightens. "I should've taken some video while I was applying it. It's good stuff. I should thank Alice for the rec."

"Looks pretty." I hold out her vest. "Will you let me put this on you?"

"I thought you'd never ask."

CHAPTER TWENTY-THREE

Grinder

HATRED CAN MAKE A MAN RECKLESS. I MADE AN EFFORT TO STOP storing hate in my heart years ago. Instead, I deal with the things that piss me off, then move on.

But tonight, an angry burn hovers in my chest. The looks a few of my brothers cast Serena's way as we enter the party leave me struggling not to throw punches.

"Finally!" Z shouts. "Our guest of honor has joined us!" He waves us toward the bar.

Growling under my breath, I keep Serena close. My hand at the small of her back, I maneuver her slightly ahead of me so I can see how people react to her. Brothers who give her anything less than a friendly hello are going on my *beatdown at a later point in time* list.

"Oh!" Lilly lets out a husky laugh and throws her arms around Serena, hugging her tight in front of everyone. "I love this dress!"

She continues fawning over Serena, curling her arm around her shoulders like a momma cat claiming one of her kittens. The two of them step aside and Z grabs me in a rib-cracking hug.

"You keep making a spectacle of me, and I'm gonna gut you in your sleep," I say close to his ear.

"Aw, come on." He slaps my back. "I'm just happy you're finally here to see the place. Lotta people want to pay their respects to you too."

I swallow my annoyance and pat Z's shoulder. "You've got a good setup here, brother. Proud of you."

"Thanks. I'm still getting used to things, but I've got a solid crew around me now." The corners of his mouth curl into an impish smirk. "Always room for improvement, though."

"Sorry, brother." Rock joins us. "I warned him not to go overboard."

Z grins wider. "I'm just so happy we're all here."

Z's love for the club and his brothers is infectious and chases away my annoyance at having the spotlight on me. "Thanks for the room you assigned us. It's nice."

"Hell, yeah. Nothing but the best for you."

My eyes find Serena, the best thing that's happened to me yet.

Serena

While Z and Gray talk, Lilly pulls me toward the bar. "Do you want a drink?"

"Just water. Are you sure you don't want me to help out?"

"Nope." She reaches over the bar and snags a bottle of water, handing it to me. "Not tonight."

I uncap the bottle and take a slow sip, careful not to smudge my lipstick or dribble water all over my chest. "Thanks." My nervous gaze scans the crowded room. "Uh, you don't know if Sway and Tawny are coming, do you?"

She rolls her eyes and points at the ceiling. "They're upstairs. Not sure when they'll make an *entrance*."

"Who?" Trinity asks, bumping up along Lilly's side. Her bright amber eyes sweep over me. "Oh, killer dress."

I touch the ruffle near my shoulder and nod at her dress which is similar to mine, except it's fire-engine red with a flared skirt. "Great minds."

"Oh" She twists and checks out the neckline. "Damn, you're right."

"You look good in red," Lilly says.

"I'll wear red now, since I chopped off the blue ends." She pats her elegantly braided blond hair. "Otherwise, it made me look like Fourth of July Barbie."

I snort-laugh into my water. "I'd think that would be a popular look around here."

"Exactly." Trinity's gaze bounces between Lilly and me. "Now, who are we hoping won't make an appearance?"

Lilly waves her hand dismissively but the corners of her mouth twitch. "That's not what I said." She leans over and squeezes my arm. "I need to check on something. Be right back. Don't worry about a thing." She saunters into the crowd, passing Z and trailing her fingers over his back. His gaze follows her for a few steps, then he excuses himself and follows.

Trinity watches them with amusement in her eyes. "*Siren* was such an appropriate nickname for her." Her gaze returns to me. "I didn't have a chance to talk to Grinder yet. How was his first ride?"

"Good, I think." I won't share my worries about his shoulder with her. "I know he'd rather ride with the club and wear his cut."

"Soon." Her expression hardens. "Are you all right being down here?"

The question leaves me tongue-tied for a moment. "Uh," I stutter, not sure what to say. Pretend it's no big deal? Confess all the dread gathering in my chest? Will Trinity respect me more if I'm honest, or will she go tell Wrath I'm not cut out to be Grinder's old lady?

"I'm not looking forward to running into Tawny," I finally answer. That shouldn't exactly surprise her.

"Oh, fuck Tawny," Trinity says with a dismissive wave of her hand. "She's called me a whore to my face more times than I can count."

"It seems to be her favorite insult."

Her eyes turn hard. "Last time, Wrath caught her and she almost shit herself."

I would've *loved* to see that.

She covers her mouth with one hand and snickers. "She hasn't had the balls since. Now she pretends we've always been *besties*," she finishes in a helium-high voice.

"Fake."

"As fuck," she agrees. "You're a patched ol' lady now, Serena." Her voice is a rod of steel shooting up my spine. "Act like it. Own it. Don't let that bitch or anyone else intimidate you."

"I know. I won't." I stand straighter and square my shoulders.

"That's better." She runs her gaze over me again. "It's gonna boil her venom that all the brothers gave you their patches too." She grins as if she can't wait to witness it. Her finger grazes Heidi's hammer that Gray sewed on for me. "I need to finalize the other girls' patches," she says absently.

"That's a really cool idea that all the ol' ladies are doing that."

"It is—"

"You must be *thrilled*," a venom-laced voice slithers into our conversation. The familiar scent of roses and powder clogs my nose. I close my eyes briefly, bracing myself for what's coming.

Ding-dong, the witch has arrived.

Steel spine time.

I don't bother searching for Gray. No matter how much he wants to protect me, he can't rescue me from this showdown.

Trinity squares up next to me, shoulder to shoulder.

"Hey, Tawny. So glad you joined the party," she says in a phony syrupy voice. She slides her arm around my shoulders and squeezes me to her side. "Lots of things to celebrate tonight."

Tawny's face screws into a scowl that used to sear my skin with fear. "Look how chummy the two of you are," she says in a slow, sarcastic tone. "Figures you two would—"

"What?" Trinity raises her eyebrows. "We would *what*?"

"Find *common ground*." Tawny's hate-filled eyes land on me. And I don't even have the heart to take pleasure in how worn-down and tired her face looks. Ten years of baggage seems to have landed under her eyes since the last time I saw her. "Proud of yourself, aren't ya? Finally, after all these years on your knees, found a brother desperate enough to patch you."

How dare she say something so vile about my man. I swallow hard and will myself not to look away. My heart pounds and beads of sweat slide down my back. Unfortunately, no clever comebacks come to mind.

"I'd watch your tone, Tawny." Trinity leans closer, all amusement gone from her usually angelic face. She's turned into a she-devil about to spew some fire. "Grinder won't take kindly to anyone showing his ol' lady disrespect."

Tawny snorts. "Grinder and me go way back, honey."

The casual way she says it sends a shiver of disgust through my stomach.

Oh, Lord. Please don't tell me she slept with Gray once upon a time. Of all the women in the world, not this one.

"I know him better than you *ever* will." She flicks one long, red nail against the collar of my vest. "He hasn't had a woman in so long, of course he's ready to patch the first pretty young pussy he stumbles into, but I bet you didn't tell him every brother in this clubhouse has taken a turn."

I roll my eyes. That's not even true. "Do you ever get tired of repeating the same lies?"

"Maybe he doesn't care since he was locked up." She flicks her hands in front of my face again. "Enjoy that patch while you can. Being pretty won't satisfy a man like him long-term. He needs more mental stimulation than *you* can give him."

"Well, I see why you two didn't end up together, then," I quip.

She glares at me. "You know his first wife was going to be a doctor, right?"

I open my mouth to tell her to fuck off, that I know all about Rose. Or defend myself by saying I actually finished my degree—except, I don't want Tawny to know one damn thing about my professional life outside of the club.

Trinity lets out a long, dramatic sigh. "Do you have a point?" She circles her hand in a *wrap it up* gesture. "You're jealous, we get it."

"Jealous?" Tawny's theatrical outrage belongs on the set of a bad soap opera. "Of what?"

"Off the top of my head," Trinity pauses dramatically and taps her chin, "that our men aren't playing daddy to porn stars?"

Boom. Talk about dropping a conversational bomb.

Tawny's mouth snaps shut. Everyone knows how Sway catered to porn star Stella before he got shot. A lot of the girls speculated the only reason Sway got the club to back Stella's porn movies was because he was planning to leave Tawny *for* Stella.

Tawny's eyes bug. She sputters. I'm pretty sure steam billows from the top of her perfectly laminated helmet of hair.

"If you stopped being such a bitch, we'd have your back, Tawny." Trinity's tone turns a shade more compassionate.

"I don't need your sympathy." Her blazing eyes leave Trinity and return to me. "Enjoy your moment in the sun, *buttercup,*" she sneers. "It won't last. I can't wait for Karma to have her way with you."

"There you are, Tawny," Lilly purrs. She hooks her arm around my waist. "Isn't this great? We have *so much* to celebrate tonight." She pulls away and strokes her fingers over Z's patch on my side. "Aw, my man's patch looks good right next to Rock's and all the upstate officers. I need to ask him what font that is, so I can incorporate it into the tattoo Bronze is drawing up for my back. Oh! Look! Rooster and Jiggy added theirs too." She levels a pointed look in Tawny's direction. "I *love* how close the two clubs are *now.*"

Trinity turns to the side and snort-laughs into her elbow.

Lilly's comments might seem random to anyone else, but each word hits Tawny like a bullet. I don't know all of the history between the upstate and downstate clubs, but I always thought it was weird having two charters not that far away from each other. Not to mention how differently the two clubs operated. Z must've shared some of the club's history with Lilly to give her the ammunition to push Tawny's buttons.

"Did Heidi come with you guys?" Tawny asks.

Maybe she assumes Heidi will join her in ganging up on me? That must be what Lilly's thinking. She nudges me to turn and taps the little hammer patch on my side. "Oh, Tawny, did we tell you we're all doing sisterhood patches? That's Heidi's. Isn't it cute? All the guys started calling her Little Hammer so we thought that was perfect." She gestures to the hammer also sewn onto her vest.

More eye-bugging from Tawny.

"Do you want us to have a little bee made up for you?" Lilly asks sweetly, gesturing to the "Queen Bee" patch on the front of Tawny's vest.

Now that I'm not quaking with fear, I have a moment to take in Tawny's shiny gold pantsuit. Reminds me of something my mother would've worn when I was a kid. Bitch or not, Tawny still has a fab figure and rocks the hell out of the gleaming lamé fabric. I'd rather cut out my tongue than say that out loud, though.

"No," Tawny snaps. "I can't believe the guys let you desecrate their cuts that way."

Lilly shrugs. "Z thought it was a great idea." She glances at Trinity and shrugs. "All the guys did."

"How nice." Seeing she's lost this battle, Tawny's gaze searches the room. "I see someone I need to say hello to." She dips away from us before anyone responds.

All the adrenaline that had been keeping me upright and stone-faced seems to leave my body in a rush. My knees weaken and I slump against the barstool at my back. I doubt that'll be the last time I tangle with her. I just hope I'm not alone for the next round.

Trinity grabs my arm and helps me onto the stool, then jumps on the one next to me. "You're okay. You survived."

"What'd she say to you?" Lilly demands.

The whole conversation recedes from my memory in a blur of bad feelings. "The usual." I flap my hand in the air, as if Tawny's words don't matter.

"You're such a clever bitch," Trinity giggles and holds out her fist to Lilly.

Lilly taps her knuckles against Trinity's. "Who, me?"

"Thank you," I mutter, feeling I should say more but not able to. Few people have ever stood up for me in my life. Especially here.

"No worries." Lilly squeezes my shoulder.

"Aw, you didn't tell me everyone was wearin' dresses." Shelby peers around Lilly's side. "Hey, Serena."

Shelby's cheery face seems to magically blot away the remainder of Tawny's negative energy.

"You look cute." I nod to her black liquid leather leggings and the sheer pink blouse peeking out from under her *Property of Rooster* cut.

"Cute?" She glances down and taps the toes of her shiny black high-heeled sandals. "I skipped wearing my favorite boots in the hopes of looking *taller*."

"You've got legs for days," Trinity assures her.

"Sorry, I wasn't sure if we knew each other well enough yet to say, 'you look sexy as fuck,'" I add.

Shelby grins. "That's more like it."

"Someone else thinks so too." Trinity points behind Shelby where Rooster's talking to someone while keeping his eyes on his girl.

Shelby's cheeks turn a shade of pink to match her blouse.

"Awww," Lilly and Trinity sing, making Shelby blush an even brighter pink.

"Y'all got any Sprite back there, or are ya gonna keep pokin' fun at me?" she grumbles while fighting off a smile.

I turn and lean over the bar, snagging the cooler door open and reaching for a can of Sprite.

"Careful, there." Someone presses my dress against the backs of my legs. "Or ya gonna flash the whole room."

"Whoops." I pop onto my seat and hand Shelby the can. "Thanks."

"Thank *you*." She holds up the can and pops the top.

While the three of them talk, my gaze wanders the room. A flash of gold catches my eye. Tawny. *Yuck.* Talking to a big, burly biker I don't recognize. Spreading more misery, no doubt. People move and I catch the Virginia bottom rocker on his cut. I've only met one or two guys from that charter.

"Oh, that's Pants!" Shelby stands on tiptoes and waves. "And Ice. I hope Anya came with them."

Tawny darts away when Wrath lumbers into the circle to greet the newcomers. He lifts his hand, motioning for Trinity to join him.

"Later, ladies." She grabs Shelby's hand and drags her into the crowd.

"They call, we come," Lilly smirks. "Sometimes literally."

I cough and almost choke on a sip of water.

"Sorry." Lilly thumps me on the back. "Couldn't help myself."

"No, it was on right on target."

CHAPTER TWENTY-FOUR

Grinder

Brother after brother stops to shake my hand and welcome me home. Some I remember. Some patched in after I went inside but still want to show their respect. I feel like a flesh and blood cautionary tale —here to warn all the brothers away from a life of crime.

"Had enough?" Rock asks me in a low voice when we have a minute alone.

"Gettin' there," I answer honestly. He'll understand. "Good thing we waited on *this* party. If you guys had sprung this on me right after I got out, I probably woulda lost my shit."

"Yeah," he answers.

The front door opens and another pack of Lost Kings enter the clubhouse. Hearty, welcoming shouts rise above the rest of the noise. My gaze lands on the tallest newcomer. "Jesus, is that Ice?"

"Looks like it." Rock raises his arm and waves him over.

"You're all making me feel old as fuck," I grumble.

"How you been, brother? It's been a minute." Ice ropes Rock into a hug, slapping him on the back.

"Not bad. Good to see you up here." Rock pulls back and angles Ice my way.

"God damn, Grinder. Real glad you're out, brother." He pulls me into a brotherly embrace. "Been a long time."

"Sure has." I look him over. "You'd barely grown into this cut last time I saw you." I slap his chest. "Now you're wearing that president's flash well. Congratulations, brother."

"It's been a journey," he says with the same humble attitude I remember.

"Heard you did time too."

He nods once. I ain't gonna ask him more about it. We can share prison stories some other time. Tonight's supposed to be about celebrating freedom.

Z swaggers over to us and bear-hugs Ice. "Glad to have you in our house, brother. Thanks for taking care of my guys last summer."

"Please, Rooster and Jigsaw helped out a lot. Rooster's still providing technical support."

"Good." Z slaps his shoulder again. "He's around here somewhere."

"I'm gonna leave you to your presidential circle-jerk." I flick my thumb toward the bar. "I'm going to grab a drink."

I'm able to wedge myself into a corner and ask for a club soda without too many people bothering me.

"Here ya go." The girl behind the bar slides a glass my way and leans over, showing off her tits in her barely there top.

"Thanks, darlin'."

"Grinder!"

Fifteen long years and I recognize that voice. Like nails scratching over my nerve endings. I turn and yup, there's Tawny mincing over to me with her arms open wide. "Welcome home, baby."

Inside, I cringe. Not a fan of being called *baby* by anyone.

Guys say hi or try to get Tawny's attention, but she's focused on me.

She envelops me in a tight squeeze, her cloying perfume an unpleasant reminder of the past. "So happy to see you, Grinder," she says. "Been a long time."

"Sure has." I pull away and look her over. Damn jumpsuit she's squeezed herself into nearly blinds me. "Still a lightning rod, I see."

"You always had the nicest things to say." She slaps my chest. "Even if you were a grumpy old bastard."

"What do you mean *were*. Still am."

"I see that." Her lips curve into the sly, snake-like smile I remember well. "I'm a little shocked to find out you patched some girl you barely know so soon."

Now we're getting down to business. Knew she wouldn't be able to help herself. "I'm shocked that you don't remember how much I hate people sticking their noses in my business."

"Grinder, you know I'm lookin' out for ya. You've been through hell. You need a woman you can trust."

"I trust Serena fine."

"I've known her for *years*. And not because she was sweet and innocent."

"Since when do you get to know any of the girls that hang around here?"

Her eyes widen and she drags her fingers over her chest. "You already know?"

"Of course I fuckin' know. You shoulda stopped and asked Steer how well I tolerated this conversation."

"See what I mean? She's already causing trouble between brothers."

"*She* hasn't done anything. People running their rude mouths are the ones starting trouble."

Her sneaky little face curls up in an imitation of concern. "You don't want to worry that she's sucking off your brothers every time you're out on a run. That's no way to live at your age."

My fingers twitch. I'd choked the shit out of Steer for less. But no matter how far I've fallen, I can't put my hands on a woman that way. Even one that's practically begging me to.

"Cut your phony concern act." I push into her space. Enough to force her to back up until she hits the bar and has to arch to get away from me. "You've always been a conniving rattlesnake. Fifteen years of lockup didn't erase that knowledge. You need to drop this. If you start shit or you disrespect Serena, there *will* be consequences. Are we clear?"

"Crystal," she hisses through her clenched jaw. Pure hatred burns in her eyes, and I don't give a single fuck.

"Good."

I back away and run my palms over my cut. We're done.

"Think whatever you want about me, but I've never betrayed the club," she says. "I've had opportunities…"

Guess we're not finished. "Never said you weren't loyal to *the club*. But you disrespect the *brotherhood* by causing trouble. Don't try to fool me, Tawny. You forget how well I *know* you."

Still miffed, she rearranges her blouse and checks her earrings. "You don't know shit. The things I've endured over the years."

"That's on you. Don't like it, you've always been free to leave."

She barks out a harsh laugh. "Leave? With the dirt I know? You think Sway would let me walk away?" she says in a harsh whisper. "Live in hiding unprotected for the rest of my life?"

She might have a point, but I just don't care. "It's not an excuse to make everyone around you miserable."

"I'm not like Rose. I didn't ignore the club and want to play house in the suburbs. I helped hold things together."

Helped run the club into the ground is probably more like it. But the fact that she has the nerve to mention Rose's name pisses me right the fuck off again. "You nailed one thing. You're nothing like Rose."

"That's right. I stood by my man when he was inside."

Ouch. That zinger of truth lands hard.

"You might've stayed, but you couldn't help sticking your nose wherever it didn't belong and causing trouble."

"Someone had to take control of things around here."

"You admitting your man was a weak president?" I sneer.

Her lips pinch. Lie and claim Sway wasn't weak or betray her man by speaking the truth? Hard choice for a woman with a skewed sense of loyalty.

"From what I've gathered, your man's ineptitude almost got him killed and put the whole club in jeopardy. So, from where I'm standing, you should be thanking every demon you pray to that he wasn't *voted out bad* or sent six feet under." I drill her with a stare she can't escape.

"The fuck do you know? You weren't here," she seethes.

"That's right. I was in *prison*. Where your buddy Ruger put me."

"Well, *your* boy settled that score when he got out, didn't he?"

The nerve of her to refer to Rock as *my boy*. But I'm not admitting or denying anything about Ruger's disappearance. "Fifteen *years*, Tawny. Think of all the things you've been able to do over the last fifteen years. Raised your kids. Fucked your man—and whoever else fell into your web—spending his money, traveling all over, eating what you wanted, doing what you wanted, whenever you wanted."

Her shoulders slump and shame clouds her expression. "I thought about you a lot."

"I'm sure you did. Probably praying I'd never see the light of day."

"That's not true," she whispers, so softly I barely catch the words. "I hated what happened to you."

"Do you really mean that?"

"Yes."

"Then show me. Otherwise, I'll keep assuming you're full of shit."

"How? What's gonna make you believe me?"

"Let go of however you felt about Serena in the past and start over."

"All right." Defeat shines in her eyes and she nods once. "I'll try to get to know her differently this time."

Don't think I didn't notice the lack of apology, bitch.

"Don't force it, Tawny." The last thing Serena needs is Tawny's fake friendship. "Treat her with the same respect you would the other old ladies."

"Old." She snorts. "I'm the oldest damn one, now. Can't mother the girls. I gotta *grandma* them."

As if she ever had a motherly bone in her body. But finally, I chuckle. I understand the feeling. "Yeah, gettin' old is a bitch but it beats the alternative."

"I guess." She peers up at me. "You're really embracing the biker stereotype of old guy going after the hot young thing, huh?"

"Going back on your word already?"

"Not at all." Her lips curve into a sly smile. "That's a dig at *you*, not her."

I choke on a laugh. For a brief second, I get a glimpse of the brash and funny twenty-something Tawny had been when I first started hanging around the club. Before she made lots of bad choices that turned her bitter. I follow her gaze to a group of club girls circling one of the younger brothers.

"You hate them because they remind you of the mistakes you made when you were their age?" I ask.

Her eyes narrow. "Don't tell me you got your degree in psychology while you were inside."

"Nah, just gained some perspective. Life is short. We should enjoy the time we have left. Staring in the rear-view mirror instead of looking at the road ahead leads to miles of misery."

"Great, you're a philosopher now, too." She crosses her arms over her chest.

"There a problem, Grinder?" Sway asks slowly as he ambles up beside his wife.

Nice timing, asshole. "Not at all, brother. Having a conversation with your wife. Wanted her to understand that if she throws her famous attitude at my girl, we're gonna have issues."

One corner of his mouth quivers. Bet he'd be smirking if he wasn't still fucked up from the bullet to the head.

I keep my expression flat. "I ain't laughing."

"Who's your girl?" His sarcastic tone pushes me toward the red zone. "Serena? Saw she's wearing your patch. When'd that happen?"

Rage coats my tongue. "Keep her name out of your mouth."

He lifts his arm as if to stop me from spewing more threats. Tremors run from fingers to wrist and he stares at his hand before setting it on the bar and pretending to casually lean. One of the girls behind the bar swings by and slides a glass of amber liquid his way.

"I don't have a problem *wiff* her," he slurs even though it looks like it's using up all his effort to get out each word.

Christ, he's more fucked up than anyone told me. "Great. Glad we cleared that up."

Tawny hooks her arm around my elbow and leans into me,

pressing her breasts into my side. "We were reminiscing about the old days."

I extract myself from her hold. "I wasn't a fan of you using me to make him jealous back then, and I ain't a fan of it now, sweetheart."

Sway lets out a harsh laugh. "Things haven't changed much."

"I don't know, brother." I shift my gaze to Tawny. "The more things change, the more they stay the same."

"I said I'd *try*," Tawny whines.

"I'm not just talking about you, Tawny. Christ, you're still as self-centered as ever."

Sway cough-laughs. "You don't know the half of it."

"Oh, shut up." Tawny steps away from me and slaps Sway's chest.

He catches her hand and yanks her to his side. Makes sense whatever strength he's got left is used to wrangle his wife. "What else you been up to since you been out?" he asks me.

"Work. Staying off my P.O.'s radar." *Knocking up my girlfriend.* But no, I promised Serena I wouldn't tell anyone this weekend. And fuck knows these are the last two she'd want me to share the news with.

"Yeah, been there. Sucks."

The few years Sway's spent in and out of prison don't quite compare to my stretch of fifteen. But I'm not here to play a game of who's had it worse. I nod instead. "Determined to stay on this side for good."

"Amen." He lifts his glass toward me and takes a deep sip. "I hear Priest is supposed to swing by. That should be interesting."

"He sure seems to shake things up whenever he makes an appearance." I can't resist poking him where it must hurt. From what I understand, last time Priest visited, he ordered Z to remain president of this charter, leaving Sway...out in the cold.

"That bitch Valentina always acts like she owns my clubhouse," Tawny grouses.

I raise an eyebrow. "Pretty sure it was never *your* clubhouse to begin with." I turn and settle my gaze on Lilly standing by Z's side in the middle of the room. "And it's definitely not yours now. So, you should chill the fuck out and enjoy the party, sweetheart."

Sway coughs and pounds his fist against his chest. "You weren't kidding about things staying the same."

Serena

I push off the barstool, intending to find Gray. Last I saw him, he was talking to Tawny and Sway. Might as well get it over with.

A firm rough hand shackles around my wrist. I don't need to turn around to know it isn't Gray. He'd never manhandle me so harshly.

I jerk and pull but his hold tightens. Spinning around, I recognize one of the bikers from Virginia.

He grins at me. Handsome, but scary. "Hey, sweetheart. We haven't met before."

Is he dense or insane? Or does the Virginia charter not recognize the importance of a brother's property patch? Wearing one is supposed to mean no one touches me.

Tears sting my eyes. What is it about me that invites people to violate every boundary? Even ones put in place by other people?

Steel spine, Serena.

"Let go of me."

"Aww, come on. Show a brother a good time." He squeezes my wrist harder. "We just had a long ride up here and you're the prettiest thing I've laid eyes on in days."

Cheap compliments like that used to be a potent elixir. A dash of sugar to ease the sourness a man was eager to shove down my throat.

Now, it ticks me off. I'm not that compliant, needy girl anymore.

"Get your hands off me." My voice quivers with old fear. The few times in my life I *did* assert myself, the punishment was quick and cruel. Somehow, I manage to keep my chin lifted and maintain eye contact, though. "*Now.*"

Asserting myself with the women associated with the club is important, but standing up to the men matters more.

"Don't be like that." He flashes a boyishly bumbling smile. "Besides, I've heard you're always down for a good time."

Shame slides over me. People here will always remember me as *that girl.* No matter what I wear or what I do, I'll never escape my club girl past, will I?

With my free hand, I tap the vest. "Are you unable to read? Grinder's my ol' man. He's going to kill you."

"Nah, sweetheart. Brothers share all the time. Those patches look all new and shiny. He won't mind." He winks at me.

"My man does *not* share." I jerk my arm again and this time he releases me.

Then, he's gone.

Just, *poof.* Gone.

"You motherfucker," Gray roars.

I drop my gaze to the floor, where he's straddling the guy, throwing punch after vicious punch.

"Fuck, I was just messing around!"

Punch.

Punch.

Punch.

The sickening thuds tumble through my stomach like spoiled meat. I stagger away. Someone's hands land on my shoulders, pulling me back even farther and I scream, jerking away.

"Shh, Serena. It's okay. It's me," Trinity says gently.

"Are you okay?" Charlotte asks, touching my arm.

The two of them form a protective bubble around me, walking us to the back corner, away from the scuffle.

"What happened?" Hope's voice breaks into our circle. "Serena, are you okay?"

Something about the soft, motherly concern in her voice breaks me. My tiny balloon of courage bursts. Tears run down my cheeks.

"Come here." She wraps me up in a hug while Trinity and Charlotte guard my back.

"I can't believe Pants did that," Trinity whispers. "We spent a lot of time out on the road with him and he was always respectful."

Something about that makes me cry even harder. *I* must be the problem.

"I hope Grinder kicks the shit out of him," Charlotte seethes. "That was ridiculous."

"Wrath's taking his sweet time breaking it up," Trinity adds with a short laugh. "Steer's nowhere in sight."

"Serena, are you okay?" Lilly asks.

I'm too embarrassed to lift my head from Hope's shoulder and face Lilly. Hope squeezes me tighter but whispers something that I can't quite catch.

"Let's go somewhere quieter," Lilly says.

The girls start moving and I have no choice but to let go of Hope and force my feet to move. I keep my head down and eyes averted from the fight. The four women keep close, blocking me from the crowd.

Lilly pulls us into the first room off of the main area, an old bedroom they seem to have converted into a television lounge. "Grab me some ice from the freezer, Trinity," she says.

Keeping her arm around my shoulders, Hope pulls me onto one of the couches with her. "Let me see your wrist."

I hold up my right hand. The one Pants had grabbed with such a punishing grip. A red circle rings it.

"Damn him," Lilly seethes. "I hope Z kicks his ass next."

Charlotte kneels next to me and curls a bag of ice wrapped in a dishcloth around my wrist. I wince and pull back.

"Sorry," Charlotte whispers.

"It's okay. Thank you."

I'd say something sarcastic like they're only protecting me because I'm patched now. But it would be a lie. The last time Shadow had attacked me inside the clubhouse, Z broke it up. Lilly and Charlotte had been there and taken care of me then too.

The last time I'd been attacked in the clubhouse. You'd think I'd learn my lesson and stay the fuck away from motorcycle clubhouses. But *noooo.* Not me. Every old scar I thought had healed, rips open and throbs.

I must be stupider than I look.

Every damn time, I fall for the lies.

CHAPTER TWENTY-FIVE

Grinder

THE SAVAGE BEAST INSIDE ME WOKE WITH A ROAR THE SECOND I SAW Pants with his hand on my woman. It took me a few seconds to make my way across the room. And that's all I needed for the red mist to cloud my vision.

In prison, violence had been a tool I used to survive. Now, it settles over me like a comforting cloak. But it isn't *my* survival at stake. It's Serena's honor and my promise to keep her safe.

I gave her that patch, explaining it meant no one would ever harm her in my club. And a few days later, a brother I share a patch with breaks my vow. That can't go unpunished. The club's own laws don't allow this violation.

Which is why no one stops me from beating Pants bloody.

When he stops trying to block the blows, Wrath finally intervenes.

"All right, Grinder," he says as if he's trying to calm a lion rampaging through the clubhouse. "He's had enough for now."

For now is just a way to get me to ease up. The promise that I'll be able to deliver more punishment later, when we both know I won't be able to go at Pants again without cause. I stand and kick him in the stomach and ribs to finalize my point.

Pants groans and rolls to his side. Still breathing. Pity.

"What the fuck were you thinking, brother?" Ice asks as he leans over Pants. As his president, it'll be up to Ice to discipline his SAA some more.

Pants groans as Ice and two other guys lift his heavy carcass off the floor. One of the club girls scurries over with a roll of paper towels and a bottle of cleaning spray and wipes away spatters of blood.

I watch the action with a detached sense of reality as the adrenaline and fury evaporate from my veins. Breathing hard, I turn toward Wrath. He holds out a towel and wraps it around the knuckles of my right hand. Now that the rage is leaving, pain sets into my fingers.

"Fuck," I mutter, shaking it off. Getting into fights at fifty hurts a hell of a lot more than it did in my twenties.

"Stop moving around and let me look at it," Wrath orders.

"You a fuckin' doctor now?"

"No, but I have some experience with broken bones, ya prick."

"You all right?" Rock asks, joining us at the bar.

"No, I'm fuckin' pissed. What the hell was that?"

"I don't know."

"Where's Serena?"

"The girls took her to a quieter location," Z says, stepping up behind Wrath. "He all right?" he asks.

"*He* is fine," I snap. "Don't talk about me like I ain't sittin' right here."

Z blows out an irritated breath and runs his knuckles over his chest. "Just worried about you, Grumpy."

I shoot a glare at Z. "I told her...I *promised* her that my patch meant no one would pull this shit with her ever again in our clubhouse."

"I know," Z says with apology in his tone. "I'm sorry. I'll talk to Ice as soon as I can."

"Doesn't matter what he says. The damage is done."

I yank my hand out of Wrath's grasp. "Am I free to go, Doc?"

He cocks his head. "Yeah, but I'd readjust that attitude before you see your girl. She's gonna think you're pissed at *her*."

"She doesn't need that, Grinder. Give it a minute," Rock adds.

"Don't fuckin' tell me what my woman needs." I turn but Z's blocking my path. He steps aside with a dramatic sweep of his hand. "First room on the left."

People move the fuck out of my way as I charge the short distance from the bar to the hallway. The first door on the left is closed. I shove it open without knocking.

Four patched ol' ladies are clustered around Serena. Trinity moves to block Serena. Then her gaze lands on me.

"You plannin' to fight me, Trin?" I ask.

"If I had to, yeah."

Damn, I love her fire.

My eyes land on Serena. She's calm now. The beautiful makeup she took such care applying earlier is smeared but there don't seem to be any recent tears. Good thing, or I'd have to go beat on Pants some more.

Hope whispers something in Serena's ear. When Serena nods, Hope pats her leg and stands. "We'll leave you guys." She offers her hand to Lilly and pulls her off the floor.

Charlotte hugs Serena one last time before joining the girls.

On her way past me, Trinity stops and squeezes my arm. "You all right?" she asks in a low voice.

"I'm pissed but yeah." I meet her concerned golden eyes. "Your husband took care of my hands."

"Good." She glances over her shoulder and squeezes my arm one more time. "Serena's made of strong stuff, but she definitely needs you."

"Thank you, Trinity."

She closes the door behind her.

Serena watches me with wary eyes as I approach. Fear flickers over her face. She shrinks against the couch. I know it has nothing to do with me, but it still wounds.

"I'm sorry," she whispers.

Her apology snaps my control and I rush closer, sitting next to her and gathering her in my arms. "What are you sorry about?"

"For whatever I did that brought that on."

"Baby, he just has a death wish. That's got nothing to do with you."

Her eyes widen and she pulls away. "You didn't kill him, did you?"

"No." I chuckle. "He still had a pulse when they dragged him away."

"I'm so—"

"Don't apologize one more time. Tell me exactly what went down."

"I don't know. It all happened so fast." She shakes her head. "He grabbed my arm and said something about not meeting before. I told him to let go. He tried telling me I was pretty and wanted me to show him a good time. I told him to get his hands off me and asked why he was ignoring my patch. Warned him that my ol' man would kill him." Her lashes flutter as she drops her gaze to her lap. "He said something about how he'd heard I'm always down for a good time."

"Hey." I place my finger under her chin and lift her head. "I'm the one who's sorry. I promised you that would never happen if you were wearing my patch."

"It's not your fault. It's mine. There's something wrong with *me*."

"There is *nothing* wrong with you, Serena." Fuck, I'm never bringing her near one of our clubhouses again.

"There is. Don't you get it? Every time you take me to one of these parties, someone will mention my past. You can dress me up however you want, but people remember and will want to test both of us."

Unease trickles through me. Serena warned me about her instinct to run. I can already feel her slipping through my fingers.

I should've punched Pants harder.

"That's not true, Serena." How can I say that with a straight face, though? I thought nothing would happen and it did. The whole fucking world seems to be spinning upside down since I got out.

CHAPTER TWENTY-SIX

Grinder

I'M PULLED FROM SLEEP BY MY PHONE ALERTING ME TO A TEXT.

By the constant beeping, it must be several texts.

"Mmm." Serena sighs and turns over, burying her head under her pillow.

I yank the phone off the nightstand and check.

Z: *Church in ten. Officers only.*

Z: *And you, G.*

Z: *About last night.*

What the fuck more is there to say about last night?

But Z's the president of this clubhouse. I can't yap about showing my brothers respect and then ignore his request.

Me: *I'll be there.*

I set the phone down and turn toward Serena, molding myself against her back. She's so soft and warm, I hate leaving her. Especially after last night.

Fear settles in my gut. That she'll be gone when I return.

"Serena?" I press a kiss against her shoulder, then behind her ear.

"That tickles." She giggles and reaches behind her, plunging her fingers into my hair. "Good morning."

Laughter. Good sign after last night's events. "Good morning, my beautiful buttercup."

"Aww." She sighs and turns, blinking up at me. "You're the sweetest."

"Sweet, huh? Only to you."

"That's okay."

I kiss her forehead. "I love you."

She snuggles up against my chest. "I love you too."

The fear that she might run recedes.

"Baby, do you have any idea how hard it is to get out of bed right now?"

She peers up at me, mischief playing over her lips. "Then don't go."

"I have to. Z summoned me to church."

"Oh." It all must come crashing back. An avalanche of memories from last night slide over her face, obliterating our happy moment.

"It's nothing bad," I reassure her, running my knuckles over her cheek. "Promise me you'll be here when I get back?"

"It's not like I can go anywhere. I rode down with you."

That's not exactly reassuring.

"I'll be here when you get back," she promises.

"Thank you." I kiss her forehead again. "Get some more sleep."

"ALL RIGHT," Z announces, starting the meeting. "Most of you know we had an issue at last night's party. Grinder dealt with it in the manner allowed in our by-laws."

Z's reminder to everyone that I didn't do anything wrong is nice and all. But why? Is Ice planning to ask that I be disciplined?

"Our code is what makes our way of life, our club, and our brotherhood, different from the way civilians live," Z continues.

Jesus Christ, I never expected Z to be one for long speeches.

"Their laws say violence is the wrong solution to a problem. Ours say, in certain circumstances, violence is not only our right, but our duty, in order to protect our loved ones. This is the code we live by."

"Amen, brother!" someone farther down the table shouts.

"Preach!"

"I've invited Ice to sit down with us and discuss." Z sweeps his hand in Ice's direction. "After today, I expect this matter will be closed." Z glances my way and raises an eyebrow.

"I'm willing to listen." After that speech, I don't think I have a choice.

Ice sits forward, placing his elbows on the table. "First, I want to say that we're prepared to offer reparations to you, brother."

"No." I hold up my hand. "I appreciate the offer, but it's not necessary. Cash or blood is how we pay our debts and penalties. I took blood last night. My *only* concern is that this *never* happens again." I shoot a look Z's way. Not that I blame him, but it did happen in his clubhouse.

Ice nods at me. "I've spoken with my SAA and gotten his side—"

"What side was there to get, Ice?" Wrath asks. "A patched brother put his hands on another brother's patched ol' lady. There's no defending that."

"No, there isn't," Ice agrees. "If it's all right with you, Grinder, I'll have him join us and explain."

"Is that okay?" Z asks me.

"Yeah, it's fine. Like I said, I'm done. Puttin' it behind me." It's working my last fucking nerve that they keep acting like I'm an out-of-control wild animal about to attack without cause.

Ice stands and opens the war room door, calling for Pants to join us.

Pants shuffles into the room with his head down and arms tucked close to his sides. I don't take pride or shame in his beat-to-hell face or stiff posture.

It had to happen. And it's his own damn fault.

As he slowly eases his big frame into a chair, a trickle of guilt slides over me. I guess that means prison didn't fully strip me of my humanity. Good to know.

Pants doesn't shy away. He's not a coward. He never would've made it to sergeant-at-arms of any motorcycle club if he was. He faces me—two black eyes, cut cheek, split lip, cracked ribs and all—head-on and looks me in the eye. "I'm sorry, brother."

"What the fuck were you thinking?" Rock asks.

"She's patched plain as fuckin' day," Z adds.

So much for letting me hear an explanation from Pants himself.

I hold up my hands in each direction. "Let him talk." I nod to Pants. "Why'd you do it? You're not new to the patch." I nod at his SAA flash on the front of his cut. "You know what a property patch means."

"Fuck, brother. This is embarrassing." He glances down at his lap. "But I got played."

"How?"

"I know you just got out of the joint. Been inside for a while," Pants says.

"Yeah, so what?" His earlier statement registers in my brain. "*Who* played you?"

"Spit it out," Ice growls.

"Tawny. I know she's an ol' lady from way back. Been running into her at club events for years. She came up to me when we first got here. Said she was worried about you. Told me she and you have history…"

"The fuck we do," I mutter.

"I didn't know." He shrugs, then winces. "She seemed sincere. Said you wouldn't take her word for it because of your shared past, but the girl you gave your patch to was bad news. Claimed she used to whore around here and—"

"Watch your fucking mouth," I warn.

Pants looks to Ice, then Z, but doesn't find shelter in their hard expressions.

"She asked me to test your girl. Said you didn't know any better because you were locked up for so long and this girl was tricking you—"

"You didn't think his own club would be looking out for him?" Wrath asks.

"Do I look like I need a dad here?" I snarl at Wrath.

"Nah, but I wanna play anyway." I don't need to look his way to know he's grinning like a smug asshole.

"It got to me," Pants continues, ignoring our outbursts. "You're a brother. Been through some shit. I didn't want some chick taking advantage of you." He gestures toward Z. "I know Tawny's the old prez's wife. Figured she was solid."

"A solid troublemaker," Z grumbles.

"I didn't realize. She said some other stuff." Pants hangs his head. "About your girl that I'm not gonna repeat at the table."

"For fuck's sake." I'm gonna strangle Tawny when I see her.

"You're right. It was dumb." Pants holds out his hands like he's pleading for mercy. "I should've known better."

I stare at him for a long minute, studying each micro-expression. He seems sincere. Takes honor to admit in front of all your brothers that you did something so fucking stupid.

"I'm sorry, Grinder. And if you allow me to later, I'll apologize to her too."

A growl bursts out of my throat at the thought of him going near Serena again. Even if it is to apologize.

"Or you can tell her," Pants adds.

"Are we good here?" Ice asks.

"Yeah, we're good."

"Can you give us a minute, Ice?" Z asks.

"Sure." He taps Pants on the shoulder.

Pants stands and leans over the table. I get up and meet him halfway to shake his hand. "Thanks for listening, brother," he says.

"Thanks for being honest."

He nods and the two of them leave.

Z waits until the door closes then turns my way. "Thank you, Grinder."

"For?"

"Being reasonable."

"I'm still fucking furious." I scan the length of the table, looking each downstate officer straight in the eye. "This better not happen again. You all might think I'm senile—"

"No one thinks that, Grinder," Steer protests.

"Shut your mouth." I glare at him until he nods that he's going to be quiet. "I'm only saying this once, so listen the fuck up. Take some notes or whatever the fuck you need to do to keep this in your brains. I *know* Serena used to hang around here. We've talked about it." I shoot a glare at Z. "I also know why she *stopped* coming to the clubhouse. If it wasn't for me, she wouldn't set foot in this place ever again. But I *promised* her she'd be safe."

"She's safe here," Hustler says. "It was a misunderstanding."

"Are you fucking kidding me?"

"What?" He casts a nervous glance around the table but when no one comes to his aid he sinks down in his chair. "Sorry."

"I'm not gonna bother with any 'back in my day' speeches because enough of you fucks sittin' in this room have been around since then. You know this shit doesn't fly. And you newer fucks never should've been voted in if you didn't respect the property patch."

"What are you asking of us, Gray?" Rock asks.

"I'm not asking for shit. I'm *telling* every brother at this table that this ends now."

"Tawny's gotta go," Jigsaw says.

"We can't off a brother's ol' lady," Steer argues.

"Who said *kill* her, you dumb fuck?" Jiggy shouts.

"Easy, brother," Z warns.

"Don't *easy brother* me. This isn't the first time she's pulled a stunt like this," Jigsaw argues. "Sway ain't our president anymore. There's no fuckin' reason for her to be here. She needs to be banned from the clubhouse. Access denied. Permission revoked."

"I agree with Jigsaw," Dex says.

"No one asked you, upstate road captain," Hustler sneers.

"I, your downstate VP, agree," Rooster says, raising his hand.

"Big surprise," Steer mutters. "You and Jiggy tag-team everything."

"The fuck did you say?" Rooster jumps out of his chair and leans across the table. "Wanna repeat that?"

"All right. Enough." Z slams his gavel against the table.

Rooster drops into his chair, still fuming.

"You can't put this all on Tawny. Pants knows better," Steer argues.

"What's your fucking deal?" Teller asks Steer.

"Yeah," Murphy chimes in. "Why are you defending that bitch so hard?"

"Great, I was waiting for the lumberjack twins to join in." Steer throws his hands in the air. "It's a matter of respect."

"Except, time after time, she's disrespected our ol' ladies," Wrath says in his deadly calm voice. "And she got away with it because Sway was your president. He's not anymore. And she's a liability."

Z raps his gavel against the table several more times. "Do I need to crack skulls with this thing?"

"Sorry, Prez," Steer mutters.

"Because of Sway's shooting, the way he got booted out of this very chair I'm sittin' in, and because Tawny seemed to have mellowed out, I wasn't going to have a talk with Sway." Z pauses and glances up and down the table. "But just like a snake ain't gonna grow legs and walk, she's never gonna grow a conscience and stop playing these petty games. Lilly's been having issues with her." He lifts his chin at me. "Nothing like what went on last night."

"Give her time," Jigsaw mutters.

"I had a very specific conversation with her last night," I say before Steer and Jiggy get into it again. "She promised me she wasn't going to start shit with Serena. For my sake." I launch into a phony high-pitched imitation of Tawny's voice. "Because she was supposedly so *worried* about me while I was inside."

Rock snorts.

"That makes it even worse," Rooster says. "She fuckin' lied to a brother's face."

"All right. I can't remember the last time we told a brother his ol' lady wasn't allowed in a clubhouse. How do we want to do this?" Z asks his officers. "Officer vote or bring it to the whole table?"

I raise my hand. "Uh, I realize I'm not a member of *this* charter, but I'd really rather not have this situation talked about more than it already has been."

"Bro, everyone saw you pound the snot out of Pants last night," Hustler says.

"I get what you're concerned about, brother." Z nods at me. "I'm going to talk to Sway first. Give him a presidential order. His wife is banned from visiting the clubhouse. If he pushes back, we'll take it to a club vote and make him sit through it."

"That's fair." Steer jerks his chin at Z. "Man-to-man conversation. We owe him that much."

Z's side-eye says he doesn't feel he owes Sway a damn thing. He blows out a long, slow breath. "Good, I'm glad you feel that way, Steer. As my SAA, you're going to join the conversation. That way he won't feel like it's a personal attack."

"No problem, Prez."

"Is this acceptable to you, Grinder?" Z asks.

Tawny's been a fixture in the club ever since I can remember. I don't take pleasure in her gettin' banned but it's what needs to happen. "Yeah, I'm okay with it. Thank you for taking it seriously, Z."

"You got it." His mouth turns down. "I know we all like to fuck around and get rowdy. That's what the clubhouse is for. But I can't stand having any of our girls treated like that. It's not what we're about. And I don't want Serena thinking she's not welcome or safe here."

"Thank you."

"Anyone know if they're upstairs?" Z asks.

Hustler shakes his head. "No, they left right after everything went down last night."

"Figures."

"You want me to call Sway and ask him to come by?" Steer asks.

"No. I don't want to give him a head's up that anything's going on. They're supposed to be here later. We'll do it then." Z flicks his hand toward the door. "Everyone's free to go."

Jigsaw squeezes behind me and rests his hand on the back of my chair. "You need anything, brother?"

"I'm good." I tip my head so I can see the tall fucker. "Thanks for having my back."

"You know it." He holds out his fist and I tap my knuckles against it.

Rooster stops by for a fist-bump as well.

Eventually everyone stops by to have a quick word and show support.

Then Rock, Z, Wrath, and I are the only ones left.

Rock squeezes Z's shoulder. "I'm not going to say I'm proud of you, but I can't think of another president who would've handled that better."

"Thanks, brother." Z taps the side of his head. "I can think of one. You."

"Nah, he would've lost his shit." Wrath jerks his chair toward Steer's now-empty seat. "The way he kept running his mouth."

"And yet, I seem to have infinite patience for *you*," Rock says.

"I don't say stupid shit like that."

"True," Rock agrees, then focuses his attention on me. "Serena all right today?"

"Yeah, she seemed to be."

As Rock and Wrath head for the door, Z stops me with a hand on my arm. "Are you at peace with this outcome?"

I blow out an annoyed breath. "Best outcome possible, honestly. I appreciated Pants being honest about how it went down. Not many brothers would admit a woman put him up to it."

"He's solid from what I've heard, so I was surprised he did that." He glances down at the table. "Rock and I were talking about having some refresher meetings before these bigger parties."

"What are you gonna do, have prospects hand out a rule book to every guest who walks in the front door?"

"Maybe." He flashes his dimples, then turns serious again. "Seriously, is Serena okay? You worried about her runnin' on you again?"

I let out another long, annoyed sigh. I seem to be forever destined to have everyone in my business. "She promised me she wouldn't leave."

"Well, she rode down with you, so technically, she can't leave."

"Yeah, she pointed that out too. Didn't really give me the warm fuzzies."

"Sorry. I know things are...precarious."

"Why are you so tuned into this, Angus?" I pat his chest. "I appreciate the concern, but you realize I'm a grown-ass man, right?"

"Yes, Grumpy," he answers with a healthy dose of sarcasm. "I just..." He taps his fingers against the back of his chair. "I didn't get to meet Chance until he was almost three."

"How? You and Lilly seem so—"

"It's a long story that I don't want to get into. Her reasons were valid." He pierces me with a warning stare to let me know he won't tolerate me disparaging his wife. "I didn't know she was pregnant, but I wish I'd tried harder to find her ass instead of letting pride get in my way."

"Serena knows I have no problem tracking her down. I've missed enough things in life, I'm not missing out on any more."

"Good. If I can do something, don't hesitate to ask."

"You did everything I could want you to do, brother. Lilly too. I really appreciate her going out of her way to look after Serena."

The corner of his mouth quirks. "She's always liked Serena. I think she's *really* happy you two are together."

"That's great. I'm proud to provide entertainment for everyone."

He smirks at my sarcasm. I hold out my hand and he takes it, yanking me in for a quick hug instead of a simple handshake. "You don't have to keep worrying about me, Z. I'm doing fine. Adjusting better than I expected because I have the club behind me. I know you keep calling me grumpy, but I hope you know how much I appreciate everything."

"Good." He pats my back one more time. "Touchy-feely time is over. Go get your girl and give her the good news."

Serena

Fake smiles may fool a crowd, but they'll never ease your pain.

I FALL BACK ASLEEP after Gray leaves. Sometime later, I wake up again but he's still not back.

An uneasy sensation rolls through my stomach. I haven't had any morning sickness yet, but I hurry to the bathroom and retch.

When my stomach stops its tilt-a-whirl impression, I sit on the floor, putting my back against the wall to catch my breath. "I'm not a fan of puking first thing in the morning, baby," I whisper, rubbing my stomach. "Let's go back to the no morning sickness thing, please."

Groaning, I pick myself up off the floor and shuffle to the sink. I flip on the taps and run my wrists under the cool flow of water for a few seconds, then lean over and splash my face. I find my toothbrush and scrub the foul taste from my mouth.

My wrist aches and I stop to check it. Last night shoots to the front of my mind. A few finger-shaped bruises mar my skin, but otherwise, I'm fine. I don't remember much after Grayson brought me to our room last night. Numb, I stood in the shower and scrubbed all my makeup off, then he tucked me into bed and I fell asleep with Gray's warm, protective body curled around mine.

I peer in the mirror. "Not too bad," I murmur to myself. My eyes are a little red and circles shade the skin underneath. Nothing some concealer won't hide. More importantly, after such a degrading event last night, I don't have the urge to do something self-destructive today.

Progress.

I smile at my reflection, hoping it will improve my mood, but I look like an idiot.

"Serena?" Gray calls.

"In here." I quickly run a brush through my hair.

Gray appears in the doorway. "How do you feel today?"

"A little morning sickness, actually."

His face pinches. "Normal pregnancy thing or stress from last night?"

Huh. I hadn't really thought it could be related to anything but being pregnant. "Normal, I think."

"Let me know if you feel worse or want to go to the doctor."

"It's nothing that serious, Gray. I should probably drink some water, though. I have a bit of a headache."

He steps away and I follow him into the bedroom. The mini fridge in the corner was stocked with water bottles when we arrived. He pulls one out and hands it to me.

"Thanks." Without taking my eyes off him, I swallow a few sips, then set the bottle down. "So, what was the emergency this morning?"

"Z called the officers to the table."

Dread settles in my stomach. "Please tell me it wasn't about...not about what happened last night." I grab my water bottle and stagger to the bed.

"Of course it was," he snaps. "Ice wanted to know if I'd give Pants a chance to explain himself. Offered me money—"

"Money? Why?"

"It's in our rules." He cocks his head. "You must've heard that before? Infractions are paid by cash or blood. Sometimes both. I declined the money since I beat the hell out of Pants last night."

"No wonder no one stopped you." Knowing how primal some of the guys can be, blood is probably the preferred method of payment.

"Right. People saw what happened. No one was going to stop me." He pauses and sits next to me, taking my hand in his. "First, I want to apologize to you, buttercup."

"Apologize to me, why?"

"When I gave you your patch, I told you it meant no one would ever do something like that to you in one of our clubhouses. I broke that promise."

"You didn't break your promise. Pants did." I think about our conversation. "Besides, you *also* swore you'd beat the crap out of anyone who touched me while I was wearing it and you certainly did that."

His brow furrows. "Did that bother you? I don't like that you saw that side of me."

The emotion in his voice squeezes the air from my lungs. I shake my head until I can form some words. "No, it didn't bother me."

"I'd never hurt *you*."

"I know that." In every other bad relationship I've had, there was always some seed of doubt or red flag early on that I dismissed. A gut reaction that my brain and heart ignored. I've never gotten any of those vibes from Gray. Not once. "So, what was Pants' excuse?"

His jaw tightens and his gaze darts to our closed door. "Tawny put him up to it."

Harsh, dark laughter rips from my throat. "Of *course* she did. I should've known it was her when he said he heard I was always down for a good time. I assumed one of the brothers told him that, but dammit, it's exactly the kind of thing she'd do."

Pure fury burns through my veins. It can't be healthy to hate someone as much as I hate that woman.

"I'm sorry. I had a talk with her last night. She promised me she'd behave."

"Must've been after she hassled me," I grumble, hating that he spoke to her at all.

"What did she say to you?"

"The usual." Heat sears my cheeks. I don't want to repeat any of it. "So how did a big, scary biker get talked into doing Scrawny Tawny's dirty work?"

The corners of his mouth twitch. "Apparently, she implied I'm too old and feeble to know when someone's using me. So she suggested he 'test' your loyalty."

"Oh, for fuck's sake. It's like she never matured past high school."

"That's Tawny." He slides his hand over mine. "In hindsight, he's embarrassed he fell for it."

"He should be," I grumble, not at all in a forgiving mood. "So, he got his ass kicked in front of everyone last night *and* copped to his poor judgment in front of all the officers this morning?"

"Of upstate and downstate."

He'll be returning to Virginia with a bruised body *and* ego. "Good."

"That takes care of Pants. But Tawny still needs to be punished."

My eyes widen. As much as I hate the woman, I don't want Gray to beat her up. Maybe tie her to a post out back, drizzle her with honey and leave her for the bugs, though.

"What's that evil smile on your face, buttercup?" Gray asks.

"Nothing." I push the vision of Tawny being consumed by mice and ants away. "So what's her punishment? Is Sway going to cut off her Botox funds?"

"No, she's being banned from the clubhouse."

Banned. Did I hear that right? "How are they going to do that? She's like the wicked witch of downstate. She'll probably use her broom to fly right over that gate outside."

He snorts. "Z and Steer will deliver the news to Sway. It'll be his responsibility to keep her away. But everyone will know she's not allowed on the premises."

Banned. Damn, Tawny's going to be pissed. She treats this place like her personal palace. And having everyone in the club know she's been banned. That's even worse for a bully with attention whore syndrome.

"Do I need to worry she's going to retaliate against me in some way?"

"Absolutely not."

We'll see about that. "The girls around here won't know what to do without being bullied and harassed by her."

"From the sounds of it, they haven't banned many ol' ladies over the years. It was common before I went inside…but that was usually so brothers didn't get caught with—"

"Their side-pieces?"

"Well, yeah."

I squint, then blurt out the worst possible question. "Did you do that when you were married to Rose? Fool around with club girls when you were at the clubhouse? The old clubhouse was next to the strip club, right? You must've had access to—"

"Never. Before she and I met, sure." His eyes take on a distant look that doesn't ease my fears. "But once we were together, I was too consumed with her to worry about anyone else."

Consumed with her. I could've happily never heard him talk about his ex that way.

"Sorry, I shouldn't have asked. It's none of my—"

"Serena, you can always ask me whatever you want. If it's club stuff—"

"You can't tell me, I know."

"I'll tell you what I can." He stares over my shoulder for a few seconds. "And don't ask me about my time inside. I really don't want to relive any of that."

"Grayson," I sigh and lean into him, wrapping my arms around his middle. "You can always talk to me about it, if you want to, though."

"Thank you, buttercup."

CHAPTER TWENTY-SEVEN

Grinder

"Do you want to join everyone for breakfast?" I suggest after delivering the news about Tawny's banishment. Being so close to her, I can't help but lean in and kiss her neck. "Or we can stay here. I'll ask someone to bring us food."

She sighs and melts against my body. "Here is good." She trails her lips over my cheek to my neck.

A shiver of pleasure runs over my skin.

"Take this off," she whispers, tugging at my shirt. She pulls away and slips off her T-shirt.

"You're so beautiful," I murmur, studying every bare inch. I reach for her breast, barely flicking my thumb over her nipple before she pulls away.

"Shirt off. Then you can touch me as much as you want."

"Feeling bossy today, huh?" I slip off my cut, then yank my shirt over my head. "Better?"

"Much." Graceful, like a ballerina, she lifts herself and settles into my lap, looping her arms around my neck. Her fingers twine into my hair, sending a pleasurable, shivery sensation traveling down my spine.

"Mmm, this is what I wanted." She presses her breasts against my chest. She's so damn soft and warm against me. I stroke my fingers over her sides and she giggles. "That tickles."

"Wasn't trying to tickle you."

A quick *thump, thump, thump* rattles the door to our room.

"What the fuck?" I growl, pulling away from her.

Serena laughs softly and presses more kisses against my chest. "This weekend *was* supposed to be a party in your honor."

"I socialized." I lean in and kiss her, then untangle myself from her embrace. "I want time alone with my woman, though."

She rolls over, pulling the blanket with her. "I'll be waiting."

The banging starts again. "G, hurry up!"

I fling the door open. "What?"

"We gotta go. Grab your shit," Rooster shouts in my face. He drags Shelby into my room behind him and slams the door shut.

"What? Why? What's wrong?" I fire off questions but I'm already sweeping my things off the dresser and stuffing my wallet in my pocket. Thank fuck I hadn't unpacked my bag.

Serena's already up and gathering her clothes.

"Got your wallet?" Rooster asks me. "Anything that identifies you?"

"Yeah." I pat my pocket. "What's going on?"

"Cops are at the gate with a warrant to search the place." He wraps his arm around Shelby.

"Shit." I stab my fingers through my hair. "I can't be here."

"No shit, that's why we're moving you." He glances down at Shelby. "She can't be here either. Tabloids will tear her to shreds."

She opens her mouth.

"Don't argue with me, chickadee," Rooster grumbles.

More knocking at the door. Rooster flings it open.

"Are they ready?" Jigsaw asks. "We gotta go now."

"Ready." Serena wraps her hand around mine and slings her bag over her shoulder.

Rooster turns and that's when I realize he's got a pink flamingo backpack over his shoulder. "Nice travel gear, brother." I slap his back.

Shelby giggles and takes his hand. "It's mine." Her gaze lands on

Jigsaw. "Aw, Jiggy, you grabbed my guitar for me, thank you." She holds out her hands for it, but he motions for her to keep moving.

"Fuck knows how long you'll be down there, you might need to entertain everyone."

"That ain't funny." She scowls. "I gotta be in the studio Monday."

"We'll get rid of 'em. Don't worry," Rooster promises.

Rooster and Jigsaw take the lead, hauling us down one long hallway after another, then down two flights of metal stairs. The scent of chlorine stings my nose and humidity clings to the air.

"Aw, you know I can't swim," Shelby says.

"No time for swimming." Rooster moves faster, slamming into another metal door and leading us down more stairs.

The air cools and an earthier smell surrounds us. Eventually we come to another tunnel. Rooster moves through it quickly, stopping at another metal door. He punches in a code and the door slides open.

"Looky here. A big ol' doomsday bunker." Shelby peers at the low ceiling and studies our surroundings as we enter. "Who knew."

"Nothin' ruffles her, huh?" I ask Rooster.

"Not much." He pulls her closer. "All right. We got rooms here." He points to the left.

Looks more like prison cells or interrogation rooms. This is more than doomsday bunker. It's the club's murder chamber.

"Sleeping bags in that locker." Jigsaw taps a large metal cabinet and a metallic echo fills the air.

The hallway opens into a larger room with dirty, stained tile. A few chairs, a big-screen television, electronics, and a collection of movies.

"I'd keep the noise and power usage to a minimum," Rooster says, eyeing the television. "We've never really tested how soundproof it is."

"So this isn't a regular occurrence?" I ask.

"This? Not since I've been a member here." Rooster swivels his head between Shelby and me. "I gotta go up there and help Z."

"Go, brother. Thanks for looking out for me."

"Last thing we want is you going back inside." He rests his hand on my shoulder. "Cops shouldn't be able to find their way down here, but I can't guarantee it."

Nothing in life is ever guaranteed. "I took the risk. I knew when I came to visit that it violated my parole, Rooster. If I get caught, I get caught. I ain't gonna blame anyone but myself." The last thing I want is him to worry about me when he needs to help protect the club.

His mouth turns down and his troubled eyes search the room. "I'll be all right." I glance at Shelby and Serena sitting at the table playing with a deck of cards. "Looks like the girls are already entertaining each other."

"There's some food in the kitchen," Jigsaw says. "A bathroom that way." He jerks his thumb over his shoulder. "No cell reception down here. There's a weapons locker, but—"

"Yeah, I ain't gonna put the girls at risk to go out like some cult leader," I assure them. "Max I'm facing is a year back inside. Ain't worth getting riddled with bullets over."

Rooster nods stiffly. "All right. Let me talk to Shelby real quick, then we gotta go."

"Come 'ere, chickadee," he calls out as he strides toward her. She jumps up and hurries over to him. The two of them talk quietly for a few minutes. When he picks her up and she wraps her legs around him, I decide to give them privacy and join Serena in the kitchen.

Her anxious face punches me in the chest. "It's gonna be all right, buttercup."

"The clubhouse has never been searched that I know of." She bites her lip. "I remember the cops coming to question Murphy once. But Sway wouldn't let them inside. Murphy left with them."

"Shit happens. Z wouldn't let anything incriminating be left around. I trust him."

Her worried eyes meet mine. "This won't look bad for Z, though, right? Sway won't try to use it against him, will he? Isn't your national president supposed to visit? Z's done a lot to fix this club up. It's not fair—" She bites her lip again. "Never mind. I know that's all club business."

"Come here." I wrap my arm around her and drag her chair closer, then pull her into my lap. "I love that you're worried about that and I love how much respect you've got for Z. Whatever happens, we'll all work through it."

"Okay." She rests her head against my shoulder and her body finally relaxes.

Rooster pops into the kitchen. "I'll be back as soon as I can."

"Thanks, brother."

He leans over the table and bumps my fist before taking off.

Shelby sighs and drops into the chair across from me. She scoops up the scattered cards and I realize these aren't playing cards. At least no playing cards I've ever seen. They've got elaborate drawings and shiny particles that catch the light. Little pieces of artwork.

"Looks like we've got time to kill." Shelby shuffles the cards and grins at me. "How about I do a reading for ya, Grinder?"

"A reading?"

"Tarot cards? No one's ever read them for ya?"

"No."

"I'll go," Serena volunteers.

"Okie dokey." Shelby grins and shuffles the cards faster.

"Oh wow, your ring is so pretty," Serena says, reaching for Shelby's left hand.

She sets the cards down and holds out her hand. "Rooster did good picking it, right? Somehow he knew moonstone would be a better engagement ring for me than a diamond."

"It still has plenty of diamonds surrounding it," Serena chuckles. "It's really beautiful. I love that it's so different."

Well, fuck. It never occurred to me Serena might want something other than a diamond engagement ring. I can't think of a way to ask her that won't alert her that I'm planning to propose, though, so I remain quiet and absorb what I can from their conversation.

"Have you seen one of those morganite rings in rose gold? So pretty." Serena's voice takes on a dreamy tone and my ears perk up. "Pink on pink with diamonds as the accent instead of the main show."

"Oh, I *love* morganite." Shelby tilts her head. "Not just because they're close to my name. They're supposed to attract an abundance of love to the wearer."

"That's neat. I didn't know that."

"Pink sapphire would probably make a nicer engagement ring than morganite, though. Durable. Oh! You know who has the prettiest sapphire engagement ring?" Shelby's voice lowers. "Mallory. Chaser's wife. Have you met her?"

"I don't think so."

Jesus Christ, I remember meeting Mallory not long after Chaser slipped that ring on her finger. My gaze strays to Shelby and Serena. These two weren't even born when that went down.

Fuck, I'm old.

Serena

If Grayson and I had to be trapped in an underground bunker for hours and hours, I'm glad it's with Shelby. She's bubbly and has tons of stories to share about touring and singing. She's really into Tarot cards and even though I'm suspicious, I agree to let her do a reading for me.

"Here, hold these for a moment. Try to clear your mind and center yourself. If you have a burning question, ask it. Or if you're just open to guidance, sit with that."

Feeling a little silly, I close my eyes and try to clear my mind. But the more I try to clear it, the more I keep worrying that I look stupid or Gray will think I'm an idiot.

"Breathe," Shelby says gently. "Focus on your breathing."

The reminder helps and I release my anxiety. "Okay." I open my eyes and hand her the deck.

"We'll do a simple past, present, and future spread," Shelby says, expertly shuffling the cards.

She lays three cards on the table in front of us from left to right. "Past." She flips over the card on the left. "Eight of Swords," Shelby murmurs. I can't tell if that's good or bad. But when I drop my gaze to the image representing the eight of swords, I'm stabbed in the chest with the pain of my past. Emotions, events, the people from my childhood who never protected me—all of it seems reflected in the image of the woman on the card. Bound, blindfolded, and trapped by the eight swords surrounding her. The gray background reminds me of the misery I felt when I thought there was no way I'd ever break free. An overwhelming sense of being powerless and helpless clings to me.

"Serena?" Shelby's soft voice pushes away the awful memories. "Are you ready?"

I'd been so wrapped up in the first card, I hadn't noticed she flipped over the other two. "Sure." I force some cheer into my voice. "Sure."

She taps the first card. "Eight of Swords. In general it means feeling trapped or victimized. Or that you feel powerless to change your situation."

My eyes burn. "That's what it reminded me of."

"Well, the good news is, see these spaces here? If she removes the blindfold, she can free herself and take back her power."

"Or find it," I whisper.

"Sure, that too," she answers quickly.

I seem to be freaking her out. This was supposed to be an entertaining way to pass the time in a weird situation and I'm sucking all the fun right out of it.

"The present, Queen of Cups," Shelby continues, smoothing over the awkward moment. "I like this one and don't see it a lot. It can represent seeing yourself in a new light. Trusting your inner voice. Thinking with your heart and using your intuition. Or she can guide you to seek help from those around you, allowing you to focus on your well-being first so that you can help others."

Gray lets out this knowing *hmm* sound. I flick my gaze his way and his mouth slides into a *told-you-so* smile.

The corners of Shelby's mouth twitch. "It can also mean your caring and kind nature helps to anchor and deepen relationships."

"That sounds right," Gray says, sliding his hand over the table and resting it on mine.

Shelby chuckles and moves on to the next card. "The future." She stares at the card for a minute. "The Empress is one of my favorites." Shelby taps the card. "Mother Earth. She represents unconditional love and abundance. Also," Shelby winks, "sensuality. For the future she could represent love, harmony, and fertility."

I almost choke.

"So quite positive if y'all are planning to make some babies in the future."

Gray sits back, laughing, while I stare at the card that depicts a goddess archetype with long, flowing hair.

"Sorry. I didn't mean to be rude," Shelby says, quickly collecting the cards.

"No, it's fine," I say, reaching for my cards before she scoops them up. "Can I write these down?"

"Oh! Sure. I'll write it down for you. *Phew.* I always worry I'm gonna poke a sore spot or something, so I try to give a general reading, you know?"

"No, it was good. Thank you."

She beams at me and reaches for her backpack, pulling out a small purple notebook. "Rooster thought I was bananas when I told him I read cards, and don't you know the motherclucker can be more intuitive in figuring them out than I am sometimes?" She shakes her head and flips through her notebook until she finds a clean page.

Gray rumbles with laughter. "That doesn't surprise me. He's a thoughtful one."

"He sure is," Shelby gushes. "Makes my little heart pitter-pat every time I see his big, bearded face." Her smile fades and she glances at the door. "Y'all think they're okay up there?"

"They'll be all right." Gray's authoritative tone is oddly reassuring, given we haven't heard from anyone in over an hour now.

I hate even thinking it, but I'm so grateful Gray's down here with us instead of upstairs possibly being arrested and sent back to prison. If Rooster hadn't gotten us out of the clubhouse in time…No, I don't even want to go there. We're safe. Gray's fine.

"I hate hiding down here and leaving him," Shelby says. "But,

Lordy, I got dragged to hell and back for photos of me at a strip club down in Tennessee. I don't wanna know what those stupid gossip sites would say—well, whatever. It's fine." She nods at me. "Before ya ask, it was one of the MC's strip clubs. Rooster needed to pay them a visit. Not my idea."

I hold up my hands. "No judgment from me."

Another couple of hours slip by. My stomach rumbles. Damn, I never had a chance to eat breakfast.

Gray opens the cabinets and searches for food. "It really is a doomsday bunker. They've got a lot of MRE packaged food stuff. Some cans of tuna."

"I can't eat tuna."

"Let's save that for a last resort. Don't wanna stink up the whole place," Shelby adds.

Gray sorts through more canned goods, stacking them all on the counter with a metallic *click, click, click.* "I guess that rules out sardines in tomato sauce."

Shelby's nose crinkles. "I'm allergic to tomatoes, so I'm out on that one too."

"Peanut butter?" Gray holds up two containers. "Canned peaches?"

"Dibs!" I shout.

Shelby laughs. "Who stocked this pantry?"

"There's a huge bag of rice, but I'm not sure if we want to test the stove yet. Some cans of beans." Gray sets a few more items on the counter.

"Ooo my," Shelby sings. "This is a tight space for a bunch of bikers to be holed up livin' off beans and rice."

I double over, laughing until my stomach hurts. "You're killing me."

"What? It's true."

We end up snacking on peanut butter, crackers, and peaches.

"Not a bad meal," Shelby declares, munching on a saltine.

"I ate so many meals of peanut butter and crackers as a kid, it's pretty much comfort food for me," I admit.

"You gotta come visit me in Texas, my momma will cook you some real comfort food."

A small prick of jealousy sticks in my side. My mom wasn't a fan of cooking or comforting. "Are you and your mom close?"

"Oh yeah. She's a hella overprotective stage mom. Kinda had to be. It was just the two of us for a long time." She takes a small bite of a peach. "Pain in my butt sometimes, but I love her. She's supposed to come up and visit soon. Hopefully you'll get to meet her."

"I'd like that. Is she coming to help you plan the wedding?" I nod to her engagement ring.

"Shoot, we probably oughta start working on that, huh?" Her smile falters. "Honestly, I'm not sure where to have it. Tradition says bride's home but we're not exactly traditional. I don't have lots of family and Rooster does, so having it here makes more sense."

"What about somewhere in between?"

She brightens again. "We thought about doing it at the Deadbranch charter in Tennessee since we spent some time there. Dawson offered us his ranch too, but I don't think he realizes what having a couple hundred bikers on his property will mean."

"Dawson…as in *Dawson Roads*? The singer?"

"That's the one." She licks peanut butter from her spoon.

The way she casually mentions her friendship with the biggest country music artist like it's no big deal reminds me that I'm nowhere near Shelby's league.

"You'll figure it out," I say lamely.

"We will." She stands and clears the table. "Right now, I've been happy to help Charlotte with some of *her* planning. At least I'll have a clue when I get to mine."

After that, Shelby wanders into the main area to search the stacks of DVDs.

"Are you okay, buttercup?" Gray's eyes are full of concern. "I'm so sorry about this."

"This isn't your fault. I'm fine." I tilt my head toward the door. "I like Shelby."

"Yeah, she's a good bunkmate."

"Oo! Serena!" Shelby shouts. "They have *Clueless*. Did you ever see this?"

"It's one of my favorites!" I yell back.

"I found popcorn…I think."

Laughing, Gray nods for me to go join her. "I'll be there in a minute."

Shelby's curled up on one end of the couch with a blanket and a barrel-sized tin of popcorn. "This mighta been a mistake. Tastes like it's been here a while," she says, passing the tin to me.

I grab a handful of cheesy popcorn. It has the texture of Styrofoam but the salty cheese dust isn't too bad.

"So, tell me more about your makeup channel." Shelby pauses the DVD. "On the road, I have a makeup person. I absolutely adore her. But when I try doing some fancier looks on my own, I end up looking like a drunk toddler who got into the glitter jar."

"I'd love to give you some tips. I didn't bring any of my makeup with me though."

"I'd love that! Next time we hang out, maybe?"

"Sure." It's on the tip of my tongue to ask if she'd let me film it for my channel, but that seems really rude, and I don't want to take advantage of her.

We're close to the end of the movie when there's a heavy metal clink from the hallway. Shelby pauses the movie and both of us sit up. Gray slashes his hand in the air, motioning for us to stay quiet and not move. He creeps toward the hallway and disappears.

"If it was one of the guys, they'd announce themselves, right?" Shelby whispers to me.

"I guess."

Voices murmur from the hallway and heavy footsteps hurry toward us.

"We're clear, chickadee," Rooster's big voice booms. A second later he rounds the corner. Shelby launches herself off the couch and runs to him.

"Logan! I was so worried about you!" she squeals.

"I'm fine. Club's fine. Lot of cleanup to do, though."

"They wreck the place?" Gray asks.

"Oh yeah. There's a few issues. Z's calling the club's lawyer to get it taken care of."

Shelby hugs Rooster tighter. "Is Jiggy okay?"

"Yeah. Just picking up his room."

"Think we're clear to come upstairs?" Gray asks.

"I think so. They didn't find what they wanted. They were pissed but wasn't much else they could do after they wrecked the place."

Rooster helps us tidy up the bunker before leading us back upstairs to the clubhouse. The pool area seems undisturbed. But once we reach the main floor, the place is ransacked.

Walls have holes hacked into them with splinters of wood paneling and insulation littering the floor. Photos have been ripped off the walls, frames smashed and shattered. We step gingerly over broken glass and sharp metal pieces.

"Lordy, would you look at this mess?" Shelby says under her breath. "What the hell were they lookin' for?"

Rooster grunts but doesn't answer.

Wrath's standing in a doorway holding up a door while Trinity helps him guide it where it needs to go.

We stop at our bedroom door where a black boot print indicates someone kicked it in. The frame is splintered but at least the door is still attached to its hinges.

Gray squeezes my shoulder. "Go check your stuff. I'm going to give Wrath a hand."

"Okay."

Shelby hugs me tight. "Thanks for keeping me sane down there," she whispers against my ear.

I swallow hard and hug her back. "You too."

"We'll finish *Clueless* together one day soon."

My lips curve up. "It's a date." I lift my gaze to Rooster's worried eyes. "Thanks for...thanks for getting us out in time." I glance at the rubble around us. "They seemed hellbent on destruction so I'm sure they would've made a big deal if they found Gray here."

"No doubt." Rooster holds out his fist to me. Laughing, I tap his knuckles with my own. Then he takes Shelby's hand and they head down the hallway.

Our room must not have looked "lived in" enough to whoever busted inside. The destruction isn't as severe. The covers are torn off the bed and the mattress askew. Drawers from the dresser, nightstands, and desk are all yanked out on the floor. But the makeup and hair stuff I left on the bathroom counter are undisturbed. My dress from last night still swings from its hanger in the closet, although my heels that I'd also left in the closet have been tossed into the middle of the room.

I work to get the drawers picked up and where they belong.

"What are you doing, buttercup?" Gray asks from behind me. "You shouldn't be lifting anything." He hurries to my side, taking the awkward but not heavy dresser drawer from my hands.

"It's an empty drawer. I'm fine." I point to the mattress. "I wanted to get that off the floor but definitely can't pick it up on my own."

He looks around the room. "How bad was it?"

"Nothing like the rest of the place. They must've thought it was just some chick staying here and moved on." I point to my dress, then tilt my head toward the bathroom. "My makeup and hair stuff weren't even touched."

"That's good." He jerks his thumb over his shoulder. "They sliced and diced Wrath's mattress but looks like they left Trinity's clothes and stuff alone too."

Someone knocks on our open door and we both turn. Dex flashes a grim smile. "You two okay?"

"Rooster got us to safety in time." Gray nods at him. "You?"

"Got the royal pat down treatment. My room is trashed but otherwise, everything's fine." He tilts his head to the side. "Z wants everyone in the main room in ten."

"We'll be there," Gray promises.

Loud voices, banging, and chaotic noises echo through the hallway. Even though it won't lock, Gray closes our door.

"Jesus Christ. What a mess." He runs his hands through his hair. "I feel like I jinxed the whole fuckin' club by coming down here this weekend."

"What? Why?" I touch his arm. "It had nothing to do with you."

"This kind of thing used to happen a lot back in the day. Club used to be involved in some…stuff that kept us on law enforcement's radar. Rock's worked hard to pull the club away from that. Sounds like Z's been fixing the damage Sway caused down here. First time I show up, they get raided? It's like the bad luck of my past followed me here." His strained voice tugs at my heart. He's really worried he caused trouble for his brothers.

"Gray, I love you, but don't you think that's a bit much?" I pull his arm down so I can see his face. "From what Rooster said, the warrant had nothing to do with you."

His lips twist. "That your way of saying, it's not all about me?"

"Well, yeah."

"Thanks, buttercup." He kisses my forehead. "I'm sorry this has been such a shit weekend. I'm sure you never expected to hide out like fugitives."

"Sounds like we were better off down there than staying up here watching the cops destroy the place." I shrug. "I liked hanging out with Shelby and getting to know her more."

A relieved smile stretches across his face. "At least something good came of it."

CHAPTER TWENTY-EIGHT

Grinder

THE MAIN ROOM OF THE CLUBHOUSE IS CHAOS WHEN WE ARRIVE. COPS trashed it so thoroughly it barely looks like the same space we were celebrating in last night. Club girls are busy cleaning up behind the bar area. Brothers are turning furniture upright and replacing cushions. Serena moves to help with the cleanup, but I hold her tight to my side.

"Gray, I should—"

"No. Stay with me for now."

"Okay." She wraps her arm around mine.

Z's talking to Rooster in his office, so I approach Rock first. "Are you whole?"

"Yeah, Hope and Heidi are at Z's place with the kids." He lifts his chin at Serena. "You're welcome to head over there with them if you want to get away from here. Lilly's making a run in a few minutes."

"I—" Serena looks at Rock, then me. "I'd like to stay and help out, unless you don't think it's safe?"

"Trinity's sticking around. Shelby's here. Charlotte should be back in a few," Rock says. "I'm sure they'd appreciate the help."

"Okay."

Z emerges from the office with a scowl firmly in place. "All full-patches to the war room table in five."

"That include me, Prez?" Ice shouts.

"Yeah, that includes you, smart-ass." Z flashes a quick smile. "If you don't mind."

Wrath and Trinity join us. "You need me to go grab Teller?" Wrath asks.

Rock shakes his head and holds up his phone. "He says he's on his way."

"How bad was your room, G?" Murphy asks as he ambles over to us.

"Not that bad."

"Good."

Charlotte joins us as the guys start moving toward the war room. She and Trinity pull Serena aside.

"Will you be all right?" I ask her.

"I'll be fine. Go ahead."

Trinity nods at me.

Uneasy but unable to say no to my brothers, I follow Rock to the table. Z takes his place at the head of the table, while Rock takes the chair at the other end. Upstate fills the spots at that end and Z's guys fill in the chairs near him. I end up somewhere in the middle between Jigsaw and Dex.

"All right." Z claps his hands to indicate he wants us all to shut up. "What I didn't want to discuss in front of everyone out there is that Tiny's not the only one who got taken in. They arrested Sway and Tawny on suspicion of child pornography. Confiscated a lot of tapes, DVDs, photos, and shit from their suite upstairs."

Absolute silence descends over the table.

Someone whistles long and low.

"Bro." Butcher's eyes widen to half-dollar size. "That is *fucked* up. Are you sure?"

"From what I gathered, they searched their suite same as they searched the rest of the place. Found some questionable photos, maybe. I don't know. Since they both claimed it was their room before the search started, cops arrested both of them."

"Sway won't have to worry about the cops," Steer says. "Tawny will fucking eviscerate him with her bare hands if it's true."

Z lets out a heavy sigh. "I don't know if it's true or not. He's been heavily involved with Stella and her films for years. But she's well-past legal. I got no idea what they found. I've been up in their room like once since I took over." He shudders. "Once was enough."

"*If* it's true," Rock says. "The club needs to distance itself from him as much as possible, as soon as possible. We can*not* have our club's name attached to that in any way."

"Distance?" Wrath sneers. "You mean *end that motherfucker.*"

"They send him to prison with a kiddie porn rap, he won't last long," Steer says.

"You'd be surprised." I can't help myself from speaking on this since I'd witnessed it firsthand. "Depending on where he ends up, he might be put in protective custody with all the other sickos. Ain't like they tell you on television. They don't always toss the pervs into gen pop for a dose of prison justice."

"Well, we'll decide what to do when we get there," Z says.

"Everyone knows Sway and I got no love lost between us. And as sleazy of a motherfucker as he can be, I've never seen him…I don't know." Rock drops his gaze and shakes his head. "We'll have to see how it plays out."

"Thank fuck I've been making sure all our girls are double and triple verified." Rooster presses his palms together prayer style and raises them toward the ceiling. "Ice's too. All of our online content is legit."

"I knew Anya's parents," Ice says. "She's definitely legal. And I know she's careful about anyone she works with."

"Then, if they find anything, Sway's responsible, and it shouldn't come back on the club," Rooster adds.

Suds raises his hand. "I got a real problem with y'all assuming Sway is guilty. We've shared a patch with him for a long time. Where's the loyalty?"

"No one's saying he's guilty," Z answers. "For fuck's sake, I just sent Charlotte to meet up with the club's lawyer to give him a hefty retainer. Got someone lined up to represent Tawny's ass too. Club's taking care of them."

"But if *we* find he's guilty by *our* code," Rock adds, "he's gotta go. End of discussion. That has always been a hard line."

"Okay." Suds sits back and nods. "That's fair. Sorry, Z. I didn't mean to question you."

"It's all right, brother." Z wiggles his fingers in the air in a give-it-to-me gesture. "Everyone's rattled after what went down today. I want my brothers to voice their concerns, whatever they are."

"Any idea if upstate will be hit next?" Rav asks.

Rock shakes his head. "So far, Swan says all is quiet."

"Malik said it's business as usual at Crystal Ball when I checked in with him," Dex says.

"That's a good sign, right?" Murphy stabs his fingers against the table. "They were specifically looking at *this* charter. Not the whole Lost Kings organization?"

"It was local PD, so it seems that way. I had to call Priest and warn him so he didn't roll up while this was going down." Z groans. "*That* was a fun conversation."

"Fuck," Jigsaw grumbles. "Just what we need."

"I managed to slip away and not show them my ID," Ice says. "But they could've run my plate outside."

"I avoided them too." Pants raises his hand. "Talked to T-Bone before we sat down, and he says all is quiet at our clubhouse."

"Not that I'm happy *we're* a target," Z says, "but it *is* good news if it's this charter alone and not the whole organization being looked at."

"What did the warrant say?" Dex asks.

"It was pretty vague. Charlotte argued with them for quite a while at the gate, so we could get things squared away in here," Z answers.

I'll have to thank Charlotte when I see her. That extra time allowed me to get my ass down to the bunker.

"Fucking Tiny and his unregistered weapon," Steer moans. "I'm gonna strangle him when he gets out."

"Drugs," Teller says, nodding at Dex. "Meth and heroin supposedly. A lot of other legal word salad but Charlotte said that's what it boiled down to."

"Two things we've never been involved with?" Steer squints. "That's fucking stupid."

"What a lovely waste of tax-payer dollars," someone else says.

"Maybe they just wanted to test out all their Rambo gear on the big, bad outlaw clubhouse." Hustler waves his hands and arms in the air like he's about to go Ghostbusting.

The guys crack up, which eases some of the tension from the morning's events.

Z lifts his chin at Rooster. "That's a thing, isn't it? Swatting? Someone makes a prank call to emergency services about a serious threat taking place, just for shits and giggles?"

"That's slightly different." Rooster taps his fingers against the table as if he's considering all options. "They would've battered down our front gate and door, not patiently waited to get a warrant and explain it to our lawyer."

"I can't decide if that's better or worse," Z says.

"You think it's possible Tawny was pissed about the ban and orchestrated this?" Jigsaw asks.

"She's a bitch but she's always been loyal to the club," I say, even though defending Tawny feels unnatural. "Her tricks are the kind of stunt she pulled with Serena. Not bringing in law enforcement."

"It couldn't have been her," Z says. "Steer and I didn't have a chance to talk to Sway before the cops showed up."

"She got arrested with Sway," Hustler says. "Even Karma doesn't work that fast."

"Besides," Steer adds. "Getting that warrant and showing up the way they did, that takes time and planning. They didn't do that on a whim."

"Our officer buddy found out about it," Z says. "But he only gave me fifteen minutes' notice." He lifts his chin at me. "At least it was enough time to get you and Shelby somewhere safe."

"Thanks, brother."

"I think they've been freezing him out," Rooster says. "We're probably lucky he found out at all."

"Or he's playing us." Jigsaw slams his fist against the table. "I've never trusted that prick."

"Same, brother," Z says.

Someone taps on the closed doors. Dex is closest, so he jumps up to answer.

Lilly's anxious face comes into view. "Sorry to interrupt. But we just buzzed in Priest and his crew."

"Fuck." Z stands and braces his hands on the table. "All right. Let's try not to show him that we're rattled. Keep working on getting the place cleaned up. He'll probably want to have a long chat, so I'll keep him busy for as long as I can." Z's gaze strays to me. He lifts an eyebrow but I'm not sure what he's asking.

As the room thins out, I approach Z. "You need me, brother?"

"Stay close. I know Priest wants to speak to you, personally."

"Where'd you think I was gonna go?"

"After this morning, I wouldn't blame you if you wanted to go the fuck home, G."

"Shit happens. We're fine. Nice little bunker you guys carved out down there. Thank you for making sure I got out in time."

He stares at me for a few seconds. "I'd go to prison myself before I let you go back inside."

"Let's not get extreme." I clap his shoulder. "You got a wife and son who need you out here."

He opens his mouth to say something else, but Rock stops next to us. "You trying to avoid Priest?" he asks Z.

Z smirks. "Like the plague."

Laughing and shaking his head, Rock places his hand on Z's shoulder and steers him toward the door. Outside the war room, Rock hooks an arm around Z's neck and yanks him close, saying something against his ear. Z nods quickly, then Rock shoves him toward the front door.

"He worried Priest's gonna blame him for the raid?"

"No." He glances at me. "You doing okay?"

"I'm fine. Just not looking forward to rehashing the last fifteen years again."

He squeezes my shoulder. "Hopefully, this is the last weekend anyone expects that from you."

Serena's at the bar and I step behind it to pull her to my side. "I want to introduce you to our national president as my ol' lady."

She glances down at her jeans and sneakers. "I feel like I should be more dressed up to meet the president."

I tug on the edge of her property patch. "You're wearing what matters most." I scan the living room. "Damn, you guys did a good job picking things up out here."

"We worked from here out." She nods to the hallway. "They're working that way. Lilly cleaned up a room for Priest, just in case they wanted to freshen up first."

There's still visible damage—holes in the wall, torn furniture—but at least it looks more like a rowdy biker clubhouse that had an out-of-control party than a place that got raided by the cops.

Still, there's a good chance Priest will come down hard on Z for landing on law enforcement's radar.

CHAPTER TWENTY-NINE

Grinder

"Grinder." Priest's low, gravelly voice hasn't changed much.

I turn, and a slow grin spreads across his face. "So glad you're on the outside, brother." He holds open his arms and gives me a slow, respectful embrace, as if he's concerned I turned feral in prison and might give him rabies.

Since there were many days inside I felt closer to a wild animal than a human, I'm not insulted. I accept the embrace and pat his back. "Damn good to see you, brother."

"You too." He pulls away and eyes my cut. "Still on parole, right?"

"For another couple of months. Been laying low and following the rules." I cast a look around the clubhouse. "Mostly."

"You shouldn't be denied family after such a long stretch inside."

I take that to mean he's not judging me for breaking conditions of my parole to be at this party. It's similar to something Serena once said to me.

Behind me, she's still as a statue. I turn and wrap my arm around her, pulling her forward. "Priest, this is my ol' lady."

He runs his gaze over her property patch. "I see that."

"Serena, this is our national president," I finish, trying to ignore his sarcastic tone. I'm pretty sure Valentina was barely out of high school when Priest picked her up, so he can fuck all the way down to fuck-off town with the judgmental smirk.

"Good to meet you, Serena. You mind if I have a word with your ol' man?"

"Of course not." With her voice barely above a whisper, I can't tell if she's intimidated by Priest, worried he recognizes her, or something else.

I lean in closer to her. "Will you be all right?"

She nods quickly, her hair tickling my nose.

"Stay here by the bar, okay?"

She turns and meets my eyes briefly. "Okay."

"Good girl." I pop a kiss on her cheek and join Priest.

He sends his hand up, catching Z's eye and pointing to the hallway opposite the bedrooms. Z nods and gestures for us to go ahead. I haven't explored this part of the clubhouse yet, but Priest seems to know exactly where he's headed.

"You've been busy since you got out," Priest says in that slick, irritating way he's always had. "Patched a girl already. Making up for lost time?"

From his mocking tone, it's clear he thinks she's a random muffler bunny I bumped into at the clubhouse or maybe an inmate groupie I met through a prison pen-pal program. And I'm happy to set him straight. "Yeah, she was my physical therapist." I touch my shoulder and roll it forward. "Went to see her for an injury I got inside and, well…" I flash a sheepish smile and shrug.

Let that reminder of how much time I did for the club sink in, asshole.

Priest stops at a door on the right, knocks, then turns the knob, motioning for me to go in ahead of him.

"Nice bonus." He closes the door behind us. It's a simple room. Stark. A desk and a couple chairs. A map of New York stapled to the wall. Priest takes the seat behind the desk and nods to one of the chairs in front.

"She's the only reason I think I was able to ride so soon," I add, to really drive home the guilt.

"That's good." He touches his leg. "Physical therapy helped me a lot after I laid my bike down a few summers ago. He didn't look anything like *that*, though."

"Serena's brains and beauty," I answer in a tight voice, irritated he feels the need to compliment her looks. "I got lucky."

"Yes," he answers slowly. "I can understand why you wanted to lock her down quickly."

I roll my eyes at the phrase, and he smirks.

After a few seconds of bullshitting, he turns serious. "I'm gonna be real with you, brother. I was concerned about how you've been doing since getting out. Making the adjustment after such a long stretch isn't easy for a lot of brothers."

Why do I suddenly feel like I'm having a counseling session with my parole officer?

"Yeah, it's been rough," I admit. "Club's made it easier, though. Every time a problem could've derailed me, they've been there to ease the way."

"By *they*, you mean Rock, Z, and Wrath?"

"Whole club, but yeah, they've gone out of their way for me. Wrath set me up with a legit job working for a friend of his. Murphy's let me borrow his truck since I couldn't ride when I got out. Teller's set up online bank accounts and straightened things out for me. Rooster's been helping me adjust to all the technology bullshit that's changed. Z's helped me with a few more personal matters. Everyone's assisted me in one way or another." Steer and Pants helped me drive home the point in a visceral way that Serena was off-limits. Don't think that will impress Priest, though, so I don't bother adding it to the list.

"I'm real glad to hear that. Especially since Murphy, Teller, and Rooster weren't even patched brothers when you went inside."

"I've known Murphy and Teller since they were kids. They were the ones who came to visit me most frequently. Got to know Rooster while I was inside. He paid me a few visits. Jigsaw and Dex visited me too from time-to-time. Steer wrote me letters. Ice sent me some care packages and shit. Squiggy kept me up-to-date on the southern gossip for a while." My list keeps growing as I recall each kindness the club's shown me over the years. "Club had to keep its distance for safety reasons. But individually, the brothers did what they could for me. Rock always made sure I had money in my accounts, which I'm sure you know goes a long way when you're inside."

"Yes, it does," he says solemnly. "Knowing that you haven't been forgotten and left to rot helps too."

"It does." *Helped me hang on to my sanity.*

He sighs and sits back, lacing his fingers over his stomach. "My preference is for brothers to never see the inside of a cell. But when that can't be avoided, it's important we pay respect to our *loyal* brothers when they find themselves incarcerated."

Meaning, had I ratted on the club, they would've found a way to end me inside. Pay another inmate to knife me on the way to the dining hall. Find someone to hang me from my bedsheets. Something painful and unpleasant.

"Never had any hard feelings toward *the club.*" *Ruger, our old president, sure. But not my club.*

As if he'd heard that last thought, the corners of his mouth quirk. "No one's heard from Ruger in over ten years. Can't be the government hiding him or they would've come down on us by now."

"Huh. Surprised he's been able to lay low for such a long time." I keep my expression disinterested and my tone neutral. "He always was a flashy motherfucker." Priest won't buy my act if I don't reveal some bitterness.

"Upstate never reported that they took a vote to put him to ground. So, I guess you're right." He drills me with his piercing stare, as if he'll strip the information from my brain with the power of his dark eyes. "He must be living off the grid in humble conditions. We'll find him eventually," he adds with a casual shrug.

No wonder Priest maintains a healthy fear of Rock, Wrath, and Z. He may push when he needs something—like Z taking over this charter in an emergency. But otherwise, he seems to stay hands-off New York.

Inside, I suppress my laughter. "I ain't losing sleep over Ruger's whereabouts." *Feel free to waste time searching 'til your dying day, brother.*

"Regardless, the club should compensate you for the time lost."

Priest reaches into his cut and pulls out several thick, rectangular envelopes a bit larger than the size of a dollar bill. He reaches into the other side of his cut and pulls out another handful of envelopes. Seems to be ten envelopes total.

"What'd you do, ride by the bank and close out an account on your way here?" I ask.

"Something like that." He pushes the envelopes across the desk at me. "It will never make up for the time you've lost, but the whole organization owes you for your loyalty."

"Rock's already—"

"That's up to the discretion of each charter. *This* is from National. It's what should be done."

"No one owes me shit." I collect the envelopes and stack them into two neat piles in front of me. "But thank you for this." I don't want to act like a greedy, entitled fuck, but I know better than to turn down a gift from Priest. He'll take it as an insult. I don't bother opening and counting the money, either. The amount doesn't matter. It's the intent behind the gesture that counts.

Serena

Every few seconds my gaze strays toward the hallway where Gray and Priest disappeared.

The intimidating old biker didn't seem too impressed with me. I want Gray to be proud I'm his ol' lady, not embarrass him. Obviously, as the national president, he's someone whose opinion matters around here.

Hope touches my shoulder and I tear my gaze away from the empty hallway. "Serena, have you had a chance to meet Priest's wife Valentina yet?"

The tall, older woman looks like something out of one of those housewives of somewhere snooty reality TV shows. Flawless makeup, long shiny hair—that's probably extensions—tight outfit, sharp, glittering nails, huge sparkling diamonds on her fingers, and a glass of wine in her hand.

"No, I haven't." I flash my most confident smile while Hope makes the introductions.

Valentina runs her gaze over me and doesn't seem any more impressed than her husband was. "So, Gray's been busy since he got out. Good for him."

Hearing another woman use his real name instead of his road name fires up my jealousy. Here's one more woman closer to Gray's age who knew him before he went to prison.

"Nice to meet you, Serena." Valentina gathers up Lilly and Hope and pulls them away.

"It's okay. I wasn't invited to the first lady pep rally either." Shelby slides up next to me and bumps my shoulder.

Her gentle southern twang erases the negative cloud left by Valentina's dismissal. "Well, at least I'm not alone."

"Nope. We newbies will form our own club." She pulls out her cell phone. "While we're at it, let's grab a photo together. I wanted to ask you before but didn't know if 'bunker selfie' was a memory we wanted to keep."

"We had fun down there." I shrug. "I've never had my cards read before. That alone was worth it."

She beams at me. "Anytime." She slips off her property patch and I do the same. Together, we lean against the bar and smile for her camera. We take a few shots and when she finds one that's acceptable, she sends it to me.

"I'm so thirsty." She slides her property patch on again and zips it up.

I turn to put mine back on too and come face-to-face with Amanda. *Shit.*

I haven't seen her in months. Our friendship has always ebbed and flowed so it's not unusual. But I never told her about Gray and me getting together.

Her eyes widen as she slowly takes me in, her gaze sticking on the patch over my heart.

"Grinder? The old dude who got out of prison? You hooked up

with him and he patched you?" Her shrill voice rises with each question.

While I lost interest in ever being patched after distancing myself from the club, Amanda never gave up hope that one of the guys would want her to stick around for more than a night.

Guilt prickles over me. But what could I do? Call her up to brag? I've been too busy worrying about the baby, moving, not having a job, and everything else going on in my life. Besides, Gray is my prize. Not the patch.

"We're together, yes," I finally answer, ignoring her obvious irritation.

"Well, I guess that explains why I haven't heard from you in so long."

The phone works both ways.

"Things have been a little hectic," I answer. "I moved into Emily's place."

Her nose wrinkles. She's never gotten along with Emily. "Seriously?"

I shrug.

Amanda sneers at Shelby. "So, what? You're too good to hang around with the peasants now?"

Thankfully, Shelby has her back to us while she orders her drink and doesn't seem to notice Amanda's snide tone directed at her.

"Not at all. I didn't realize you were here tonight."

"Were you here for the raid?" she asks. "I heard about it and that's why I came over. To help with the cleanup."

"That was nice of you." I glance around the main room. The furniture has been righted. Posters taped over the places where holes were punched in the walls. Debris swept away. A vast improvement from earlier. I hadn't run into Amanda while I was fixing up this part of the clubhouse earlier. Maybe she was cleaning one of the bedrooms. "Everything got messed up pretty bad."

She leans in closer. "I heard Sway and Tawny got arrested."

That can't be right. It's so loud in here, I must have misunderstood.

I ask her to repeat it and she does, her hot breath wafting over my cheek as she whisper-shouts in my ear.

"Holy crap. Really?"

Don't think mean thoughts.

Don't think mean thoughts.

It could've been Gray who was arrested for violating his parole, so I *will* not take pleasure in Sway and Tawny's troubles. It'll bring bad luck.

Amanda nods solemnly, although her mouth is twisted with barely restrained glee. Tawny's never been nice to her either.

"Here ya go!" Something cold brushes my arm. I turn and Shelby's holding out a champagne glass to me.

No. No. No.

Why hadn't I come up with a prepared excuse sooner?

"What's in it?" I ask carefully.

She shrugs and takes a sip. "Champagne, sugar cubes, and brandy? Somethin' like that."

"Oh, I'm watching my sugar." I hand it to Amanda so fast, liquid rises dangerously close to the lip of the glass. Amanda shrugs and takes a long sip.

Shelby stares at me for a few seconds. "I try to avoid sugar when I'm on the road but since it's my downtime, I'm gonna indulge a lil'."

"No, no, you should," I insist.

Since I know my way around the bar, I slide behind it and grab a can of ginger ale. So I won't seem out of place, I pour it into a champagne glass and drop a wedge of lime in it.

Shelby eyes me as I return. "You know ginger ale has sugar in it too."

Nervous laughter bubbles past my lips. "So it does."

Get it together. You're the one making it obvious.

"Hey, I'm Shelby." She nods at Amanda.

"Sorry," I interrupt. "Shelby, this is my friend Amanda. Amanda—"

"Yeah, Rooster's girl." Amanda's voice sounds closer to accusation than recognition. "I've seen you around."

"Oh." Shelby's gaze flicks my way. "Okay. Nice to officially meet ya." She sips her drink.

"You're that singer who got kidnapped last summer, right?" Amanda asks.

Cold mortification slides down my spine. *Jesus, Amanda. Really?*

Shelby rolls her shoulders and lifts her chin. "That's me. But I'd rather not talk about it. We've all had enough unpleasantness around here."

"Serena!" Someone squeals my name. Two seconds later, a tall, slender, energetic body crashes into mine. I bump into one of the barstools to brace myself and catch her.

"Lala! Oh my God. Are you trying to knock me out?" Laughing, I pull her in for a longer hug. "How've you been, you nut?"

"I've missed you!" she shouts, squeezing me again. "I heard you were here." Her gaze drops to my vest and she grins even wider. "And that you'd been patched. Congratulations!" she squeals again while jumping up and down.

"Thanks."

"Hey, Shelby!"

Shelby reaches for Lala, pulling her in for a hug. "Good to see you. Where you been hiding, Lala?"

"All over." She nods at Amanda. "Hey, can you finish helping me in the kitchen?"

"Sure." Amanda sends a frosty look my way. "I guess you're too good to help out now?"

My cheeks burn. "No. Not at all." I move to follow the girls but Shelby yanks me backward by tugging on my vest.

"Her man asked her to wait here with me," Shelby says. "We'll come help when we get the all clear."

Lala nods and skips off to the kitchen, while Amanda sends me a death-glare.

"What's up with your friend?" Shelby asks after they're gone. "She ain't real nice to ya."

"I...uh..." Shelby didn't hook up with Rooster until after I'd already left the club scene. Unless someone told her, she doesn't know

I used to be like Amanda and Lala. Part of me doesn't want to tell her and risk losing our budding friendship. The rest of me knows she'll find out eventually, so I might as well just say it now. The other ol' ladies seem to have accepted me, Shelby will too. "I used to, um, you know, hang around here and come to a lot of the parties."

She blinks and glances in the direction of the kitchen. "By yourself?"

"Well, with Amanda."

"I thought you and Grinder hooked up after he got out?"

"We did."

She sips her drink slowly, watching me over the rim of her glass. "Did ya know Rooster back then?"

Well, damn, this girl isn't playing. "I was always friendly with Rooster and Jiggy but not in the way you're thinking."

Pink stains her cheeks and she sets her drink on the bar. "Shoot. I'm sorry. I wasn't trying to be rude." Her lips curve in apology. "It just comes naturally sometimes."

"No, I get it. I…uh…was usually with the old VP. He was possessive but…not in the nice way."

Sympathy shines in her eyes. "I think Rooster's mentioned him before."

Whatever Rooster told her was enough for Shelby not to ask any questions about Shadow.

"Before that, I had a terrible crush on Murphy. But Heidi knows that," I hurry to add. "It's water under the bridge." *I hope.*

"Gotcha" She holds up one hand. "You don't owe me any explanations, Serena. I had to hang out with Rooster's ex when we visited Washington. It was weird, awkward, and for some cockamamie reason her husband felt compelled to punch Rooster at one point."

"Oh shit." I slap my hand over my mouth. "What'd Rooster do?"

"Punched him back." Her lips curl into an evil smile that looks totally out of place on her wholesome face. "Multiple times."

"That sounds like Rooster. I'm surprised Jiggy didn't get in a few punches of his own."

"Oh, believe me, he tried." She launches one foot forward, bumping one of the barstools. "I woulda kicked the guy in the dick myself if Rooster woulda let me."

"I bet." Damn, she's little but fierce.

"Anyway, it's none of my business. Sorry for prying." She lifts her chin toward the kitchen doors. "I just didn't care for your friend being rude to ya."

Emily's the only other person in my life who's ever worried about how anyone treated me. "Thanks."

"You got it." She gives me that mischievous little grin again. "The guys may say 'Kings forever' but I say, 'Queens stick together.'"

CHAPTER THIRTY

Grinder

I<small>T'S BEEN ONE HELL OF A LONG WEEKEND AND</small> I'<small>M EAGER TO GET ON THE</small> road. Unfortunately, Priest has other ideas. I've spent more time in church downstate than anything else. Z seems to read my irritation as I pass him to go into the war room.

"Get some rest last night?"

"Yeah." I glance around then lean closer to Z. "You hear anything about Sway yet?" I ask in a low voice.

"Nothing."

"Shit."

"My sources think they're gonna focus on him now instead of the club."

"Well, I guess that's something."

He claps my back and sends me on my way. As I glance over my shoulder, I catch a glimpse of Priest and his enforcer, Blink, approaching Z. No wonder he wanted me to move along.

With Priest and Blink visiting, brothers settle into their seats faster than usual. Z walks Priest to his seat at the head of the table. They seem to argue about it for a minute, but then Priest takes Z's place.

The noise in the room falls to a hush.

I run my gaze down the length of the table. Rock catches my eye and lifts his chin. The corners of his mouth are tight with annoyance. The only signal that he'd rather be anywhere else.

"I'm honored to be able to sit down with *all* of our New York brothers," Priest says, standing at the head of the room. "Thank you for allowing me to join you for church."

As if Z had a choice.

"I'm proud to be your national president and don't take lightly the trust you've put in me over the years." He glances at Rock and then Z. "Both charters *now* embody what our brotherhood was always supposed to be."

He just had to get that *now* in. Too bad Sway's not here for that little dig.

"You've done so much good work, especially over the last year. It hasn't been easy and I'm proud of all you've accomplished."

I'm on the edge of my seat waiting for the "but."

He pauses. "But now I'd like to do something for the whole organization."

Here it comes.

"I've been approached to be interviewed for a television documentary about outlaw bikers. Given some of the recent troubles our brothers in Washington and Tennessee have faced, I think it would be a good way to tell our side of the story."

Fuck me to hell and back. I did not see *that* coming.

"This show would give us exposure to an audience we don't normally have a reason to interact with. We'd have a chance to show that bikers are not as threatening as the media portrays us."

The Priest I knew fifteen years ago was all about avoiding the spotlight and publicity. The outlaw bikers I grew up around didn't give a fuck what society thought of them. Where is this need for fame coming from?

Rock must be sitting with the same bewilderment. The intensity of his stare deepens but he doesn't say a word. Z is similarly stoic. I think we're all waiting for the punchline.

Priest's gaze slides toward Rooster. "Rooster and I had some discussion about this, given the nature of his high-profile ol' lady. Doing what we can to put the club in a good light in front of the public benefits everyone."

By the frown and side-eye Rooster launches Priest's way, I think he has a different memory of their conversation. He doesn't nod or speak to acknowledge Priest's comment, nor does he contradict him.

The lack of response seems to frustrate Priest. He frowns and glances over his shoulder at Blink.

"We've seen clubs do interviews before," Teller says in a strong but still respectful manner. "It never ends up painting them in a good light. The interview gets chopped and edited to fit the 'biker gang' narrative."

Taking one for the team. Good boy, Teller.

"I think we're better off keeping our heads down, doing our thing, and staying off anyone's radar, like we always have," Murphy adds.

Rock's jaw tightens and he slides a "shut your yap" look at the two of them, but there's also pride shining in his eyes.

"I'd obviously work with the producers ahead of time to set the parameters of the conversation." Priest's tone is full of irritation at being questioned.

"Is this something other clubs are taking part in?" Wrath asks. "We're not that large of an organization to focus an entire show on."

"Other clubs have been approached." He nods at Rock. "Including your friend, Chaser. I think he turned them down."

"I'm sure he did." Rock's clipped answer borders on disrespect. "I think he sticks to writing songs and staying out of the spotlight these days."

As much as I've witnessed Rock busting Rooster's balls for his friendship with Chaser, he doesn't take the opportunity to throw Rooster under the bus with Priest.

"Since you brought up Shelby," Rooster says, raising his hand. "Any publicity I've taken part in was carefully curated to keep the focus on her. I've always kept the club's name as quiet as possible."

"Right. I respect that but I no longer think such extreme caution is necessary," Priest answers.

Maybe not for *us*. But I can't imagine it'll look real good for Shelby to be associated with outlaw bikers. I may have been locked up for fifteen years but even I can see that would be bad for her image.

"What are you suggesting we do? Mainstream?" Steer asks.

"With all due respect," Dex pipes up before Priest answers—or shoots—Steer. "I see this going off the rails fast. Whoever it is and whatever they promise you, we all know they'll only focus on the 'seedy' aspects of biker life—the strip clubs we own—"

"The porn we finance," Jigsaw adds. "Our girls have been really careful to keep those ties separate. But a documentary crew might dig into our business ventures. Are we prepared to be labeled the porn kings of the biker world or whatever stupid title they'll come up with?"

"Sex sells." Dex nods at Jiggy. "We all know that's how they'll frame the story."

"Not to mention they'll want to do some dramatic segment on property patches and yap about how we're all sexist pigs." Steer rolls his eyes.

"Well, that's not exactly a lie." Z laughs. "But yeah, Steer's right. They're going to twist something sacred to make us look like cavemen assholes and imply that our women are brainless bimbos." His face hardens like he's already thinking of murdering anyone who talks shit about Lilly.

"I'll deflect the property patch issue easily," Priest counters. "It's no different than wearing a wedding ring—"

"Sorry, but there is a *huge* difference between a band around your finger and a patch on your back saying *property of*," Dex says. "You'll look insincere as fuck if you try that play."

Damn, Dex is laying down the hard truths today.

"You have a problem with our traditions?" Priest asks with a raised eyebrow and dangerous tone.

Dex isn't intimidated by Priest. He sits up and looks him right in the eye. "Not at all. It's a private ritual that *we* understand. It has meaning in our world and that's all that matters. I don't like having something so important to us opened up to outsiders to ridicule, question, and make assumptions about." He crosses his arms over his chest. "It's disrespectful to our women who wear the patch."

Murmurs of approval go around the table. Even Blink cocks his head like he hadn't considered that before.

"I'll keep that in mind." At least Priest sounds more thoughtful than annoyed now.

"Um, can we go back to the bringing attention to our businesses thing?" Sparky asks. "I don't see that being good for us. Like, at all."

Z nods, picking up Sparky's thread. "Not all clubs are completely legit. Washington may be out of the press for now, but they're still waging a war with other clubs. Thumbing your nose at the government in such a public way might not be the wisest choice. Just because Washington beat one case doesn't mean the government won't cook up another."

"I think that only gives us more of a reason to do it," Priest insists. "They can focus on the so-called seedy aspects like the strip clubs and porn all they want. Distasteful or not, they're *legal*. Let the world think that's our only source of income. It fits the biker image and moves the attention *away* from other revenue streams."

Rooster shakes his head. "Except, down in Tennessee you had girls trying to pull a hustle on the customers by druggin' and robbin' them. Digger cleaned up that mess. We got lucky that most of the marks were too embarrassed to come forward and press charges. But if you put the Royal Dolls on television, you're bound to have more people coming out of the woodwork with stories to share. That could bring a *lot* of heat to the club."

Priest stares at Rooster as if he's trying to decide if he should thank him or murder him. "That's a good point. We can use our place in Mississippi as an example. Or Crystal Ball. There hasn't been any misconduct that I'm aware of *there*."

Dex's eyes are screaming *over my dead body,* but he looks to Rock to take the question.

"The club is a front for laundering money," Rock says. "I doubt a film crew's gonna want to dig into our taxes, but you never know."

What a diplomatic non-answer with a side of thinly veiled sarcasm. Proud of Rock for maintaining his cool during this fuckery of a meeting.

"Ice?" Priest lifts his chin at our Virginia charter's president. "It might bring your girl's website some extra traffic."

"Anya does fine without adding extra heat," Ice answers.

Priest's jaw tightens.

"I doubt Stella will care one way or another." Z nods at Hustler. "You can run it by her if this goes any further."

"Sure, I can do that," Hustler agrees. "She might be the best one to showcase since she's got all those other legit writing gigs and stuff she does. A classy chick like her could help tone down the seedy image."

Priest narrows his eyes at me and my skin prickles. "Grinder, you have any thoughts on this?"

None that you want to hear. "I'm still struggling to adjust to all the changes in the world. Technology hasn't been my friend since I got out. Not sure my opinion is valid here."

"Your opinion is always valued. As an older member your perspective is important," he insists.

Since you asked. "I'm used to the old days where we didn't give a fuck what society thought of us and kept to ourselves. Courting the media feels unnatural. Begging the public to see us as cuddly teddy bears in leather seems undignified for a biker." *That might've been too harsh.* "But maybe modern times call for modern solutions," I finish, striving for a respectful thought to end on.

"Modern times call for modern solutions." Priest nods slowly. "I like that."

That's all you took from what I said?

"Well then, I'll keep everyone updated on how this moves forward. *If* it moves forward." Priest slaps the table. "That's all I had to share. Thanks for allowing me to take over your meeting."

"Anytime." Z scans the length of the table. "Does anyone else have any matters they need to discuss?"

"I'll be around if anyone wants to speak to me privately," Priest offers. He jerks his head toward the door and Blink follows him out.

Z watches the door for a second, but I doubt he's going to say anything with Priest lingering so close. The slow, what-the-fuck eye-slide he sends around the table says plenty.

CHAPTER THIRTY-ONE

Serena

"Ready to hit the road?" Trinity asks me while we're waiting for the guys to finish with church. Since she can't seem to sit still, she's sweeping and cleaning up random bits behind the bar. I grab a bottle of water and perch on one of the barstools to stay out of her way.

"Am I ever." I've never been so eager to return to my non-MC world.

She frowns and sets her broom to the side. "Is something wrong?"

I shrug and glance around. "Can I talk to you for a sec?"

She flashes a warm smile. "Sure. What's on your mind?"

Hell, I don't know how to say this without being offensive. But she's the only one who I think has been in a similar situation. "Uh… you used to hang around the club before you and Wrath got together, right?"

Her smile flips to cool. "Not exactly. He and I met before I moved up to the clubhouse."

"Oh."

"What's this about, Serena?"

Trinity's always been so confident and in control, she'll never respect me if I break down and cry. I steel myself, drawing in a deep breath. "How did you get people to *stop* bringing it up?"

"Who said something to you now?"

"Amanda...Tawny...Pants...Steer. God only knows who'll be next."

"Fuck 'em."

"What?"

"Aren't you and Amanda supposed to be friends?"

"Kinda."

Her lips flatten to an angry line.

"I don't care what anyone else thinks. I just don't want to cause Gray any embarrassment."

Finally, she seems to soften. "Listen. If Grinder doesn't have a problem with it, it's no one else's business." She blows out a breath. "I really hate talking about this, so let this conversation be your sign that *I* care about you and accept you."

Wow, that's some raw honesty. "Okay."

"Wyatt and I were young, stubborn, damaged, and really bad at communication when we met. I didn't exactly come from a loving or safe family, so the idea that someone might actually care about me as a person and not a human Fleshlight was hard to wrap my mind around."

That's vivid. "I can relate to that." Oh, how I can relate.

"I thought you might." She sighs. "Anyway, we did a lot of stupid shit to each other and it took a while to get to a place of forgiveness."

"Did people ever say anything?"

"I'm sure they did." Her lips twist into a wry smile. "Heidi was younger, so she could be a little testy." She touches the hammer patch on her cut. "She's grown up a lot in the last few years. Charlotte and I had some words at one point but we got over it."

I remember how territorial Charlotte was over Teller the first time *I* met her, so this isn't a surprise.

"Here's what I think might be the difference, though. Wrath's the SAA. Not many people were going to risk giving him *or* me attitude once he patched me. Grinder, on the other hand, has been away for a long time. And while everyone will talk about how much they respect him—and most of the brothers absolutely do—some of them still have that urge to test him." She stops and shakes her head. "To see if he still has what it takes to roll with the club's code. And because, let's face it, they're assholes."

This time, I laugh with her.

"But," she continues. "Grinder's handled it every time. Quickly and mercilessly. Word will spread. People forget. It's really no one's business anyway. I mean, it's not like either of you knew the other existed until he got out."

"Well, that's true."

"You love Grinder?" she asks.

I don't even hesitate. "A lot."

"Good." Her lips twist into a pained smile. "I have a few vague memories of him from when I was a kid."

"You knew him?"

"Sort of." She waves her hand in the air like she's batting away a pesky old memory. "My Dad was in a different club and they mingled from time to time. Anyway, I remember Grinder as sort of gruff with the guys but he'd always have a smile for me."

"Somehow, I'm not surprised."

"What I'm trying to say is, I'm glad you two found each other. You seem to make him happy." She tilts her head. "And I like the way he looks out for you."

"You mean, punching people when they call me a whore?"

She lets out a harsh laugh. "Yeah." More seriously, she adds, "Anyone who thinks that, let alone *says* it, deserves whatever they get."

"Thanks."

"Stop worrying about the past, okay?" She pulls me in for a quick hug. "You can't start reading the next chapter if you're still focused on the last one. And you don't want to miss all the exciting adventures coming up."

"I like that. I'm going to write it down and tape it on my mirror with all my other motivational quotes."

She busts out laughing and releases me. "Anytime."

Grinder

I'm almost to our room when one of the doors across the hallway opens a crack. Wrath peers out, his serious gaze landing on me, and he jerks his head. "Get in here." He opens the door wider. "Hurry."

The fuck is up now? I just want to see my girl and get home.

I glance up and down the hallway before hustling my ass into his room. "What's with the spy games?" I grumble after he closes the door.

I turn and find Z, Rock, Dex, Rooster, Jigsaw, Teller, and Murphy scattered around Wrath's room. "Thanks for thinking of me, guys, but despite the rumors of what goes on in prison, I'm not interested."

"Hilarious," Wrath answers without a shred of humor. He jerks his chin toward an empty spot at the foot of the bed.

I run my gaze over the assembled group again. 'Where's Steer?"

"Keeping Priest busy," Z says.

"I'm not an officer, so why am *I* here?"

"For your *older perspective*," Z answers in a realistic impression of Priest's earlier comment.

"Stop acting like I'm the fucking Crypt Keeper, would ya."

"We don't have a lot of time," Rock says. "Let's argue about this later."

I hold up my hands to let them know I'm here to listen.

"What Priest wants to do is a big fucking problem," Wrath says.

That's what I figured this was about.

"I never saw the day comin' where Priest would want his face on television," I agree.

"I got the feeling he was more open to publicity over the summer," Rooster says. "I didn't think he meant filming a fucking documentary."

"Why didn't you warn me?" Z asks.

Rooster's eyes widen. "I told you he implied it was fine if people knew Shelby was under Lost Kings' protection by wearing my colors when I was on the road with her. 'Quietly let the world know there would be consequences to fucking with my girl' was how I think he put it."

"Right," Z says. "This is *way* past a photo in a magazine."

"Or a magazine *cover*," Jigsaw adds.

"Shut up." Rooster leans over and shoves Jigsaw.

"My problem," Rock says, "is that this is a network producing the documentary. We have no way to control the narrative or how it will be presented."

"We all know it's not going to be presented in any way that flatters us," Teller says.

"When has this ever gone well for an MC?" Murphy asks. "Didn't that dude who founded the Club-We-Won't-Name try and turn himself into a celebrity? Club stripped his patch and put a hit out on him."

"He's still hiding in the New Mexico desert somewhere," Dex adds.

"I know who you're talking about," I say. "And that's a good point." I glance at Rock. "If Priest does this, it might be the end of the road for him as national president. And I think you're the best one suited to take his place."

Good thing Rock can't shoot fire with his eyes or I'd be burned to a crisp on the spot. "Shut your mouth, old man. I don't want any part of that."

"He's right, Rock," Z says.

"Careful, Z, he'll draft you as his VP," Wrath warns.

"No, no, no. I need to stay right where I am." Z slaps the wall to punctuate his statement. "Murphy will make an excellent national VP and Teller can run upstate."

"What now?" Teller's eyes widen. But this can't be the first time someone's suggested he should lead the club.

"Let's not tap dance on Priest's grave, yet," Dex says. "That motherfucker won't go down without a fight."

"He won't have a choice if this documentary backfires." Wrath paces in front of the bathroom door.

"Can you try to get a moment alone with Blink?" Rock asks Wrath. "See where his head is at?"

"He thinks what Priest tells him to think," Z says.

Jigsaw reacts with a raised eyebrow—the one with the scar slashed through it. "I don't know about that."

"You tell him about Sway's arrest?" Rock asks Z. "Because if that goes further, you know damn well it'll end up in the documentary. Then being sleazy porn kings will seem like a compliment."

Z's eyes narrow. "I mentioned it. Didn't get into a lot of details. He didn't seem surprised."

"Sway's not in a position of power now, so I don't think Priest gives a fuck what happens to him," Rooster adds. "But Rock's right, that info will get dug up and used to smear *all* of us."

"What's our game plan?" Murphy jumps out of his seat and swings his arms back and forth like he can't sit still another second.

"Wrath's gonna talk to Blink," Rock says.

"I am?"

"Yes," Rock growls. "I'll talk to Ice and see where he's at, although I think we already know."

Rooster raises his hand. "You think Washington knows what's up yet?"

"You feel like riding out there to give 'em the good news?" Z asks.

"Fuck no. But I established a rapport with the guys when I was out there. I can try reaching out if you want me to."

Z stares at him for a few seconds before answering. "Yeah, do that. Just call to chat. Mention Priest visiting. See what comes up."

"You got it."

"All right." Rock claps his hands and stands up. "It's been fun, but I'm ready to hit the road."

"Same." I stand too.

"I'm hurt, guys," Z pouts. "Didn't you enjoy the raid and hospitality?"

"It was a blast," Teller sneers. "Cops digging through my fiancée's underwear was the highlight of my weekend."

"Yeah, the one who stopped to ask me about the condom size I use was a real gem," Dex adds.

"What? He'd never seen them that small before?" Jiggy asks with a straight face.

"You wish."

"Actually, the size of your dick is the last thing I've ever contemplated in my life," Jigsaw says.

"Yeah, but the more you talk about it, the more we're starting to wonder." Murphy holds his palms up. "See the problem?"

"They tossed Lilly's drawer of toys all over the place. I think she threw everything out." Z lifts his chin at Murphy. "Tell your wife to expect a large order soon."

"Takes a lot of gadgets to keep your wife satisfied at your advanced age, huh?" Jiggy nods solemnly. "Good to know."

"Fuck off, clown."

"Well." I slap my hands together like I'm cleaning off this conversation. "Now that I know more about your...personal issues than I ever wanted, I'm ready to leave."

"Right there with you, G," Dex says.

"Come on, now," Z protests. "We could all use a little humor."

Laughing, I reach for Z and yank him in for a hug. "Proud of you, Prez," I say against his ear. "Thanks for everything."

He pulls back with a serious expression creasing his face. "Are we good, brother?"

"We're good," I assure him.

"You'll return?"

"Yeah, I'll be back."

"All right." He cracks a hint of a smile. "I'll let you leave, then."

"Aww, this is touching." Jigsaw leans in and hugs both of us.

"All right, get off me," Z laughs and pushes both of us away.

Across the hall, I push into my room. Serena's sitting on the bed, scrolling through her phone. "Hey, I was getting worried about you."

"Wrath wanted to have a sit-down. Grabbed me before I could make it in here."

"Everything okay?"

"Just some shit national threw at us. No one expected it." I shrug off my cut and hang it over the back of a chair. "Are you all packed?"

"Yup."

"Good." I reach into the desk drawer for the envelopes Priest gave me. "Think you can stash these in your purse for me? I'll get them from you when we get home."

She blinks at the envelopes as I hand them to her. "Is this all cash?"

"Guilt gift from Priest." I nod at the pile now in her lap. "Doesn't even add up to what I would've earned makin' minimum wage for the last fifteen years. But it's the thought that counts."

"I had no idea."

"Not all clubs give a crap. But we always wanted to be different. A real brotherhood. Not a bunch of bozos who claim to be a brotherhood but don't lift a finger to help out their brothers when it counts." I want her to understand the club is more important to me than the money.

"You trust me to hold this much money?"

"You're already carrying something that matters to me a hell of a lot more than money, so yeah."

Pink sweeps over her cheeks. "Gray."

"What?" I rest a finger against her chin and tip her head back.

"I'm not doing anything *that* special."

"To me you are." I kiss her cheek. "Now, let's get the hell out of here."

As much as I hate it, I have constraints that I have to follow. We still need to stop in Catskill and "check out" of our cabin. Setting up a "cover story" and hiding in the basement this weekend has tested the limits of my freedom.

That's the problem with being caged, you don't feel the bars holding you in until you try to push against them.

CHAPTER THIRTY-TWO

Serena

A LIST OF THINGS I NEED TO DO CROWDS MY MIND BEFORE I'M EVEN fully awake. I blink and stretch, staring at the light leaking around the edges of the blinds in Gray's room. His warm, solid presence comforts me, but since he's almost always up before me, I don't want to wake him. My bladder demands my attention, though. I creep out of bed slowly, scooping up my phone as I go. Gray's still sleeping as I close the door.

After a quick trip to the bathroom, I drop down on the couch and check Instagram, like I do every morning.

"What the hell?" I scroll through hundreds of notifications. It doesn't make sense. All I posted before going to bed last night were simple before and after makeup take-off selfies. But for some reason, much older posts are getting likes and comments, and my list of followers has exploded.

At the bottom of my notifications, I find my answer.

@MsShelbyMorgan tagged you in a post.

"Oh my God." I tap the link to Shelby's post. It's a photo from last weekend. The selfie of Shelby and me, carefully cropped and filtered to obscure the clubhouse's background.

@MsShelbyMorgan: Hanging with the makeup QUEEN @TranquilSparkle go check out her flocking fab tutorials!

"Holy shit!" I slap my hand over my mouth, conscious of my loud voice in the quiet apartment.

I quickly navigate to my YouTube channel, which has also received tons of new views, likes, and comments. "Oh my God," I repeat over and over. This is huge.

"Why aren't you in bed with me?" Gray rasps.

I tear my gaze away from my sky-rocketing numbers and almost drop my phone.

Gray fills up the bedroom doorway. Shirtless, with his arms raised and braced against the doorframe. Why did I get out of bed when this sexy beast of a man was waiting for me? He yawns and stretches, showing off toned muscles and inked skin.

"I'm having trouble remembering."

The corner of his mouth slides up. "Like what you see, huh?"

"Very much."

"All right. I'll forgive you for letting me wake up alone." He glances toward the kitchen, a playful smile flickering over his mouth. "And not starting the coffee."

"Look." I thrust my phone at him. "Shelby tagged me in a post and my socials are exploding."

"I definitely need coffee to figure that one out." He kisses the top of my head as he passes me. I scroll and scroll through new comments. Deleting mean ones and answering nice ones. "I better thank Shelby. She said she'd tag me, but I didn't really expect her to."

"You got her number?" Gray asks.

"Yup." I tap out a quick text.

Me: *Thank you so much for the mention!*
Shelby: *Anytime!*

A second text comes through from her with a flamingo, crown, and sunflower emoji. Grinning, I send her back a heart.

"Okay, so tell me what put that glow on your face this morning?" Gray sets a mug on the coffee table in front of me and takes a seat.

"Tea?" I peer into my mug and give his a forlorn look. "I feel it's unfair for you to drink coffee when I can't."

He pauses mid-sip. "I didn't think you'd want to blow your one cup this early in the day."

"I'm not going to bother with the one cup." I pick up the tea and stir the spoon through it. "I don't want to risk it. I'll stick to tea."

"I'll knock back to one cup a day, then."

"Now, that's true love." I lean in and kiss his cheek.

"When we're together," he adds.

Shaking with laughter, I set my mug down. "Fair enough." I pick up my phone again. "This was so sweet of Shelby."

"That she mentioned you?"

Gray doesn't quite understand and I'm not sure how to explain without adding a bunch of details that won't mean much to him. "She has a much bigger audience than I do. Theoretically, a large part of her audience should consist of teenage girls or young women, who may also be interested in makeup. So by tagging me like that, she just gave me exposure to a whole audience I might not be able to reach otherwise."

"So, free advertising?"

"Exactly."

"What does that mean for you?"

"The more I grow my audience, the more I'll attract companies who will pay me to make videos about their products. More ad revenue from my channel. Stuff like that."

"That's great." He scratches his hand over his beard. "So you actually make money with that?" He flicks his hand toward my phone.

I duck my head. It always feels so weird or silly to talk about this with people who don't understand. "It started out as a hobby, but yes, I earn enough to pay some bills with it. Not enough to match my PT salary or anything."

A pained expression creases his brow. Damn it. I wasn't trying to make him feel bad about losing my job.

I glance at the clock. "Do you need to get to Strike Back?"

"Yeah, I'm supposed to open."

"You're sure you don't mind me going to class with Emily?"

"Of course not." He rests his hand on my leg. "I just want you to be careful."

"Em knows I'm not ready to tell anyone I'm pregnant yet. She promised to be my partner and go easy on me."

"I'll remind Jake not to single you out for anything."

"Wait, what reason are you going to give him?"

He stares at me for a few seconds. "That I don't want another man's hands on my woman."

I snort-giggle into my tea. "That's believable. Especially with that face you're making."

He pulls the cup from my hands and sets it on the table again. "It's believable because it's true." He tugs me into his lap, cuddling me into his protective embrace. He lifts my shirt and rests his hand against my stomach. "Why aren't you ready to tell anyone?" he asks quietly.

My gaze narrows on his large, rough hand protectively curled over my pale stomach. "I'm scared," I whisper.

"Of?"

I rub my thumb over his and he twines our fingers together. "I don't want to jinx things. It's still early and I'm so scared of losing..." *Don't say it. Don't say it.* "Of something happening," I finish.

He lets out a slow breath. Only as his body relaxes underneath mine is it obvious he was worried about my answer. "So, it's not me."

"You? No, why would you think that?"

He lifts his hand, like he's preparing to list a number of reasons. "Ex-con, old enough to—"

"No." I wrap my fingers around his and bring his hand back to my stomach. "That's never crossed my mind."

"Never?" He raises his eyebrows in disbelief.

Frustrated, I sit up and slide out of his lap. "You're not 'ex-con' or 'older guy' to me." I cup his cheek and turn him to face me. "You're just 'man I love very much.'"

He tips his head and brushes his lips against my wrist.

"I'm a little embarrassed how soon it happened," I admit. "I hate people thinking I tried to trap you or that I'm careless or something." I shrug, feeling silly now that I said that out loud.

"Since it's my kid, my opinion's the only one that matters. And I don't think that at all."

"Good, glad we cleared that up." I pop another kiss on his cheek, grab my tea and head to the kitchen.

"What are you doing? I'll make you breakfast." Gray follows me.

"I just want toast."

"You need to eat protein. Let me make you an egg."

The thought of an egg sends a wave of revulsion rolling through my stomach. "Nope."

"Peanut butter on the toast at least?" He opens a cabinet and pulls out a glass jar. "It's that organic, only-peanuts-and-salt-not-in-a-plastic-jar kind you said you prefer."

Laughing, I take the jar out of his hand and set it on the counter. "You remembered that?"

"It seemed important to you."

"I read this thing about pesticides and allergies. I just don't want to eat something that might not be good for junior." I grab a spoon from the drawer and twist the lid on the peanut butter. When I can't open it, Gray pries it from my hand, gives it a quick twist and screws off the top.

"And I love that about you." He slides the jar over to me. "None of that stuff would ever occur to me."

"I can't stop thinking about it." I take a small lick of peanut butter, then spread some on my toast.

"That's the kind of stuff I was talking about when I said I want you to let me help you."

I pause and set my spoon down. "You help me with lots of things."

"Okay. Well, if there's more I can do, tell me."

"You're late!" Emily shouts.

I close the front door and kick off my shoes. "Give me five minutes to change."

She races over to meet me, thrusting her phone in my face. "How do you know Shelby Morgan?"

Laughing, I grab her phone and check out the photo of Shelby and me. "She's engaged to one of Gray's friends."

Her eyes widen. "By friend, do you mean one of his biker brothers?"

"Yes. Rooster."

"Rooster." She raises an eyebrow. "I bet there's a cock joke in there somewhere."

"Probably," I laugh. "He's a really nice guy, though."

"Gee, this must be some club if all the guys are *so nice*." Her mocking tone prickles over my skin.

"They are…well, to club family."

"Be prepared." She snatches her phone away. "Libby's going to grill you big time. She *loves* Shelby Morgan."

"Really?" I don't know Shelby well enough to ask her for favors. And she's already done me a huge one. But maybe she wouldn't mind signing something for Libby. I'll have to ask next time I see her.

CHAPTER THIRTY-THREE

Serena

"Ready for our big day, buttercup?" Gray leans in and kisses my cheek.

"I think so." I open the front door wider and shout, "Em, I'm going!"

"Okay. Good luck!" she calls out.

I pull the door closed behind me and join Gray outside. "You didn't have to come to the door to get me."

He stares at me as if I shook a can of soda in his face and popped the top. "What do you want me to do, sit at the curb and honk the horn like a teenager?"

"Well, you don't have to be so formal. That's all I meant."

He holds the passenger side door open for me and helps me into the truck. "No one's ever called me *formal* before."

I sigh as he closes the door and rounds the truck.

"Are you nervous?" he asks once we're on the road.

"Honestly, yes." I smooth my long skirt over my legs. "I'm not a fan of having wands shoved up my vagina."

Gray chokes. "Is that what we're doing today?"

"You didn't read any of the stuff I sent, did you?"

"I skimmed it."

I roll my eyes and stare out the window. "The baby is maybe a couple centimeters long at this stage. That's the best way to see it. It's uncomfortable but doesn't hurt. Just awkward."

"Well, I'm going to be right there with you, no matter what."

His calm assurance chases some of my anxiety away. I reach over and rest my hand on his leg. "Thank you."

My appointment's later this time, so we have to wait. Gray's full of happy energy. God, I don't want to disappoint him today.

While we're waiting, I pull out my phone to show Gray a crib that I like.

"You want to look for that after we're done here?" he asks.

"Maybe. There's a baby store in Slater that's supposed to have one. Do you think it's too soon, though? I hate to lug it to Emily's and then…" My voice trails off. The reminder that our situation is still up in the air seems to zap Gray's cheery mood.

Good job, Serena.

Another patient loudly gushes about the baby shower her mother-in-law threw for her over the weekend to the receptionist. "Oh, we did the blind-folded baby food test! It was such a hoot. Maryanne almost threw up the pureed chicken. It smells like cat food. But we made out like bandits…"

I stare out the window and try and tune out the long list of baby presents she rattles off. It's not the awful games or gifts that bother me. I don't need *stuff*. Gray's been more than supportive and active in buying whatever I need and I've never been a fan of goofy party games.

What I can't stop thinking about is that I don't have women in my family to plan a shower for me. Not for the gifts, but for the stories and advice they'd share. My grandmother would've had all sorts of warm memories to tell me. She would've knitted a dozen pairs of baby booties by now. Damn, I miss her. Emily's been more than supportive. But she can't give me baby advice. Besides, she's done enough for me. I wouldn't dare even hint to her about a baby shower. I haven't spoken to Amanda since I ran into her downstate and she's definitely not a baby shower person either.

"You all right?" Gray closes his hand over mine. "You look so sad all of a sudden."

I force a smile. "Still nervous about the appointment." At least that's true.

"Serena!" the nurse calls out.

"Thank God." I grab my bag and hurry to meet her.

This time I'm less embarrassed about having Gray there watching everything. He's a large, calm, comforting presence.

"So, how do you feel today?" Dr. West asks as she breezes into the exam room.

"I've had a few episodes of morning sickness."

"Hmm. Okay." She taps her tablet a few times. "Tired?"

"Yes."

"That's normal, right, doctor?" Gray asks.

"Yes. Perfectly normal at this stage. Her body's going through a lot of changes."

She runs through more questions and then squeezes my blood pressure out of me. For some reason the compression of the cuff annoys me more than usual.

"Better than last time but still elevated," Dr. West says. "We'll keep monitoring."

"I'm watching my salt, taking my vitamins, exercising—"

"All good," she assures me. "It's just something I want to monitor as you progress, Serena. You're not doing anything wrong."

The part I'm tied up in knots over comes next. Gray's right next to me, holding my hand, watching the doctor's every move. His anxious eyes dart to the dark screen every few seconds.

I twitch and shift on the narrow table.

"Stay still," the doctor murmurs.

A soft *whooshing* fills the room, then what sounds like a dozen horses galloping. I squeeze my eyes shut, so grateful for that sound. A tear slips from my eye, rolling into my hair.

"There it is."

The doctor's soft voice opens my eyes and I find her pointing to the screen.

"Is that our baby?" The awe in Gray's voice wraps around my heart. He reaches for my hand, curling his fingers around mine and squints at the screen.

"That's it." The doctor traces her finger over a small dot. "It's too early to see much."

"Everything looks okay?" My voice shakes as I get out the question.

"Yes. This gives me a better idea of your due date too."

"It's so fast." Gray's grinning from ear to ear.

"The heartbeat is strong," the doctor agrees.

Once we're finished, she gives me some leaflets about childbirth classes and ways to manage blood pressure.

"That was amazing," Gray says when we're alone in the truck together. He reaches over and takes my hand. "Thank you."

"Thank you for coming with me."

"I wouldn't have missed this for anything."

"Well, I really liked having you there. I feel so overwhelmed sometimes." I flip through the pamphlets the doctor gave me. "Most women have parents and in-laws to help them. Or at least share their wisdom."

"Sorry, buttercup. My folks are long gone and they weren't wise."

"My mom's probably still out there running around somewhere." I flip my hand at the windshield. "But I sure as fuck wouldn't let her near my kid." I stare straight ahead, feeling childish. "Sorry I'm being so whiny today. I'm just in a mood."

"We got good news. Doc says the baby looks healthy." He slides his hand over mine. A soothing gesture to go along with his gentle, coaxing voice. "Why don't we start telling people now? I think Hope and Lilly would be happy to share some advice with you."

"You think so?"

"Yes, I do. Heidi's pregnant too. Only a few months ahead of you. She can probably give you a lot of current info."

Are Heidi and I ready for that kind of friendship? "Maybe."

"How about Thursday?" he suggests. "Family dinner night. We can tell everyone at once."

"Let's see who shows up first."

"Are you worried?"

"That someone might say something snarky about me getting knocked up so quickly? Yes, I've already told you that."

"Then you should know," he pauses and glances over at me, "the first person who opens their mouth and utters an ugly word is getting punched in the throat."

For some reason, that cheers me up. Impending motherhood must be making me bloodthirsty.

CHAPTER THIRTY-FOUR

Serena

"Are you sure this looks okay? I'm barely showing. No one's going to believe me."

Gray studies me with a critical eye. It only makes me fidget more. "Stop staring at me."

"You asked me to look at you." His voice holds only a fraction of frustration. "Yes, you look lovely. I like that shade of blue on you."

I reach up and fiddle with the straps of my dress. "It might still be too cold. I'm going to grab a sweater."

Gray follows me up the stairs to my room. "You've done a nice job in here." He stands in the doorway.

"You can come in. Sorry I haven't had you come up since we moved my stuff in. We're always in a hurry to go somewhere."

He steps inside, closing the door behind him. "We're not in a hurry tonight."

"No?" I push hanger after hanger aside, not finding a sweater that will match my cobalt blue dress. "Doesn't dinner start at a certain time?"

Gray's strong, rough hands grip my hips and yank me against his hard body. His warm breath skates over my shoulder and neck. "Don't know. Don't care right now."

I laugh and jerk my shoulder as his beard tickles over my skin. "That tickles."

"Yeah? How about this?" He nips and sucks at the sensitive spot between my neck and shoulder.

My knees turn to jelly and I sag against him. "Tickles in a different way," I murmur.

"When's Emily coming home?"

"I don't know. Not for a while."

"Mmm," he growls against my neck. "Whole place to ourselves?"

"Yes," I whisper.

He slides his hands under my dress and trails his fingers over the backs of my legs.

I dance in place, wiggling but not really trying to get away. "That tickles even more."

"Trust me, I'm not trying to tickle you." He hooks his fingers in my underwear and tugs.

"I shouldn't bother getting dressed before you pick me up."

He releases me and steps back, the warmth of his body disappearing.

"What's wrong?" I turn to face him.

"Nothing. You're right. I shouldn't start groping you the second I see you."

By the crinkle between his eyes, I can tell he's serious and not trying to lay a guilt trip on me. "I was kidding." I step closer and pull my dress over my head, dropping it on my dresser. "I like your hands on me."

"That's one thing we have in common, then." His greedy eyes roam over my body and his mouth curls at the corners. "Your underwear matches your dress."

I stare down at my sheer mesh and satin bra and panty set. "I like to match inside out sometimes."

"I like. Very much." He curls his finger at me. "Come closer."

I stop to take off my sandals first.

"I liked them on. Puts you at a nice height for me," Gray says.

"Sorry."

He holds out his arms, waiting for me to come to him this time.

I happily close the distance, snuggling up against his chest.

"Mmm, that's better." He kisses the top of my head, then wraps his arms around me and lifts.

"What are you doing?" I squeal, grabbing onto his shoulders.

"Exploring my girl."

"Exploring?" I kiss his cheek and tease my fingers through his hair. "Have I ever mentioned how much I love your hair?"

"I don't think so."

"I'm a bad girlfriend, then."

He laughs, a low, happy rumble, and sets me on the bed. "You're welcome to run your fingers through it anytime, buttercup."

I reach for his belt but he closes his hand over mine, stopping me. "Not yet. Stretch out on the bed for me."

"Stretch...how?"

He cocks his head like it's a silly question but I'm really not sure what he's asking.

"Lie back and stretch your arms over your head."

"Oh, you want me to pose for you?" I arch my back, trying to be as graceful as possible.

"That's nice."

I can't see him now but I hear the clink of his belt buckle. The ticking of his zipper and the rustle of his pants. Tingles of anticipation skitter over my skin.

The bed dips as he eases next to me. "Hey, buttercup." He slides his arm under my head, encouraging me to cuddle up to him. "Ahh," he lets out in a contented sigh. "That's better."

I close my eyes, inhaling his clean, crisp scent—evergreen and mint. "You need skin-on-skin time with me?"

He tilts his head, looking down at me with an amused smile playing over his lips. "Exactly."

"Will we do this every night if we live together?"

"What's this *if* business about?" He slides his free hand over my side, stopping to rest on my stomach. "I want us all under the same roof."

If only Gray understood how many promises I've heard in my lifetime. Promises that were always broken. "I know."

He tilts his head, studying the room. "I meant what I said. It looks really nice in here."

"Thanks." I let out a frustrated snort. "It's not like I have a job to worry about going to. I've cleaned and organized my room an embarrassing number of times."

"You need money or anything else?"

"No, I'm good."

I close my eyes for a second, just enjoying the steady thump of his heart under my cheek. The soothing way he strokes his hand through my hair and over my back shifts me into a dreamy state.

"Tired, buttercup?"

"A little," I mumble.

"We don't have to go tonight."

I've been mentally preparing myself for making this announcement all day. "No. I want to go."

"Have you thought about baby names?" he asks.

I prop my chin on his chest so I can see his face. "Only since I was like ten years old."

He chuckles, jostling me. "Tell me."

"Well, I like Lincoln for a boy."

"Interesting. That was my grandfather's name."

"Really?"

"Yup. I like it. How about for a girl?"

"I like the name Bliss."

"Serena and Bliss...yeah, that makes sense."

"I thought about Bliss Lauren for my grandmother."

"She was good to you, your grandmother?" he asks.

"Yes," I answer, careful not to open a door to my past. "She let me live with her when I wasn't safe with my mother."

"Why weren't you safe with your own mother?"

Warning. I sit up, instantly on the defensive. "Gray, remember how you told me talking about prison stuff was off-limits? One of those things you're not comfortable with me asking you about?"

"Yeah," he answers slowly.

"Well, talking about my family and past trauma is off-limits for me. Besides the stuff I've already told you."

"Wait a second, Serena. That's not the same thing."

"I've dealt with it in therapy." I want to argue that my past won't affect my ability to be a good mother, but he hasn't suggested that. Yet.

He hesitates, then nods. "Okay. But if you ever want to talk to me about it, you can."

I doubt it will be the last time he brings it up, but for now he respects this boundary. And for that, I'm grateful. "Thank you."

Downstairs, the front door slams, ending this conversation. "That must be Libby."

"Does she bust into your room without knocking?" he asks, reaching for his pants.

"Sometimes, yeah."

I cock my head, listening for any other sounds. "She must've gone into the kitchen."

"It's fine. We should get going, anyway."

I scoot off the bed and collect my dress, slipping it over my head. Gray's buckling his belt when I turn around. "I was enjoying our cuddle time."

"Same, buttercup."

"Serena!" Libby knocks on my door, then flings it open. "Oh, shit! Oh, no! Sorry."

"Great, I was hoping to avoid that," Gray grumbles. He slips into his T-shirt.

"We're both dressed. She'll live." I try to sound casual, but inside I'm cringing. Emily never said I couldn't have Gray over, but I feel like *no male guests* was implied. I grab a denim jacket and open my door.

No Libby in the hallway. "I probably scarred her for life," I mutter.

Behind me, Gray snorts.

I hurry downstairs and find Libby tucked into a corner of the couch. "Sorry, sorry!" She holds up her hands. "My fault for not waiting for an answer."

There's no point in protesting that nothing happened. "What's up?"

"Hi, Mr. Lock." She waves at Gray. "Sorry 'bout that." She focuses on me again. "I wanted to ask for a ride. But I'll just wait until Em gets home."

"No, we can give you a ride," Gray offers. "Where do you need to go?"

"My friend's house." She rattles off the directions and it sounds like it's on our way.

"Thank you," I whisper to Gray on our way to the truck.

"No problem."

Libby chats the entire way to her friend's house. I can't tell if it's because she's embarrassed about before or she's just in a chatty mood. Either way, Gray doesn't seem to mind. In fact, he actually seems to listen. Every now and then he asks her a question or to explain some teenage lingo.

He stops the truck in front of her friend's house. "Do you have a ride home?"

"Her mom will drive me home." Libby shoves the door open. "Thanks, guys." She waves as she races up the driveway.

Gray waits a few seconds until Libby disappears inside and then puts the truck in drive.

"Thanks for doing that. Helping Emily out with transportation was the one thing she asked me to do when I moved in."

"It's really not a problem." He glances over. "Feels like it's good practice, anyway."

"I think we have some time before our little peanut is bursting into our room and asking us for rides."

He shakes his head sadly. "Time has a way of slipping out of our grasp."

CHAPTER THIRTY-FIVE

Grinder

FAMILY NIGHT AT THE CLUBHOUSE IS ALMOST AS LOUD AND CHAOTIC AS chow time in prison. The big difference is how happy everyone is to see each other. I'm also not worried about anyone stabbing me. Food's better too. Maybe it's just the noise setting me on edge.

Serena seems to be agitated too. She's been fidgeting with her hair or dress every few minutes since we arrived at the clubhouse. No matter how many times I tell her she looks beautiful. I shouldn't force her into making this announcement. But what she said after leaving the doctor's office really got to me. She needs some knowledgeable females who can help her with pregnancy stuff.

"Hey." I pull her closer. "Instead of announcing it to everyone, would you rather just talk to Rock and Hope?"

She seems to contemplate that for a second. "No, I geared myself up to make the announcement. So we might as well."

That's not encouraging but I take her at her word.

"Is this a Spring Thanksgiving?" Z asks, pointing his knife at the four turkeys lined up on the table. "What's going on here?"

"We let Sparky pick the menu," Trinity says.

"I thought meat was murder?" Wrath shouts down to Sparky.

"Tasty, tasty murder!" Sparky yells back.

"Were the Brussels sprouts your idea too?" Jigsaw picks one up and chucks it at Sparky who catches it in his open mouth.

"Don't start throwing food," Rock warns. He lifts his chin at Alexa whose eyes gleam as she reaches for a Brussels sprout.

"No, no," Heidi says, placing the bowl farther away.

"Apologies for setting a bad example for the little ones," Jigsaw says, dipping his chin at Heidi.

"Bad example for *humanity*, you mean," Murphy says.

Jiggy reaches over and stabs a sprout with his fork. "That too."

"If that goes anywhere but your mouth, I'm gonna stuff every one of your holes full of Brussels sprouts until you're airtight," Z warns.

"Don't threaten me with a good time, Prez." Jigsaw grins and sticks the sprout in his mouth, chewing slowly. "Mmmm, bacon grease. These aren't bad."

"That's how my mom made 'em," Sparky says.

"You have a *human* mother?" Steer gasps. "I woulda sworn you were hatched from an egg."

"It's going to be a while until we get to the adult conversation," I mutter to Serena. "So don't lose your nerve."

She's too busy shaking with laughter, an improvement from earlier.

As we start on dessert, Rock taps his glass. "All right. Anyone have good news to share this week?"

"I won my trial," Charlotte says.

A round of applause goes around the table.

"You help set some poor helpless criminal free, Char?" Wrath asks.

"You know it." She raises her water glass in his direction. "Seriously, though, no. It was a defamation case for a private client."

"Very nice, Charlotte." Z looks around the table. "Who else?"

"One of my book covers won a contest," Trinity says. "I've had a lot of new jobs come in from the exposure."

"Was it one of your hot man-chest covers?" Rav shouts.

"Was Wrath on the cover?" someone else asks.

"No and no. It's something new I tried, that's why I'm extra excited about it doing so well."

She gets a loud round of applause.

"Anyone else starting to feel like our women outshine us a little?" Dex asks.

"Yeah, but that's nothing new," Murphy points out. "We're used to it."

"Speak for yourself," Stash says.

"Oh yeah? What'd you accomplish this week?" Murphy asks.

"I ate an entire family size bag of cheese puffs all by myself in one sitting." Stash stands and pats his stomach.

"Is that where my cheese puffs disappeared to?" Sparky's face twists with outrage.

Butcher raises his hand. "I raised my kill-death ratio in Call of Duty to a solid three-point-oh."

"I rest my case," Murphy mutters.

Rav raises his hand next. "I went two whole days without watching any porn. Like, none."

Across the table, Charlotte's jaw drops. "You need a good therapist who enjoys a challenge."

Rock closes his eyes and takes a long, slow breath. "Let's save whatever kind of achievement that is for the *after dark* segment of the night."

I stand and pull Serena up with me. "Serena and I have news." I curl my arm around her waist. Her body trembles slightly and I give her a squeeze. "We're having a baby."

Our news explodes like fireworks. The dining room erupts in a flurry of excitement and congratulations.

"Oh my God!" Lilly jumps out of her chair and runs over to us, hugging Serena fiercely. "This is so great. I'm so happy for you guys. How do you feel?" She peppers Serena with a breathless list of questions. Hope and Heidi join them, pulling Serena slightly away from the table.

"We had a pact," Rav moans and pounds his fist against the table. "No more babies for a while."

"Absolutely no one signed onto that," Teller answers with an eye-roll.

"We're still team 'no babies' down here," Wrath says, pointing to Trinity, and then himself.

"Hear, hear." Shelby leans over the table and gives Wrath a high five.

"Thank you, brother!" Rav shouts. "You too, sister!" He points at Shelby.

Rock walks over with a smile stretched across his face and shakes my hand. "I had a feeling something was up with you two. Congratulations."

"Thanks."

Two heavy hands land on my shoulders and yank me backward. "You know I'm just fucking around, right?" Wrath rumbles. "Congratulations, brother. Happy for you."

"Thanks."

"I hope you have a girl, though, because I still want to be your favorite son."

"You're the only one with an ego big enough to come up with that," Z says.

"It's a gift, right?" Wrath grins at us.

Teller joins us and hugs me. "You're gonna be a great father, Grinder. Congrats."

"Thanks."

As the excitement dies down, most of the club returns to discussing other things. The girls still have Serena in their circle, reinforcing my gut feeling that this was a good time to share our news.

"Take a walk with me." Rock wraps his arm around my shoulders, not giving me a chance to say yes or no, and steers me toward the hallway.

"Where you taking me, Prez?"

"Somewhere quieter, that's all. How are you doing with all this?"

Now that we're far enough away from everyone, I blow out a breath. "Honestly? Scared shitless. I'm worried I'm way too fucking old to be having a kid."

Rock nods knowingly and opens the war room door, motioning for me to go in ahead of him.

He stops at his cabinet and raises an eyebrow at me. "Yeah, I'll share a toast with you. Ain't seeing my P.O. until next week."

He sets two tumblers on the table and adds a neat pour of less than two ounces to each. "Worried I'll go wild on ya?" I joke.

"Trying to ease you in slow, Gray." He lifts the bottle, silently asking if I want more.

"This is fine." I nod to the bottle. "Fancy stuff. Didn't realize you'd acquired such expensive habits."

"Hope buys it for my birthday."

"Ahh, figured she was the one with the classy taste."

He huffs a short laugh. "Got that."

I take a slow sip, savoring the smooth burn. Been a long time. "Glad we finally told the club."

"Serena didn't want to?"

"She was worried."

"Yeah, Hope didn't tell me right away." He lifts his glass and stares at it for a second. "We waited to tell everyone, too. Just in case."

"I've barely figured out the landscape of how the world works these days. Now, I'm going to try to raise a kid for the first time? At my age. It seems crazy."

"Being an older first-time parent isn't all that bad." Rock's gaze shifts to the closed door. "At first it's annoying. Everyone feels the need to point it out to you. In case you're not aware."

"I hear that," I grumble.

"But hopefully with age comes wisdom and patience. Fuck knows you'll need both."

"How can you say that? Grace is a doll."

He huffs with laughter. "She's sweet ninety-nine percent of the time. That one percent is murder, though."

"I believe it."

"What I mean is, things you might not have understood when you were younger, or cared enough to figure out, will be easier to accept." He holds his hand high in the air, parallel to the table. "Our life experience gives us an ability to see things from that thousand-foot perspective we don't have when we're younger."

"Yeah, but kids think they know it all and don't give a shit about life experience."

"That's exactly what I'm talking about. You're old enough to understand that about kids and react accordingly." He smirks. "Seriously, Gray. You're going to be fine."

"I'm scared to death I'm gonna fuckin' die and leave her alone with a kid who won't have any memories of me." Wow, I finally found the words to express what's been eating at me the most.

"That's a harsh possibility." As usual Rock doesn't sugarcoat things to soothe my feelings. "I worried about that a lot at first too."

"You're not as old as me, fucker."

"I'm aware." He drills me with a shut-up-and-listen stare. "I hope, by now, you know I keep my promises. Anything happens to you, the club will take care of your family."

Shit, yeah. He sent money to Rose for years at my request. Even when she told him to fuck off. Things are different now, but I'm still confident he'd do right by Serena. "It's the only thing that allows me to sleep at night."

"That's what the brotherhood's supposed to be. What it was always meant to be. We live hard, the way we want, and accept the consequences because we know our brothers will take care of us."

"Amen." A sense of peace settles over me. It's a relief to finally get some of this stuff off my chest. "Thanks, Rock. Appreciate talking this out with you."

"Anytime you need to talk, I'm here to listen." He hesitates for a second. "I know you're worried about burdening Serena while she's going through this, but she's a smart woman. She can handle it."

"I'm sure she can. But I don't want her to worry about anything else. I'm trying to make things easier on her, not harder."

"Believe me, I understand. But one way or another, you two are in this together for a long time, so don't shut her out."

"I'll try. I'd really rather not keep reminding her of the age difference if I can help it."

He bites his lip, as if he's trying not to laugh. "Like I said, she's a smart woman. I'm sure she's noticed by now."

"Don't be a jackass."

"It's only a problem if *you* make it a problem."

"Yeah," I grumble. "Hey, thank Hope for me. Appreciate her talking to Serena. She's been a little down that she doesn't have a lot of female relatives and stuff to help her out. I'm trying to support her as much as I can but…"

"Of course." He cocks his head toward the door, listening for a second. "Can't have a strong brotherhood without a strong sisterhood. Took a while for that to sink in."

"Well, you all seem to have chosen well." I drain the last of my scotch and set the glass down.

"Better go find her or Hope will be loading her up with more baby stuff than you're prepared to take home tonight." He stops and frowns. "Where are you planning to call *home*?"

"Don't know yet. She's still at her friend's place. I was hoping to get off parole, then figure out the living situation, but I might need to figure it out sooner."

"If you need…assistance with anything, come talk to me."

"I ain't borrowing money from you, Rock." I force a wry smile. "Besides, didn't I tell you about the consolation cash Priest gave me?"

He grunts in acknowledgment. "I'm not saying borrow money from me." His gaze slides to the door again. "Club's done well with some investments that we've kept…close to home."

"So, not reported to National."

He lifts one shoulder but doesn't confirm or deny. "Teller's the one who did the hard work. He's the investment genius. But you would've been a member upstate if you'd been out, so you should—"

"You've given me more than enough, Rock."

"Listen, if *you* want to be stubborn, that's fine. Go sleep in the woods for all I care. But you're gonna have an ol' lady and baby to think about soon. I'm not saying pick out a million-dollar mansion and I'll finance it for you. I'm saying, you might have trouble getting credit, a mortgage, or whatever. And if that's the case, let me know. Teller and I can help you sort it out."

"No wonder you're such an effective president. Got all the right words at your disposal to bend me to your will."

"It's my superpower."

I slap my hand on the table and stand. "At least you're humble."

Laughing, he stands too, then pulls me in for a hug. "Congrats, brother. You two gonna find out what you're having or wait?"

"Shit, I don't know. I didn't ask Serena what she wants to do yet."

"You've got time. I know Z's itching for another boy to come into the family."

"Fuck, I don't even care, as long as the baby's healthy." I eye him closer. "You two gonna have another? Try for a boy?"

"Nope. Didn't think we'd be able to have one, so we don't want to press our luck." He glances around the war room. "Always said I didn't want kids because I already felt like I was raising a bunch of 'em."

"Shit, if that's not fucking accurate."

"But Grace is something else." His usually hard face softens. "Well, you're going to find out soon enough."

"You got any other advice for me?" My how the tables have turned. Me coming to Rock for life tips.

"Have you gone to her doctor appointments?"

"Yeah, we had the first ultrasound the other day. Things looked good."

His mouth curves. "Hearing that heartbeat the first time..." He shakes off whatever memory came back to him and turns serious again. "Keep going with her if you can. You'll learn a lot."

"Yeah, been real enlightening so far."

"You'll be fine. No doubt." He slaps me on the back and walks with me to the door.

Lilly is waiting outside of the war room. She tosses an anxious glance over her shoulder. "Grinder, can I talk to you for a sec?"

"Sure."

"Z still in the dining room?" Rock asks her.

"I think so."

After Rock leaves, she wraps her hand around my arm and pulls me to the side. "Congratulations. We're all really happy for you two."

"Thanks, sweetheart."

She flicks another nervous look around the room. "Can you give me the number of Serena's friend…Emily, right? The one she's staying with?"

"Uh, yeah, I guess. Why?" I pull my cell phone out to search for the number.

"Well, from what she's said, I understand Serena doesn't have other family? It sounds like Emily's the person she's closest to." Her eyes dart around the room and she lowers her voice. "I wanted to ask her if she's throwing Serena a baby shower. If not, I'd like to offer to host it at our place. But not if I'm stepping on Emily's toes or anything."

My chest tightens and I have the strongest urge to hug Lilly. I keep my cool, though. "Thank you. I don't know what, if anything, Emily has planned. I don't know how any of that stuff works."

Lilly laughs softly. "Of course you don't."

"Let me know what you need—money, whatever—so I can help out."

"There's no need." Her expression shifts to serious, almost sad. "I never had a baby shower. And I missed Hope's. We already threw one for Heidi. It's different when you're a first-time mom, though. I'd really like to do this for Serena."

Now, I can't stop myself. I pull her in and give her a gentle squeeze. "That means a lot to me, Lilly. Thank you."

"Of course." She pulls her phone out of her back pocket.

I find Emily's number and recite it for Lilly.

"Perfect." She jams her phone in her pocket. "I'll reach out to her tomorrow."

"That sounds good."

Music and happy shrieks from the kids echo down the hallway.

"Oh, boy. Sounds like they're getting into it," Lilly laughs. "We're supposed to herd them into the living room for movie night and snacks."

"Bet that's not easy." I escort her to the dining room where the little ones have taken over the entertainment part of the night.

Shelby has her guitar out, leading a sing-along.

Lilly winces as Chance and Alexa hit a few off-key high notes. "I don't think either of them will be touring with Shelby in the future," she whispers to me.

"You never know." I lift my chin in Shelby's direction. "She seems willing to give them lessons."

"Aren't they adorable?" Serena joins us, hooking her arm through mine. "Even little Grace is into it."

"Oh, yeah, she *loves* Shelby's singing," Lilly says.

A scuffle breaks out between Chance and Alexa. I can't see how it starts but it ends with Chance pushing Alexa on her butt. She's tough though, and jumps right back up. Unfortunately, her revenge is thwarted by Murphy scooping her out of the fray.

Z sweeps Chance into his arms for a stern lecture.

Lilly sighs and holds out her hand to her son when Z sets him down. "Come here, buddy, let's chill for a minute."

"Why'd you scold him?" Rav asks. "She started it."

Z stares at Rav like he's grown two heads. "I'm not teaching him it's okay to put his hands on women."

"Yeah, but Alexa started it," Rav insists.

"I don't fuckin' care."

"And I'll talk to her about *that*," Heidi says as Murphy sets Alexa in her lap.

"But—" Rav protests.

Z thumps his chest. "Look at me. I'm not fucking tiny. Chance is gonna end up as big as me if not bigger. Right now it's kids rough-housing but when he's older, he'll end up doing some damage. I don't want him thinking it's okay to hit girls for any reason." A little calmer, Z adds, "His job is to protect and provide. Not be some douche who thinks fairness means hitting women. Fuck that." He points at Murphy, then Rock, and Teller. "One of you needs to have a son for him to rough-house with soon."

"I'm trying," Murphy says.

"Bro, why you so worried about everyone's parenting styles?" Teller asks Rav. "Stay in your porn and chicken nuggets lane."

Rav shrugs. "Someone who still has his balls attached has to look out for the little dude."

"My son will be fine," Z snaps. "Worry about yourself."

"Fuuuuck," Sparky groans. "Chance is *such* a lucky dude. He's got all the chicks around him."

"Watch where you're going with that thought," Murphy warns.

"All I'm saying is, it's cute. They'll all grow up together, be sweethearts. It's so storybook."

"Who knew Sparky was such a romantic?" Serena whispers in my ear.

"Nah." Ravage leans over and pats Chance's head. "You're gonna get friend-zoned and have to watch them date everyone *but* you. But don't you worry, there will always be plenty of bunnies around to return the favor."

"I think you said the quiet part out loud, bro," Stash says, running his fingers over his mouth like he's tugging on a zipper.

"All right, fuckstick." Z lifts his son into his arms. "Get away from my kid. I don't need you filling my son's head with garbage."

Chance scowls at Z.

"Let's go walk it off, buddy," Lilly says, leaning up to kiss Chance's cheek.

Shelby watches them leave the dining room and shakes her head. "I didn't even get to the moshing songs." She tucks her guitar in its case. "Little hellraisers ya'll got there." She catches sight of Grace snuggled in Hope's arms. "Except you. You're a lil' angel."

"Not always," Hope laughs.

"I'm a unicorn," Alexa insists, running over to Shelby.

"Yes, you are." Shelby squats down to Alexa's level and talks to her in a lower voice that doesn't make it over here.

Serena's eyes sparkle and there's a glow on her cheeks that was missing earlier. I pull her closer. "Feeling better about telling everyone?"

"Yes, actually." She watches Shelby and Alexa for a second. "I want our baby to grow up surrounded by family and other kids to play with."

"Even Ravage?"

She shifts her gaze toward him. "Well..."

"Hey!" Rav swaggers over to us. "I just enjoy yanking Z's chain. He's so easy to rile these days."

"There *are* worse things in the world than taking fatherhood seriously, you know," Dex says.

Rav shrugs. "Maybe I'm still pissed with him for moving downstate."

"Is hell freezing over?" Murphy shouts. "Did Rav just correctly identify a feeling?"

"Shut up, ginger. No one was talking to you."

"Romper room's been a blast," Hustler announces, "but are we all going down to CB and the new clubhouse tonight or not?"

"I'm headed down there to *work*," Dex says.

"Grinder, you still haven't seen the new clubhouse or been to CB," Rav points out. "What's up, bro?"

"Did you miss his earlier news?" Stash coughs in his fist. "Obviously, he's been getting *busy*."

Serena titters with laughter and presses her face against my chest. "Yes, you have," she says between giggles.

"G was locked up for fifteen years and *still* has better game than you two clowns, who gotta pay girls to talk to you," Jigsaw says to Rav.

"I ain't payin' them shit," Stash mutters.

"You better be tipping our girls if you're in the club wasting their time," Dex growls.

Rock walks up next to me. "As I was saying earlier..."

"Yeah, it's like raising a bunch of kids who never grow up."

"Grace should be a piece of cake after these guys," Serena says.

Rock chuckles. "Amen to that."

Hope, holding Grace, walks around the others to join us. Grace reaches for Rock when she's within grabbing distance and he pulls her into his arms. "I think you've had enough exposure to these degenerates for the night."

Grace bobs her head up and down.

"Hah." I laugh. "Smart cookie already."

"You heading home or taking Grace to the living room for movie night?" Z asks, rejoining our group.

"I'm not sure she'll be awake much longer," Hope says. "But we'll start the movie with you guys."

Grace waves at Serena over her dad's shoulder as he carries her out of the dining room.

"Ohhhh, she's so sweet." Serena sighs and melts against my side. "Now I hope we're having a girl."

"Hey." I nudge her shoulder. "When can we find out *what* we're having?"

"Ahh, there's a blood test to check for chromosomal conditions that can be used to tell if you're having a boy. I think I can do that in another couple of weeks. Otherwise, it's a longer wait until you can tell on an ultrasound."

"Do you want to know ahead of time?"

A little crease forms between her eyebrows. "Of course. Why wouldn't I?"

"Just wondering." I hug her to my side again. "We haven't talked about stuff like that, is all."

Her body relaxes against mine. "Oh, sure. Do *you* want to know?"

"Absolutely."

She blows out a breath. "Okay. Good."

Trinity joins us and drapes her arm over Serena's shoulders. "Is this whole scene making you rethink kids?" She paints her hand in the air in front of us.

Serena slaps her hand over her mouth and laughs. "No, but it's making me rethink letting Rav or Stash ever hang *around* my kids."

"Got that right," Z mutters next to me.

I elbow him in the side. "I think Rav just misses you."

Z smirks. "Whatever."

"No thank *yooo*," Shelby sings loud enough to draw our attention to her conversation with the guys. "Can't stand anyone yanking on my hair."

Serena winces. "I hate that too. I have a fear of going bald."

Trinity fluffs her hand through Serena's hair. "I don't think you have to worry about that anytime soon. You have beautiful hair." She winks at Serena. "Besides, it all depends on who's doing the pulling and *how*."

Serena casts a quick glance my way. "That's true."

"Ding-dong! We found the vanilla couple!" Rav points at Shelby then Rooster like a demented carnival barker.

"Fuck off, clown," Rooster sneers.

"Since when is vanilla a bad thing?" Dex steps forward, drawing everyone's attention, and holds out one hand. "It's a common flavor for a reason. Stands on its own, compliments other flavors, or it can be a building block to create new flavors."

"Mmm...have you ever had a really good French vanilla or bourbon vanilla?" Shelby squeezes her eyes shut. "Exquisite. I'd go for that any time."

"See." Dex nods at Shelby. "Vanilla is a classic for a reason."

Rooster slings his arm around Shelby's shoulders. "Yeah, brother. I get where you're going with your analogy, but stick to discussing ice cream with my ol' lady."

"Come on." Dex dismisses it with a wave of his hand. "You know me better than that."

"That's 'cause Dex is asexual." Rav grins like he came up with something clever.

"Jesus Christ," I mutter.

"Being community dick isn't exactly something to brag about, bro," Jigsaw points out. "It suggests you can't satisfy a woman so none of them come back for a second round of disappointment."

"Oh, shit!" Steer snaps his fingers and points at Rav.

"You're the last one to be pointin' fingers," Hustler reminds Steer. "Your dick's so toxic, I'm surprised it doesn't glow neon green."

Shelby slaps her hands over her ears. "*Lalalalala.* I don't want to hear 'bout anyone's willy."

Her silly plea is enough to cool the escalating insults that were bound to get someone punched soon.

"I'm just saying," Dex holds up both hands, then points at Ravage. "Quit yucking other folks' yum. Not liking something isn't a bad thing."

Rooster pulls Shelby into his lap and kisses her cheek. "I dunno. She threatened to mule kick me if I pulled her hair once."

"Right. Once. I didn't have to say it twice," Shelby agrees.

Steer lifts his chin at Shelby. "I can see why, if you wear those cowboy boots in bed, Shelby. They'd put a hurtin' on a man's nuts."

"Maybe." She kicks one foot out. "Come on over and let's see."

The guys roar with laughter, even Rooster, although he keeps sending Steer murderous glares in between chuckles.

"The two of 'em screech like barn owls in bed, so if that's vanilla, sign me up," Jigsaw says.

Shelby's eyes bug and her jaw drops.

"So, so many things wrong with that sentence, my dude." Sparky shakes his head. "So many."

"Z makes these horny bear noises." Murphy lifts his chin and grins at Z from across the room. "I legit thought we had a grizzly problem when we were living next door."

Z rolls his eyes. "We can't all sound like a wheezing Yeti."

"See." Sparky points at Murphy, then Z. "That's how you do it. Mock your brother, but leave the ladies out of it so you don't embarrass them."

"I don't *screech*." Shelby gives Jiggy a haughty chin lift. "I vocalize my pleasure."

"Loudly," Jigsaw agrees. "It was meant as a compliment."

"You're sleeping outside next summer." Rooster wads up his empty coffee cup and launches it at Jiggy's head.

I shift my gaze to the clock on the wall. "We better head home, buttercup."

"Sure."

"I'll walk out with you," Trinity says.

"Are ya leavin'?" Shelby races across the dining room, the soles of her boots clunking against the hard floor. "I barely got to talk to ya." She hugs Serena fiercely. "I knew I drew that Empress card for a reason. Congrats, you two. You'll have to let me do another reading for you soon."

"Anytime." Serena hugs her back. "Thank you again for the shout-out. I'm still seeing new followers from it."

"Oh my gosh, any time!"

Trinity reaches for Shelby, pulling her into their huddle. "Shelby mentioning my designs has given me a whole new side-business."

Shelby ducks her head, pink racing over her cheeks. "Gotta support my girls. You're both hella talented, I'm happy to be the megaphone givin' ya a boost." She gasps. "Oh, that reminds me! Rooster is building me this fan-flocking-tastic vanity room. It'll be a great backdrop if you still want to let me film a tutorial with you."

"Wow." Serena's eyes widen. "Yes, yes. I still want to do that," she stammers. "If you do."

"What is this 'Rooster's building me' bullshit?" Jigsaw says, slowly approaching our group. "I think you meant, 'Rooster suckered his best friend into doing lots of unpaid labor,' didn't you?"

"Aw, you know I appreciate it, Jiggy." Shelby pouts and reaches up to pat his cheek.

"As annoying as he is, he's good at putting stuff together," Rooster says, slapping Jigsaw's back so hard, he lurches forward.

"Easy, fucker."

Rooster lifts his chin at me. "You two heading out?"

"Yeah."

The girls go through another round of hugs and goodbyes. It's another half-hour until we finally make it out the front door.

Outside, under the stars, Serena takes a deep breath and closes her eyes, tipping her head back.

"Are you all right?" I ask.

"Yes, that was…better than I thought it would be."

"I'm sorry we have to leave." All these small tastes of freedom are dangerous for me. I can't wait until I don't have to worry about a curfew.

Soon, I hope. Soon.

CHAPTER THIRTY-SIX

Grinder

A *GET YOUR ASS TO THE CLUBHOUSE* TEXT FROM WRATH HAD HIT MY phone about an hour ago.

"I'm here, what's the emergency?" I push open the war room door. Only Wrath, Teller, Murphy, Dex, and Rock are seated at the table. "I got here as fast as I could."

Rock side-eyes me as if he's annoyed I didn't get here faster. Too fucking bad. He knows I live almost an hour away.

"Loco called," Rock explains. "He wants to meet up."

No wonder Rock's annoyed. He hates anyone demanding things from him, let alone the leader of some trivial street gang.

"He specifically requested your attendance," Wrath adds.

"It's about fucking time we heard from him. You think he has a lead on what's up with Grillo?"

"We'll find out." Rock stands and opens the closet door. Something beeps and there's a metal clank. Rock slips on a shoulder holster.

Teller's eyes narrow as Rock stuffs a pistol in each side of the holster. "You worried you might have to shoot someone tonight?"

Rock turns his head and stares at Teller for a beat. "No," he answers, slow and packed with sarcasm, "I'm packing Glocks in case we want to stop and go bowling. The fuck's wrong with you?"

Murphy doubles over, wheezing with laughter.

"I think if we start rolling in to visit Loco unarmed, he'll get offended," Wrath says. "It'll tarnish the gangster image of himself he has in his head."

Dex chuckles. "You should've been a psychologist. Nailed that one."

Teller throws a scowl at everyone. "Whatever. I'm just glad we're meeting him at the diner tonight instead of the whorehouse."

"Big amen to that, brother." Wrath reaches over and slaps Teller's arm. "Hoping he gives us a minute for dinner before we get down to business. I'm starving."

"Aw, poor Wrath." Murphy pulls a sad face. "Trinity didn't feed you today?"

"Actually, no. She's working late."

"Are your hands broken?" Teller asks. "Feed yourself, ya lazy bastard."

Wrath glances at his phone. "My feeding window starts at six."

"Jesus Christ," Rock mutters.

"Feeding window?" I cock my head at Wrath. "What are you, a fucking dog now?"

"Don't ask, Grinder," Murphy warns. "You get him started, he'll never shut the fuck up about intermittent fasting."

Wrath shoves Murphy to the side. "Don't be cranky with me. Not my fault you're gaining weight with Heidi pound-for-pound. She's having the baby, not you."

Teller snickers into his hand. "It's sympathy pounds."

"Shut up, both of you." Murphy lifts his shirt and smacks his abs. "Still harder than a brick wall."

"So is your head," Rock comments.

"Put your hairy belly away," Wrath groans. "You're gonna give me nightmares."

"Can't believe I missed fifteen years of this," I say to Rock.

He lifts his gaze to the ceiling. "Hasn't always been this colorful."

"Yeah, Wrath only learned to speak in full sentences recently," Murphy adds.

"Probably around the time your balls dropped," Wrath shoots back.

"What does that...what the...you know what, never mind." Dex slaps his hand on the table and stands. "We ready to go, Prez?"

"Yes, for the love of fuck, can we please." Rock waves his hands toward the door.

I fall in next to Murphy. "You trying to goad Wrath into killing you?"

"He knows I'm messing around."

Quick like a cobra, Wrath wraps one of the tree trunks he calls arms around Murphy's neck and choke-hugs him. "I don't know. You're extra mouthy today."

Murphy gags and tries to pry Wrath's arm from around his neck.

"I need my VP in one piece for this meeting," Rock warns.

Wrath releases Murphy and thumps him on the back.

"Thanks, Prez," Murphy croaks. "I felt your concern."

"I'll choke you myself if you don't settle the fuck down."

"Calm yourself, Rock," Teller says. "You're wound a little tight tonight."

"And you're begging for an ass-kicking. Watch your fuckin' mouth."

"So fucking glad I rushed up here for this bullshit," I mutter to Dex.

He shrugs. "They've been at it for days. Murphy runs his mouth. Rock calls him out. Teller mouths off to defend Murphy. Rock bites his head off." He waggles his hand toward them. "Then Wrath pokes his nose in it and makes it worse. Rinse, repeat."

"That ain't good."

"They'll get over it."

We finally get on the road. I decide to take my chances wearing my cut and riding with my club brothers, because fuck am I tired of worrying about every little thing. Dex rides at the back with me. Rock sets a lazy pace through the mountain roads leading to Loco's diner. It's old school. One of those buildings that looks like someone dropped a silver sardine can in the middle of a field. Parking lot could fit an entire city of cars in it.

Rock circles to the back of the building, backing his bike right up to the wall next to the door. Loco steps out with a big grin stretched across his smooth, dark face.

"Heard you all comin' about a mile away."

"That's the idea," Rock says, taking off his helmet and shaking Loco's hand.

"Kings ain't afraid of no one," Loco shouts in his highly animated way. "Gotta love it."

"Should we be afraid of someone around here?" Wrath asks, taking a slow glance around the parking lot.

"No. Fuck, no. You think I lost my fuckin' mind? That's not what I meant." Loco wiggles his fingers at us. "Come on inside."

Whatever bullshit was going on at the clubhouse has evaporated. Murphy and Teller remain stone-faced and silent as they fall in behind Rock. I follow behind Dex.

We enter what seems to be a hallway behind the kitchen. Hot stuffy air presses on my skin and the scent of grease and onions permeates the area.

"Grinder." Loco sticks out his hand. "Good to see ya again, Mr. Savage."

"I heard you wanted me here."

"I sure did."

Now that we're all inside, Rock slips off his shades and gives Loco a slow once-over. "No suit today?"

Seems like our first clue that things are about to get messy.

"This is dress-down day here at the diner." Loco sweeps his hand over his black baggy cargo jeans and long, plain black T-shirt. Pristine white sneakers peek out from under the hem of his pants.

"So, what are we doing here, Loco?" Rock asks. "I know you didn't gather all of us here for the Monday night meatloaf special."

"Actually, our meatloaf is the best in the Capital Region," Loco says in an offended tone. "I'll send you home with a to-go bag if you want."

"I'm good, thanks."

"I'll take a burger to go." Wrath elbows Rock. "The burgers are good here."

Rock glares at him but Loco lights up at the compliment. "Thank you, Wrath. I'll let our cook know you appreciate his creations."

"He was singing the praises of your burgers all afternoon," Murphy says with a straight face.

"Yeah?" Loco's eyes dart between Murphy and Wrath like one of them's yanking his chain.

"True story." Wrath pats his gut.

"Why don't you come visit more often, then?" Loco asks. "I'll comp you a burger or two any time you want, Mr. Wrath."

Rock sighs. Loudly.

"Right, right, follow me." Loco taps a series of numbers into a keypad. The silver door to our right slides open. I study the mechanism as we pass through.

"Interesting lock."

"State of the art. You'll understand why in a second."

He leads us to a narrow set of metal stairs. The metallic thud of our boots follows down into what feels like a meat locker. At the bottom of the stairs, Loco pauses and flicks a row of switches. Blinding lights flash on, illuminating the basement. It's not a meat locker, just a damn cold room—in temperature and feeling.

The floor, walls, and even the damn ceiling are covered in gleaming black tile. Pipes run overhead, grates in the floor for drains. Fanciest damn murder room I've ever seen.

The six of us stand there expressionless but I feel the waves of *what the fuck* rolling off my brothers.

Maybe it's all the glossy black tile, but the room seems bigger than it should be given the size of the restaurant above us. Loco swaggers straight through the middle of the room, heading for a shadowy area toward the back. We pass a row of round blue metal drums with warning labels. Then a line of black metal drums. Chemicals to assist with body disposal, I assume.

I fall in step with Rock. "You starting to think bringing all the club officers here maybe wasn't the best idea?"

"Not yet."

Teller brushes against my arm. "Does *everyone* we know have a murder room?"

"Probably," Rock answers.

"Necessary in our line of work," Wrath adds.

"What's that?" Loco skids to a stop and turns around.

"We're admiring your murder room," Wrath answers. "Impressive attention to detail." He points to the tiled ceiling with sprinklers strategically placed every few feet.

Loco's wide, maniacal grin hints at how he got his nickname. "When we had the fire, I took the opportunity to upgrade our establishment." He lifts his chin at Wrath. "You know what I'm talking about."

"Yeah, but I missed my opportunity to install a murder room in the basement of Furious."

"Eh." Loco waves his hand through the air. "You got locker rooms, right? Just as good." He turns and continues walking.

Murphy's been quiet the entire time, but now he slides up on Rock's other side. "Kinda wish Z or Rooster had come with us," he whispers.

Rock raises an eyebrow.

Murphy tilts his head toward a shadowy section where the wall and ceiling meet. Every few seconds a row of red lights blink on and off.

"Recording?" Rock asks.

"Maybe." Murphy shrugs.

I pull a pair of leather gloves from my pocket and slip them on.

Loco stops walking and unlocks a large steel door. A cloud of piss and fuck-knows-what-else air bursts over us. The lights flicker on and the stench becomes obvious.

Grillo.

Banged up, bloody, sitting on a filthy old mattress, and tethered to the wall by a hefty length of chain.

Gotta say, it does my heart good to see him in this condition.

"Get yourself a new pet, Loco?" Rock stands back and crosses his arms over his chest.

"Yeah, caught me a big rat." He squats next to Grillo and grins. "Been squeaking all sorts of secrets for me, right?"

"*Thuck yooo,*" Grillo slurs through his swollen lips.

"A fighter until the end," Loco cackles. "I respect that."

Grillo blinks and seems to focus on us. "You." His eyes widen when they land on me.

"Guess you made an impression, old man," Loco says.

"Thrilled to hear it." I crouch down next to Loco so I can look Grillo in the eyes. "Why'd you come after an innocent woman who had nothing to do with any of this?"

"Who? Your blonde tart?"

I whip my hand in a short, quick arc, connecting hard with his cheek.

"You got a thing for blondes?" Loco asks me. "Serenity's gonna be heartbroken."

I slowly turn my head and stare at him, then over my shoulder at Rock. "You kiddin' me?"

He grumbles something I can't quite catch.

"I got what I needed from him," Loco informs me. "You need something?"

"No. I'm fucking *out* of prison business, and I intend to stay out." I grab the length of chain piled next to Grillo, pull it taut and whip it around his neck, yanking until it chokes off his air. "This is what your errand boy did to my girl. Choked her. Scared the shit out of her. Embarrassed her at her job. All for nothing."

He struggles and claws at my hands.

I give one last squeeze, then let him go, dropping the chain to the floor with a clatter. Standing, I brush my hands off and back away. "All yours, Loco."

"That was intense." He jerks his head toward Teller. "Not as bloody as Teller's handiwork, but impressive."

"He a rapist?" Teller asks.

"Not that we know of." Loco pokes at Grillo. "Count your blessings. That motherfucker over there would slice off your jewels and jam 'em down your throat." Loco stands and pulls out a pistol. "I'm just gonna shoot you in the head."

I back up a few feet.

All foolishness disappears from Loco's expression. He stands tall, points the pistol at Grillo's temple and squeezes. Once. Twice. Three times.

Blood, bone, and brain splatter all over the mattress, wall, and floor. Grillo crumples against the mattress. Loco looms over the body, staring at the blood soaking into the mattress. "Gonna have to burn that," he mutters.

"You need help with the cleanup?" I ask.

"Yeah. I don't want to bring any of my other guys in on this."

"All right."

It's long, dirty wet work but at least Loco has the right equipment.

"I like this method," Loco says. "I like to think I improved upon the way you guys handle disposal."

Rock levels a cool look at Loco. "We use several different methods."

I glance at Loco's shoes. "Got some splatter on those sparkling white kicks of yours."

"Ah, fuck. I should've known better."

It's late when we finally trudge up the stairs into the land of the living.

"Sorry, Wrath. Kitchen's closed," Loco says.

"That's all right, brother. I'll stop by another time."

"You do that. Any time you want."

We go through a round of the ritual handshakes but I think we're all too tired for much conversation.

I straddle my bike and wait for the others. Rock pulls out first, then Wrath, Murphy, Teller, Dex and I take off. The grisly images from the night recede as I ride into the wind. Guilt and remorse don't enter my mind. Only relief that it's over. We ride slow, taking it easy, riding the dark back roads.

After what we just witnessed, it's almost as if we're daring the devil to follow us home.

CHAPTER THIRTY-SEVEN

Serena

Gray won't reveal his plans for today.

"Wear something nice," is all he told me last night.

Emily and Libby left early this morning, so I had the whole house to myself. I filmed a tutorial while I got ready for wherever Gray was taking me. Took my measurements. I'm finally actually starting to show and I'm proud of my little bump. I spent an embarrassing amount of time staring at my profile in the full-length mirror this morning. Since I wasn't sure where we were going, I chose a short, loose dress and my knee-high Dr. Martens.

"Can't you give me a little hint?" I ask.

Gray flips on his blinker, moving into the right lane. "If I do, then you'll guess and I don't want to ruin the surprise."

"Are you taking me to Sephora?"

"I don't know what that is, so no."

"Maternity clothes shopping?"

"No, but we can do that this week, if you want."

"I'm starting to show." I smooth my dress over my stomach. "See?"

He glances over with a soft smile flickering over his lips. "I noticed. You look beautiful." The aching sincerity in his voice takes my breath away.

It doesn't matter where we're going. I'm just happy we're together.

A little while later when he takes the same exit we'd take to go to downstate's clubhouse, my anxiety returns.

"Are we going to the clubhouse?" I ask quietly.

"Nope." He glances over. "Sounds like it would bother you if we were."

"Bother isn't the right word. I'd just like a head's up so I can mentally prepare myself."

He sighs. "I would've told you if that's where we were going."

At the end of the exit he turns away from the clubhouse. That's a relief.

Eventually, he guides the truck to a posh residential neighborhood that looks like dozens of others. "Who are we visiting?"

His lips curve but he doesn't answer. He stops in front of a massive house with a long driveway already full of cars.

"Isn't that Rock's SUV?" While there are plenty of GMC Yukons on the road, Rock's extra-long edition has a distinctive blacked-out look that's hard to miss.

"No, I don't think so," Gray says absently, shutting off the truck. "Wait for me."

I study the vehicles and the house while waiting for Gray. He helps me out of the truck and closes the door behind me.

"Gray, who are we visiting?"

"You'll find out in a minute." He gently nudges me up the long stone path leading to the front steps of the house.

Gray lifts his hand to knock on the front door but it swings open before his knuckles touch the wood.

Lilly, beautiful in a royal blue wrap dress, her long dark hair tumbling in waves over her shoulders, beams at us. "You're here! Welcome." She reaches for my arm, tugging me inside.

Duh, this is Z's place. I should've figured that out. But why didn't Gray just say so? There's no chance to ask him now.

He follows with his hand at the small of my back. The house is huge and it takes a few seconds to get my bearings while Lilly leads me into the cavernous sitting room to the left.

Balloons in a variety of pastel shades, streamers, and other baby-themed items fill the space.

All the upstate old ladies, a few women from the upstate and downstate clubs, Emily and Libby are all standing in a semi-circle. "Surprise!"

Lilly claps her hands and hugs me. "Happy baby shower!"

"Oh," I breathe out. "This is…" I turn and stare at Gray, hoping he'll explain what's happening.

His lips curve into a gentle smile as he leans closer. "Lilly and Emily planned this for you. They consulted me for the best time, but the party was Lilly's idea," he says against my ear.

Still confused, my gaze tumbles around the room. My vision clouds with unshed tears. Gray hugs me to his side. "You all right?"

"I'm fine," I whisper. I force a shaky smile to reassure him.

"The guys are downstairs," Lilly says, taking Gray by the elbow. "I'll show you. They're hammering up some drywall or painting or something." She waves her hand in the air and laughs.

"I'll find my way. You guys go on."

"Oh my God! It was killing me to keep this a secret!" Emily shouts, bouncing on her toes. She squeezes her hands together as if she's really proud of herself for not spilling the details. Her antics push away my tears and finally pull laughter from me.

"You nut." I reach for her, hugging her tight.

"She didn't tell me until yesterday." Libby elbows her sister. "I'm offended, you know. I can keep secrets."

I'm having trouble processing everything. "How did you and Lilly even…"

Emily turns, searching for Lilly. "Your friend called and asked what we were doing for your shower. We've been conspiring together."

"Guilty." Lilly grins. "I know you still have a way to go but since it's your first baby, we wanted to get our hands on you early." She turns, reaching for Hope and tugging her closer. "We wanted to share all the stuff that worked for us."

"And warn you about the things to avoid," Hope adds.

Twin trails of warmth slide down my cheeks. I quickly swipe the tears away. "I'd like that."

Shelby squeezes in and hugs me. "Hiya."

"Hey, thank you for coming. I know you're not into baby stuff."

"Yeah, but I like *you*."

Libby's eyes are bugging like she's about to burst.

"Did you get to meet my friend, Libby?" I ask.

"Sure did." Shelby grins.

Laughter ripples over Trinity's expression as she approaches. She leans in and hugs me. "Are you surprised?"

"Completely shocked. Gray wouldn't tell me where we were going. I was starting to wonder…" I still can't believe they did all this for me.

Charlotte hugs me next. "Trinity and I made sure there were no weird baby games."

"Oh, please," Lilly says. "We wouldn't."

Shelby wrinkles her nose. "I went to one back home once where they had a contest to see who could chew a piece of gum into the shape of a baby." She sticks out her tongue and pretends to retch. "Couldn't get outta there fast enough."

"That's…gross." I glance at Lilly. "Thank you for not doing *that*."

"Fair warning," Heidi says, "Hope had a magical unicorn birth so take what she says with a grain of salt. Not everyone is so lucky."

"Well, after losing two, I was relieved something went right for me," Hope murmurs, glancing at her feet and smoothing her hands over her dress.

"Oh, shoot." Heidi's eyes widen and gloss over. "I'm so sorry, Hope. I…"

"It's fine." Hope wraps her arm around Heidi's shoulders. "I know what you meant."

Charlotte stands and quietly leaves the room.

"Alexa came a little early." Heidi squirms in her seat. "And I was *not* quite prepared for how gruesome things would be."

Hope's green eyes fix on me. "You have youth on your side, and all of us to support you. You're going to be fine. And," she flicks her gaze to Lilly, "Lilly will fight me on this, but I swear by the prenatal yoga program Swan put together for me."

Swan blushes and glances at the floor. "Thanks, Hope."

"I seem to remember you having a different opinion during your pregnancy, Hope," Trinity says, tapping her finger playfully against her chin.

"You hush." Hope leans over and swats Trinity.

"I believe it," Shelby says. "Yoga's good for lots of things."

"It is," I agree. "I recommend it to a lot of my patients when they finish physical therapy. Sometimes we combine the two. It can be really beneficial to anyone managing a chronic health condition."

"I didn't fight you on it," Lilly argues. "I said, dragging my ass out of bed for yoga during the last trimester was bullshit." She winces and bites her lip. "Sorry, Serena, we're not trying to scare you."

"After some of the things I've survived, this will be a piece of cake."

"I'm already sold on the yoga." Heidi rubs her hands over her stomach. "I've been meeting with Swan every morning."

"You've been very diligent," Swan agrees.

"Well, having a husband who's supportive and actually *helps* makes a big difference too." Heidi snaps her mouth shut and nervously glances around the room.

My heart squeezes. I'd forgotten about her first husband, Axel. Murphy and Alexa seem to have such a tight bond, it's hard to think of him as anything other than her dad.

"I'm going to go help Charlotte with the cupcakes." Heidi stands and rests her hand on Hope's shoulder. "Do you need anything?"

"I'm fine, honey." Hope pats her hand and gives her a warm smile.

"Grinder seems very involved, Serena," Lilly says tentatively.

"This might sound weird, but he's so *sweet*." I sigh and look away, unsure of how to put my feelings into words. "He's so happy about the baby. He doesn't let me lift a finger. Just spoils me rotten." No matter how hard I try, the darkness from my past creeps into my present to whisper that I'm not good enough. "I'm not used to being treated that way."

"You absolutely deserve to be treated with love and respect," Hope says, as if I'd projected my ugly thoughts into her head. "No matter what, Serena."

"This makes my heart happy." Lilly clasps her hands over her chest. "Z keeps teasing Grinder, calling him Grumpy. It's good to know he has a sweet side."

"Don't they all, though?" Trinity's mouth quirks. "It's always jarring when I run into someone at the gym, or anyone really, who works with Wrath. They'll talk about how gruff or scary he is, and I have a moment of 'wait, are you talking about *my* man?' I don't see that side of him at home."

Lilly holds her arms at her sides in an imitation of a wrestler. "It's his size."

"And the death scowl," Hope adds.

"He also doesn't have patience for bullshit," Trinity says. "And ninety-nine percent of those sales reps who stop by the gym are full of shit."

"I used to find Rock intimidating too." Lilly nods at Hope. "I was worried about you that first night you let him take you home."

Hope snort-laughs. "I was drunk." Her smile fades. "But I knew I was safe with him."

"Z only seems slightly more approachable because of his dimples." Trinity taps her cheeks. "And he likes to joke around."

"But hell help the person who threatens anyone in his family." Hope shivers. "Then, he's pretty terrifying."

Lilly's lips curl. "One hundred percent true."

"Sorry, Serena." Hope reaches over and pats my hand. "We were supposed to be talking about you and Grinder."

I can't help laughing. "It's okay. I like listening to you guys." For once in my life, I actually feel included and accepted. I don't want to open my mouth and say anything that might disrupt that.

Trinity cocks her head, like she's listening for sounds of impending doom. "We shouldn't have left Heidi alone with the cupcakes."

Hope shakes with laughter. "I think Shelby and Charlotte are there to supervise."

"Murphy mentioned her sugar cravings have been out of control this trimester."

I clutch my stomach. "Oh God, is that what I have to look forward to?"

"Everyone's different," Lilly assures me. "I barely wanted to touch food my first trimester. Then, I wanted salty stuff one minute and sweet the next."

"I just liked slightly odd combinations," Hope says. "Apple pie and strawberry ice cream was my favorite for a while." She sticks her tongue out. "Sounds awful now, though."

"Well, that makes me feel better about all the peanut butter and peaches I've been craving lately," I mutter.

Lilly's nose wrinkles. "That's an interesting one."

Shelby returns carrying a tray of blue and pink cupcakes. "I couldn't help it. These flamingo cupcakes were so flocking cute."

I burst into laughter. "Oh my God, these are amazing. Did you make them?"

"Heck no. You don't want me baking a dang thing. I ordered them from a bakery near us. That place is gonna be the death of my waistline."

"Give me a break, Shelby." Lilly plucks a cupcake off the tray. "You have a perfect figure."

"Thanks." She sighs. "It's hard to know since every week some jackass is posting a photo of me with some piggy pun as the caption."

"That's horrible," Hope gasps.

"*Wah, wah*, I know I shouldn't be complainin'. I'm lucky anyone gives a damn about me at all, but frick it's annoying."

"You shouldn't have to put up with that just because you're a singer," I say. "But I kind of know what you mean. I got a few uh, less than flattering comments on my last couple of videos. 'I knew you must be pregnant, your face looked so much fatter lately.' Like, who on Earth thinks that's an appropriate thing to say to anyone?"

"Appropriate went out the window a while ago," Shelby mutters, biting into a cupcake.

"Too bad some of those people don't realize that if Rooster ever hunts 'em down they're gonna be in for a world of pain," Trinity says.

Shelby frowns and cocks her head. "Ya know, there *was* one yahoo that used to print a ton of crap about me. Haven't heard a peep from him in months."

Lilly and Hope snort and burst into giggles.

"Rooster probably tracked him down." Trinity smirks. "Poor guy. Let us all pray he still has the use of his legs."

"Let's pray he isn't six feet under." Swan presses her palms together for a brief moment of silence. Her mouth slides into a sly grin.

"That really shocked Grinder," I say. "Some of the comments people leave for me. He was livid."

"He *does* give off big murder daddy vibes," Shelby mutters around her mouthful of cupcake.

Lilly squints. "What?"

Emily has her hand pressed to her lips like she's trying not to laugh. I narrow my eyes at her. "What's so funny?"

"She's right!" Emily bursts into laughter. "I thought the same thing when I met him. The way Serena described him, I expected some soft old dude—"

"Hey!" I smack her arm.

"You know what I mean." She waves me off. "Then she shows up with hard-bodied Santa."

Hope snorts and coughs a spray of cupcake into her napkin. "Oh my God."

"Easy, mama bear." Trinity thumps Hope's back a few times.

"Sorry," Emily says to Hope. "But I thought to myself, this is a *murder daddy*. He's sweet to Serena but I bet he'll yank someone's spine out through their throat if they say something mean to her."

"Amen!" Trinity lifts her hands toward the ceiling.

"That is almost exactly what Gray said when he read those comments on my Instagram. I don't think he realized the people leaving them could be anywhere in the world."

"Social media wasn't a thing when he went inside," Trinity says in a sympathetic tone. "I barely have a grasp of it myself, so I can't imagine what he thinks."

"I know he's surprised I make money from my makeup tutorials and postings. But he's never belittled it or anything. He seems fascinated, almost." I squint, thinking over my life. "I've never dated a guy who didn't make fun of my makeup hobby."

"And what did I tell you about those kinds of guys?" Emily leans forward. "They can either appreciate your art or get the fuck out of your museum."

"Whoa!" Shelby pumps her fist in the air. "That's the best dang quote I've ever heard."

"That really does perfectly sum it up," Trinity says. "I'm so happy Grinder supports you like that. It took a lot for me to tell Wrath about photography and designing book covers when I was treating them as a side hobby. And oh my God, when I came clean—no judgment or scorn from him. He couldn't have been more supportive. Went out and bought me every single thing I could ever need to take it from a hobby to a career. Rented me studio space…That's love."

Hope reaches over and squeezes Trinity's hand. "I love you guys."

"Rooster bought me a whole-ass RV to tour in since my record label wasn't concerned about my comfort or safety," Shelby says. "I will *never* get over how matter-of-fact he was about it, either." She pulls her shoulders back. "You need this. I bought it. This is what we're doing," she imitates Rooster's deep voice.

"Men of action. That's what we have," Hope says. "They're a rare breed."

I lean over and nudge Libby who seems enraptured by the whole conversation. "This is what I was talking about. *If he wanted to, he would.*"

"What was that?" Emily asks.

Libby makes big pleading eyes at me.

"Just some advice between besties," I explain in a vague way that won't betray Libby's confidence. "Actually, I think I got it from *you*. If he wanted to, he would."

"Ohhh." Emily nods. "Accept no excuses. If a man's into you, he'll show you he cares. Period."

"Oh, I like that," Swan says. "No excuses."

"Marcel found a house for us that included a guest house for *my brother*." Charlotte plops down on the couch next to Lilly. "My little shit of a brother who pulled a *gun* on him the first time they met."

"Why haven't I heard *that* story before?" Shelby asks.

"Were you mad he bought a house without asking your opinion?" Emily asks Charlotte.

"Mad? Hell no. I couldn't jump him fast enough. Right there on the kitchen counter."

"Gross." Heidi clutches her stomach. "I don't need to know *that* about my brother."

Charlotte grins at her, then focuses on Emily. "I don't think it was quite a done deal. He brought me there for final approval. But he knew me well enough to know I'd love the place."

"That's sweet," Emily says.

"It's romantic as all get-out," Shelby sighs. "I wanna write a song about it, now." She pulls the little purple notebook I've seen her with before from the back pocket of her denim skirt. "In fact, y'all have given me lots of inspiration. Don't mind me." She taps her pen against her chin. "I wonder if Dawson will let me release a song called *Murder Daddy*?"

Laughing, Hope turns to me. "Serena, if your side business is doing that well, you should probably think about incorporating. It'll help you deduct items on your taxes."

"Ugh, no work talk, Hope," Charlotte says.

"Hey, I need to keep my skills sharp somehow." Hope playfully swats at her. "Right now, Trinity is my only official client."

"I feel so *fancy* having my own corporate counsel." Trinity shimmies her shoulders.

"I pay my taxes," I say quickly. "Learned that the hard way my first year. I barely made a couple thousand dollars, and the IRS was looking for their cut."

"Anything over a certain amount gets reported," Hope explains. "I know a good business CPA I can put you in touch with. And I can help you incorporate if you want to do that."

"Sure. I wouldn't know where to start. I'll pay you, of course," I hurry to add, so she knows I don't expect her to do free legal work for me.

She waves off the offer, though. "We'll talk."

Charlotte leans over and whispers something in Lilly's ear and Lilly nods.

"Okay." Charlotte stands and claps her hands together. "This is the best part of the shower," Charlotte announces. "Or so I've heard. Presents!"

"This way!" Lilly stands and motions like a flight attendant for us to move into the room across the hall.

This seems like the family room, with a plush sectional, wide-screen television, gaming consoles and more lived-in furniture. A round table in the corner is stacked with boxes wrapped with pastel paper and gift bags.

"Oh my God. You guys didn't have to," I protest, feeling overwhelmed again. "The party…everything is already so…"

"Nonsense, that's the whole point." Hope steers me into a recliner near the table. "We had fun with it."

"Gray said you hadn't put a baby registry together yet or anything," Lilly explains.

I hadn't seen the point since I didn't expect anyone to throw me a baby shower.

"So Hope, Heidi, Winter, and I put together a list of everything we found the most useful after coming home from the hospital."

"When the 'hard part' is supposedly over and you get the baby home and think, 'what the fuck do I do now?'" Winter elaborates.

Heaven help me, I haven't thought that far ahead. "I haven't gotten there yet."

"You will," Lilly assures me.

"Sooner than you think," Hope adds.

"A crib and stroller are pretty personal," Lilly says. "Plus, you already know you need those. We tried to choose stuff you won't realize is important until you're stuck."

Even if I hadn't put together a registry, I'd done a lot of looking and reading online about baby gear. After opening the first few boxes, it's clear they didn't choose random, generic baby bibs or throw a handful of onesies in a bag.

Shelby hands me two boxes. "They gave me a list but then I saw this other thing and couldn't resist. It said zero to three years old, so I hope it's okay." She bites her lip and looks at Heidi.

I open the gift Shelby chose on her own. *Vibrating Guitar Grasp Toy.* "Oh my gosh, this is so cute!"

"In case your little rock star is musically inclined." Shelby bounces on the couch cushion in her excitement to show me the features. "It's got little textured 'tuning pegs' and it vibrates. I couldn't resist that."

"I love it." I lean over and give her a one-armed hug. "Thank you."

"You won't use this until about three months or so but time's going to fly fast," Heidi says. "Alexa loved this."

I open the box she hands me. *Tummy Time Water Mat.*

"You fill it with water, and it's got all these cool shapes floating inside the mat," Heidi explains. "Makes tummy time a little comfier."

"That's so cute. I love it. Thank you."

Heidi added a bundle of hooded towels with the mat. I pull each one out of the bag and shake them out—a panda and a fox.

"I begged her to get the flamingo one." Shelby runs her fingers over the soft black terry cloth. "But Heidi said we should do gender neutral items."

Heidi laughs. "It was *super* bright pink."

"Boys can like pink," Shelby protests.

"It's fine. I love pandas *and* foxes," I assure Heidi. "Thank you."

I'm overwhelmed with all the boxes and packages the girls pass to me. Some of the things they chose were on my radar. Other things—like baby mittens—had never occurred to me.

"If you ever need advice on something or want someone to go shopping with you, just call me," Lilly says.

"Thank you."

By the time Hope hands me the last present, I'm buried under a mountain of tissue paper, bows, and ribbons. We hear squealing from the hallway and feet pattering over the floor.

"Mommy!" Alexa bursts into the room and launches herself at

Heidi.

Charlotte catches Alexa in her arms and picks her up. "No love for your auntie?"

"Yes!" Alexa presses her hands to Charlotte's cheeks and kisses her nose.

Chance lingers in the archway, observing the room.

"What's wrong?" Lilly asks him.

"Nothin'."

"Who set the little guys free?" Heidi asks. "Hmmm?" She kisses her daughter's cheek. "How'd you get loose?"

"Daddy!"

"Uh-huh. I suspected."

"You can join us, Chance," I wave my hand at him. But he glances over his shoulder and runs away.

"He suddenly has this aversion to anything too girly," Lilly explains in a low voice. "I swear, if he picked it up from Ravage, I'm going to strangle him."

Z appears in the archway, carrying Chance. "We kept them entertained as long as possible."

"We're fine." I stand and excuse myself to find the bathroom.

In the hallway, I run into Gray. "How's it going?" He stops and kisses my forehead.

"So great. Let me pee and I'll be right with you."

He chuckles as I hurry away. When I emerge a few minutes later, he's waiting outside the door for me. "You didn't have to wait."

"Come here." He pulls me into his arms, his big, warm body providing comfort and security. "I missed you."

I sigh and loop my arms around his neck. "I'm right here."

When we return to the living room, the kids are busy picking up the paper and stuffing it in a bag.

"I'm going to be so sad when they stop thinking this is a fun game," Lilly whispers.

"You want us to help you load your truck?" Murphy asks Gray.

Gray finally notices the pile of presents. "What happened here? Where are we going to put all that?"

"Sorry." Lilly hugs Hope to her side. "We went a wee bit overboard."

"Little bit," Hope agrees.

"We have the spare room you can use, Serena," Emily says.

Gray's jaw tightens for a second but he nods.

While the guys work on taking things to the truck, I pull Lilly into the hallway. "I really can't thank you enough."

"It wasn't just me."

"I know but hosting at your house was a lot. Thank you so much."

She hugs me tight. "Anytime. And I meant what I said. If you need to talk or want advice, don't hesitate to call me."

I feel the sincerity in her words. Lilly's always been kind to me. She's not offering only because I'm with Gray. "Thank you."

Outside, it's almost dark.

Gray walks me to the truck carefully.

"You had a good time?" he asks.

"I really did," I gush, still buzzing with happiness. "You know it was bugging me that I don't have anyone to talk about this with. Any female relatives, I mean."

"Feel better now?"

"Yes. Everyone's experiences were so different, so that helped a lot."

He opens the back door and tosses one last bag inside, then stares at all the stuff. "What...are we going to do with all of this?" He shakes his head. "My parents brought me home from the hospital and used a dresser drawer as my crib."

I can't tell if he's joking or really annoyed. "Well, today we have no need for dresser drawers. We have soft cuddle blankets shaped like pandas, rainbow bouncy cushions, and a generous family who gave us lots of useful gifts."

He steps back, and one corner of his mouth twitches. "I love you." He curls his arm around my waist, and gently pulls me closer. "Thank you." The emotions in his voice are clear—hope, sincerity, and true gratitude.

Like *I'm* the one who's given *him* the most precious gift.

CHAPTER THIRTY-EIGHT

Serena

Certain people are meant to be part of your history. Not your destiny.

"I MIGHT HAVE EATEN TOO MANY CUPCAKES." I CLUTCH MY STOMACH. "By the way, did we bring any of those home with us?" I twist and try to search the back seat under all the baby shower gifts.

Gray rumbles with laughter. "Yes, I think there's a couple containers of goodies back there."

"Uh-oh." I squeeze my eyes shut. "I need to pee."

Gray glances over. "The next rest stop is maybe five minutes ahead. Will you be okay?"

I squirm in my seat. "I'll make it."

He presses the accelerator down harder. A few minutes later, he guides the truck to a stop at the curb. "I'll be right in," he promises.

"Thank you." Even though I'm in a hurry, I pop a quick kiss on his cheek.

I wiggle my way out of the truck and hurry inside. The scent of greasy fast-food stirs both my appetite and my nausea. My gaze lands on the ice cream shop as I hurry to the bathroom. I'd kill for a strawberry milkshake.

When I emerge a few minutes later, Gray's waiting close to the entrance. As if he's concerned someone might try to steal me away. I clasp his hand and press myself against his side.

He smiles down at me. "Feel better?"

"Much." My eyes stray toward the ice cream. "Except, now I want a milkshake."

"Let's get you a milkshake, then." He flicks his gaze toward the burger joint. "You sure you wouldn't rather have real food first? You've been eating sugar all day."

My stomach rebels at the thought of a greasy fried patty. "No."

"All right."

We walk up to the counter. I'd been dead set on strawberry but now that I'm up close with ten different flavors, I want them all.

"Oh, they have butter pecan. I wonder if that would make a good milkshake? Chocolate peanut butter..." I all but press my nose up against the glass window of the freezer staring at the large tubs of ice cream.

Gray rumbles with laughter and turns toward the cashier. "Can you make small sizes of the butter pecan, chocolate peanut butter, and strawberry? And one large chocolate peanut butter."

The cashier glances over his shoulder. "It might take a minute."

"That's okay."

The guy rings up the order. Gray pays for it, then hands over a generous tip and thanks him.

"That was nice," I say, sliding closer to him.

"I know it's probably a pain to make all three."

"You didn't have to—"

"No." He curls his arm around my waist, drawing me closer. "Whatever my girl wants, she gets."

I hum a happy noise and rest my cheek against his chest.

"Strawberry." The cashier sets a small cup and straw on the counter.

"Why don't we find a table and I'll bring the shakes," Gray suggests.

I scoop the cup off the counter, poke the straw through the top and take a sweet, cold sip of strawberry milkshake. "Ah, so good," I murmur, closing my eyes to savor the fruity-creamy sweetness on my tongue.

Gray chuckles softly and rests his hand at the small of my back, gently steering me away from the counter.

I'm so focused on my shake—I might need to order another one in a larger size before we go—I don't notice Gray's body freeze in place.

I bump into him and have to take my attention off my cup.

A beautiful, polished woman maybe in her late forties blocks our path.

They both stare at each other. Mouths slightly open. Eyes wide.

A fist of fear squeezes around my heart.

This is his ex-wife. Rose. It has to be her. I know it in my bones. The man *I* love used to be *in love* with this attractive, elegant, put-together woman.

Her gaze slowly shifts to me. Her eyes widen slightly but otherwise her expression doesn't change. I fidget and brush my hand over my dress, wishing I'd worn something that covered more of my legs. While she's giving me the slow once-over, Gray tightens his arm around my waist.

"Rose." His tone is stiff. Formal. As if this is painfully awkward for him. Somehow, that eases my tension. "How are you?"

Rose shakes herself out of the shock or whatever she's feeling at seeing her ex-husband. Her wine-red lips curve into a genuine smile. "I'm okay. How are you…adjusting?" She casts a quick look around as if she doesn't want to broadcast Gray's business all over the place.

Maybe she's not so awful after all.

Still, I stand there mute. Waiting for Gray to introduce me. Is he embarrassed to be seen with me? Reluctant to claim me as his girlfriend?

"Uh, Serena," he says, "this is Rose. Rose, Serena."

My hands are clutching my milkshake for dear life, so I nod at her. "Nice to meet you." What else should I say? *I think you suck for ditching Gray when he went to prison but thank God you did. He's mine now.* That would probably be overkill and a little rude.

"Order up!"

"Well, I should let you go. Good to see you're doing well, Grayson." Rose nods at me. "Serena."

Finally, we move past her and she walks up to the counter to place her order. *Dear God, please don't let her come sit with us.*

Gray leads me to a table in the corner. "You all right, buttercup?" he asks in a low voice.

"Sure. Yeah, of course." Too bad I can't keep my voice steady.

He pulls out a chair for me and I drop into it.

"You need anything else while I'm up there?" he asks.

"Napkins." I lift my milkshake. "Somehow I'll end up spilling this all over myself."

"You got it." He leans down and presses a quick kiss against my forehead.

My back's toward the counter and I don't bother turning around to see if Gray and Rose share some chitchat. I'm secure enough in our relationship not to feel threatened by her.

Instead, I suck down my milkshake so fast, my brain freezes and my stomach cramps.

"Ugh."

Gray returns and sets three cups on the table. I grab one of the smaller ones that looks like the butter pecan and, queasy stomach or not, take a sip.

"How is it?" he asks as he stabs his straw into the lid of the largest cup.

"Perfect," I mumble.

"Sorry about that. I never expected..." his gaze shifts to somewhere behind me, "to run into Rose. I haven't thought about..."

I'm on the edge of my seat, waiting for him to finish that sentence. "What?" I prompt.

One corner of his mouth curls into a pained smile. "I haven't thought about her since the day I saw her." He gestures toward the parking lot. "But we're not far from where she lives."

"Me and my impatient bladder," I mutter into my milkshake. Wait, did he say he hasn't thought about her at all?

"You haven't thought about her even once?"

"Except for whatever questions you've asked me…" This time his smile warms his whole face and he rests his hand over mine. "I've been too consumed with someone else to linger on the past."

"Oh." My jaw hangs slack as I process his words.

"There's no room for anyone else in here, buttercup." He taps his chest, over his heart.

Too emotional to respond with words, I wrap my fingers around his and squeeze.

Still holding hands, we return to sipping our shakes. At least for a few seconds.

"Ugh." I set my cup on the table and clutch my stomach.

"What's wrong?" Gray frowns and bangs his cup on the table.

"I might have ingested too much cold stuff too fast." Another icky sensation slithers through my stomach. "Uh-oh."

"What do you need?"

I push myself away from the table. "Bathroom. I'll be right back."

Everything I pass as I speed-walk to the restroom is a blur. I narrowly miss bumping into a family with what seems like fifteen unruly children. I make it to a toilet just in time to lean over and heave. I refuse to kneel on the dirty bathroom floor so it's painful and damn near impossible not to puke all over myself.

Cold, clammy sweat bursts over my skin and I whimper, hating how horrible I feel.

Finally, the tumbling in my stomach stops. I clean myself and stumble out of the stall. The sinks look so far away. I lurch over to them and turn the cold water on full blast, practically sticking my whole head under the powerful burst of cool, liquid relief to rinse out my mouth. The awful taste seems to cling for far too long.

I don't know how long I'm standing there bent over with my head craned under the faucet, but I finally straighten and run my hands and wrists under the water as well. A ghost stares back at me in the mirror. *Jeez.* My skin's so pale. Dark circles ring under my eyes. Well, at least none of my YouTube followers will recognize me.

Out of the corner of my eye, I catch movement behind me.

Rose.

Damn.

"Are you okay, Serena?" she asks softly.

"Not really." I twist the tap off.

Rose gathers a handful of paper towels and brings them to me. Even though I'm a few inches taller than her, she dabs one of the towels against my forehead in a kind, motherly sort of way.

"How far along are you?" she asks.

Her voice is barely above a whisper but it crashes around the tiled walls like a bowling ball.

"A couple of months." I run my hand over my dress. God, I hope I didn't puke on it. I'm barely even showing but she noticed right away.

"The milkshakes." She flashes a kind smile. "The sickness. I remember very well what that was like."

"Oh."

"Gray seems happy."

Heat explodes over my cheeks. She's going right for it, isn't she? I shift my gaze to my shoes. "I hope so."

"Have you been seeing each other long?"

"No," I whisper. For some reason I'm even more embarrassed admitting that. But it's not like she isn't aware that he was recently released from prison. "We didn't….this wasn't planned."

She chuckles. "It rarely is. You're not alone there." Only kindness, maybe even affection, colors her tone.

Don't I know it.

"What do you do?" she asks.

Is she trying to make polite conversation? Or does she actually care about the answer? Why?

"I'm a physical therapist." *Or, I was. Now I post videos of makeup looks online full-time.*

"Oh." She raises an eyebrow. "Interesting field."

"It is, yes. I like helping people." I hesitate, not sure why I'm going to ask this. "Gray said you wanted to go to medical school?"

A sad sigh passes her lips. "I did, yes. I'm sure he still thinks it's his fault I didn't go."

"What do you do now?" If she can be nosy, I can too.

"I'm a dental hygienist. My husband and I have a small practice."

"Oh, that must be nice to work together."

"It has its moments." She pats my shoulder. "Feel better?"

I concentrate for a moment. "Yes, I think I do."

"Good. It was nice to meet you, Serena." She turns toward the stalls.

Did she come in here specifically for me? Or did she happen to run into me? The answer doesn't matter, I suppose.

I wash my hands again, replaying the odd conversation over in my head. Why is it so odd? Did I expect her to come at me flying squirrel style, yanking on my hair and laying claim to Grayson? Why would she? Supposedly she's happily married. Maybe she really does care about Gray and wants him to be happy too. Not every woman in the world is a psycho ready to throw down for a man.

Gray meets me outside. "Are you okay?"

"Yes." I glance over my shoulder. "Rose, uh, helped me out."

"I saw her go in."

We're quiet while we walk out to the parking lot.

"Do you want me to bring the truck and pick you up?" Gray asks.

"No, the air feels good. I want to stretch my legs a little before we get on the road."

Inside the truck, Gray turns and faces me, taking my hand in his. "You seem troubled. Did Rose say something to you?"

I don't detect anything but concern for me in his question. "Just small talk. She noticed I'm pregnant. Asked how long we'd been together."

"What? Why?"

I duck my head. Should I bother telling him?

There's no point in keeping secrets. He's not going to leave me for his ex-wife. I know that. "I think she wanted to know if you're happy."

He sits there staring at me.

Fear tightens my stomach. "You *are* happy, Gray, right? I know this isn't what you planned—"

"I said goodbye to the life I'd *planned* a long time ago, buttercup." He brings my hand to his lips and kisses my knuckles. "*Happy* doesn't scratch the surface of how I feel. I'm looking forward to our future together, not worrying about the past."

CHAPTER THIRTY-NINE

Grinder

"Just a few more months of this," I mutter to myself as I head to my appointment with my parole officer. At least I ain't worried about dealing with Grillo ever again.

That thought infuses some pep into my steps.

"Mr. Lock, good morning," Ms. Lewis greets me, even friendlier than usual.

"Morning."

We get the humiliation part of our visit out of the way first. Drug test. When we're finally seated in her office, I roll up my sleeve. "Ah, Mr. Grillo had mentioned I'm supposed mention any new ink."

Her eyebrows lift. *Yeah, lady, I feel like a brownnoser too.* Must be all the guilt, since I happen to know she's getting stuck with Grillo's caseload—*permanently.*

"Yes. Thank you for being so up front." She slides open a drawer and pulls out an instant camera.

"Finally, technology I'm familiar with," I joke, nodding at the camera.

She snorts. "Budget cuts don't care about technology." She takes the picture and returns to her desk. "How's work?"

"Good. I was thinking about getting back into welding, though."

"I think that's a great idea. I can give you information about a couple of programs if you want to get re-certified."

"Yeah, that'd be good."

"To be honest, Mr. Lock, I almost feel like these appointments are only holding you back."

You and me both.

"I'm going to recommend that you're released from parole early. That way you're free to move about, look for a better job, do what you need to do."

Is this real? It almost seems like too much to hope for. If I seem too eager, will she deny me? "I would really appreciate that."

"All right. It may take a while, so we'll schedule another appointment, just in case. You should get a letter in the mail, though."

"Thank you."

"One more thing."

I knew this was too good to be true.

"Would you have any interest in maybe mentoring other parolees? I think you could provide a good example to them."

You have no idea how wrong you are.

"Would I be allowed to?"

"If it's through a program, yes. It wouldn't be an issue."

"What would I do?"

"Just talk to them about the importance of staying out of trouble. Working a steady job. Avoiding bad influences. Things like that."

Well, now I just feel like shit. Most people getting out of prison don't have family bending over backwards to help them out the way I have. Job —club found it for me. It would be dishonest as fuck for me to tell some poor schmuck to "avoid bad influences" when I've been socializing with my club from day one. A wheel of hypocrisy—not supposed to associate with my club, yet without them, I wouldn't be a successful parolee being asked to mentor other criminals. Z's going to love this slice of irony.

"Saying yes or no won't impact your early release from parole," she hurries to add when I remain quiet for too long.

"Yeah, I might not mind doing that." It probably wouldn't be much different from how I tried to help other inmates when I was inside. "Let me think about it."

"Great." She hands me a card. "This is the coordinator. Give him a call if you're interested."

I take a quick glance at the card and shove it in my pocket.

At least by the time I leave I'm feeling a lot more optimistic about my future.

MIDMORNING at the clubhouse means it's quiet. Everyone's either at work or sleeping. Pretty soon I'll be able to spend time here without any pesky feelings of remorse.

I open the door to my room upstairs. Forget my apartment, *this* place almost feels like my first real "home" after getting out of prison. After everything I've gained and lost in my life, I can't help feeling sentimental about something as silly as a bedroom. The first night I spent with Serena was right here. In this bed. Regret tugs at me for how conflicted I felt that night. Part of me knew the second we met she was meant to be my future. Thank fuck she gave me a second chance. Running into Rose the other night didn't hurt a bit. Felt like closing the door on my past once and for all.

Serena and I will be together *every* night soon enough. I grab what I came for, close the door and head downstairs.

I open the entryway closet, searching for a pair of gloves, when shouting from outside draws my attention. I cock my head, trying to figure out who's out there.

"Murphy, stop!" Rock's voice thunders with more concern than anger.

Murphy answers in an angry tone, too low for me to make out what he says. He and Rock seem to go back and forth. Their voices quick and angry followed by stern and pleading.

"I don't want to hear it!" Murphy finally roars.

More back and forth. Alexa's wails in the background tug at my heart. These two fuckers need to calm down before they scare the crap out of that little girl.

A door slams. More yelling.

Jesus Christ, where the fuck is Wrath? He should be de-escalating this situation before it gets out of control.

Another door slams.

As much as I don't want to intrude on what sounds like an extremely personal matter, I don't want one of these boneheads getting hurt.

I fling the clubhouse door open as Murphy slams his truck into gear and spins his tires. The truck catches and lurches forward. The brake lights flash once as Murphy steers around the clubhouse. Then the truck's gone, roaring out of sight down the driveway.

"Fuck!" Rock shouts, standing in a cloud of dust.

I pound down the steps and cross the gravel. "The fuck was that all about?"

He doesn't seem to notice me at first. I touch his shoulder to get his attention. "Rock, what happened?"

He clenches his jaw and shakes his head. "Nothing but some nuclear fallout."

Fuck, I can guess what went down. "Everyone okay?"

"Not at all." His jaw tightens again, and he stares at the ground. "Murphy took it harder than I expected."

No shit. I coulda seen that one coming.

Rock already looks miserable. No reason to pile more guilt on his shoulders.

"Give them time to cool off." I slap his shoulder. "I was heading out, but I'll stick around if you need me."

"Nah, brother. Thank you, though." He glances over his shoulder in the direction of his house. "Everything okay?"

"Yeah, got some good news today. P.O. says she's going to recommend I'm released early from parole."

At least that seems to cheer him up a fraction. His lips quirk at the corners. "Damn, that is good news, brother. About time."

"Z didn't—"

"Nope. You asked us not to interfere, so we didn't. This is all because of you."

"Well, also her hefty caseload, courtesy of Grillo 'being out on leave.'" I let out a dark chuckle.

He smirks at my sociopathic humor. "The world's a better place without him and you don't belong on parole. Win all around for everyone involved as far as I'm concerned."

"My thoughts exactly."

At least my news seems to take his mind off whatever ruined his morning. He huffs a short laugh. "It's good to have you back, Gray." He cocks his head. "Serena okay?"

"Yeah, she's doing well." I pat my pocket. "Trying to plan my big surprise for her."

"You'll know when the time's right." He jerks his thumb over his shoulder. "I'd rather stay and talk to you, brother, but I better head back and deal with this."

I don't envy the conversations waiting for him back at his house. "If you need something, let me know."

"I will, brother." He reaches out and squeezes my shoulder. "Thanks."

CHAPTER FORTY
Serena

"We had our talk with Sway. Tawny knows she's not allowed on-site. You don't have anything to worry about, Serena," Z assures me as soon as we arrive downstate.

I'm an idiot for returning here after what happened last time.

But Gray said it was important.

"It ain't Serena who needs to be worried," Gray says. "Tawny shows her face, I might put a bullet in it."

"Easy, G."

"Fuck that."

"You mind if I borrow your ol' man for a minute?" Z says, nodding at the bar to indicate that's where I should go wait. "We'll be right in my office."

Within screaming distance is what he seems to be saying.

Steel spine. I have to show Z I'm confident. "Sure. No problem."

Gray steers me to the side. "You all right?"

I allow my gaze to bounce around the main room. Not many people are even here and the ones I recognize I've always been friendly with. "I'll be fine. If I need you, I'll yell."

"All right."

I perch at the bar, facing Z's office so I'll see Gray the minute he

399

emerges. Lala hands me a glass of seltzer water and I sip it slowly, hoping I won't have to run and pee anytime soon.

"Serena?" A prospect everyone calls Fiddle swaggers toward me with his hands stuffed in his pockets. He eyes my property patch carefully. "Grinder's ol' lady?"

"Yes." Lala and I are the only two women in the area, so I don't know why he seems so tentative.

She flutters her lashes at him and sticks her chest out. "Hey, Fiddle."

"Hey, girl." He flashes a crooked smile her way before focusing on me again. "Uh, Tawny's at the gate. Prez said I'm not supposed to let her in, and she's pretty pissed."

Lala erupts into a fit of snort-giggles.

"Okay," I answer slowly. "What does that have to do with *me*?"

"Well, ah, she said since *you* had her banned, you were the one who could give permission for her to come in."

"Wait a minute." I slide off my barstool and Fiddle backs up a few steps. "That's a load of bull. I didn't have anything to do with it. Her shitty behavior got her banned from the clubhouse." The more I think about what he said, the angrier I get. "Besides, an ol' lady can't overrule an order given by a club *president*. You should know that, prospect."

His posture tightens, fists clenched at his side, and he opens his mouth like he's about to blast me into the next room.

"Think it through, prospect," Murphy warns, coming up behind Fiddle. "She's right." He steps in front of Fiddle and glares. "You best be respectful to our ol' ladies."

"I was," he protests. "I just asked." He waves his hand toward the front door. "I don't know what to do about Tawny. She's out there screaming her head off."

"Well, Sway's busy, so she's just gonna have to wait," Murphy says. "Out there. If you're not man enough to tell her that, then maybe you should hand in that cut."

"I told her. But it's *Tawny*." The poor kid is dangerously close to whining.

"Are you more afraid of Tawny than you are of Z?" Murphy asks.

"Fuck no."

"Then gather those marbles you call balls and go tell her to fuck off."

Am I evil for wanting to follow Fiddle outside and dine on that scene like a five-course meal? Tawny being told *no* by a prospect. It's too delicious.

There must be an evil gleam in my eyes that betrays my craving for revenge. Murphy smirks at me. "You wanna go watch?"

"Kinda." I bite my lip. "Is that bad?"

He laughs and shakes his head. "Nope."

"Hell no," Lala says.

"Come on, Serena." He jerks his head to the side and turns around.

I hurry to catch up to him. "You're not serious?"

"Sure I am." He stops at Z's office and knocks on the door. After a second, he opens it and leans inside. I catch a glimpse of Gray. They exchange a few words, then Gray comes to the door.

"Are you okay?" he asks me.

Unsure of what exactly Murphy told him, I shrug. "I'm fine but I don't like her trying to get me in trouble. I just want her to leave me alone."

"Why would *you* be in trouble?" Gray asks.

"She told the prospect that since I had her banned from the club, I could let her in. It's not my fault she was banned." I wave my hand toward Z who's still seated behind his desk. "Why would I ever try to contradict the president? Especially for her."

"I'll go get Sway and tell him to handle it," Z says.

As he passes me, I touch his arm. "I'm sorry."

"Nothing for you to be sorry about, sweetheart. This has nothing to do with you. She broke the rules and she got banned. She shouldn't be dragging you into it."

My thoughts exactly.

Murphy steps into Z's office and chuckles. "She's giving Fiddle hell out there." He gestures toward the line monitors displaying video of the front gate. "Asshole deserves it for being so dumb."

"She ain't gonna leave until one of us makes her," Gray says to Murphy.

"More than happy to help. But you wanna wait for Sway and Z?"

"Sway's…occupied." Z returns pinching the bridge of his nose and shaking his head. "No good ever comes from me going up to their room," he mutters. "Why do I keep doing it?"

"You want to wait until Steer gets here?" Gray asks.

"Nah, she'll cause a big scene and probably sneak through after him if she can." Z jerks his head to the side. "Come on, let's go." His gaze lands on me. "You wanna watch?"

"Uh, don't think less of me, but yeah, I kinda do."

Z lets out an evil chuckle. "My kinda girl. Come on."

Gray takes my hand. But he and Z move so fast, I have trouble keeping up and end up shaking myself free.

"You can't be here, Tawny," Z shouts as he approaches the gate. "Sway was supposed to have a talk with you."

"He talked!" she shrieks. "This is bullshit and you know it, Z."

"My orders are bullshit?" He takes a slow, sarcastic look around, finally looking down at the president patch on the front of his cut. "Well, would you look at that? I'm the fuckin' president of this charter. My club. My rules. Period. It's not up for fucking discussion."

"Z, you've known me for years," she whines.

"Yeah, I have. And someone should've done this a long time ago." He leans in closer and lowers his voice. "You think you were gonna fool one of my prospects to let your ass in? That ain't gonna work for you no more, sweetheart."

Her wild gaze lands on Gray, then me, and her face twists into outrage. "You're taking *her* side? Over mine?"

"There are no sides here, Tawny. You fucked up big time. You disrespected a brother and his ol' lady."

"You lied to my damn face, Tawny," Gray says. "Swore you'd leave Serena alone."

"I'd already talked to Pants before I made that promise." Her eyes bore into me. "Oh my God," she says slowly, dropping her gaze to my stomach. "You're fucking pregnant? Already. Your whore ass finally trapped a brother permanently. Good for you," she sneers.

Since I'd been expecting that reaction from her all along, it has almost no effect on me.

"Christ, Gray," she continues, as if she's determined to dig her own grave with her mouth. "What I told Pants wasn't that far off. You're fucking pathetic—"

Gray whips a pistol from the small of his back and points it at her head. His face twists with a rage I've never seen from Gray before.

Terror shakes me down to the soles of my feet.

"Bitch, I'll fucking end you if you utter another word," he says with an eerie calm.

She freezes and sticks her hands up.

"You've got five seconds," Z warns. "Then I'm lettin' Gray shoot you. That's the only way you're getting on this property again. To bury your body in the woods."

A tear—an actual fucking tear—rolls down her cheek. "Fine." She lifts her chin. "Tell Sway I was looking for him."

"Yeah, I'll get right on that." Z jerks his chin. "Go."

She hops in her black Buick and peels out, leaving a cloud of dust in her wake.

Numb, exhausted, and humiliated, I turn and trudge toward the clubhouse. I doubt it's the last I'll ever see of Tawny.

But at least she's gone for now.

CHAPTER FORTY-ONE

Grinder

EVEN AFTER WE FINALLY GOT RID OF TAWNY, I'M IRRITATED AS FUCK.

Not in the mood for another party.

Serena steps out of the bathroom. "What do you think?" She holds out her arms and sways from side to side.

Goddess. That's what I think. A motorcycle club party isn't where she belongs. Not in that innocent pink dress. Well, it would be innocent except for the deep cut in the front. The rest of it is made up of sheer, floaty layers of pink the shade of cotton candy. The material waterfalls over her bump in a simple, flattering way.

"Gray?" she prompts.

"You're beautiful."

She honest-to-God reaches up and squeezes her tits. "My boobs are getting a little big and they're too achy to mess around with taping them into submission, so," she crosses her fingers. "Let's pray they behave."

I help her into her property patch and then zip it all the way up. "There. Your rogue tits can stay safe."

She snort-giggles. "You like the dress otherwise?"

"I love it. I feel like you should be twirling around in a field of wildflowers, though. Not hanging out with a bunch of beer-guzzling bikers."

"Oh, stop."

I plant a careful kiss on her cheek and take her hand. "Are you comfortable in those shoes?"

"For now."

"Well, tell me if they bother you and I'll run down here and grab something else for you."

"Thank you."

We run into Rooster and Shelby in the hallway.

"Oooo, Lordy. Now that is an Empress dress if I've ever seen one," Shelby drawls. "Look at you, lil' momma."

Serena blushes. "I thought it was pretty."

"Pink sure is your color. I'm so glad you're here tonight. My momma's coming and I want you to meet her."

I lift my gaze to Rooster, and he shakes his head.

"I can't wait," Serena says.

It's not Shelby's mom we run into first, though. It's Chaser and Mallory.

"Grinder." Chaser holds out his hand and pulls me in for a slap on the back. "Good to see you again." His gaze strays behind me and his mouth curls up. "This your girl?"

The one I had to get involved in my brother's gang squabbles for? his smirk seems to say.

"This is Serena." I pull her forward. "Serena, this is an old friend of mine. We go way, way back. Chaser Adams."

Serena dips her chin and offers a quiet hello.

Mallory squeals and runs up from behind Chaser with her arms out. "Grinder, you're here." She gives me a fierce hug. "It's so good to finally see you. How are you? You look good."

I hold her at arm's length. "Well, god damn. You haven't aged a day, sweetheart."

"Oh, stop." Mallory ducks like I'm embarrassing her.

"I'm serious. Same as the first time I met you." I peer at her closer, making her laugh. "A little more wisdom and less tolerance for bullshit in those eyes, but otherwise, same."

"You have *no* idea." Her gaze lands on Serena and her face brightens. "I see you've patched your ol' lady. Congratulations."

"Damn right. Serena, this is Mallory. Mallory, Serena."

Mallory squints for a second, like maybe she recognizes Serena from previous visits. But she has too much class to say anything rude. Instead, she pulls Serena in for a gentle hug. "Congratulations to both of you."

"Thank you," Serena says, returning the embrace. "I've heard so many nice things about you from Shelby and the others, I'm so happy to finally meet you."

"That's so sweet to hear. Thank you."

Mallory's gaze strays to Serena's stomach but again, she's too classy to ask.

"How long have you been out?" Mallory asks me.

"Not long enough. Still dealing with bullshit." I catch Chaser's eye. "You know how it is."

"Unfortunately, I do."

Serena

"They were nice," I say to Gray after Chaser and Mallory move on.

"Yeah. She's a sweetheart. Glad they're still together after all this time."

I'm not sure how I feel about his obvious affection for Mallory. Then again, it doesn't seem like her husband takes his eyes or hands off of her, so I'm being silly.

"Grinder, may I borrow Serena?" Shelby asks. "I want to introduce her to my momma."

"Of course. Where's Rooster at?"

"Kicking Jiggy's ass last I saw."

Gray chuckles as Shelby pulls me over to the bar.

"Momma, this is my friend, Serena," Shelby introduces. "Serena, Lynn Morgan."

"Shelby's told me so much about you, it's nice to finally meet you," I say.

She leans in for a quick, stiff hug. "Nice to meet you."

"You never told me Chaser was still so fine," Lynn says to Shelby in a hushed voice but still loud enough for me to hear.

Shelby's cheeks turn pink. "Momma," she scolds. "Please."

"What? It's a compliment. Lotta them rockers didn't age well. At all. He more than aged well. Doesn't hurt his wife is still so pretty. You know, when we first started dating, your father had the biggest crush on her—"

"Lordy, please take me now," Shelby mutters to the ceiling.

A laugh slips out of me and I cover it with a cough. Shelby squints in my direction. "It's not funny." Her lips quiver like she's trying to hold in her own laughter.

Jiggy saunters over to us, stopping in front of Lynn. He leans in and says something to her too low for me to hear.

"Sure, Jensen." Lynn slides off her stool and promises Shelby she'll be back.

"Stay outta trouble," Shelby warns. When Lynn turns, Shelby reaches and snags the edge of Jiggy's cut, gently tugging him backward.

He turns and flashes an utterly deviant smile at her. "What's wrong, songbird?"

"Jiggy." Shelby spears him with a serious stink-eye. "I'm watchin' you."

"Watch away." He waggles his fingers at her and takes off after Mrs. Morgan.

After he's out of earshot, she shakes her head and laughs. "I can't tell if he's tryin' to get my goat, genuinely likes my momma, or has a runnin' bet with his brothers to see who can bed her first." She lifts her gaze to me. "I ain't a fan of any of those options."

I chuckle at the amused note in her voice. "Hard to tell where Jiggy's head is at." I lean sideways to get a better view of him but he's busy talking to Steer. "He's a good guy, though."

"Oh, I know." She glances over her shoulder. "I just don't want things to be too awkward between Rooster and him."

The more time I spend with her, the easier it is to see why Rooster patched her so fast.

"He could use a good woman to look after him," she says. "It just don't gotta be my momma, you know?"

"I hear you."

Her mother bustles in between us to grab her purse from the bar, say a few words to Shelby and then leave again without acknowledging me.

Shelby sighs. "Sorry, don't take it personal. She has this borderline obsessive fear I'm gonna get knocked up and ditch my career for raising babies." She rolls her eyes. "She's probably worried you're contagious."

I snort, then laugh. "I feel like she should know you better than that."

"Right? I mean, seriously." Her smile falters. "You know I'm only jokin' right? I'm excited about *your* lil' guy. Can't wait to smooch the crap outta him when he gets here."

"Shelby, no worries. At all." I felt the same way at her age.

CHAPTER FORTY-TWO

Grinder

"That's it for now." Z slaps the table to dismiss everyone. "I need my officers to stick around." His serious blue gaze swings my way. "You too, G."

I blink and sit my ass back down. Not sure what the fuck he needs me to stick around for.

Even though Z didn't ask for their presence, Rock and Wrath join the remaining members at the table. Z nods at them.

This thing's starting to feel like a setup, but I can't figure out the end goal.

Z stands and paces to the double doors, pushes them closed until there's a soft click, then returns to his seat at the head of the table.

A serious air descends over the room.

I push forward to the edge of my chair, resting my elbows on the table. My body's on high alert for some reason and over the years I've learned to listen to those instincts.

"It looks like Steer's going to be moving on as the SAA to our Deadbranch, Tennessee charter." Z nods at Steer. "Congratulations, brother."

It's a lateral move, so not really something to celebrate in my opinion, but I keep that to myself.

"Congrats, brother." Rooster reaches across the table and shakes Steer's hand. "What happened to Squiggy?"

"Apparently, he's moving into the prez position." Z casts an irritated look at Rooster. "Although Priest strongly hinted he'd prefer *someone else* there. Seems you did *too* good a job while you were on the road."

Rooster shrugs. "What'd Digger do, retire? Or *get* retired?"

"Didn't sound like a voluntary retirement," Rock says.

"After what was going on in their strip club, I'm not surprised," Rooster says. "He's cleaning house to gear up for that documentary he wants to do. That way he can claim it was a 'few bad apples' who are no longer part of the club. Last I knew Digger wasn't sure Squiggy was solid, though."

"Well, whatever job Squiggy was off doing must've been good for the club," Z explains, "because Priest seemed happy with him." He gives Rooster another pointed glare. "For now."

Again, Rooster ignores the implied accusation. "Gonna miss you, brother." He nods at Steer. "We had a good time out on the road."

Steer nods. "Figure this will make things easier. This summer, Z won't lose half his officers going out on tour with you and your girl."

Z chuckles. "*I* might take off with you fuckwits this summer and leave Hustler to run the club on his own."

Hustler sits up, shaking himself out of his lethargic state. "What's happening?"

"Lilly and I could use a road trip before Chance starts school." Z lifts his chin at Rooster. "She loves Shelby. Said she wouldn't mind helping her out."

"Fuck yeah, I'd love having you guys out with us," Rooster says.

Jigsaw cackles and rubs his hands together. "Greg will piss his pants when he sees Z coming."

"And Z won't infringe on the pussy spree." Steer reaches his fist across the table for Jigsaw to bump. After a second of hesitation, Jigsaw taps his knuckles against Steer's. "Win-win."

Still not sure why the fuck my presence was required for *this*, I sit back in my chair and cross my arms over my chest. Next summer, my only plans involve being elbow deep in diapers, and spoiling my *wife*.

"Don't worry, old man." Z's attention returns to me. Fucker misses nothing. "There's a reason I asked you to stay."

Out of the corner of my eye, I catch Wrath grinning. That's never a good sign.

"I'd like you to step into the role as my SAA." Z's tone is solemn. He's not yanking my chain.

I jolt upright again. "What? I've been out of the life for fifteen years. Barely getting my boots wet. Can't wear my cut in public. Had to hide in the basement like a coward when the cops were here. How the fuck am I supposed to protect your back, brother?"

"I'd argue being in prison only heightened your senses. Made you *more* aware of danger and how to protect the club," Steer says in a lazy, smug tone that pushes all my irritable buttons.

"No one asked you," I snarl without looking at him.

Jigsaw does this long, slow, dickish scratch of the side of his head. "Didn't Quill's guy say you had a rep for being a *savage* inside?"

"Says the guy who collects the fingers of his enemies," I shoot back. The pain I inflicted in order to survive in prison isn't anything I want to brag about.

Not offended in the least, Jigsaw pats his breast pocket as if he might have a digit or two stored inside. "Takes a savage to recognize a savage."

Fucker.

Z chuckles. "Brother, I trust you one hundred percent."

I gesture toward the closed chapel doors. "What about the rest of your crew? Ain't some of them gonna be pissed off? They've been here, putting in the hard work. Gonna be looked at like favoritism, passing over other brothers who've earned it more than I have."

"No one's earned it more than you." Wrath's deadly serious baritone rumbles from the other end of the table.

"You've protected the club for fifteen years. Sacrificed the most." Rock's observation is equally somber.

"I don't need a consolation prize for doing the right thing," I argue.

"It's not a consolation prize." Rock glances at Wrath. "I don't want you to leave upstate, Grinder. But we all agree having you as SAA down here would benefit the whole club."

"How? I'm rusty as fuck. I'm old. I haven't even decided where I want to live. My apartment is way the fuck out of downstate's territory," I point out.

"I moved. You can too," Z says in an irritating tone, similar to how he explains shit to his son.

"Yeah, grandpa." Jigsaw clutches an imaginary steering wheel in front of him and rocks from side to side. "They have these fancy things called moving trucks these days—"

"Shut up."

"I get to nominate my replacement," Steer cuts in, suddenly the voice of reason. "And I want it to be *you*."

"Because Priest ordered it," I argue. No doubt that sneaky old fuck put them up to this when he visited.

"He didn't *order*." Z wiggles his fingers in the air in front of him. "He *suggested*."

"Same fucking thing where Priest is concerned."

"No decisions need to be made today." Z raises an eyebrow. "Just consider it. You're supposed to be off parole soon. I'll help you and Serena look for a place closer to here."

Hustler snickers behind his hand. "Jesus fuck. Please say yes. Tawny's head will *explode* when she finds out Serena's patch outranks her."

Z snort-laughs.

"Not that club decisions should be made that way," Jigsaw grins, "but it *is* an added bonus."

Steer shakes with laughter. "You're all mean."

"Only because it's fuckin' true," Wrath adds.

"Not gonna lie, I'd love to see the look on her face when it's announced," Rooster says. "It's almost worth lifting the ban just for one night."

"Fuck. You're all conniving little fuckers." I stand and slap my hand on the table. "Am I free to go, Prez?" I sneer at Z.

"See, look at that. You're already getting the hang of it." Z sweeps his hand toward the door as if he's granting me permission.

SAA. The patch I wore when I was sent to prison fifteen years ago.

Do I even want the responsibility now?

Back then, it wasn't the title that got me thrown inside. But in the future, it could be. A brother sworn to protect the club and specifically to protect the president has to get his hands dirty.

Wouldn't I do that anyway, though?

If someone threatened Z, SAA or not, I wouldn't hesitate to put a bullet between their eyes. Same for any of my brothers.

Serena's at her makeup table when I push into our room. The various lights she uses when she's filming light up the space like a sunny summer afternoon. She's definitely more comfortable here now than she was the first time we visited. How will she feel if this ends up being my home charter?

"And now, take your fluffy brush and—"

"Shit, sorry, buttercup."

She snaps the camera off and jumps up, hurrying over to me. "No big deal. I'll edit it later."

I study her half made-up face and can't help my lips from sliding into a smile. Everything about her always calms and centers me. Makes me happy. I thought this feeling was a myth.

"I don't think I understood what happiness was until I met you, buttercup," I blurt out like a sentimental fool.

Her anxious expression softens.

I reach for her, curling my arm around her waist and dragging her closer. "How are you feeling?" I rest my hand over her getting-bigger-by-the-day bump.

"Good, actually. I woke up feeling all glowy, so I thought I'd film some content and get ahead."

"Sorry I interrupted."

"It's okay." She moves my hand to a slightly lower spot. "He was kicking earlier."

"Damn." Hate that I missed our little guy's kicks. Love making that connection with him whenever possible.

"He'll be at it again." She frowns and reaches up to stroke my cheek. "What's wrong?" She slides one finger between my eyebrows, chasing away the tension gathered in that exact spot. How does she always know? "Was church okay?"

"Church was fine. After church is when things went sideways."

"Why?"

I drop onto the edge of the bed and pull her into my lap. Should a brother discuss things that happen at the table with his ol' lady? Every biker I've ever met has had a different opinion on this. When it's something that will impact *her* life, yeah, I think I should.

"Z asked me to be his SAA."

She's quiet for a moment, absorbing the news. "Wow. What happened to Steer?"

"Looks like he's moving on to our Tennessee charter."

"Huh. If anyone was going to move to Tennessee, I thought it would be Rooster."

"I got those vibes too. But Rooster denied it. Besides, if he goes, Jigsaw goes, then Z loses most of his officers in one exodus. We can't have that."

"It makes sense. You and Z have a lot of history. His trust in you runs deep and that's what a president needs." Her gaze slides away. "Especially after what Shadow did to Sway. The guys respect Z and I know he trusts them, but it's still not the same as the bond you two have."

God damn, she gets this stuff better than some brothers do.

"Will you be upset if this is my home charter?"

"Will *you*?" she counters. "You're close to Rock and Wrath too."

"Yeah, they won't be far away. They were all for it."

"I'm sure it was because it's good for the club. Not because they want to get rid of you."

"That's what they said."

"Tawny's really gone, right? The ban won't get lifted?"

I won't tell her about Rooster's joke that we should lift the ban. "Not on my watch. Not on Z's either. You saw how pissed he was."

She tilts her head, looking around the room we've claimed as ours when we visit downstate. "I'll be okay with it. On one condition."

"What's that?"

"That we don't live *here*." She presses her hand to her stomach. "He needs a happy, peaceful, real home."

I wrap her up tight in my arms and press my forehead against hers. "Absolutely. I'd never, ever expect my family to live at the clubhouse. No matter how nice it's been fixed up. I want a home where I can just be with my wife and kids."

She gasps at the word *wife*. *My sweet Serena, you didn't think a property patch was enough for me, did you?* I'm not ready to propose today, so I ignore her reaction.

"I'll tell Z yes, then?" I want to be sure she's okay with this.

"You didn't already say yes?"

"No, I wanted to talk to you first."

"Gray," she sighs. "Thank you."

"It's not set in stone, yet." For all I know, Z will be pissed I didn't accept immediately.

The corners of her mouth lift. "The future never is."

CHAPTER FORTY-THREE

Grinder

"All right, I'm in," I announce at church that evening. "On one condition."

Z raises an eyebrow. "A little soon to be making demands, but all right. Let's hear it."

"This twice a day, sitting down for church bullshit *stops*."

Everyone chuckles at that. Even Sway, who's seated as far away from me as he can get. As he should be.

"But I love seeing your grumpy mug." Z waves his hand at the table. "Besides, it's a special occasion."

"You didn't know I was going to say yes."

His lips twist like he's trying to restrain himself. When he's finally in control he lifts his hand. "Sway, you had something to share?" Z nods to Sway.

Sway stands and drops his *Downstate, NY* bottom rocker on the table.

It's a cloth patch. Doesn't weigh much but it hits the table with the force of years behind it.

"Already talked to Z about this, but my ol' lady and I decided to move on down to Florida." His mouth slides into a distorted half-smirk. "This last winter was rough." He taps the side of his head.

"With the hole in my noggin and all. Tawny and I are thinking Florida weather would be better for *both* of us."

Weather my ass. Tawny must still be steaming mad she's forever banned from this clubhouse.

"Fuck, we're gonna miss you, brother." Steer stands and embraces his old president.

"The fuck you are, traitor. You're moving to Tennessee anyway." Sway laughs and returns the embrace.

This is less of a meeting and more of a farewell to Sway. Everyone shakes his hand and shows respect. No one mentions how strange it is not to have a send-off party for him. He seems to want to go as much as we want him gone.

He stops in front of me last. "Somehow we're still standing, brother," he says.

Some of us steadier than others. "Yes, we are."

"Good luck. You're coming full circle. I feel good with you watching Z's back here."

"So do I." We shake hands and he even pulls me in for a too-long-for-my-taste hug. Neither of us mentions Tawny.

Then, he's gone.

Rooster closes the war room doors. "What's this mean for Stella, think she's going with him?" he asks in a low voice.

Z stretches in his chair, propping his feet on the edge of the table and lacing his fingers behind his head. "Don't know. Don't care."

"We'll lose a lot of money," Hustler says.

"The fuck we will. I—" Z snaps his mouth shut. "You know what, I don't care. I'd rather wash my hands of her anyway. That other chick is starting to gain popularity and she comes without the drama."

"Oh, she's dramatic when she comes," Steer says.

"Charming," I mutter.

Z glares at him. "I'll take your word for it, thanks."

Rooster drops into the seat closest to Z. "We might be helping Loco with his girls, so we'll take a cut of that action too. The club can absorb the hit of losing Stella if she goes."

"You wanna be treasurer, Rooster?" Hustler asks.

Teller chuckles but doesn't say anything.

"No thanks. That's all you, brother."

"So we're really not having a party for Sway tonight?" Steers asks.

Z jerks his thumb over his shoulder. "Did he look like he was in a partying mood?"

"Nah, guess not." Steer lifts his chin at Rooster. "Shelby's mom coming by the clubhouse tonight? Never saw her last night."

Jiggy sits back with a shit-eating grin and rests his ankle on his knee. "Lynn was *preoccupied* last night."

Rooster rolls his eyes and stares at the ceiling. Counting to a hundred, maybe?

"Bullshit." Steer slaps the table. "No way she spent the night with you."

"A gentleman doesn't share details." Jiggy's devilish eyes slide Rooster's way. "But there's a solid chance that next year this time, Rooster's calling me 'Daddy.'" He covers his mouth and snickers into his hand.

"The fuck I will," Rooster growls. "You don't even believe in marriage."

"I'm willing to make an exception for a special woman," Jiggy says.

"That'll be so cute, Rooster." Steer shakes with laughter. "One big happy family. You can all live together."

"Shut up," Rooster groans. "For real. I'd reconsider that plan, Jiggy. Shelby will never forgive you."

"Why?" He turns his puppy dog eyes on Rooster. "She wouldn't want me to be happy?"

"Not with her momma."

"Does she have strong feelings about *me* getting together with her mom?" Steer asks. "I *definitely* don't want to marry her if that helps my case."

Jigsaw jumps out of his chair, but Rooster yanks him back by grabbing a fist full of his cut.

"All right. No one's fucking anyone's mom," Z says, "so knock it off."

Murphy raises his hand. "You know, technically, that's not true for all of us."

Teller groans and rolls his eyes.

Z points at Murphy. "Nice one."

Steer eyeballs Rooster's tenuous hold on Jiggy's cut and skirts around the edge of the table, grinning like a big, bald idiot. "Later, fuckwad."

Hustler, Suds, Butcher and the other brothers slowly file out of the room.

"If I let you go, will you behave?" Rooster asks Jigsaw.

"Probably not."

"Whatever." Rooster releases him and Jigsaw runs out of the room.

Z motions toward the door and nods at Rooster. "Would you, please?"

"Yeah, yeah." Rooster groans and takes off.

Then it's just Z, Rock, Wrath, Teller, Murphy, Dex, and me. Much like the old days. Rock stands and grabs glasses from the wetbar in the corner, setting one in front of each of us. He pours a small amount of amber liquid in each one, then takes the seat next to Z.

"Took years and Sway's *finally* leaving." Z closes his eyes and tips his head back, staring at the ceiling. "A-fucking-men."

Rock snorts. "Fractured our entire charter to form this one." He slaps Z's shoulder. "Only to leave it in your hands, anyway."

"That's some delicious irony," Teller smirks and lifts his glass in Z's direction.

"Gotta love it." Wrath taps his glass against Teller's.

Murphy seems to be keeping his distance from Rock *and* Teller. He paces behind Z for a few minutes before finally settling into a chair next to Wrath. "Would you take over National, Rock?"

"No. And stop putting that idea out in the universe."

"You might not have a choice," Dex says.

"Let's worry about New York business," Rock snaps. "How's your crew doing?"

"Fine. They've handled themselves well. I've been treating them like prospects and I haven't had any pushback."

"You talking about Remy?" I ask.

"Yup."

"They're support club material. No hesitation," I volunteer. "I'll sponsor them."

"Look at you jumping in with both feet." Z nods approvingly. "Good, because I nominate you and Jigsaw to mentor them with Dex."

"Fine by me." I shrug off the extra assignment. "You want me to tell Jigsaw?"

"Later, when he's cooled off."

"Are we toasting something?" Murphy lifts his glass. "Or did you pour these for looks?"

"Grinder, why don't you do the honors," Z says.

"All right."

We all raise our glasses.

The words come automatically.

"Kings forever, forever kings."

CHAPTER FORTY-FOUR

Serena

THE TRUCK ROLLS TO A GENTLE STOP.

"Hey, sleepyhead. Time to wake up," Gray whispers.

I open my eyes.

Where the heck are we?

Lights. Hundreds of tiny, twinkling white lights line a stone walkway, leading to a lovely front porch covered in more sparkling lights. Sturdy white columns frame an elegant black front door.

"Gray?" I blink and stare at the house, trying to pick out any identifying details. "Where are we?"

"You'll see." He steps out of the truck. "Wait for me."

He opens my door and carefully guides me to the ground.

"This is so pretty," I whisper.

"I'm glad you think so." He takes my hand and leads me along the path to wide stone stairs and a porch that extends the length of the house. At the front door, he stops and pulls out a piece of paper. He punches a code into the box on the door and it beeps.

"Whose house are we breaking into?" I ask.

"That depends." He pushes the door open and motions for me to go in ahead of him.

The soles of my boots squeak against the shiny wood floors. Gray bends down and unlaces my boots, slipping them off one by one, then taking off his own.

"They're neat-freaks like me, huh?" I ask, trying to figure out where the heck we are or who we're meeting. This will teach me to fall asleep in the truck.

A long staircase winds to our left. To our right a comfortable living room with a generous blue stone fireplace. Everything is white with black accents. We pass a pretty powder room, a dining room, laundry area, another den or living room, and a room in the corner of the house with glass doors.

The black and white theme carries throughout. Although, the kitchen adds stainless appliances and gray cabinets. "Wow, this kitchen is amazing." During the day, the wide windows must let in tons of light.

"I thought so too. Enough room for two people to cook together."

"Definitely."

He pulls me toward the room with the glass doors. "It's being used as a home office now," Gray explains as he turns the handles.

"Some office." Pristine white shelves and drawers from floor to ceiling line the walls, with a built-in desk facing one of the three windows. The other two windows have low, comfy benches built into them. "Oh, window seats! I always wanted one in my bedroom."

"I remember."

A metal desk on a pretty pink rug sits in the middle of the room. A stab of envy pokes me. I could arrange this into one hell of a makeup studio. All the natural light would be perfect for filming tutorials. The shelves and drawers would more than hold all of my supplies.

"It must be a woman's office. What does she do?"

"I didn't ask." He shrugs.

I wander to the window facing the backyard. With the outside lights on, I can make out a stone patio and flat expanse of neatly trimmed grass. To my right, another building catches my eye. "Is that another garage?" I ask.

"Yup." He rests his hand on my shoulder and tugs me away from the window. "Follow me."

Anxiety creeps over me as we ascend the stairway to the second floor. "Are you sure we're not going to scare the crap out of someone?" I whisper.

"I'm sure."

We emerge in the middle of a wide square landing. Thick, fluffy carpet cushions our steps. Each corner has a room. Gray starts at the farthest one.

Here is where the black and white scheme ends. Soft blues and greens cover the walls and ceiling. Gray ducks into the attached bathroom and we emerge on the other side in a room painted pink and purple. "Oh, how cute! It must be a brother and sister sharing a bath?"

"I think so."

We leave the pink bedroom and pass another bedroom, a closet, a bathroom and, at the other end, double doors. "I was told this is the primary suite," Gray says as he twists one of the handles and pushes the door open.

"Oh, wow! It's huge." I can't help gawking as I cross the threshold. "Oh my God, is that a spiral staircase?" I run over to the narrow, iron stairs. "Does it go somewhere?"

"There's a small room up there."

"Oh my God, I could live out my Rapunzel fantasies here."

He chuckles as I carefully climb the twisting stairs. At the top, it opens into a circular room with enough room for a chaise lounge and side table. White built-in shelves similar to the ones downstairs line one wall. These are stuffed with books and candles arranged in rainbow order. Lights dot the dark hills and valleys visible beyond the one large, round window.

"This is so cute."

"I thought it was a neat touch," Gray says from the staircase. "The stairs would be a deterrent for me though, I'd worry about rolling down them and cracking my skull."

"Yeah, if I get any bigger, they'd be an issue." I rest one hand on my stomach and hold tight to the railing as I descend. "Wow, look at the rest of the bedroom though. My whole apartment could've fit in here."

Under the spiral stairs, there's a large walk-in closet. "This is nice. I always wanted a walk-in closet."

"Don't get attached. That's supposed to be the 'husband closet.'"

"Like, the husband lives in there or stores his clothes in there?" I tease.

"Maybe both."

A king bed takes up most of one wall and on the other side another door opens to an even larger walk-in closet. "I think I found the 'wife closet'! Holy crap!" The racks where clothes would normally hang are empty, but rows of shoes line an entire wall. "A woman after my heart," I sigh.

Gray chuckles. "Thought you'd like that."

The closet is so long, there's a door on the other end. I pop out near the spiral staircase. "I'd never make it out of the bedroom to the rest of the house."

"Come see the bathroom."

"There's another one?" I hurry to his side.

A long vanity counter with mirrors and drawers takes up the space outside of the bathroom. "I'd be in heaven there. Look at all those perfectly placed outlets."

"It has a steam shower, whatever that is," Gray calls from the bathroom.

I follow his voice, stepping onto the cool, white tile floors. The entire bathroom is shiny white tile with pops of gray accents. Silver fixtures. A large soaking tub and walk-in shower. Another vanity counter and sinks. "Are the owners some sort of celebrities?" I ask.

"I don't think so." Gray shrugs. "Do you like it?"

"I never knew I had such strong opinions on bathrooms before. But I love it."

"Good." He takes my hand again. "Let's go outside."

"Gray." I stop in my tracks, tugging on his hand. "What are we doing here."

"Let's go outside and I'll tell you."

Confused, anxious and a tiny bit hopeful, I trot down the stairs after him. After a quick detour to grab our shoes, he slides one of the glass doors in the kitchen open and flicks a switch. Lights burst over the stone patio.

"Someone's serious about their security lights," I mutter. "Emily would love this."

"Yeah, I liked that too."

Now that we're outside, I notice the covered pool in the center of the patio. An iron fence surrounds the immediate pool area, then leads to the backyard. "They even have a pool, oh, and a pool house! How cute."

"I think it was a kid's playhouse." Gray nods to the short front door of the little house. "Not quite grown-up size."

"Oh, yeah. How adorable." I lean over to peer in the window. It's too dark to make out much, though.

To our right, the patio widens into a hidden space with a canopy and bench. "They called this the love nook," Gray says.

"Cute." Tired from our tour, I plop down on the bench and admire the little lights over the canopy. I sense Gray ease into the seat next to me.

"Serena." Gray's serious tone snaps my attention away from the lights.

He slides his hand over mine. "Serena, you've given me hope when I had despair. You've brought light into my world that I thought would be forever dark. I wasn't truly free until the day we met. You're the key that unlocked my heart. Whatever years I have left, I want to spend loving, protecting, and cherishing you. I want to raise a family with you. I'd rather go back to prison tomorrow than be free for the next fifty years, if you're not my wife."

Shivers race over my skin.

"Will you marry me?" He slides a white and gold box open.

Through the twinkling lights and tears suddenly clouding my vision, I can't see what he takes out of the box. But it doesn't matter. I already know the answer to the question.

"Yes!" A torrent of tears burst out of me, along with the happiest laughter to ever pass my lips. "Yes. Yes, I'll marry you."

His warm hand curls around mine. He gently guides a ring down my finger. The cool metal slides against my skin and rests firmly in place. I blink to clear the tears and stare at my hand. "Oh my God! It's pink! And rose gold. How did you know? It's so beautiful." The most perfect peachy-pink, cushion-cut stone twinkles on my finger. A halo of tiny diamonds sparkle around the stone and over the band. "It's huge."

"Well, when I realized you wanted a sapphire instead of a diamond, I thought bigger would be better."

I can't stop staring at it. It's the prettiest thing I've ever worn.

"If you don't like it, we can get something else." He lets out a dry laugh. "The jeweler and I are close buds now."

"No! I love it. It's exactly what I would've chosen if I knew something this pretty existed." I tear my gaze away from the ring and meet his concerned eyes. "Really, I love it." Forget the ring. "You really want to get married? To me?"

He glances around as if he might have misplaced his patience. "You see anyone else here carrying my kid?"

Of course. *I'm having his baby.* "Gray, we don't have to—"

"Don't finish that sentence," he warns. "You said yes."

I swallow my words and nod. "Wait a second, what are we doing here? *Where* are we?"

"Do you like the house?"

"I love it."

"It's about half an hour from the downstate clubhouse. Rooster's place isn't too far from here. About ninety minutes from upstate's clubhouse. I thought it would be a good location. Although, if you end up taking that job in Union, it's a good forty-five minutes away. Might be an annoying commute."

I blink while I try to do all that travel math. "And?"

"I put in an offer on the house. But I've got three days to get out of it if you don't want to live here."

"What?" I jump out of my seat and scurry backward until the whole house comes into view. "How can...what are you talking about?"

Gray follows and grabs my arm to steady me. "Do you like it?"

"Like it? I love it. The room with all the windows." I wave my hand toward the downstairs room with the great light and all the shelves, "And the," I flap my other hand toward the little turret that I'm sure is the room above the bedroom. "Rapunzel room."

Gray seems to understand my wild train of thought. "Yeah, the second I saw the room on the first floor, I thought it would be perfect for you to film your videos. You can make a great backdrop with those shelves."

"You want to buy a house based on my side-hustle?"

He frowns. "That's not the only reason." He pulls me closer and leans down, nuzzling against my neck. "The bedroom is big enough to keep a crib in for the first few months, so little Lincoln can be close to us. And you can make yourself a library up there when you need an escape."

"What about you? You've put all this thought into rooms that I'd like. What about what *you* want?"

"I *want* my wife to be happy."

"I'm serious."

He sighs and stares at the house. "I always wanted a fireplace like the one in the living room, but what I really want these days is to be outside as much as possible." He tilts his head. "Besides, you still haven't seen the garage, buttercup."

I thought he meant the two-car garage attached to the house, but he means the matching building a couple hundred feet away from the house. He leads me to the backyard's gate and onto the paved driveway. "Three garage bays? We don't have that many vehicles."

"Not yet." He opens the side door and flips on a light. Pieces of an old Ford Mustang are in stages of reconstruction in one of the bays. Steel drawers and cabinets seem to be overflowing with tools. "I don't think all the tools are staying. Shame, he's got a nice collection. I'll have enough room here to get back into welding and do some other stuff."

"Is that what you did…before?" *Why didn't I know that?*

"Yup. Made a decent living at it, too."

I walk to the middle of the garage and spin in a slow circle. It's so big, it almost has a warehouse quality to it. "This seems like the perfect place for us. Like it was made for Grayson and Serena."

"I thought so. That's why I jumped on it as soon as I saw it." He steps up behind me and settles his hands on my hips. "But I want you to love it too."

"I do. I really do." I hesitate, knowing he won't like my next question. "But can we afford this? I don't have any savings to help with a down payment and the mortgage—"

"I have it covered."

"Gray, I can't—"

"Didn't you just say yes to being my wife?"

"Yes."

"Then trust me to take care of you."

I can't help opening my mouth to protest again. "You shouldn't bear all the responsibility—"

He silences me with a finger against my lips. "Use your money to decorate your studio the way you want."

"That's it?"

"You're going to be plenty busy in a few short months."

I glance at the house again. "Can we be all moved in by the time the baby comes? I'd love to be able to set up a nursery and—"

"That's my plan." He nods to the disassembled car. "As you can see, they're already partially moved out. They want a quick closing too. Nasty divorce or something."

I hate the idea of benefiting from someone else's unhappiness. "You think that's bad luck?"

"Nope. We make our own luck."

THE EXCITEMENT of the evening keeps me wide awake the whole way home. I can't stop staring at my pretty ring and thinking about the house. Our baby will have a safe neighborhood and beautiful yard to play in, although we'll have to do some serious babyproofing to certain parts of the house.

"I know we have a lot of things coming up but when do you want to get married?" Gray asks when we return to his apartment. "Soon, before you're showing more? After baby gets here? When?"

I squeeze my hand into a fist. "We don't have to…"

He shakes his head. "Come here, I want to show you something." He tosses his coat over the couch and stalks into his bedroom.

Curious, I follow. "I've seen it all, Gray."

"Cute," he quips. "I'm serious, though." He stops in front of his dresser and pulls open the top drawer. Paper crinkles and he withdraws a yellow handwritten receipt. Folding it in half and placing a finger over part of it, he thrusts the paper at me.

I reach for it, and he yanks it away. "No. Look at the date."

My eyes scan the visible text. *Exquisite Baubles.*

I gasp when I read the date. "That's the day I found out I was pregnant."

"Yeah." He folds the page again and tucks it away in the drawer. "I stopped there and put a deposit on a ring *before* I came back to the clubhouse and found you *missing.*"

"You…you did?"

"Yes. So, I want you to understand I didn't ask because you're pregnant. I already planned to propose. I wanted time to figure out how and when, get the ring right, all that stuff, first. But I already wanted to make you my wife."

"Really?" I squeak.

"Yes, really."

I launch myself at him, wrapping my arms around his neck. He gently lifts me.

"I'm very excited about our baby, but that's not why I want to marry you." He presses a quick kiss to my lips. "Thank fuck I overheard you and Shelby talking about rings before yours was finished. I had time to have him change it."

"Wait, what was the one you picked?"

"Doesn't matter. Do you like yours?"

"I love it."

"If you don't, I give up. I'll take you to pick out whatever you want."

"No, this is it." I glance at the ring over his shoulder. "I can't believe you got it this perfect from overhearing one little conversation."

"It pays to be nosy."

In his arms, I feel cherished and loved. *This* is the special spark that's been missing my whole life. Plenty of men have desired me, and I confused that with love. But it always burned fast and left me feeling empty and used—or worse.

The love Grayson and I share, the way he treats me, it isn't frantic, rushed, or desperate.

It's lasting, secure, and *permanent*.

EPILOGUE

Grinder

"IT FITS! IT FITS!"

I glance up from baby Link as Serena runs out of her closet, heels clicking over the hardwood. She throws her arms wide and sways from side to side, making the bright yellow plaid skirt swing against her upper thighs.

My gaze slowly travels up to the white T-shirt clinging to her chest. "I thought we agreed no student-teacher role-play scenarios?"

"No." She huffs, not finding my joke as funny as I meant it to be. "It's like Cher's outfit in Clueless. But I couldn't find a matching blazer." She swings a bright yellow cardigan around and slips her arms into it. "It's cute, right?"

"It's sexy as fuck. What's the occasion?"

"The Clueless theme party we're having at Shelby's." She shrugs. "I bought it before I got pregnant and didn't think I'd ever fit into it again." She tugs on the waistband of the skirt. "It's vintage. No spandex."

Link coos and gurgles, waving his little hands in the air.

"Aw, I'm here Lincoln." Serena kicks off her heels and hurries over, scooping him into her arms.

"Careful he doesn't spit up on your outfit," I warn.

She shuffles closer and thrusts her hip my way. "Unzip it for me?"

"Gladly." I help her strip off the skirt and set it to the side, leaving her in the T-shirt and her underwear. I tease my fingers around the edge of her shirt. "This too?"

"I don't care about the T-shirt," she says without taking her eyes off the baby. "But I think I'm going to feed him."

I help her get situated in the rocking chair in the corner and leave them for a bit.

When I return, Link's stone-cold asleep against Serena's breast.

"Here." I hand her a bottle of ice water.

"Thank you," she rasps. Her eyes land on the box in my other hand. "What's that?"

"Well, I was going to give them to you for your birthday." I set the box on the end of the bed. "But you looked so frickin' cute in that skirt, I don't want to wait. And I want you to have them for your party. I think they'll match."

Her eyes widen and a soft smile lights up her face. "You got me a present?"

"I'm always thinking of you." I smirk at the box. "Had a devil of a time stuffing that box in my saddle bag, so it's a little banged up."

Link squawks and fusses as she hands him to me. "Shh, give your momma a break, little man." I tickle my finger over his cheek. He blinks up at me, big blue eyes the same shade as Serena's. Everyone keeps saying they'll change. I hope not. He smacks his lips a few times and closes his eyes again.

Paper rustles behind me and I turn, wanting to see her expression.

"Oh my God." She slides her hand over her open mouth. "They're so pretty!"

"You like them?"

"I love them!" She pulls the tall, black leather boots out of their tissue paper wrapping and studies the yellow embroidered flowers trailing along the side, from ankle to knee. "They're beautiful."

"I don't think the flowers are buttercups, but close."

She grins at me. "You're like a shoe fairy. First, Libby, now me."

I'd gotten Libby something similar for her birthday. She took it hard when Serena moved out.

"Yeah, I know. That's why these come with them." I hand her the baby and pull a smaller velvet box from my back pocket.

"Gray, I was only kidding." Her eyes widen and she takes a step back.

I open the small velvet box in my hand, pleased with the way the small diamond earrings sparkle in the light. "I know you're worried about him grabbing at your earrings. But these are small and have a secure clasp."

"They're so pretty," she gasps. "They look like little flowers."

"They are."

"Really?"

"Here." I open my arms to take the baby back and hand her the box. "I don't think you want me jabbing at your ears."

"You're the best husband."

I heft my baby boy in my arms, staring at his sleepy face. Love and awe twine through my chest. "You've given me a precious gift I never thought I'd get to experience. I plan to spoil you for the rest of my life, Serena."

"I don't need presents." She finishes slipping the earrings in and pulls her hair back so I can admire them. "Just you."

"Do you like them?"

She peers into the mirror covering the door to her closet. "I love them."

I set Link in his crib and walk over to Serena. "You put them on before the boots, you must like them."

"I really do."

I wrap my arms around her waist, untying the short robe she'd put on earlier to feed the baby. She exhales a shaky breath and leans against me, staring at our reflections in the mirror.

Sometimes, I still think I have no business with this woman. Or maybe I'm still in prison, sleeping through the best damn dream ever. If that's the case, I hope I never wake up.

"What are you doing?" she asks as I open the robe.

"I want another one," I whisper against her ear. "A little girl who looks like you."

"I don't think you can place an order," she teases.

I kiss her shoulder, tugging the fabric out of my way. "Or a brother for Link. I don't care."

She tilts her head, studying me with serious eyes. "Two is my limit. So you better make it count."

Laughing, I strip the robe off the rest of the way. "Is that a yes?"

"Yes."

"Answer something for me, first."

She turns to face me, waiting for the question.

"Do I make you happy?"

"*Happy* doesn't come close. I always feel cherished in your arms."

"You've given me a life I thought I'd lost." I kiss her temple. "I'll cherish you until the day I die."

And even then, it'll never be enough.

THE LOST KINGS MC® WORLD

Sometimes I'm asked where the standalone fit into the Lost Kings MC world.
This would be my suggested chronological reading order.

1. Kickstart My Heart (Hollywood Demons #1)
2. Blow My Fuse (Hollywood Demons #2)
3. Wheels of Fire (Hollywood Demons #3)
4. Renegade Path (A Lost Kings MC World Novel)
5. Slow Burn (Lost Kings MC #1)
6. Corrupting Cinderella (Lost Kings MC #2)
7. Three Kings, One Night (Lost Kings MC #2.5)
8. Strength From Loyalty (Lost Kings MC #3)
9. Tattered on My Sleeve (Lost Kings MC #4)
10. White Heat (Lost Kings MC #5)
11. Between Embers (Lost Kings MC #5.5)
12. Bullets & Bonfires (A Lost Kings MC World Novel)
13. More Than Miles (Lost Kings MC #6)
14. Unhinged (Iron Bulls MC #5) by Phoenyx Slaughter
15. Warnings & Wildfires (A Lost Kings MC World Novel)
16. White Knuckles (Lost Kings MC #7)
17. Beyond Reckless (Lost Kings MC #8)
18. Beyond Reason (Lost Kings MC #9)
19. One Empire Night (Lost Kings MC #9.5)
20. After Burn (Lost Kings MC #10)
21. After Glow (Lost Kings MC #11)
22. Zero Hour (Lost Kings MC #11.5)
23. Zero Tolerance (Lost Kings MC #12)
24. Zero Regret (Lost Kings MC #13)
25. Zero Apologies (Lost Kings MC #14)
26. Swagger and Sass (Lost Kings MC #14.5)

...and many more to come!

ABOUT THE AUTHOR

Autumn Jones Lake is the *USA Today* and *Wall Street Journal* bestselling author of over twenty novels, including the popular Lost Kings MC series. She believes true love stories never end.

Her past lives include baking cookies, bagging groceries, selling cheap shoes, and practicing law. Playing with her imaginary friends all day is by far her favorite job yet!

Autumn lives in upstate New York with her own alpha hero.

www.autumnjoneslake.com

facebook.com/autumnjoneslake
goodreads.com/autumnjoneslake
pinterest.com/autumnjoneslake
instagram.com/autumnjlake
bookbub.com/authors/autumn-jones-lake
tiktok.com/@authorautumnjoneslake